Night of the Witch

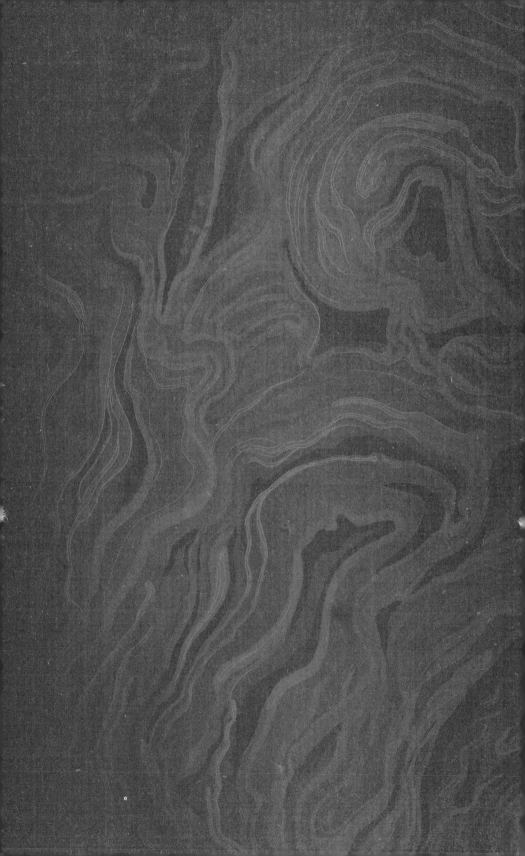

NIGHT OF THE WITCH

SARA RAASCH
AND
BETH REVIS

sourcebooks fire

Cover and internal design © 2023 by Sourcebooks
Jacket design by Erin Fitzsimmons and Liz Dresner/Sourcebooks
Jacket art © David Curtis
Internal illustration and design by Laura Boren/Sourcebooks

Sourcebooks and the colophon are registered trademarks of Sourcebooks.

Published by Sourcebooks Fire, an imprint of Sourcebooks
P.O. Box 4410, Naperville, Illinois 60567–4410
(630) 961-3900
sourcebooks.com

Cataloging-in-Publication Data is on file with the Library of Congress.

Printed and bound in the United States of America.
LSC 10 9 8 7 6 5 4 3 2 1

To every witch that burned,
and every witch that watched,
and every promise they made in the smoke.

CONTENT WARNINGS:

Domestic abuse (memories), unjust imprisonment, body horror, murder, physical torture, psychological torture, emotional manipulation, loss of body control through magical means, child abuse (memories/aftermath), animal abuse (one memory)

1

FRITZI

DECEMBER, 1591

My mother's eyes are fire embodied, smoldering with such fury that I feel their heat on my skin. That fire burns straight to my core, spearing me, as I stand helplessly in our little kitchen, arms splayed, empty potion vials clutched in my fists.

"Go, Friederike," she tells me, a growl of command. "Get in the cellar."

The shouts of battle outside haven't waned. How long has the fight lasted? And still, each cry of attack is as jarring as a crack of thunder, surging alertness into my veins, a building stockpile of *wake up* and *danger* and *go.*

Mama tells me that again. "Go, *now*."

I only came in here to restock my supplies and regroup. Our coven needs help—

"Mama, you cannot ask me to hide. You *cannot*."

She throws a glance through our warped front window. A protection talisman hangs against our single pane of fogged glass, ash tree twigs knotted into a triangle, limbs strung with rosemary bundles still fresh and floral-sweet.

A lot of good that talisman has done.

A lot of good *any* of our protection spells have done.

I grab for the herbs spread on our kitchen table. Birchbark for protection, fennel seed in a cedar box for defense; what will work, what will be *enough*? I brought everything that we had out of the cellar, all our last remaining herbs, but I turn back to the open hatch helplessly, like something else will appear, some great solution I'm too panicked to see.

"Mama," I try again. I am faltering, my voice is too high, my movements too unsteady. When I reach for the herbs again, the cedar box tips, spilling dozens of tender fragrant fennel seeds across the wood. "Let me make more potions. I can do it quickly. Let me try—"

The wrinkles around her usually smiling mouth tug down. She smooths back her unruly blond curls, identical to mine, hoping to wipe away some of her uncappable sorrow. I have seen that look before; it is branded on my soul, and I know, a flash of realization, what's changed in the last few seconds.

This battle teetered on the edge of hope before it even began. We always knew the witch hunters would come for us, so we had defenses, strategies planned, but success relied too heavily on luck.

And every ounce of luck turned its back on us from the start.

Whatever my mother saw outside has told her: We can't win. We *won't.*

I pull the empty vials to my chest. "We're still standing. We have to keep fighting!"

Mama surges forward to cup my cheek in her palm. She smells of sweat and gunpowder.

Outside, screams. From my family. From hexenjägers, the vile witch hunters. Spells explode and rifles pop.

"Mein Schatz," Mama whispers, her thumb soft on my face. "I don't need you to be brave now. I need you to *listen.*"

I shove the potion vials into the leather pouches hanging from my belt and grab her wrists. "Mama, please—I need to tell you—"

She presses a kiss to my forehead. "I love you, Friederike."

Then she pushes me. *Hard.*

I stumble back, stunned, and trip on the open hatch door.

It's my fault, that's what I was going to say. *The battle outside, the witch hunters being here, is my fault. You cannot save me from it—*

I fall, hands tearing on the rough wood ladder, knees banging against the wall until I drop with a jaw-clacking thud on the dirt floor of our cellar.

Pain pierces through my body, bright and shattering, as I look up at the hatch and see Mama gazing down on me, backlit so there is only darkness where her face should be.

"Wait!" I cry. "*No—*"

She slams the hatch door shut. I hear the chain lock, hear the rug drag over it.

"Wolf and fox and strength of bone," Mama says above me, the words muffled. "Help me here keep safe this home. Protect and care, shield and cover, lend your might for this desperate mother."

"*Mama!*" My screams will be useless. Her protection spell means that even if someone was standing right on top of the door, they wouldn't be able to hear me. If they knew the cellar was there before, they would forget it as long as the spell lasts.

The strength of my mother's protection magic is renowned, but that doesn't stop me from tearing up the ladder and thundering my fists on the door.

Though the sounds I make are deadened, I can hear what is happening outside—the shouts of fighting still echo throughout our little village.

Tears stream down my face, but I viciously ignore them. I do not get to cry. I have to *act*.

Still on the ladder, I whirl to face the front corner of the cellar. The window—Mama and I installed it to help ventilate when our food molded last year. It's blocked by crates and barrels now, but it should be big enough that I can crawl through—

The door to our cottage bangs open, and my whole body seizes. I know it is not Mama leaving—her footsteps patter overhead, a hurried whirl of reaction as she turns on the intruder.

I go rigid on the ladder, every muscle in my body attuned to listening, heart stunted, breath held. I don't even dare pray.

"Kommandant Kirch," Mama says, her tone utterly emotionless.

A shout tries to escape. I press my palm to my mouth and gulp it down.

"Did you think you could hide from this battle?" the kommandant asks.

"I am not hiding," says Mama without hesitation. "I was waiting for you."

There is a long moment of silence between them. I can imagine the way they stare each other down—my mother, every bit of her bearing saying that she is the most powerful witch for leagues; and Kommandant Jäger Dieter Kirch, barely two years my senior, emitting the bold, irrepressible spirit that made one so young the head of the hexenjägers.

The prize she will make him. The praise that will be heaped upon him. He's rounded up a whole coven, the last in the area, and killing my mother means killing an elder. A powerful one.

My terror subsides into fury, breath coming in tight pants against the tears still streaking down my face.

He will not *touch* her.

But when he says, "Take her," I cry out again.

I slam my shoulder into the door, but it won't lift, and no one above is even aware that I'm here. Except for Mama, and I know she won't look down as hexenjägers stomp into our cottage for her.

Irons clank. But there is no fight or resistance; she goes willingly.

She knows we have lost.

She knows Birresborn is fallen.

Her arrest is swift—they'll take her to the main city, to Trier, where a mock trial will be held before they tie her to a stake.

All her protection spells. All her wards. Years of watching our neighboring covens get whittled away or flee to safety until here we are, the last of the covens in this corner of the Holy Roman Empire, finally taken out, finally decimated.

Many of our elders pushed to leave in recent months. The hexenjäger threat was too powerful, and we were growing weaker and weaker.

"We should go to the Black Forest," my aunt Catrin said a week ago; she was getting bolder in her defiance of my mother. "The forest folk of the Well will take us in."

"And transport the dozens of people of our coven across hundreds of miles?" Mama replied, trying to be calm in their meeting with the other elders. "How far do you think we would get with the hexenjägers on our doorstep already? They would pursue us into the very heart of our magic. We cannot risk it. Besides, the hexenjäger threat is our responsibility."

"Maid, Mother, and Crone." Aunt Catrin sighed, her face going slack. "Our only other option is to die here, then? To wait for the jägers to break through our defenses?"

"No," Mama promised. "No. We will find a way to reach them. We will find a way to end this."

We will find a way to end this.

Our responsibility.

My stomach spasms with that responsibility, toxic and consuming as I scramble down the ladder.

We cannot give up.

I cannot give up.

I tear down the stacks of crates and barrels in front of the window, our stores of food dumping at my feet, beets and radishes and rolling potatoes.

"Maid, Mother, Crone," I pray out loud as I heave the last barrel away. But I don't know what I'm even praying for. Salvation? Strength? Comfort? Everything, I need *everything*, and no prayer is sufficient.

I leave a single crate to use as a stepladder and leap up onto it. The window is barely the size and width of my head—will I be able to crawl through? Did Mama's spell extend to this exit?

We didn't waste money on glass for this window, just a series of iron bars shoved into the dirt. A better witch would stop and form a spell to break the bars, but I'm not my cousin, skilled with controlling lit flames; I'm not even my mother, who can call animals as easily as she breathes. What do I use? Herbs. Useless, stupid herbs, and how will they help me now? I have none left, anyway—we had pulled the last of our herbs up to the kitchen when Mama told me to hide, so in this moment all I have is myself and empty potion vials.

I work faster, fingers bleeding as I free clumps of earth and rock. Thank the Three that Mama and I aren't exactly skilled architects. I'd joked about it then, how this window would one day collapse, but schiesse, I never thought I'd be grateful for our shoddy craftsmanship.

One of the bars breaks free.

The shouts outside heighten.

I look up before I can think not to. My eyes lock on a group not four paces from this hidden window: two hexenjägers are fiercely locked in battle with two witches. Their fight is a mimic of others happening all over the town square, witches embroiled in extricating these intruders from our coven.

The jägers use swords, hacking and slashing.

Witches fight back the only way we know how: with magic. We have physical weapons as well, some of us, but a well-placed spell can be as effective as a blade.

One of the witches is Agathe, whose affinity is in weaving. Her loom makes our fabrics, threading spells into our wool. The blue kirtle I wear now has a hem embroidered with green in a repeating pattern of an ash tree, for protection.

Now, she swings a net in a mighty arch, ensnaring one jäger. He screams, and I hear sizzling, his skin boiling against the magic Agathe wove into the fibers.

Next to her is Gottfried, whose affinity is with animals, like Mama. He whistles, and a dozen ravens break from a tree line, making a sharp dive for the other jäger. He shrieks in tandem with his comrade, and for a moment, hope wells—how can simple humans stand against us? We'll push them back; surely Mama's worries were misplaced—

Then the jäger in Agathe's net twists. No warning cry.

He impales Agathe on his sword.

Head to toe, I go utterly immobile, a horror I've never known pinning me in place.

Gottfried wails. His distraction is enough—the other jäger frees himself from the ravens and hurls his body at Gottfried, tackling him to the ground. I see the flash of metal, the bite of blade scraping the air between them, and then Gottfried's wail plummets into silence.

The two jägers leap to their feet and race off, throwing themselves into the next fight with furious, single-minded drive.

I am a body without thought too.

I use the freed iron bar to hack away at the dirt beneath the remaining two bars, heart bruising on my ribs. If I can get this window open wider, I can get out there—I'll get out there and—and—

More screams float into the cellar, more garbled shrieks as battles are lost, as jägers slaughter my family, and with them drifts a single thought. A single, shattering question.

Where is my mother?

I should have seen jägers drag her across the square. Shouldn't I have? Where did they take her?

"Keep that one!"

The voice—Kommandant Kirch.

My eyes seek out the source. There, across the square—the kommandant stomps toward a prison wagon. He points at a girl one of his hexenjägers is dragging away.

"Liesel!" I shout for my cousin. It gets swallowed in the battle cries that have pitched into outright screams. "Liesel—"

She shrieks in terror as the kommandant grabs her from the hexenjäger and throws her into the prison wagon himself. He says something to her, something that makes her tiny body cower back, a wraith of blond hair and pale eyes, and then he slams the door on her.

My focus widens so suddenly, so aggressively, that I teeter in the shift.

I thought we could wrest victory from this battle—I thought Mama's fear had been misplaced—

But I see now what she did, what she knew: we are lost.

Between my window and Liesel, the town square is a massacre. Blood coats the ground. Bodies lie in piles, the few remaining witches getting cut down in harsh, thrusting blows from jägers lost in their hunger for war.

So many are fallen.

Too many.

I drop to my knees in the cellar, clinging to the freed iron bar, and vomit on the dirt floor.

Maid, Mother, and Crone, forgive me, forgive me, please, forgive me—

The prayer comes easily, but I feel its uselessness. The Three won't hear me.

It's too late. Anything I do—it's too late.

The iron bar drops from my fingers, thuds against the cellar's floor under my knees. Powerlessness seizes my muscles so unrelentingly that I start shaking, vibrations I can't stop, terror I can't control.

You know how to help.

Sweet and jarring all at once, the voice slithers up the back of my neck, pounds on my head, equal parts seduction and sting.

I knot my arms around myself, eyes squished shut, ears deafened to the screaming outside, the primal, guttural cries that go beyond pain.

You know how to help, Fritzi.

No. No, I don't.

Without needing herbs. Without needing a conduit at all.

STOP!

Just say the spell. You know the words. You remember them.

My mouth opens. I hate the part of me that does that, the part of me that always leans in to listen to the darkness whispering its saccharine promises, temptation brushing my cheek like it isn't responsible for one of the greatest traumas of my life before this one.

Muscles shaking in terror now tremble with tension from the way I hold myself against the voice, the promises of wild magic always lingering, always waiting to pull me over the edge. The cellar is dark, shadows creeping in, night coming fast and cold in winter—those shadows loop around my quaking body, and I am all fear and weakness.

Everyone is dying out there. Liesel is in a prison wagon.

What can I do?

"Do all witches hear the voice, Mama?" I asked years ago. I been about ten. "The one asking them to try wild magic? Is that a goddess talking to me like Perchta talks to you?"

The goddess Perchta, the Mother, long ago chose my mother as one of her favored witches. It means nothing more than Mama has her ear, is blessed and guided by the Mother Goddess—but to be chosen by a goddess! For a young witch, the idea had been all I wanted.

But my mother's face. Save me, I'll never forget that look on her face, a flinch of disgust that she smothered with a too-wide smile. "The goddesses do speak to us, but they would never tell us to use wild magic. Don't think on it, mein Schatz. Think only on how you will resist its pull. Tell me now, what are you?"

My heart sank. A goddess hadn't chosen me? Not even Holda, the Maid, young and fierce and bright? Surely I was worthy of Holda's blessing!

"I'm a good witch, Mama," I said, and smiled. "A green witch!"

She nodded. "A good green witch, indeed."

I say that to myself now. A good witch. A green witch. I use herbs and create spells. I do not hear the voice in my head; I do not feel its pull; I am a good witch—

Will a good witch survive this?

I scream and fly to my feet, the iron bar back in my hand, and with my last fleeting remnants of strength, I pry the other bars free and gouge enough dirt out to widen the opening.

I will not give in. Not today. Not tomorrow. *Never*.

I throw that word up against the voice in my head. *Never, never, you will never get me; you've taken enough.*

A stream of smoke floats through the cellar window.

It could be mist on an early morning breeze, common enough now in winter—except for the smell. Wood and cinder, earthy and rich, a fire on a summer night, a smoldering kitchen flame under a boiling pot—and it isn't innocently gray. It's heavy, choking black.

The oddity doesn't make it past my focused terror.

I need to get out of this cellar. *Now*.

The smoke blows, obscuring the town square, filling this cellar until every blink is grating sand on my eyelids and every breath burns.

Once the bars are freed, I stack more crates back beneath the window and haul myself up to the opening.

My body scrapes against the edges of the window hole as I wiggle free. Streaks of dirt drag along my coarse blue kirtle, my square-necked shift beneath splotched with grime and sweat as I roll to my feet outside.

"Mama!" I scream into the smoke, coughing each breath. "Aunt Catrin! Liesel!"

Why haven't any hexenjägers swept in on me yet? I'm out of the cellar; they might not be able to see me in the smoke, but they should be able to hear my screams now. I don't care. I'm too overcome with panic, and I shout the names again.

The wind shifts.

The sky clears first. Brightest blue, high afternoon, a crisp December day as any other.

Liesel wanted to make sweet zwetschgenkuchen today but use apples instead of plums. *No*, I told her, *I'm sorry, Liesel, I can't. Mama needs my help with the chores I didn't do yesterday, on my birthday.*

My birthday.

The thought of it cracks my heart, shatters what's left, and it's in that state that I see what has become of Birresborn.

Bodies lie everywhere, left to fall where they were killed. Some hexenjägers; not enough. Mostly my family, my coven, shot with rifles or stabbed with blades.

I stand still for a moment, the world off-balance, and I realize—I'm the only thing standing now in this village. The surviving hexenjägers have left. My coven is...

In the center of the square stands a single stake.

How long did I cower in that cellar? Too long, not enough.

The wind whistles, catches, puffs smoke higher, and I hear only the thud of my shattered heart beating in my ears. I hate the absence of noise more than screaming, this incessant, defeated *silence*.

I drop to my knees in front of her stake. Her burnt remains are held to the charred wood by a great iron chain.

They didn't take her back to Trier. Didn't give her the sham of a trial.

They branded her chest. A curved *D*, for dämon. *Demon.*

I did not hear her scream when the kommandant lit her fire, when he branded her—she would never have given him the satisfaction

"Mein Schatz."

My body bends double. I cannot will it to stay upright. I claw the earth, nails digging deep into ashes and mud, and from the pit of me, the core of me, I scream.

It is a promise.

It is a beginning.

2

OTTO

The city of Trier smells like fear and shit.

I wrap my black cloak over my shoulders, securing the pierced-heart brooch at the neck. My leather boots are polished to a mirror shine. My belt is heavy with my sheathed sword hanging on my left and a wheellock pistol holstered to my right, but before I open the door to the headquarters of the hexenjägers in the Porta Nigra, I mentally pause, feeling each hidden weapon on my body, thinking of what I would need to do to reach each one instantly.

A dagger at my back and a smaller one in my boot. A silver knife beneath each shirt cuff, the cost of such blades immense, but paid for from the archbishop's own coffers.

A vial of holy water around my neck. A scroll of parchment with a verse from Exodus written in Latin, blessed by the Pope himself, sewn into my cloak. A jar of dirt from Jerusalem, tiny and clinking in my pocket next to a golden crucifix, the only thing I have left of my father's.

Witches need more than blades to pierce them before they are cast into hell.

Our weapons are designed to rend the flesh and burn the soul.

I sling open the door and step onto the stone corridor. As I expected, there are fewer witch hunters here than normal. My plan to get regular updates from the city while I was on patrols meant that I cut my most recent tour of the southern part of the diocese short.

"Kapitän!" One of the lower-ranked men shouts, running toward me.

It's a new recruit, Johann, too junior to have been included on patrols outside the city yet. He's a kid, really, fifteen or sixteen. I'm no more than a few years his senior, but that age difference feels...wrong. He has peach fuzz on his chin, a gleam of innocence still alight in his eyes.

"What is it?" I growl.

"Kommandant Kirch is not yet back," the boy stutters. "I—we were not sure of the changes to the executions?"

"Changes?"

The boy bobs his head. "Ja, Kapitän." He holds a paper out to me.

I snatch it from him. It bears the archbishop's seal, as well as the stamp of the executioner, that pompous ass. Both men are far older, and yet they cower behind boys like Johann.

Like me.

There is a reason why the hexenjägers are young. They say it takes youth and the strong muscles of good holy boys to fight the devilish strength of the witches. The oldest among us is Kommandant Dieter Kirch, and he is in his early twenties. I, at nineteen, am the captain, second-in-command. To be fair, I have only been elevated to this position because I had my father's name behind me. Nepotism worked in my favor, as did the kommandant's personal approval of me.

And, well, Trier is running out of good holy boys willing to wear the black cloaks. What started as a mania has settled into something even darker. There are rumblings of rebellion. The archbishop may lead the charge against the witches, but the parishes have started to question whether or not the man is correct in his crusade. There is, after all, far more gold on his fingers and around his neck than what is used for alms.

Unfortunately for them, the archbishop has been known to hear blasphemy among the doubters, blasphemy that is often treated with the same fire as the witches face.

The archbishop sits upon a literal throne, watching the burnings from afar. The executioner, he lights the fires, but it is the hexenjägers, the children he trains, who bind the hexen to the stakes. Who haul their crying, fighting bodies to the pyres.

Who root out the evil as if it is a foul weed that will wither and die in the sun.

There is always fire between the others and the hexen. Fire, and the children like Johann who they have trained to dirty their hands.

Fools.

I snap the parchment out, scanning the words quickly. The archbishop has written the decree in Latin—it is, after all, a mandate from the Church—but it's also a precaution. Few of the lesser-ranked boys can read even in German, fewer still in the language of God.

"I knew about this," I state flatly.

Bright red splotches stain Johann's face. He's nervous around me. "It's just that...with Kommandant Kirch gone..."

I start walking toward my office, and Johann races to keep up. I insisted early on that the only way the hexenjägers could truly be efficient at purging evil from the diocese was through efficient communication, and it became my role within the unit to create that system of messengers. It is often a tedious task, and not without its trouble, but it also means that I am the first to know when the next burning will be and where the next patrols will be sent out.

So I know Kommandant Kirch left Trier with more than half our men, a sudden mission that had been prompted by necessity when a large and powerful coven had been uncovered. It must have been a surprise to the kommandant, who otherwise wouldn't have left the city during an important time. I know he's been obsessed with finding covens that still have elders; it's no wonder that he would attack as soon as he heard, even if that left the city without its main hexenjäger forces.

And I already knew about the burning, scheduled for the solstice in a few days. We typically have burnings of one to two witches every few weeks, but the archbishop put a hold on them, intending to have one large burning at the end of the year to showcase the triumph of good over evil, letting the smoke of the bodies of burned witches scent the cold December air.

It is for these reasons that I've rushed to the city, cutting my own fruitless patrol short.

There is, after all, much to do when you're about to help murder a hundred people.

Witches, I remind myself as I enter my office. *They're not people. They're witches.*

"But sir—" Johann lingers at the doorway, unsure of whether he is allowed to step inside the tiny stone room that serves as my office.

"What is it?" I demand. There's a *lot* to plan before the solstice, and I have no time for mewling boys who do not know what to do other than *hesitate.*

"Kapitän Ernst, we have held the witches in prison for weeks. No burnings. It's...getting crowded."

"Yes," I reply acidly, "when you don't burn witches alive and instead leave them in a cell, they do tend to not simply disappear. What do you want me to do about it?"

Truth be told, I dread the day. The streets will choke with the stench of rendered flesh. My stomach twists, although my face betrays no emotion.

All the Holy Roman Empire will see the smoke rising from Trier, and all will tremble with fear. Exactly as the kommandant wants.

If the archbishop's order goes as planned.

"If Kommandant Kirch does not come back before the solstice..." Johann starts, his words fading out as he tries to put a cohesive sentence together, "we aren't sure what to do. Perhaps you could authorize a new location for the prisoners, or..." His voice trails off at my quelling glare.

I narrow my eyes, considering the options. "I'll inspect the prison," I say. It would not suit my plans if the prisoners were moved. I shove past the boy and march down the stone corridor. When I do not hear the younger man's boots following my own footsteps, I bark, "Come along!"

Johann scrambles to keep up as I descend the massive winding iron staircase.

The headquarters of the hexenjägers is in the Porta Nigra—the Black Gate made by the Romans when they occupied the city-state of Trier hundreds of years ago. The building has been remade into a church, the upper level used by the blessed witch hunters.

But I continue down the iron stairs, winding round and round, dizzyingly descending past the church, deeper, deeper underground.

"Sir?" Johann squeaks, but I ignore him.

There is no part of Trier that is untouched by Rome. The Germanic nations are the Holy *Roman* Empire for a reason—centuries have passed, but our stones were cut by Roman laborers, our streets mapped by Roman cartographers, our religion seeped into the people by Roman Emperors. Constantine the Great himself lived in Trier.

And his men carved out the aqueducts.

The enormous tunnel system under the streets of Trier is ancient but still good, designed to bring the clean waters of the Moselle River into the city. Not many remember it now, centuries later. There are rumors that the aqueducts are haunted, and Johann crosses himself as I approach the entrance underground. He truly is still a child.

The only ones who haunt the aqueducts are the witch hunters.

I hand Johann a torch, and he holds it while I use my flint to light the greased bundle atop the stick. I let him go first, and although the torch trembles in his hand, Johann enters the narrow passage, shoulders hunched but without any hesitancy to his steps.

Once inside, no light reaches through the tunnel. Cold water sloshes over our feet. Johann's dim light barely flickers.

It doesn't matter. I close my eyes, embracing the darkness. I know these routes better than anyone. Johann peers nervously into the side tunnels, shoulders hunched, eyes squinting.

What would have been a twenty-minute walk or more meandering through the winding streets above is a quick ten minutes through the aqueducts. The tunnel branches off and then opens up to a sort of sub-basement with pillars of brick holding the floor above our heads. Stone steps lead to a door.

"I'll never figure out these tunnels," Johann says mournfully. His torch flickers as I fit an iron key into the door.

I glance behind him as he swings the torch idly. "Watch it!" I bark.

The boy jumps, nearly slipping on the damp floor.

I grab the torch from him. "See those?" I point to the barrels stored on raised planks under the brick pillars to protect them from the water. Johann nods, eyes wide. "They're full of gunpowder, you unverschämt. Be careful with your torch."

"Why would they store that here?" Johann grumbles, but at my withering look, he says no more.

After letting the door at the top of the stairs swing open, I shove Johann through and then stash the quenched torch on a hook. We climb the steps, leaving wet boot prints on the stone. Once inside the main basilica, the guards on duty nod to us in greeting as we stride into the hall.

I stare about the prison in horror, although my face shows no emotion. Some of these witches have been behind bars for a month already. The hay at their feet is scant, stained brown, molding and musty where it's not putrid and wet.

I harden my heart to pity. In order to contain the evil, this holy building was selected as the most secure and blessed. Where a congregation would typically gather, there are now iron bars extending from the cut stone floor, trapping the hexen. There is only one door facing the altar, with heavy chains and three locks keeping it secure.

"You can see, sir," Johann says in his too-high voice, "there's hardly any room left. If Kommandant Kirch comes back with more people from his raid of the coven in the north..."

"Kommandant Kirch can deal with it," I say.

"Should we relocate some? There are cells in the Porta Nigra..."

"Monk's cells, not prisoner cells," I snap. Prior to the formation of the hexenjäger units, the upper part of the old building was a monastery. "Would you put a witch beside the bones of Saint Simeon?"

Johann blanches. "It's just...it seems..." Johann's voice fades to a whisper, but I still catch his words. "It doesn't seem right, does it? It's inhumane."

He should be afraid to speak so foolishly. If Kommandant Kirch heard such presumptuous remarks from a recruit, the lad would be lashed at the very least.

I slam my fist against the boy's jaw, the blow coming hard and fast and without warning. He spins in a circle before crashing down to the stone floor with a tooth-clacking snap of his head. Blood spurts from his lip as he looks up at me with wide, fearful eyes.

I crouch down in front of him before he has a chance to right himself.

"Are you suggesting, recruit, that these hexen be given better quarters?" I speak loudly, my voice carrying. Every single person in the vast room—witch or soldier—hears me. "A witch sells their soul to the devil," I boom. "Each and every one of them will stay here. Behind this cage. Until they burn. Their *comfort* is of little concern to any true hexenjäger." I stand, towering over the recruit, peering down my nose at the boy. "Am I understood?"

"Yes!" he squeaks. "Sir!"

I tilt my chin up and peer around the room. Roughly a hundred witches, crammed into a cage meant to hold only two dozen at most. Fewer guards than usual—most are with Kommandant Kirch, in his raid to the north. But enough.

My words settle over the basilica. The hexenjägers standing guard at the doors or patrolling the cage walk with proud steps, their spines straighter, their jaws more determined.

The witches—the ones still sensible to their plight—weep softly.

My words have ripped the last shred of their hope away.

I feel them watching me as I stride past the cage toward the main doors of the basilica. Dim light filters through the windows cut high above in the stone.

"Like his father."

I hear the whisper behind me, but I don't pause to see which fellow hexenjäger spoke. Everyone sees my father in me. A zealot, full of passion, a warrior of the faith. His death was ignoble, but his reputation outlasted him. He is the reason I was able to advance so quickly in the ranks of the hexenjägers, despite never having held a torch to a pyre. I may be second-in-command, and everyone else has forgotten the truth of it, but I have not: I am untested.

I have organized patrols, I have worked as a guard, but I have not yet lit a single fire.

I wonder: what would my father think of *that*?

I bite back the smile threatening to twist my lips, knowing exactly what he would think of the solstice and what I shall do on that day.

The young recruit skulks behind me. Already, a bruise blossoms across his jawline.

"You are right, Johann," I announce without turning to face the boy. "The prison is crowded. But not so crowded that it cannot handle one more witch."

"Sir?" he asks.

I reach the front of the prison. Wilhelm is the highest ranking hexenjäger on duty. He snaps to attention when I stop in front of him.

"How many units remain in the city?" I ask. While I know many men went with Kommandant Kirch, I am unsure of the exact number.

"Four, sir."

"Gather five men," I tell Wilhelm. "It will not take much to bring down the witch I have in mind, but she is crafty." I don't want the city left defenseless, nor can I risk facing a witch alone.

Especially this one.

Wilhelm salutes me, nodding once and then turning to gather the men I asked for.

"Fetch my horse," I tell Johann. The boy takes off at a run toward the stables.

While they work, I step outside into the fresh air, blocking the witches from my senses. That is, after all, the purpose of the walls. To let the foul evil remain unseen before it is scoured from this earth.

"Sir, your horse." Johann arrives moments before Wilhelm returns with five men—four astride, one leading a horse cart with a cage built into the back. The wooden box has one narrow door off the rear with iron bars providing the only light and ventilation. An adult could not fully stand in such a cage, the rough wood and shoddy construction not even fit for animals.

I slowly cast my look across each of the waiting men. They're loyal hexenjägers, among the best. Black cloaks cover broad shoulders; the gleaming enameled badge of the witch hunters provides the only spot of color.

I grab the reins of my horse's bridle from Johann's outstretched hands. "You ride on the cart," I tell the boy.

His eyes widen with eagerness, and he scrambles up to sit on the rough bench.

"Where are we going, sir?" he asks as I mount my horse.

"Bernkastel," I say.

There's noise behind me as some of the men realize the weight of our mission. Johann is the only one willing to speak what the others are thinking. "Bernkastel?" he says. "Isn't that the town where you are from?"

"Yes." I bite off the word. Some of the guards from inside the basilica have stepped out to see what the commotion is, where the Kapitän is heading off to so soon after returning to the city, so near to the date of the mass solstice burning.

I feel their eyes on me. Most of the witches that the hexenjägers rooted out came from Trier itself, but as the witch hunt has stretched from a season to a year to a decade, the hexenjägers have cast their net broader and broader, into the surrounding villages and towns, dragging the evil back into the city for proper disposal.

Still, it's rare these days for the home of a prominent hexenjäger to come under scrutiny.

I heave a sigh, my shoulders bowing to the weight of what must be said, what must be done.

I turn to the men. "We go to Bernkastel," I say. "A day's ride east. There is a witch there, living alone by the river. A young maid." A muscle twitches in my jaw. "My sister is the witch. We go to arrest her."

3

FRITZI

The forest's undergrowth snags around my legs as I trudge forward, huddling deeper into my cloak. It's too big—I stole it off a line two villages ago, along with a wide-brimmed hat to ward off the chill alongside my thick wool kirtle and linen shift. The cloak smells like horses.

Just keep walking. One step. Another.

I should have stayed in Birresborn long enough to get supplies. *Real* supplies, warmer clothes and food and more than the handful of empty potion bottles in the leather pouches that hang from a belt around my hips.

But every moment I waste is another moment that the hexenjägers get Liesel closer to Trier.

So I walk. And I keep walking.

Another step.

Another.

"*We should go to the forest folk,*" Aunt Catrin begged my mother and the Elder council.

I hear the echo of her plea now.

We should have gone to the Black Forest. Why did we let it get this far?

Elders whisper the command to children from the moment they can recognize the dangers around us. "Go to the Black Forest if anything happens," they say. "The forest folk will keep you safe."

But asking to be taken in by the forest folk, the goddess-chosen guardians of the source of our magic hidden in the dark deep of the Black Forest, is only a solution used by the most desperate of covens and witches. The thing we are to do when we have no other options—getting there requires traversing the many, many miles between us and the Black Forest, evading hexenjägers and whatever other prejudices lurk in the surrounding territories.

And most of it sounds like a bedtime story, anyway. Too good to be true.

Especially for a witch like me.

The forest folk guard the source of our magic, the Origin Tree—one colossal fixture composed of three trees braided together, each older than time itself, one birthed from each goddess and infused with their magic. The Origin Tree's power gives all magic life, and the forest folk ensure that the Well of magic that springs from the Origin Tree stays protected from corrupting forces—like wild magic.

Witches—good witches—access the Well's magic through the rules laid down by the goddesses and enforced by Elders.

But other witches—bad witches—can access a different sort of magic, a magic of chaos and corruption, spoken of in just as hushed tones as the forest folk, but fearful tones, cautious and terrified.

A witch can do anything, *anything* at all with wild magic, the sorts of magic that the hexenjägers fear us for. But a witch can only draw on one source, so to access wild magic, they must sever their connection to the Well, then connect to wild magic through evil acts of sacrifice, revenge, and murder. The longer they draw their power solely from wild magic, the more their soul twists and rots, until they are that which they seek: evil, through and through.

When I mix potions, the spells I speak tether me to that Well of uncorrupted magic, and infuse the potions with power.

When Liesel speaks her spells over lit flames, the words connect her to the Well and pour magic into her veins and let her see the answers to questions in the heat of the fire.

When Mama speaks her spells over bones or fur or animals, those spells tether her to the magic, and let her control creatures or portend warnings in bones and more—

Or she used to. She used to be able to do that.

My heart bucks, bruises, and I push on my chest, hand fisted.

The forest folk and the Origin Tree are protected by the goddesses, hidden away in the impassable bulk of the Black Forest. It's almost a fairy story, but now...

Why didn't we leave sooner?

Why did we stay in Birresborn?

The thought has been a persistent itch in the back of my mind since I left. Mama's words roll through me: *The hexenjäger threat is our responsibility.*

There are no other covens left to stand against them now. A few burned; more fled to the Black Forest. We have failed in that then, too.

No—*I* failed in that. I led everyone to slaughter.

Guilt is iron, it is lead, a weight in my lungs, invisible and intangible but relentless. So when I shake myself to focus, or focus as much as I can in my exhaustion, the guilt does not go away—it shifts, retracts, but there it waits, like my grief, watching and patient. Both know they will conquer me eventually. Both know I am as good as decimated under their power. They are in no hurry.

I swallow a spurt of nausea, my mind flashing with images, the grotesque transformation of people I loved into corpses. The hexenjägers were thorough; I couldn't find any trails taken by others who might have gotten away.

But someone else had to have escaped. Right? And if they did, they would be heading to the Black Forest. My aunt. My cousins. Any of the little ones. They all knew, from the moment they could talk, *"If the hexenjägers come and Birresborn is no longer safe, go to the Black Forest. Go to the forest folk. They'll take you in."*

But Liesel didn't escape.

My eyes blearily drift to snatches of sky through the canopy, gauging my direction, but I'm tired, and I ache. Keep walking, keep going—

I imagine my cousin shivering in a cold, dark cell, her little body racked with sobs as she awaits an unjust trial at the hands of the hexenjägers in Trier.

Another step. One more. Everything in me hurts, battered in the coming winter chill, but the pain is deeper than surface discomfort, my muscles wrenching in a way that reminds me, with every beat, I am alive.

The grate of ashes in my lungs—I am alive, I lived through the plumes of smoke.

The cuts on my fingers and arms—I am alive, I lived through clawing my way out of the cellar.

The grit in my eyes—I am alive, I lived through the sobbing as my mother burned.

Alive. Alive.

The word taunts me, and I keep walking.

How many days has it been since Birresborn? My stomach rumbles, and I pull one of the tubers I foraged out of my leather pouches. It's crunchy and tasteless, but it silences the hunger pains, one small relief in the endless thunder.

It's well past midnight, whatever day it is. Winter is thinning the forest's canopy, but enough of it remains that even the palest moonlight is kept at bay. The air is crisp, mixed with the humidity of a recent rain-not-quite-ice that lingers on my cloak in mushy droplets. There is moisture in every breath that smells of coming snow and decaying plants and dense, saturated dirt.

I feel my way onward, relying on touch and sound to move. There are no shadows even here; all is impassable darkness, so I wouldn't know if I was being followed, would I?

No. I'm scaring myself unnecessarily—if I was being followed, the hexenjägers would have set on me when I stole these clothes. It's just the darkness playing tricks on my mind.

And exhaustion. That ache is beginning to go deeper than the rest.

Stop thinking. Stop complaining. Just walk.

I check the sky for my direction; I cannot see the stars. Darkness only, everywhere. Am I still going south? My heart hammers, pushing panic through my limbs.

"Folk of the forest, herbs and charm," I say the lullaby to myself as I take another step. My voice sounds foreign and rough to my own ears. "Keep good children safe from harm. Folk of the forest, grass and bark. Leave bad children in the dark."

That's a lie. *Leave bad children in the dark.*

The bad ones aren't in the dark. They're right here, right next to us.

It's such a lie that I hiccup a laugh, but it cracks in my chest, and pain shoots out, choking me until I sob—verdammt, not again, *not again*.

The sob begets more, and my eyes burn with tears. How does it burn still? Haven't I cried out all the smoke and ash?

I find a tree trunk, lean my weight on it. I'm so tired; keep walking.

Another step, and something tethers around my foot.

I scream. It's a hand—a hexenjäger grabbing my ankle, face in a monstrous snarl—

My arms flail, and I slam to my knees. Nothing more happens, no clawlike fingers dragging me for a stake, and when I turn, feeling over what tripped me, I find only an arched root.

A root.

Not a hexenjäger.

My whole body deflates, and schiesse, how I hate myself. A tree root. I screamed and gave away my position because of a *tree root.*

The chilly dank darkness closes around me, thicker than a quilted blanket. My limbs start to give way, and in a wash of calm fuzziness, I droop closer to the damp undergrowth.

A shake, and I scramble to my feet and slap my cheeks, hard. *Stay awake, unverschämt!*

Another step. Another. I spot a gap in the foliage overhead—I'm still heading south. Mostly. Good.

Another step.

Another.

One by one, all the way to Trier.

4

OTTO

It is a solemn ride to Bernkastel.

The witch hunts have been going on for half our lives. No hexenjäger—no person in the entire diocese—is untouched by the trials.

It started when I was ten years old. For years, we'd heard of the villages who purged evil from their squares by burning witches. The archbishop sanctioned the deaths, then formulated the hexenjäger units for more efficient trials and executions.

For a time, despite the terrors outside our town, there was peace. Joy, even. I went from a boy to a man under my stepmother's guidance. She was the only mother I truly knew, and I loved her as such. She often tempered my father's rages.

For a while, we were a family.

Then the trials swept through my town. An old woman was first to be suspected of witchcraft, her land desired by a cousin. My mother usually had a calming effect on my volatile father, but the trials enraged her. She ranted about heresy—but not the heresy of the accused witches. The heresy of the zealots who burned them.

That was not the first time my father hit my mother; it was not even the first time he'd broken her nose. Blood streamed down her lips, and she spat at him, calling him a man who knew only fear, not God.

Father went into a quiet fury at my stepmother's rebuke. I still remember it. Hilde and I were in the upstairs loft, hiding, holding hands, trembling as Father turned on his heel and left our cottage.

He came back with hexenjägers.

He made us watch her burn.

"I will kill him," I whispered to Hilde that night. "You wait."

But in the end, I did not have a chance to follow through with that promise. Father developed a cough. First, he said, it was the smoke that had ruined his throat. But the wheezing and sputtering didn't go away. Then he claimed that my mother had cursed him in her death, making a deal with the devil.

"Then pray," I told him coldly. "Or is your god no match for a single, innocent woman?"

He tried to hit me, but his body racked with a fit of coughing. Blood splattered with mucus. "One day, boy," he choked out, his voice raspy, "you will thank me. You will see how much this world needs purging."

He was dead the next day.

And that, more than anything else I have ever seen in my life, proved to me that God was real.

Hilde and I survived on our own for a time. Mother had brewed beer to supplement the coins Father poured into the golden coffers of the cathedral, and she'd taught Hilde well. I dug out a garden behind the house. Hilde and I both hunted—mostly setting rabbit snares in the forest.

We survived.

But we didn't forgive.

And we never forgot.

When I got a little older, when our money started to run out, when some of the folk in town started speculating on when Hilde would be married and to whom, I went to Trier.

I trained with Dieter. I moved up the ranks, my position handed to me thanks to my father's reputation among the holy men.

I became Kapitän of the guard that killed my mother.

And now I'm coming home.

For my sister.

The cottage is just as I remember it. Despite moving to the city, I used to visit Hilde often. Later, it became necessary for distance and time to separate us.

Smoke puffs up from the chimney.

That first winter without Mother, Hilde never lit a fire. But there's smoke now, and little wonder as it's cold, and Hilde would need flames to brew her beer.

I slow my horse. The men behind me do the same. The cart rattles on the deeply rutted road. I imagine my sister riding in the cage built in the back, her thin arms and legs knocking against the rough wood as the cart lumbers back to Trier.

One of the men kicks his horse, pulling up beside me. Bertram, I trained with him.

"Sir, you can stay outside," he says. "It is no easy thing to arrest a relative." He meets my eyes, and I see sympathy there.

I shake my head. "No. I want her to know it was I who turned her in, I who condemned her. I cannot let evil exist in my own family."

Bertram's jaw is hard as he nods deeply, respectfully.

I dismount quickly. Best to be done with it.

I unlatch the brooch that fastens my cloak to my shoulders, letting the cloth drape over the saddle, careful to keep the dirt from staining it. My men follow suit—despite the cold air, the churning smoke from the chimney indicates that it will be sweltering inside.

Hilde learned from Mother well—keep the blaze going while brewing beer.

A pang hits me at this memory of home, and what that meant. Once.

Three short strides, and I'm at the door, my men behind me.

I feel the weapons hidden all over my body.

"God bless the righteous," Bertram says as I reach for the door. His words make me pause, just a fraction, my fingers cold on the iron ring that opens the wooden door.

There's a flicker by the window. Soft brown hair. White cotton kerchief. Hilde, inside. She's singing to herself, the fire roaring—she has not noticed the loud horses and men who have arrived.

My eyes settle on the windowsill where a clay bowl sits with cream inside the house. Bertram has followed my gaze. He makes the sign of the cross. Bowls of cream like that are little offerings to the forest folk, the old ways.

The long-steeped habits of the Celts that have not yet been purged from society.

I throw the door open.

My sister spins around, eyes wide. For one fraction of a second, I am met with a look of love. My sister and I share blood only through our father, but we grew up together, happy children who truly loved each other.

But then her hazel eyes move past me.

To the men.

The horses.

The cage on the cart.

And when she turns back, I see only fierce rebellion in her gaze. She knows.

It's time.

"What are you doing here?" she snarls.

"I have turned a blind eye to your practice for far too long." I stand in the doorway. I can feel Bertram and the other men crowding behind me, trying to get inside, but I don't let them. Not yet.

This is my sister.

This moment is ours.

"What evidence have you?" Hilde spits. Behind her, the firelight casts her in flickering shadow. Her defiance and the stifling heat do nothing to appease the hexenjägers gathered in her door tonight.

My gaze lingers on the cauldron at the fire. It's copper, not iron. "A vessel for potions?" I ask, arching a brow.

"For beer, you damn fool, as well you know."

I lift the tall, pointed black hat that sits on the little table by the door. It's called a hennin—Mother wore one too, to stand out in the crowds when she sold beer in the town market.

Another sign of a witch.

"And a broom by the door!" Bertram says. He tries to press it into my hand, but I drop it. It lands softly on the earthen floor.

"You can condemn a woman for a pot, a hat, and a broom?" Hilde asks, hand on hip. "I make my living with beer. How else am I to brew and sell it?"

The broom is a sign all the women in the diocese use—putting one outside the door indicates that the brewer has surplus to sell. Most people can't read, but the signal is common enough, an invitation to come up to the house and buy homemade goods.

I can feel the men behind me shifting uneasily. Every man with a mother has a home with a cauldron and broom inside it. Hennins are old and out of fashion, but common enough in the towns with markets.

At that exact moment, a ginger cat streaks across the floor.

"A familiar!" Bertram says, pointing.

Hilde growls in frustration. "I brew with hops! Mice love hops, but the cat loves mice."

I shake my head. "Witches hide in plain sight," I say. "But the little details add up. You seem to have an excuse for everything."

"There is nothing to excuse." Hilde's voice is fierce. "My only crime is not yet marrying. I am a maid who dares to live by herself, and—"

"Do you?" I let the words drop easily from my mouth, as if they do not matter, but they still Hilde's rant. "Or do you reside with the devil? Does your coven visit often?"

She cringes before me, finally aware that there's nothing to make this—me—go away.

"Your mother burned as a witch," I say without inflection or emotion. I speak as if she were not a mother to me too. "I had hoped, Hilde, that you would not follow in her cursed footsteps."

"*Bruder*—" Hilde's voice cracks with fear.

"I am no brother to you," I say, glaring at my sister.

That is what breaks her. Her rash responses and spitfire curses die on her lips. She is reduced to the little girl who used to come to me after skinning her knee or burning her fingers. Her eyes plead with me, her whole body seems to shrink with the dawning realization that I will not save her.

Not this time.

"Hilde Ernst," I announce, "I hereby arrest you for the heinous crime of witchcraft. You will stand trial in Trier, and then you will be condemned to die in fire here on Earth before God sends your soul to burn in hell."

5

FRITZI

"Are you excited for tonight, mein Schatz?"

Mama kneads dough at the table, flour coating her arms to her elbows. Sunlight slants through the kitchen window, pillars of light that catch on the white dust in the air, the wave of excess flour that comes when she tosses a handful onto the dough mound. Her schupfnudeln is my favorite dish in the world—potato dumplings that are buttery and crispy and eye-rollingly *good*.

She also has my favorite stew—Gaisburger Marsch—simmering in a huge cauldron over the fire, which makes our cottage smell like savory broth, and she had Aunt Catrin buy my favorite apfelwein at the market.

A girl only turns eighteen once, after all.

I hold a glass of that wine and force a smile at Mama.

"Of course," I say and take a sip. It washes over my tongue, liquid golden honey with a sharp tang at the back of my throat.

The smoothness of the alcohol almost makes me tell her. The words are on my tongue, nestled beside the wine's sweetness.

I almost say it. *Mama, I invited him. He's coming back.*

Mama pauses to swipe hair out of her face. It leaves a trail of flour across her forehead.

"Soon enough, you'll be an elder with me," she says with a proud grin. "You grow up so quickly. I can hardly believe it."

I give her a sardonic smile. "I'm hardly *elder*-old yet."

"*Old?* You think I'm *old*?"

I laugh as she does, giggling into my wine.

"Besides," I say, "maybe I won't be an elder at all."

Mama starts rolling half the dough into a long tube. Her eyes go from her work to my face and back again. "Oh? Are the Maid, Mother, and Crone calling you elsewhere?"

I lean forward, apfelwein sloshing. Some of it puddles on the floor. "What if they haven't spoken to me at all yet?" The words gush out of my mouth, just as accidental as the spill, another sticky mess I'll have to clean up. "What if the Three never speak to me?"

Abnoba, the Crone, wise and ageless and bright, protector of our forests, and prime guardian of life.

Perchta, the Mother, goddess of rules and traditions, of the hunt and beasts.

Holda, the Maid, guardian of the afterlife, of winter, of duality and coming together.

They guide us, bless us, watch over us—and speak to us, sometimes. It is a quiet whisper, I've been told; a settling of your soul, a rightness you can feel to your very core. It was how Mama knew she would become our coven's leader; Perchta, the Mother, appeared to her in a vision. It was how my cousin Liesel, just ten, knew from practically infancy that she would be the most powerful augur in a generation; Abnoba, the Crone, took great interest in her.

I have an affinity, like all other witches—the Well's magic channels through me when I use herbs and potions, but every witch has an affinity that they hone from an early age, chosen through interest or need or aptitude. It is one of the laws that governs how we keep the Origin Tree's magic uncorrupted: witches adhere to their affinity and the rules laid forth by the forest folk for how each affinity may be used. Plants and potions have always come naturally to me.

But no goddess has spoken to tell me of a mightier destiny. Nothing more has stirred in me at all.

Well—that's not true, is it?

I shake the voice away, flinching at the shiver that races down my spine.

Mama sees the way I twitch. She braces her hands on the table to give me a level look, one that instantly makes me want to defer to her, bow my head in surrender. But I hold her gaze.

"Friederike," she says, and her voice is full of such tenderness that tears warm the backs of my eyes. "Do you trust me? Do you believe I am a worthy leader of our coven?"

I sag in my stool, my spine hitting the wall. "Yes. And I know what you're going to say—since I'm your daughter, my blood will ensure that the Maid, Mother, and—"

"Absolutely not. Blood has nothing to do with the Three connecting to you. Don't speak for me, child."

I go silent, lips pressed together.

"I was *going* to say," her eyebrows lift, but she's smiling, "that I do not allow anyone unworthy in our coven. Even my own kin. If you don't trust yourself, trust me, and my necessity to protect this family. You've seen the sacrifices I have made to keep us safe. The Three will speak to you when they are ready to guide you; be patient."

Her eyes peel away from mine.

After a moment, she adds, "Do you still hear the voice asking you to use wild magic?"

There is no emotion in her words.

Will you lie to her, hm? What use is there in lying? She sees your truth.

"No," I say instantly. "Not for years."

She nods with a grunt. A breath catches in my throat as she punches the remaining dough, hard, shaking the table.

"If you were someone unreachable to the goddesses," she tells me, "I would have thrown you out long ago."

Smoke billows.

I cough, running through the haze—*no, no, Mama! Liesel—I'm coming, I swear, I'm coming—*

I run, and run, but the smoke swirls and thickens, swelling all around, and I wheeze in it, lungs filling only to deflate in hacking coughs—

A jolt rips through me, and I fly awake. Hard. The reality of lurching out of sleep hits me like I drank too much apfelwein, jagged tendrils of a headache pulsing across my scalp and down my neck.

I sit there, gasping, hands on my head.

I fell asleep.

Unverschämt, you idiot!

I must've tripped again sometime last night. I'm sprawled over the roots of a tree, tucked up alongside a gnarled bush and at least out of sight of anyone passing by. There are no main roads around, but that doesn't mean there aren't other travelers hoping to avoid soldiers or hexenjägers.

A groan, and I crouch forward, trying to will my headache away. A layer of frost coats my jacket, skirt, and boots. The solstice hasn't yet passed, but winter is approaching hard and fast and relentless.

I need to forage—if it frosted last night, most useful herbs will soon die off under the winter chill.

But Liesel could be in Trier by now, if the hexenjägers who took her didn't detour.

What few hours of restless sleep I managed have cleared my head enough that I realize I can't very well show up in Trier sleep-deprived and manic. The headache thuds dully across my scalp, and I wilt between my bent knees.

Schiesse. How have I survived even this long? I've let grief drive my every action, and look where it's gotten me.

Deep breaths. Just take a moment to—

I breathe again. Sniff tentatively at the air.

Smoke.

I didn't dream that.

I fly to my feet. My body seizes from the hard ground, and I bite down a wince, rubbing a kink in my back and warmth into my limbs as I try to figure out where I am.

The sun is not yet high—barely dawn. I'm still angled more or less south, maybe a little more east now, and I sniff again, tracking the direction of the smoke like a morbid hunting dog.

There—that way.

I stumble forward. Sleep hazes my mind enough that I only half-think to ask myself why I'm going *toward* a fire. But I'm hooked, drawn like a fish up a line.

The forest pulls away a few paces later into a small tidy clearing. A single thatched-roof house sits far back from the trees, its plaster walls white and clean, its crisscrossing wood boards in need of paint but solid. A chimney at the rear belches smoke into the air over the soft brown slopes of the dried straw roof.

I hover at the edge of the forest. My mind is still in a fog, and I stare up at the smoke like it will unfurl answers across the sky. Liesel can read signs like that.

My stomach grumbles, pointing out another area I've failed spectacularly in. I haven't kept a steady supply of food.

Well, where there's a house, there's people; and where there's people, there's food.

Mama drilled our coven's laws into my head before I could even walk. We put good into the world, and our Well of magic feeds on that good. Putting negative into the world feeds wild magic, and we do not *touch* wild magic.

But I've already stolen a few things since leaving Birresborn. And stealing isn't really putting *bad* into the world, is it? More like...taking good.

I survey the clearing, see no one from this angle, and creep up to the house.

There's a back door that opens into a small garden, and the wall has a few haphazard windows strewn across the back. Whoever is inside could easily look out and see me, but my stomach flips again.

I'll risk it.

The garden's dirt is upturned, soft with recent harvesting. There are a few crops left, the sturdier late-autumn ones that can withstand frost and chill. Winter greens and squash.

I drop to my knees, rip two orange squash off their vines, and start to duck back for the forest's edge.

From inside the house, something slams. A table overturning maybe, or a chair smashing to the floor.

"You monster!" a woman screams.

I scramble, but not for the clearing; closer to the house, flat against the wall and out of sight of the windows. But it isn't me she's yelling at—there's more crashing within, clear signs of a struggle.

And in that noise—boots. The jangle of swords, the unmistakable rattle of weaponry.

Heart in my throat, I ease around the corner of the house and stop just before the front yard. Slowly, so slowly, I lean around—and spot a group of horses pawing the road, tied to the yard's fence.

Latched to them is a prison wagon.

Liesel.

Tears sting my eyes. Maybe the Three haven't forsaken me after all.

Or, at the very least, they haven't forsaken Liesel, but whatever the reason, I'll take their gift.

I throw down the squash. Within the house, I hear now the gruff, taunting voices of men who think they're in control. The woman they're arresting is putting up a fight, spitting all kinds of vile insults at them—I'd laugh, if I was still capable.

There are a number of windows that look on the front yard, and the open door too.

I take off at a full sprint, running as hard as I can for the horses. They're war horses; my approach doesn't faze them in the least. I slide to a stop beside the prison wagon, the slickness of the dirt road sending me to my backside, but I'm hidden now from view of the house, and no one calls out *Hexe!* or *After her!*

Still, I hold for a breath, two, willing my heart to slow.

"Liesel?" Her name comes out of my throat croaked and trembling. "Liesel?"

I knock on the outside of the wagon.

No answer.

She could be unconscious. Or tied up. Or—

She's alive. He wanted her alive. She has to be alive.

Shaking, I push to my feet and round to the back of the wagon. There's a small window with iron bars across it, and I use the step at the back to hoist myself up and peer within.

"Liese—"

I don't even finish saying her name.

It's empty.

This isn't the group that arrested my cousin. That killed my coven.

My stupidity heats my chest. That I thought the Three could have turned a blind eye to my sins. That they would have rewarded me, even if to reward Liesel more.

What will I do now?

I know what I *won't* do.

I won't keep trudging through this forest, lost, desperate, scared.

Hexenjägers stomp through these lands, lands they *stole* from the tribes that came from these hills, and they incite fear and terror into all who hold to the ancient ways. And now they're arresting yet *another* innocent woman, dragging her back to Trier for a faux trial and gruesome death.

It's time *they* trembled.

It's time *they* feared.

Deep in my mind, beneath the surge of righteous fury, I swear I hear the voice sigh happily.

That should give me more pause than it does.

I wouldn't be the first witch to crack like this. To give in to wild magic out of anger and well-earned rage, only to become exactly that which the hexenjägers preach against: a murderous demon that could bring down curses on whole herds of livestock, make men blind where they stand, and mutilate flesh with a snap of their fingers.

Their fear of us is not entirely unjustified.

And I feel that now more than I ever have. It would be so very, very easy to destroy them all.

But I would destroy *myself* in the process.

Wild magic is corrupting. It is poison. It draws its power from all the foulness of the world, and to touch it is to let your soul shrivel in its rot.

I jump down from the prison wagon. The hexenjägers haven't come out of the house yet—there's a raised argument happening now, one of the jägers shouting at the woman, trying to calm her down.

She *shouldn't* be calmed. She's right to be furious.

I am furious.

And I'm going to *act*.

Yes, the voice says, giddy. *Yes. Act! Make them suffer!*

Not with wild magic, I snap back. *I don't need you to be powerful.*

I hurry back behind the house. The small garden waits for me, and my eyes cast over it, searching, searching—

Something bumps my leg.

I nearly scream. But the moment I look down, a small ginger cat stares up at me, and any noise falls flat in my throat.

Mama loved cats. We had dozens over the years.

The cat makes a low grumble of a purr in her throat. She coils away, tail flicking, before she bounds over the garden fence—

And right into a small bush of rosemary.

I scramble for it. There's nettle too—and witch hazel—

All powerful protection herbs.

I pull out one of the empty vials I had on me when I left Birresborn. From the house, I hear a scream. The telltale sound of irons locking around wrists.

Hurry, hurry—

I stuff the vial with herbs and add a pinch of snow on top, a crude, quick potion.

Please work.

Then I rush for the cottage. A bracing breath in, a slow breath out, and with the heel of my boot, I kick in the back door.

All attention swings on me. The hexenjägers. The woman they're arresting.

The lot of them throw ferocious glares, all assuming I'm a threat, either another witch or another hexenjäger. The woman's wrists are in manacles, the center chain held by a hexenjäger who has a look that isn't just angry—it's panicked.

Good. Let him writhe.

"Herb and plant with roots that roam," I start the spell that will channel the Well's magic and turn these herbs into a protection potion. "Help me here keep safe this home. Protect and care, shield and cover, lend your might to this lone daughter."

Tears sting my eyes as I weave the words around my vial. Mama's spell mingles with mine, the one she used on me.

Raw, aching grief pours into my spell, and I feel the power build and build, so I say it again—

"Herb and plant with roots that—"

"Stop her!" The hexenjäger holding the chain shouts. "*Hexe!*"

"—keep safe this home. Protect and—"

The hexenjägers tear toward me.

"Shield and cover, lend your might to this lone daughter!"

I shout the words.

I *scream* them.

They rip from the center of my being, that tight knot of fury *they* planted there, and my palms grow warm around the vial, burning, *burning*.

Too hot. Too much. I lurch back, hands opening, and my vial launches out like a ball from a cannon. The glass hits the floor and shatters, spraying the potion up in thick green smoke.

This potion shouldn't *smoke.*

Thicker and thicker—more and more—

The hexenjägers cry out. I can't see the woman, but when I scramble forward, the density of the spell shoves me back, out of the kitchen, out of the cottage, launching me across the garden.

I slam against the ground, my head striking a garden post, and all goes black.

6

OTTO

Where is she?

I scramble up. Smoke is everywhere. Gagging, my eyes bleary, I try to look around.

"Hilde?" I choke out.

No answer. But a quick scan of the one-room cottage tells me she's not here. The rest of the hexenjägers are still sprawled on the floor, knocked out. I don't remotely care about them. I don't even bother to check if they're still alive as I race past their inert bodies, launching over the broken chair and upturned table.

Some of this smoke is *green.*

Images scramble in my brain.

Where is my sister?

And also: *Who was that?*

The back door is wide open. Someone—a young woman—burst into my sister's cottage and threw something...green smoke? At Hilde. And Hilde's gone.

She's…gone.

No. No, no, no, my brain screams. Hilde *can't* be gone. The whole plan will go to shit if—

There. By the garden post. A woman. Hilde?

No.

The *other* one.

I rush, boots thundering across the garden as I race to her form. My mind can't keep up with my body's actions, but it feels good to act. The woman doesn't appear conscious, but I don't risk it. I throw myself on her, pinning her shoulders to the ground with my knees. She moans, eyelids fluttering, and I flick my hand out, calling for the silver dagger hidden in my sleeve.

I may be the kapitän of the hexenjägers, second-in-command, but I have never, not once, believed that witches were real.

Until now.

"What are you?" I growl at the thing beneath my knees, blade held to her delicate white throat.

Her eyes focus slowly. Then they narrow, full of hatred.

She works her mouth, tongue running over her teeth as her lips twist derisively. I mirror her snarl unconsciously, then apply pressure to the dagger. She swallows, the up-and-down of her neck muscles making her skin redden under the blade's edge. They say silver hurts witches.

Good.

"Where is she?" My voice is harsh, hurried. I think I hear movement from behind me. The other hexenjägers are waking up.

"Who?" The witch has the audacity to look confused.

I spit out a curse at her. "My *sister.*"

"Your…?" The rest of her words die as I lean harder against her throat. A thin red line of blood sprouts under the dagger.

It would be so *easy* to kill her.

And I would be praised for it. Lauded as the hero who single-handedly killed a witch that blasted a whole hexenjäger unit with magic.

But I *need* Hilde.

"Yes, my *sister*, you witch." I grind my knees down, not caring at the way the girl cringes in pain. "What did you do to her?"

"You were trying to arrest your own sister?" she gasps out in utter disdain.

I ignore the question. She kicks her legs at me, as if she could buck me off her, but I'm far stronger than her and, what's more, I don't care in the least how much I hurt her in return. Not as long as she answers me.

"I *protected* her," the girl grinds out when I lean in harder. Her words come as little pants—she cannot breathe with my weight bearing down on her chest. "From monsters like you."

Before I can ask her what the hell that means, Bertram bursts through the garden, racing toward me. "Kapitän!" he shouts. "Kapitän Ernst!"

I toss a glare over my shoulder. The blundering fool has crushed all my sister's cabbages in his attempt to rush to my aid.

The witch beneath me squirms, thinking that I may be distracted enough for her to escape. I almost laugh at her feeble attempt. In one swift motion, I push myself off her, my hand pressing into her clavicle so that she's blinded by pain. Before she can move, I yank her to her feet, grabbing one slender wrist in my hand and twisting her arm. She cries out as I pin her there, her arm wrenched so solidly that if she tries to flee, it would take only a little pressure from me to dislocate her shoulder.

"Get the irons," I order Bertram.

"What are you going to do," the girl says in a hollow voice, "burn me?" She speaks as if she doesn't care, but I see the sweat that breaks out on her forehead, the flash in her eyes. "Did you pack a brand to label me a dämon too?"

She's seen a burning before. The thought comes unbidden to my mind, and I push it away. The branding of witches is something new, something the kommandant devised only a few months ago. If this witch has seen the consequences of black magic, she should have known not to perform it in front of an entire verdammt hexenjäger unit.

Through the cottage's broken door, I can see the other men finally struggling up. Bertram is shouting for aid—there's clinking iron from the chains, a wooden thump as the cage door on the cart is banged open in front of the cottage.

Meow.

I almost stumble on the cat. A ginger cat, winding its way through my legs.

"Get away, Rose," I order. Only my sister would bother to name a mouser, but she has a soft spot for the thing.

The witch mouths the cat's name. *Rose.* Her pink lips form a perfect little circle, like she's surprised at the sweetness of it. Rose rubs her head against the witch's ankle, and my stomach turns, remembering the legends of how witches turn cats into familiars. Has this hexe somehow corrupted my sister's innocent pet?

"You will tell me where my sister is," I say, my voice a low whisper.

"Why?" the witch snaps back at me. "So you can burn her, too?"

The other men are approaching now. Bertram has the iron shackles in his hands. I cannot say much, not with them so close.

"You're not going to burn, hexe," I whisper, my voice liquid.

Her eyes widen.

"But you'll wish you had by the time I'm done with you."

7

FRITZI

The prison wagon sways, occasionally hitting a rut in the road that sends my body thumping against the wall, the iron manacles on my wrists shifting, smelling of old metal and rust. The jägers aren't going particularly fast, and I wonder if it's because the lead one thinks they'll stumble across his sister.

Maybe we will.

But I'm hoping she got away. She probably saw the smoke from my spell—I still have no idea why it *exploded*; maybe there was something hidden growing among those herbs?—took the opportunity, and bolted into the forest. Now that the hexenjägers are gone, she has to be back at her cottage, picking up the remains of her trashed home.

While I'm serving out her fate.

Guilt seizes me. Guilt and fear and bone-shaking dread.

No. I won't think about that. I won't think about how I set out to save Liesel only to end up exactly like her.

My head falls back against the wall, a defeated sigh whimpering out of me.

Everything about the past few days has rapidly spiraled into the worst case scenario, so perfectly and with such lethal precision that I'd think I'm cursed if I didn't know the truth.

It isn't a curse.

It's *me*.

My own actions have come to demand reparation. My own past has come to poison my future.

I force a brittle laugh. Schiesse, being stuck in this damp, dark box does nothing but seep exhaustion into my brain. I'd been surviving the past day and night on action only, moving forward, drowning in my mission to save Liesel. But here, now, the abyss of grief is waiting for me, the yawning stretch of everything I've been outrunning finally tripping my heels.

It's good, though. I'll gladly fall into this self-deprecating nothingness if it means distracting myself from the fact that I'm a prisoner of the hexenjägers. That I'm on my way to Trier, bound for an even worse fate than my coven.

A tremble rocks through me. My throat grates, a scream or a sob bubbling to life. No, no, *no*—I will not give these jägers the satisfaction of falling apart. I'm not in a Trier prison yet, am I? So all isn't lost, and it's at least a half day's trip still, and they'll likely have to camp for the night, or at least stop to relieve the horses. Once they do, the moment they let me out of this box—they'll have to, won't they?—I'll act. Run. Fight them. Steal a pistol. They took my empty potion vials but left my coat and hat, so I can easily hide and survive in the forest, no matter how cold it drops. *Anything* to get away.

Liesel is counting on me.

And I will *not* let her down. Not again.

The wagon heaves to the side, throwing me bodily off the seat, my manacled wrists making it impossible to catch myself. I land on the rough wood floor with a tumbling crash, pain forcing a cry from my lips.

But the wagon stops.

I stay on the floor, staring at the barred window at the top of the doors. Sure enough, footsteps sound outside. Gruff voices.

"There's a campsite a few paces off the road," says the kapitän. The hexenjäger whose knees I can still feel on my shoulders, a line of blood now dry on my neck from his blade. "Scout it. We'll stay here tonight. And you three, span out. Hilde Ernst may yet be in these woods. She couldn't have crossed the river—if she ran off in the chaos and smoke this hexe made, she could be somewhere nearby. It's a long shot, but worth it."

"Kapitän, what about..." The voice peters off. Then, quietly, he adds, "The *witch*?"

I cut a gruesome smile. That's fear in the young jäger's voice. It bolsters me like a rope tossed into a long, jagged chasm.

"Scared, are you, Johann?" someone else teases. "Should we leave you on guard, then?"

A pause. "If that is my duty." But Maid, Mother, and Crone, he sounds *petrified*.

I heave my shoulder into the side of the wagon, rocking the whole structure, which earns a satisfying chirp of terror from Johann and a scrambled muttering of prayer.

One of the other jägers laughs.

Another thunders his fist on the side of the wagon. "Quiet in there!" The kapitän.

"I didn't actually make any noise," I cut back. If I wasn't so exhausted, so hungry, so downright strained with grief, I'd be able to think more rationally. But right now, the only thing keeping me at all level is the sound of disgusted irritation the kapitän emits.

"I will stay on guard," he says to his men. "The rest of you, go."

There's a resounding chorus of "Ja, Kapitän!" before feet trudge off, stomping from the road into the tangled undergrowth.

The moment I know we're alone, I leap up and kick the door. "Are you going to let me out?"

No response.

I wrap my fingers around the bars—I can't stand up straight in this wagon, so to look out the window, I have to crouch a bit—and see the kapitän with his back to me.

His arms are folded, his spine rod-straight, a spotlessly clean black cloak slung over his broad shoulders. That cloak, his dark hair, his eyes—he is all shadow, save for the pale wash of his skin, and the presence he gives off is one of utter control. He looks like he was formed from a cast iron mold of what the perfect hexenjäger should be.

Fury roils in my gut. "Hey, I'm talking to you!"

Nothing.

I yank on the bars. "You can't keep me in here all night, jäger. Where am I supposed to piss?"

That makes him flinch.

"Oh, did I upset your delicate expectations for how a woman should talk?"

His head shifts toward me, showing him in profile, his mouth in a snarl.

"You aren't a woman," he says. "You're a witch."

"I'm a *person*." He won't meet my eyes, but I glare at the side of his face. "My name is Friederike—"

He cuts up a hand. "Your name isn't necessary to our—"

"And my friends, my cousins, the people I love, they call me Fritzi, you absolute arschloch."

His jaw bulges. I can see my name in his mind. Humanizing me.

Was he part of the brigade that attacked my coven? It was chaos: fighting and frantic spells, and then the cellar, the burning, the smoke—

"Does knowing the names of the people you murder make it harder to condemn them? Good. Should I list the names of the witches you burned nearby? I'll start with those most recent, in Birresborn," I say, probing.

He glances at me, away. "I have been traveling. That patrol was Kommandant Kirch. And simple *names* would not affect any good jäger in their duty."

Kirch rings through me, a struck bell, a dozen emotions keening high and loud.

"Ah, yes, Kirch, your almighty."

"He is not the Almighty."

"No? Oh, that's right, he reports to the archbishop. Your kommandant, the ever-eager right hand of that walking plague you dare call a holy man. Tell me truly, is it the archbishop's face you jägers see when you close your eyes in prayer? Or merely when you close your eyes for *other pursuits?*"

His face turns purple. "Weigh your words carefully, hexe. I will not stand for blasphemy."

"Speaking of—how is the kommandant? Back in Trier?" I'm toeing a dangerous line, but I have to know. Did he get Liesel back to Trier? Or is she still rolling through the countryside, like I am? Is she close by, even—maybe this caravan is due to reunite with Kommandant Kirch's?

The kapitän doesn't respond. The muscles in his face bunch tight, the tendons in his neck flare, and he works his lips in a scowl that doesn't feel like the typical hexenjäger hatred for my kind—it runs deeper. It feels almost personal.

"Are you *mad* at me?" I guess. "Grumpy that I'm getting under your skin, or that I didn't let you arrest your own sister? Having yourself a good pout, are you?"

The kapitän whips around to face me and takes a single step closer to the wagon. I don't miss the way he glances at the woods, checking that we're still alone.

"You have no idea what you've stepped into," he spits at me. "Years of planning, and—"

"You have no idea what an absolute disease you are," I throw back. "The world would be better without your presence. Think about that, jäger—if you died, no one would mourn you, and the land would rejoice."

"And who would mourn you?"

My lips part, but the answer is raw and recent: *no one.*

He can see he's hit something. He doesn't smile, though; no reveling in his verbal victory.

He studies me. Narrow, cold brown eyes. Eyes that have watched a hundred people burn. Eyes that saw his sister fight.

There is nothing in him, a blankness that sends a shudder down my body.

Hatred, I can handle. Power-hungry dominance, I expect.

But this indifference? He looks like he could stab me in the heart and leave me for dead on the road without a second thought.

Which begs the question—

"Why didn't you kill me?" I ask, staying back from the window, in the shadows of the wagon.

He may not have been at Birresborn, but he's no better than the men who were.

Some of the tension in his brow smooths out. "Why did you use magic in a room filled with hexenjägers?"

"Do you ever answer a question straight?"

"You are not worthy of answers, hexe."

"*Fritzi.* Maid, Mother—" I drop my chin to my chest. "Talking to you is like speaking to a wall."

I think we're done, so I turn to sit again.

But the kapitän makes a gruff hum in his throat. "What spell did you use on my sister?"

I go rigid. My lip curls, and I press back against the window, letting him see my anger, my determination. "Protection. Enough to let her get away."

"That's the thing I can't place," he says, lips tight. "My sister would not have fled."

"From her crazed brother trying to arrest her? You're right, she should have embraced you with open arms."

The kapitän's eyes narrow. He shakes his head like I'm simple, like *I'm* the one refusing to give him straight answers.

Footsteps draw closer; the other hexenjägers back from scouting.

"Why do you care if your sister got away?" I spit at him. He doesn't look at me now, waiting at attention for his men to rejoin him on the road. "You still got a witch to bring back to Trier."

Something about his posture changes. I can't tell what it is; is he standing straighter? Is his anger returning?

Whatever it is, it makes me flinch again when he throws me one last glare.

There's calculation in his cold eyes now. A thought playing out that I can only guess at.

I hear his words come back: *You're not going to burn, hexe. But you'll wish you had by the time I'm done with you.*

I feel suddenly like I should beg for my life. Like he has a pistol aimed at me, and I have only seconds to live.

But I clamp my mouth shut and scowl at him, fuming, drawing on the swell of anger his presence stokes.

I will not fear him.

"Kapitän? The site is clear," one of the jägers says.

"Good." He turns away from me. "Set up camp."

He takes a few steps off into the forest before he adds, "Bring the witch."

Relief sweeps through me, but it's short-lived.

The wagon door opens. I stare out at two hexenjägers, their faces brittle mixes of fear and disgust, only to realize that while the wagon kept me in, it also kept them *out*.

And now, if I don't manage to escape, I'll have to spend a whole night in a hexenjäger camp, relying on their disgust to override any other impulses they may have.

One of the hexenjägers reaches in to seize the chain between my manacles. He yanks me hard, and I go careening out of the wagon, slamming to my knees on the dirt road, a cry bursting unbidden out of me.

The other hexenjägers laugh. Something breaks in them, tension evaporating for one terrifying second—I see the change in their eyes. Their fear is now aggression.

A jäger grabs a rough handful of my blond curls where they peek out beneath my hat and wrenches my head back. I whimper—I can't help it, can't stop it, my body reacting to this change viscerally.

If they don't fear me.

If they aren't repulsed by me.

I have no way to protect myself.

Terror is cold and consuming and splays through my chest in a sharp wave.

"Bertram! *Stand down!*" The kapitän's shout thunders over the road.

I gasp an inhale, wincing at the way Bertram's hand twists in my hair.

The men go stiff. They eye Bertram and take a noticeable step back.

The kapitän squares himself directly in front of me. His glare is fixed to Bertram's grip on my hair, his cheeks stained red.

"No one," he sweeps that glare across his men, "is to touch the witch. Understood?"

A pause, then the men sullenly agree.

Bertram drops his grip on me. "It's just a *witch*, Kapitän. We've had our fun with others."

The men shift, uneasy. Their fear is returning, and I can practically hear their thoughts.

Others, yes. But others *never used magic.*

However brave these hexenjägers think they are, they haven't dealt with real magic. A few of the older ones likely encountered real witches in the early days, but the first victims of the witch hunts were mostly true witches—now, after years of my people burning or fleeing to the Black Forest, the only victims that remain are innocents who are no more magical than the hexenjägers who condemn them.

My panic starts to ease, the tense muscles in my chest releasing slowly. I can see their unease creeping over them like frost over frozen ground.

The kapitän's glare flashes to Bertram. "This witch is tainted with evil. It is a prisoner of Kommandant Kirch, and I will not have any of my men falling prey to its guiles. Understood?" He takes a threatening step toward Bertram, a silent reminder of how tall he is in comparison, the sheer weight of his presence.

"No one is to touch the witch," he repeats. "*Understood?*"

"Aye, Kapitän!" the men say in unison.

Bertram bows his head. "Aye, Kapitän."

The kapitän juts his chin at me. "Now secure the hexe," he commands and stomps off.

The campsite is little more than a clearing with a charred pit for a fire. The hexenjägers set to work efficiently, putting out bedrolls, gathering wood, stoking flames to life. Soon, the clearing is a sole orb of warmth against the encroaching dark and chill of night.

And I'm lashed to a tree at the edge of the clearing, hands above my head, just far enough from the fire that every stray wind makes me shiver. But I'm sitting, at least, and I'm not in the direct line of sight of any of the jägers, so as they start dividing evening chores—doling out rations, tending the horses, organizing a watch—I take stock of my surroundings.

The manacles are looped to the tree via rope—easy enough to get through, if I can find something sharp. I can just make out bumps of vegetation on my left, but the firelight doesn't reach—are there herbs I can use? Likely just grass. But there are plenty of rocks on this flattened space, and one is bound to be sharp enough to saw through the rope.

How will I grab one? If I can bend, maybe I can use my foot to flick one up and catch it...

Four of the hexenjägers are centered around the fire, eating, passing a sheepskin, and bellowing the type of laughter that comes with camaraderie. The kapitän is off talking with the three hexenjägers who were searching the area for Hilde. They didn't find anything, and I smile. At least that innocent woman is safe.

One of the jägers by the fire jostles the shoulder of another who can't be older than fifteen. "Johann—the witch looks hungry. Why don't you feed it, eh?"

Ah, the scared one.

Johann's face pales. But he picks up a bowl and extends it for another to ladle in stew.

His arm is shaking. He spills some of the stew, and the men roar laughter.

"Schiesse, Johann, how green are you?" Bertram roughs his hair. "Barely off your mother's breast!"

More laughter. Johann's face reddens, but he stands, dutifully, and his eyes flash up to mine.

He balks.

"It isn't *that*," he says to the men, fighting for composure. "I've never—it's *powerful*. Isn't it? I've never seen magic like that."

There's a wash of silence through the men. Despite their banter, I see Johann's terror in all of them, briefly, and I can't stop my feral grin.

Their fear is holding.

Good. I trust their fear more than I trust their kapitän's order.

They're all trying not to look at me and failing. When I bare my teeth at one, he crosses himself.

The kapitän chooses that moment to stomp into the firelight. He takes the sheepskin from one of his men and the bowl of stew from Johann. If he's aware of their tension, their conversation, he doesn't show it.

"First watch, take your stations. The rest of you, sleep. We have an early start tomorrow."

No one argues, and they disperse. I clock where the two on patrol go—one to the north, one to the south, and they'll likely walk in a slow rotation until they're relieved. But there'll be enough space between them to slip through. I can even wait until Johann is on watch and use his fear to my advantage.

I just have to get out of this verdammt *rope*. Even manacled, I'll be able to run away.

I look up at it, shifting for a better view—

When a shadow slashes over me.

"You won't escape."

Slowly, I shift to frown at the kapitän, but he's backlit by the fire. I can't see his face.

A blink, and I see Mama. Standing over the cellar hatch. Her face in shadows.

My pulse surges into a gallop, and I fist my frigid hands.

"Your sister won't be the only woman running free from you today," I snap.

His shoulders go rigid. "She did not run. You did something to her. And you will tell me what, exactly, you did."

"Verpiss dich, jäger," I say in as sweet a voice as I can manage.

I shouldn't antagonize him. I should be doing everything I can to be small and forgettable and unthreatening.

But my quickened pulse courses hatred into every part of my body, and I can barely see through the swell of rage. I want to lash out at him, kick him in the groin; I want to spit in his face, tear his eyes with my fingers.

He drops into a squat before me. I scramble back, pressing myself to the tree, and all that anger sharpens into cold, relentless fear.

The kapitän tips his head, surveying my position: huddled against the tree, eyes wide, legs pulled up against my stomach.

"No one will touch you," he tells me. "We are not brutes."

"No, you just burn people alive. Far more civilized."

He holds out something to me. The bowl of stew. The sheepskin.

"You're hungry," he says.

I'm so tempted to tell him to piss off again, but I bite my lip and shake my manacled hands in response.

"And you'll only feed me if I tell you where your sister is?" I ask. "Because that is definitely the behavior of someone who is not a brute—"

He sets the sheepskin down and lifts the spoon out of the bowl.

He's not really going to—

He is.

The kapitän holds the spoon to my lips.

I stare at him, stunned.

"Don't let stubbornness make you stupid," he tells me. "Eat."

"It would be mighty inconvenient if your prisoner passed out from hunger before you could properly torture her, wouldn't it?"

His jaw bulges. He bumps the spoon against my lips. "Eat," he repeats, his tone of command so second nature that it sounds well-worn.

The stew is something crude and easy, road rations mixed with melted snow, but the scent drives my stomach to rumbling. I've only eaten bits and pieces while traveling from Birresborn, and if I'm going to make any progress tonight, I'll need my strength.

I part my lips and take the proffered bite.

"There," he says. "Is that so hard?"

Oh, I will *kick him* the moment I've had my fill.

I still can't see his face in the dark, the fire at his back. He drops into silence as he feeds me, just dips the spoon back into the bowl and lifts bite after bite, nothing in his movements saying he's impatient that I'm eating slowly or that he's offended having to feed me at all. It's so in contrast with the bitter, angry man he's been that I can't help shrinking from him, my eyes dropping, each bite I take now feeling like he's won something, like I've conceded to him.

"You're wrong," he whispers to the dark.

I don't answer.

"I have never burned someone alive."

I can't help myself—my snort of derision is more like a snarl. He would lie about the thing he must be proudest of? There's a trick here.

He opens his mouth as if to speak, but then seems to decide it's pointless. He turns to pick up the sheepskin and offers it to me.

I tip my head back and beer slides into my throat. It's hoppy and rich and immediately warms my whole body, which is a problem—exhaustion creeps up over me again. My ever-present companion. But I blink furiously and sit up straighter, willingly myself to alertness.

The kapitän pushes the cork back into the sheepskin. "You can sleep. I told you, no one will touch you."

I laugh. It's bitter and sharp. "Forgive me for not thinking your word has any bearing whatsoever, *jäger*."

He holds a beat. "You're not going to escape either."

I refuse to look at him, glowering at my lap. "Just leave me alone."

His nearness is disorienting. Is that why he fed me? So I'd be full and too tired to run? My arms shake, and I do look up now, only to scowl.

Maid, Mother, and Crone, I've never hated someone as much as I hate this one man.

"Leave me *alone*," I say when he lingers.

He stands. I think he's going to walk away, but he just tosses the now empty sheepskin and bowl toward the fire. Then he pulls a length of rope from a satchel at his waist and knots one end to my wrist.

"The manacles aren't enough?" I snap.

Silently—the Three save me, this man barely *speaks*—he unwinds the rope and loops the other end to his wrist.

We're connected now.

Any move I make in the night, he'll feel. Unless I can somehow saw through this rope without waking him. How heavy a sleeper is he? Maybe—

"I'm a very light sleeper," he says at the look on my face. "And until you tell me what I need to know, you're under my command."

I can't stand it anymore; I rear back and thrash out to kick him, but he sidesteps it easily, and when he does, his face catches in the firelight.

He isn't smiling. Not laughing at my feeble act of rebellion.

He looks…in pain.

The kapitän drops to the ground next to me—out of kicking distance—and positions his back against a tree. He folds his arms over his chest, pulling taut the rope between us, and closes his eyes.

I yank on the rope, hoping to make him tip over, but it barely fazes him.

The Three help me, I want to scream. I want to attack him. I need to expel this fury, because if I don't, I'll realize it isn't fury at all.

It's fear.

I won't escape tonight.

Which means tomorrow, I'll be taken into Trier as a prisoner, and any chance I had at freeing Liesel will be lost.

The fire sizzles down to embers, casting the area in a hazy orange glow. It's that softness that pushes tears down my cheeks. I can't stop them; I can't even wipe them away, helplessness urging more, careening my grief out of control.

My mother died yesterday.

I haven't let myself feel it. Not truly. And I grind my teeth against it now, begging myself not to think about it, not yet; I'll mourn, but not *yet*—

I sob there in the darkness, fighting to keep my gasps quiet.

Maid, Mother, and Crone, the prayer comes unbidden, and it *aches* now knowing they won't hear me. That I'm well and truly alone.

Are you, though?

Go away, I push at the voice. *Not now. Please. Just leave me alone.*

I've come this far and not given into wild magic. What makes the voice think I ever will, if I haven't by now?

There is no response.

8

OTTO

I lead the caravan back to Trier. My horse is a pace ahead of the others, and I value the silence this affords me. I tune out the other men and the creaking of the prisoner cart, leaving me with only my own voice in my head.

And the echoes of my sister's screams.

Nothing has gone to plan.

And now Hilde is...

I don't think she's dead. The witch, she calls herself Fritzi—she didn't seem to think that Hilde is dead. Just missing.

"And safe," she insisted. She clearly thinks Hilde ran away, but I know without a shadow of a doubt she did not. *So where is she?*

Damn the witch, I can almost see the events from her point of view. An innocent woman being arrested for witchcraft, with a sure sentence of death from either neglect or burning. This real witch overheard, acted to save her, and...

And now all my plans are shot to hell.

I factored in everything, measured the odds, weighed the chances. I considered every single possibility.

Except *actual, real* witches.

They're not *supposed* to be real! That was the *point!*

Bertram kicks his horse, picking up his pace to ride abreast with me. The roads are wider the closer we get to the city. We've passed some merchants getting ready for the Christkindlmarkt, but everyone gets out of the black-cloaked hexenjägers' way.

"It's still a bit hard to fathom," Bertram says to me in a low voice after a few moments.

He's the closest to my age and the highest-ranked jäger beneath me, although he clawed his way to the top, a history riddled with arrests and pyres, signing up for the jägers when he was younger even than Johann. Perhaps he feels a bit of camaraderie toward me due to these facts, despite my lack of desire to chat.

"We've been doing this how many years?" he continues blithely.

Too many, I think.

"And despite all this time, I have yet to see an *actual* witch's power," Bertram continues. "Although," he adds in a musing tone, "I met one of the first hexenjägers, and he swore magic was real."

My eyes go wide at that. It's no secret that the archbishop employs young men to be hunters. The excuse has always been that youths are stronger in body and more innocent in soul, both of which are needed to take down a witch. But it has only just occurred to me that while the trials have been ongoing for years, I have not interacted often with any of the original hexenjägers.

"He said, in the beginning, that the witches fought back with magic," Bertram continued. "Said he saw it with his own eyes. Some of the men went mad; the archbishop retired them to a monastery. I reckoned he'd gone mad, too, to be spouting such nonsense about magic." Bertram paused, glancing back at the cart. "Now I figure the first round of hexenjägers might have fought real witches, and the ones left must have gone into hiding or something like that."

I still don't speak. If given half a chance, I know Bertram would prattle on for hours. I'm used to ignoring him, but for once, I find what he's saying to be worthwhile.

"But, well…" Bertram eyes me. It's clear he's testing the grounds, trying to see how much I will allow. Whether I will leap to the defense of the mission of the hexenjägers, whether I will chastise him for not showing blind obedience.

I say nothing. Just yesterday, I struck Johann in the face for blasphemy, but Bertram at least has the sense to speak in tones so low only I can hear.

"I've always sort of thought it was a bit of a scam," he says in a lower voice. "I mean, I cannot help but notice that if a man wants a different wife, it's easier to get her burned as a witch than to get the pope's approval for divorce. If there are two bakers in a town, one will accuse the other of witchcraft so that there's less competition."

The accusations that fly around Trier are fed by greed and fear. If you stand to profit from a burning, you hold out the match. If you are different from the societal norms in any way—too loud, too quiet, too strong, too weak—you are sent up the pyre.

We all—every citizen of the diocese—are complicit. While the archbishop preaches about purging the city of sin, we all see the order of operations. First, he banned all Protestants, then all Jews from the city. Trier was to be Catholic—Jesuit—only.

But that wasn't enough.

Witches came next. And they were not banned—they were

murdered. Now that it's too late, there are hints of rebellion seeping throughout the city. There *are* good people left in Trier, ones willing to fight. But their rebellion is a whisper now.

They need something louder than the roaring flames to spur them into revolt.

But for now, fear holds the resistance back. The archbishop was smart in that. Divide the people, make them feel alone. Make them know that if you do not conform, you are called a witch.

And you are burned for it.

I have seen the truth of it from the start, from the moment my mother was cast screaming into the flames.

But I had thought that perhaps others—even in the hexenjäger units—were merely swept up in the panic and ignorant of the truth. That is why, I had assumed, the units cast boys into the roles the men could not stomach. Easier to radicalize the young, easier to expect obedience.

Hilde understood this. And, bless her, she had pleaded with me in the cottage before her arrest not in an attempt to save herself, but to try to save the others. To make the hexenjägers see—not only was she innocent, they *all* were.

But Bertram clearly knows the truth. Despite being told of witchcraft, he never believed before.

And he lit the fires anyway.

"I wonder if she'll burn differently from the others," Bertram says idly, simply curious.

I glance at him from beneath my cloak's hood. "If you knew all along that the witches burned were not truly witches, why do you still wear the cloak?"

Bertram shrugs, the black cloth over his shoulders rippling. "It's a job," he says.

Bile rises up my throat.

I have seen evil—Kommandant Kirch did not rise to the top of the units without knowing *exactly* what he does. The executioner flaunts the wealth he's gained from working the witch trials; he knows what he does; he *relishes* the cruelty that profits him. The archbishop—he may be the most evil man I know, orchestrating it all.

I have seen evil.

But until this moment with Bertram, I had not realized how often it wore the face of apathy.

The city of Trier rises to the west, spires of churches pointing into the midmorning sky, gleaming in a veneer of holiness behind the city walls.

The bridge over the Moselle leads straight to the city wall on the eastern side, and it's where the heaviest flow of traffic into and out of the city is. There are buildings beyond the city wall, though, some made of crumbling stone from centuries before, others wooden structures that weren't built to last.

And then there are the Roman ruins.

Rather than head toward the city gate by the bridge, I direct our caravan off the main road, winding toward the eastern side of Trier, outside the wall. The vast remains of ancient Roman baths, partially debris and rubble as people scavenged stone blocks from the structure, rise up to our left.

Our city is built on the bones of a fallen empire.

Giant stone blocks tower over the side of the road, creating an entrance I veer the caravan toward. I hear a thump and a curse from the prisoner's cart as Fritzi is tossed around inside the rough wooden box.

I circle my horse back to the tail end of the caravan, waving off

Johann, who'd been riding in the rear. The hexenjäger unit moves with practiced ease. We have, all of us, even the youngest, been a part of prisoner transports here.

The Romans killed the Celts for sport after enslaving them to build the amphitheater in the first place. There are mocking stories of how the gleaming, armed gladiators strode into the arena with polished metal weapons shining as they faced starved, abused Celts armed with nothing but sticks and rocks. Sometimes the Romans captured bears or worse, wild boar, and let nature kill the nature-worshipping tribal members.

Sport.

I wonder if those Celts would think their deaths better than the ones we offer to their witch descendants today.

I dismount, tossing my reins to one of the boys. I wave the others off as I approach the wooden prisoner cart. My boots thud as I mount the little step, using the iron bars in the only window as leverage so I can stand and peer into the box.

The witch—*Fritzi*, I remind myself—is backed into the farthest corner. Slants of light cast her in shadow, but even from the darkness I can see the fierce rage in her eyes. Recognition flashes across her face as she realizes which hexenjäger is peering down at her.

It is quickly replaced with hatred.

I had not been sure of what I would do until I see her now. I had the idea first when she snapped at me about not caring as long as I had a witch to imprison. She's right—I *do* need a witch to imprison. But still, I debated it all this long morning. Witnessing her hate now gives me the resolution I need to act.

I joined the hexenjägers after they burned my stepmother. Not because I believed in them.

Because I wanted to destroy them from the inside out.

Over the years, I worked my way up, hiding the little rebellions—the cells that weren't locked, the children who disappeared before they were arrested, the warnings to families to flee before they were accused. I had my father's zealous legacy to give me credibility within the hexenjägers, but my stepmother's loving heart to always ground me outside of them.

Nothing I did was ever enough, though.

Especially once I leveraged my father's name and sat beside Herr Kommandant. It has always been evident that Kommandant Dieter Kirch is not simply following orders from the archbishop. He does not act with faith or any presumption of doing good.

He loves the murders. He *relishes* them. He actively works to make them more torturous, cramming the accused in inhumane prisons and branding them with the letter *D* for dämon before executing innocent people.

He never wants to see the witch burnings stopped. No amount of blood spilled on the streets of Trier will be enough for him.

I had thought, before, that the mania of the witch hunts would die down, and I hoped only to save as many as I could before the hexenjägers inevitably failed. But once I got close to Kommandant Kirch, once I saw the full depths of his depravity, I knew...

Nothing short of insurrection will stop the witch hunts.

So I hatched a plan with my sister.

Everything was in place. Months of preparation—pilfering keys to hidden doors in the tunnels, laying out routes for escape, sabotaging messages—all of it hinged upon the idea that I would arrest Hilde, and I would put her into the witch trials myself. She would organize the prisoners; I would set them free.

This mass burning the archbishop planned seemed the perfect tipping point. Release *everyone* right under his nose, at the height of the Advent season and Christkindlmarkt where everyone would see.

While I was on patrol in the south, I cemented the last of my plans, even going so far as to arrange a boat that would take Hilde and me from Trier to Koblenz, using the branching river to fully leave behind the last vestiges of this life. I would never be able to stay in the diocese once I broke into the basilica and freed a hundred or so accused witches, but I had to hope that such a large rebellious act would be enough to spur the public into rejecting the cycle of terror and evil the archbishop holds in his iron fist.

The plan had been to fight from within for as long as possible, save as many as possible, and then escape to some other principality or diocese, somewhere I could hide safely and start a new life with my sister.

But with Hilde gone, wherever the hexe sent her—I have lost my connection to the prisoners.

And I've lost my sister. I push the thought down, even though it causes a physical pain in my heart. The witch seemed certain Hilde was safe. I *know* Hilde would want me to focus on saving the innocents. But all I feel is broken and lost when I think of how she is...elsewhere.

Focus, I remind myself. I have worked for years to appear to be nothing but a ruthless hexenjäger. Above suspicion.

I will not fail now.

I glare at Fritzi. There's not enough room for her to stand, but nor does she cower.

She's my last hope.

I press my face against the bars. "Listen," I say urgently, my voice low so that only she can hear. "Do what I say—*exactly*."

"You can't make me—"

"If you want to survive, listen to me. I can save you, if you obey me."

I can save you all, I tell myself.

And I hope that it's still true.

9

FRITZI

I blink at the bars after the kapitän jumps back down.

I can save you, if you obey me.

A threat like that isn't unexpected from a hexenjäger.

I've heard stories from witches who passed through Birresborn, most just looking for a safe place, others on the run to the Black Forest after most of their coven was lost. All would grow quiet when the visitors told their tales. Where they had come from. What they had escaped. Even the children, huddled at their parents' legs, weren't sent away from the gruesome realities; we all had to listen, because we all could feel the overhanging threat.

This could be you. This could happen to any of us.

Listen, and take heed.

And so I know exactly what hexenjägers do to us. Even to those who aren't witches, who found Birresborn by accident, not knowing they'd stumbled into a coven—Mama let them in anyway, and we sent them off with supplies and full bellies. The stories were all the same.

Hexenjägers who came with irons and scowls.

Hexenjägers who didn't wait for a trial, who killed or burned their victims on the spot.

Hexenjägers who slipped into houses with "early warnings" of an arrest and promises that they could make it go away if they were granted certain…favors. *Give me one night*, they said, *and you'll live.*

Each story was more heart-wrenching than the last, painting a picture of a world beset by power-hungry men all high on their claims of righteousness and purity.

So I have no illusions about the kapitän's threat. That's what it is: a threat.

But what of the earnestness on his face? The fear in his eyes?

I dig my fingertips into my temples and rub in slow circles. I'm sleepless, that's all. It happened so quickly; I misread his expression. Earnestness could easily be eagerness. Fear could easily be mania.

The door to the prison wagon bursts open. Bone-deep exhaustion has numbed me, and I come up to a crouch before the hexenjägers have to reach in for me.

Outside, I see we're in ruins of some sort, long ago remains of the Romans who were the first colonizers of these lands. The first to look at my people and deem us little more than fodder. My eyes cast over the rocks and rubble, the wall of Trier running beyond the length of this space, and my numbness settles deeper.

The kapitän is sending the bulk of his men back up the road, leaving only himself and two others with me. One is the boy who even now won't meet my eyes, Johann.

The other is Bertram.

He grabs the chain between my hands, his eyes all disgust as he sizes me up in the harsh, cold sunlight. "Let's get her locked up. I need a pint."

Johann moans his agreement. It's the kapitän who hesitates, something gruesome and dark on his face, before he turns without a word.

I don't know what I expected. For them to lead me straight into a prison? For there to be a set of stairs that would take us up and over the wall of Trier? But when Bertram pulls me toward a small arched entrance set directly in the sheared stone beneath the wall, I seize up.

A tunnel. A tunnel under the city.

Is this how they bring in all the witches, or have they planned something special for me?

My brain rattles with information—the old Roman aqueducts, just more verdammt *ruins*—but panic has my heels dropping into the dirt, my arms trying and failing to rip back and out of the hexenjäger's grasp.

Bertram growls at me. "Go ahead and try to flee," he snaps as he yanks me forward. "I'll take pleasure in running you through."

He shifts his hip, drawing my attention to the sword strapped there, but my panic doesn't calm, and we walk closer, closer, closer to that tunnel entrance. It's all darkness, a small door of nothingness, and I can't convince my lungs to draw breath.

I'm hit with the iron-tinged sensation that once I go into that tunnel, I'll never come back out again, and of all the horrors I've endured the past days, this looms over me, swallowing me whole.

What do you fear in the dark, Fritzi? You know how to escape. You've known all along.

A cry bursts out of me. I'm desperate, on edge; this is the exact sort of situation where the voice could get to me, I know it could.

I could give in. So easily.

I could escape. Save Liesel. Save myself.

Just say the spell. Start the words. This can all be over.

Others in my coven knew the words too. We had a communal

building to store our most sacred texts, spells passed generation to generation on scrolls and rare bound books; but there were a few writings that Mama kept under lock and key in her room and forbade us from reading.

So of course we did.

It became a dare from the oldest cousin *You're not scared to see what it says, are you?*—until a group of us needed to prove our bravery.

We snuck into my mother's room in the cottage, a group of insolent cousins and friends, giggling the whole while, not knowing what we were truly set on finding. We'd heard the worst stories about our goddesses already, tales whispered around dying flames late at night to make us behave: *Perchta will come in your sleep! The Mother knows all you've done. If you've been naughty, she'll slice open your belly and stuff you full of straw!*

But this was no story. No fable meant to scare and instill obedience.

It was a spell.

I remember the words, flowing in thin, curling script across the parchment, on a page labeled *Wild Magic.*

Below the spell, it spoke of the balance Mama drilled into my head. How witches must put good into the world, because our Well of magic builds with good deeds; the more we do, the more magic our coven has to draw on.

That was why Perchta, the Mother, was so absolute in her rules and traditions. Why Abnoba protected the forests and life so fiercely. Why Holda guarded the barrier to death with such devotion.

The Well protects us. It's a tap to allow a trickle of uncorrupting magic through.

But wild magic is a flood, and it ruins or drives a witch mad, drowning them in the wake.

To cement the connection to wild magic, a witch must sever their connection to the Origin Tree and its Well, the page said. *This is the spell that must be recited to do so.*

Only a few of us saw the page. The rest crouched around, wide-eyed and giggling still. Liesel had been there; she was about four years old, tiny and plump and observant.

"Are you all right, cousin?" she'd asked in her soft little voice.

I'd slammed the book shut.

Say the spell, the voice demands now. *I can help you in ways you can only imagine. You need not suffer, you need not be a prisoner. Say the spell!*

Had I heard the voice before I read the passage in Mama's forbidden book? I can't remember. I can't remember a time when I *didn't* hear it, and right now, being dragged for senseless darkness beneath a hexenjäger city, I am closer than I ever have been to giving in.

I drop my heels again, but Bertram is ready for my protest; he hauls me toward the tunnel, and I go, helpless, as I have been all this time. Even when I turn, I see the kapitän behind me, and Johann behind him.

Reality crashes down on me, sharp and jarring.

There will be no leaving these tunnels.

I will be entirely at Kommandant Kirch's mercy.

My lips part. A word is on the edge of my tongue, the first in the spell.

Say it, the voice pleads. *Use me!*

I could kill these hexenjägers.

I could use wild magic to wreak unrestrained havoc on these foul men—and be precisely the sort of monster they believe me to be.

My body shakes with self-hatred. I'd say the spell *now,* to save my own body, but I wouldn't say it to save Mama and my coven?

That silences me.

Tears prick my eyes as the hexenjäger drags me the first few paces into the tunnel. There's rustling behind, a shift, and then the smell of acidic smoke.

The kapitän has lit a torch.

It does little to chase away the dark, and with each step we take farther inside, the light from outside fades until we are in a world all our own. The tunnel is only an arm's length over my head. The kapitän must crouch to fit, his broad shoulders caving forward to not brush the laid stones. The sound of water dripping echoes tinnily, a distant, steady tick, and my boots push through the occasional puddle, shallow and smelling of molded water.

I focus on those things. The way the air stinks of cold stone, iron and earthy; the feel of the chill on my skin, icy below ground. My boots slip on a grimy rock, and I falter, catching myself by the tight grip Bertram holds on me.

I feel the kapitän at my back, one firm hand going to my shoulder.

"Steady," he says, gruff and low.

I shake him off and keep walking. Bertram glances back, once, and I catch a flash of discomfort on his face.

He doesn't like being in this tunnel either. *He* isn't walking to imprisonment and death, but still, I revel in knowing my captors are sharing even a small part of my misery.

A tunnel branches from our main one. As we cross the intersection, I feel a gust of wind from somewhere to the left. I shiver in the chill of it. Bertram shivers, too, and I get the feeling it's more from fear.

"What is that?" Johann asks from the rear.

"Ventilation," the kapitän says. "Keep going, Bertram."

Bertram yanks my chain, and I stumble two quick steps. But another breeze blows, and he glances back at the kapitän questioningly.

Bertram's eyes go to me, thin with accusation.

Does he blame me for a cold wind? What power I hold over this man. If only I could use it.

I keep walking, head down, not wanting to instigate Bertram at all—

The kapitän's sharp cry is the only warning before the torch hisses out into nothingness.

Sinking, consuming darkness rushes around me, choking, thick. I see nothing, eyes strained wide in fruitless searching, breathing stunted as every muscle in my body goes rigid.

"What happened? Where's the light?" Johann is frantic, his tone high and grating.

"The witch bespelled the wind!" the kapitän snaps back. "Bertram—"

Arms clamp around my body. A scream builds in my chest, but a thick hand plants over my lips, holding me silent as the weight around me pivots sharply to the left, yanking me hard.

Feet splash. "I've lost her!" Bertram's voice from ahead rings against the walls. And if he's not holding me, then—

I buck, manacled hands going up to grab the kapitän's arms, but I can't pry him off—and to what end, anyway? Cold sweat washes down my body as I feel his muscles tense around me, keeping me flush to his front, his limbs like stone, encasing me.

"The witch ran off!" the kapitän says like he isn't holding me in his arms. "She can't be far—Bertram, go on ahead; it's a straight shot to the Porta Nigra from here, so if she went that way, she'll end up nowhere good. Johann, back to the entrance—let nothing out, you hear me? I'll search these side tunnels. *Go!*"

The booming shout rings in my ears, dizzying me. I long for numbness again, but fear rears up, a relentless hand snaking around my chest, squeezing the air from my lungs in a cool, quick rush that condenses against the kapitän's palm.

What is happening?

Why did he *lie*?

Footsteps part in stomping rushes—Bertram racing ahead, Johann going back the way we came. The kapitän holds me motionless for one second, two, three—

Then he drags me back a few paces, to where the tunnel split. Or, at least, I think that's where we go—I still see nothing, but clearly he knows the route even without light.

My skin prickles with terror. A tight winding of dread, my body feeling too exposed, too soft.

I'm alone in an underground tunnel with a hexenjäger kapitän, and no one on earth knows he has me.

You said no one would touch me, I think, but I can't get the words to form. *You said you weren't brutes.*

I can't stifle my cry as he shifts me higher against him, his hand slipping from my mouth.

"Don't make a *sound*," he hisses into my ear.

I would if I thought that would improve my situation at all—but who would come running? More hexenjägers?

One hexenjäger, I can handle.

One hexenjäger, I can kill.

He's focused on wherever he's taking me, his breath huffing fast, his heart hammering against my back. We take another turn, his boots sloshing through puddles that sound deeper now—another sharp turn, more water sloshing. How will I find my way out?

Never mind that now. Get *away*.

I lift my manacled arms and slam my elbow back into the kapitän's stomach. He huffs a startled breath and releases his grip, but only barely—I manage a single step forward before he seizes my arm, a predator's instincts, and slams me against the wall of the tunnel.

Terror shoots through me, a white fog across my mind, and all I want, all I am, is the need to scream. The kapitän's forearm presses across my chest, his elbow and fist connecting with the bruised spots where his knees pinned me in the garden, and I wince, teeth flashing in the dark.

"I won't make it easy for you," I spit, terror disintegrating into anger. I fall backward into it; anger, I can use, and I thrash against his weight. "I may not have magic right now, but I have claws and teeth. Every moment, every *breath* will be a fight, jäger—"

"A fight? Schiesse, that's not what I—*stop*. I know it's hard for you," he tells me, and for once, his voice is almost sorrowful, "but unless you want to end up on a stake, stay quiet and *trust me*."

"Trust you?" I gasp, bucking. He's incredibly strong. So strong I know I have little chance of overpowering him, and that realization sends a shudder through me, fed by the icy water soaking into my boots.

I have been manacled, bound, and locked in a prison wagon, but it's his display of strength that reminds me how much of a prisoner I am.

"Yes," he says, his breath warm on my face. He's a voice only. A voice and a press of weight in the dark. "Trust me. And if that's too impossible, then know that this is the only way to save everyone."

"By purging the city of—"

"No. The people locked up by the hexenjägers. I'm going to save them, and you're going to help me."

I stare into the darkness, my eyes wide, brows to my hairline.

He doesn't wait for my reaction. He grabs the chain between my manacles and hauls me on, and I go, because I can't fight him off, because I have no other options, because his words are dancing through my head.

He's trying to *save* the people he helped imprison?

No. This is a trick. This is some kind of final test before the hexenjägers burn me, before Kirch returns and has his fun. He's trying to break me. That's it—this is him, this is all Kommandant Kirch—

My mind is heaving, roiling. A panic, a delirium, a final shattering as the kapitän stops.

There's rustling, the sound of keys rattling. I hear one go into a lock, twist.

Dim, hazy light pushes into the tunnel. I lurch forward, drawn to the light like a moth, my panic momentarily hesitating as my eyes adjust, and I can *see*.

Beyond lies a small square room, crates stacked against one wall, a distant, steady dripping breaking the silence. There's a shaft in the ceiling where a ladder might go and no windows or doors beyond this entrance—it's a cellar.

I don't get a chance to ask a question. The kapitän shoves me into the room.

"Stay *silent*," he says, and I hear the grate of his words fully now, see the desperation on his face. In that moment, he's not just a soulless hexenjäger; he's a boy, wide-eyed and scared.

He's pleading with me. *Begging* me to stay quiet.

"What is going *on*—"

But he slams the door on me.

I throw myself at it. There's no handle from this side, just a smooth outline, and when I hammer my fist on it, it doesn't even rattle.

"Jäger!" I shout at the wall. No response. "*Jäger!*"

Nothing.

I kick it. It only sends a jolt of pain up my foot, and I dance backward until my thighs catch on a crate. I sit, heavy and shocked, staring at the door.

The shaft above dumps foggy light down on me—there must be windows up there, an exit. Around me, the crates are mostly whole, some dampened from moisture, the floor slick and the walls unbroken by other openings.

I glare at the opening in the ceiling.

Whatever game this hexenjäger is playing, whatever test Kommandant Kirch is putting me through…

I'm *done.*

I'm getting out of this cellar, and I'm going to find Liesel, and we're going to the Black Forest.

Are you really going to them? asks the voice. *Why go all that way when I am right here to help you?*

I snort. *Where were your useless questions when the kapitän had me in his arms?* I shoot back. *You're slipping, Darkness.*

I'm talking to the voice more than I ever have before.

This can't be good.

I pull to my feet. My hands are still manacled—I'll have to take care of that too. But for now, all I need to focus on is getting out of this cellar.

There are enough crates stacked against the wall that I can create a crude tower to climb.

Grim, I cast one last look at the impassable cellar door that leads out to the tunnels.

"I'm getting out of here, jäger," I promise to the silence. "Then I'm getting my cousin and we're going to the forest folk."

10

OTTO

If God had to send me a *real* witch to contend with, why did he have to send me one that was such a pain in the arse? Her magic was strange, and I can only hope she told me the truth when she said she had protected Hilde, not hurt her. Magic, I can handle.

Her mouth? Not so much.

I take a deep breath. That's not fair. She's scared and alone, and how is she to know the black cloak of the hexenjägers is a disguise to me and not a truth? Still. It would be easier if it were Hilde here, Hilde helping.

Sorrow makes my steps falter, my breaths stutter in my chest. *Hilde.* If I can get this witch to trust me, she'll tell me where my sister is. I don't think she did anything to harm Hilde, just...sent her elsewhere. Perhaps far away. But that doesn't matter. I will find and save her and...

One thing at a time. I rush through the aqueduct system. First to Johann—he's closer.

"No one came through, Kapitän!" Johann says, a tremble in his voice—partly from fear, but mostly from cold. It's winter, and we're both wet to our knees from icy river water sloshing over our boots.

He's right to be afraid, though.

"What happened to your torch?" he asks as I brush past him and retrieve a fresh one from the basket by the aqueduct entrance.

I'd tossed it. Had to. If I'd taken the torch out of the tunnels, it would have been apparent that I quenched the flame in the cold river water, not that it died in some witch's wind. Plunging the torch down had been the quickest means to getting the darkness I needed to hide my actions as I took Fritzi.

I knew Johann and Bertram wouldn't be able to navigate the dark as I could. I am more familiar with the tunnels under Trier than anyone, even the kommandant. I have often walked them without any torches, counting my steps and feeling for the cues to know which tunnel is which.

The dark never scared me. I have lived too long in it.

"Come on," I growl without answering his question, leading him back through the tunnels after lighting the new torch.

Johann makes no comment as we head toward the Porta Nigra, one of the few paths he knows. Had the hexenjägers looked at the tunnels as more than a means of transporting prisoners, they would know that Fritzi could only have gone in one of six different tunnels that didn't lead into a dead end. If any of them had bothered to map out the tunnel system, they would know where each of those six tunnels goes, and how a person can escape through them.

But no one knows those routes except me.

Johann sniffles behind me. I don't look back, but I know the boy is truly scared now. Not of the dark. Not even of the witch. Of the repercussions of losing her.

I don't speak, setting a quick pace through the cold water. Soon enough, the tunnel opens up, broadening at the base of the Porta Nigra.

Bertram stands there in his sodden boots, eyes straining. There's some light from ventilation shafts here, and his gaze roves over us, hopeful and then crestfallen.

"So, Johann couldn't catch the witch," Bertram growls.

What an arschloch. I don't bother hiding my contempt. "Johann wasn't holding the witch's chain," I snarl. "She made the torch go out, but you were the fool who let her go."

"She had demons' help!" Bertram protests, eyes going wide. "Something slammed into her with the force of ten men, ripping her from my grasp!"

Johann squeaks in terror, but I have to bite the inside of my cheek to keep from smirking. A demon with the strength of ten men? My shove against Fritzi had not been gentle, but Bertram is letting his fear overtake his senses.

Good. That will work in my favor.

"Come on," I growl to the two others as I lead them out of the tunnels and toward the long iron spiral staircase that goes from the aqueduct all the way into the Porta Nigra. Our steps echo in the stone chamber as we ascend.

By the time we reach the top of the Porta Nigra, I know the silence has done more work than anything I could have said. That's one of the few valuable lessons I've learned from being a hexenjäger—even an innocent will confess to a crime if left with nothing but guilt and silence. Johann's eyes are as wide as a saucer. Bertram's face is downcast as he mutters a prayer—one that will not be answered.

Because, much to all of our terror, Kommandant Dieter Kirch has returned to Trier.

Even before we reach his office, I can tell that he's back. A cold fear crackles among the hexenjägers on duty here. Everyone is on high alert;

the salutes that follow me as I lead Bertram and Johann down the corridor snap like whips.

I knock on Kommandant Kirch's door.

"Enter," his voice calls, deep and resonant.

I push it open.

Kommandant Dieter Kirch is a tall man with broad, rectangular shoulders. His blond hair curls at the end and brushes his starched shirt collar. Everything about the man screams strength and power, from the muscles straining against his clothes to the hard edge of his jawline as he inspects us. But the thing about the kommandant that gives him more power and respect than other men is his eyes.

There's something...eerie about his eyes. They are a simple blue, a common enough color, nothing remarkable, but...it's as if shadows move behind his irises, the colors seeming to swirl if you look at them too long. It is impossible not to feel uneasy under his unflinching gaze.

Kommandant Kirch takes a moment to drink in our appearance. Wet boots, stained breeches, waterlogged cloaks.

"Where is the witch?" he demands.

I have worked with Dieter Kirch for years; he knows what I mean when I sweep my hand toward Bertram.

The kommandant glares. Bertram actually takes a step back, bumping into Johann.

"From what the other men in your patrol said, this witch was...powerful," the kommandant says.

I nod once, sharply.

Dieter turns to me. "You went to fetch your own sister to be burned?"

I nod again, slower this time.

Dieter strides forward. "It takes a...strong man to turn in his family."

"She was not family," I lie. "She was a bastard child; my father whelped her with a witch. *Not* my birth mother," I add, reminding everyone in the room that unholy blood does not run in my veins.

Dieter nods slowly. "Still," he says, and there's a tone in his voice I almost don't recognize. Pride? "And then a powerful witch took her." His voice is grave. "That witch ensorcelled your sister and sent her..."

"Elsewhere," I finish. "Perhaps to hell, where her kind revel."

"Perhaps." He smiles impishly. "My, what fun my men have been having. The troops I took with me burned a coven that fought back with *magic*, and now this little witch is spiriting other witches away!" He giggled, the sound pitched high, but then his shoulders slumped. "I suspected some of the men were feeling a bit...disheartened. Unaware of the depths of their mission. Now they see what we are up against, though, now their passions are stoked."

Dieter walks slowly past me, toward Bertram. "You," he says.

Bertram looks as if he's about to piss himself, but he squares his shoulders. "Yes. Sir."

"Do you doubt the holiness of our cause?"

"No!"

"But you are to blame for the witch's escape."

"No! No, I—"

Dieter shakes his head, and Bertram closes his mouth so quickly his teeth clack. "It was not a question." The kommandant's gaze flicks to me.

"I held the torch as we went through the aqueduct. Johann guarded the rear. Bertram held the witch's chains."

"She caused a wind to blow out the light!" Bertram says, stepping forward in his own defense, his eyes wild with fear. "And demons—there were demons that ripped her from my grasp, demons that spirited her away!"

Kommandant Dieter Kirch raises an eyebrow and stares at Bertram with the full force of his pale eyes until Bertram's voice stutters to silence.

There it is. The guilt and quiet that does all the work for him.

"There were no demons," Dieter says finally, his voice brooking no argument. "You are a hexenjäger blessed by the saints. No demon could lift a hand to you. Unless you invited them in?"

"No!" Bertram says immediately. "I'm pure. I've been to confession; I have no sin for them to exploit!"

Dieter raises one finger, and Bertram is silent again, trembling. We all watch as Dieter strolls around the room, his boot heels clacking on the stone. "This room was once the cell of a saint, did you know that?" Bertram nods, but Dieter's not even looking at him. He continues speaking, casually, as if this were a chat. "Saint Simeon. He became an anchorite, enclosing himself into this very chamber as if it were his tomb, dedicating every moment of his life to prayer."

Dieter turns to face us fully, opening his palms toward us as if in veneration. "And then," he continues, "a flood happened. The Moselle River rose and rose, and the people of Trier? They blamed Simeon for causing the flood. They called him a witch."

Dieter crosses the room, toward a window made of glass pieces held tight with lead solder. He touches one of the panes. "They threw stones at this building, trying to get to him and kill him. And then the waters of the river receded. All was well."

"*Was* he a witch, sir?" Bertram asks when Dieter does nothing more than stare at the glass pane.

Dieter strides back over to Bertram, footsteps heavy, and slaps him across the face.

"No, you fool," he spits, his tone no longer casual but enraged. "He was a saint. And you—*you*," he snarls, "are the unverschämt who cannot tell the difference between a witch and a saint! You are the unverschämt who drops a chain and blames made-up demons."

Before any of us can react, Dieter grabs Bertram by the collar and drags him across the room. Bertram's hands scramble to his neck, choking, but that's not the punishment Dieter has in mind.

He kicks open a door to a small stone chamber and throws Bertram inside. Bertram crashes into the wall, spinning around even as Dieter slams the door in his face, turning a large iron key.

"Saint Simeon purposefully chose to become a recluse and dedicate himself to God," Dieter tells the locked door in a calm, even tone. "May you learn something from his strength."

I swallow, looking at the stone closet. It is narrower even than the aqueduct. There's not enough room inside to sit on the floor. Bertram will be unable to spread his arms out—he would barely be able to lift them in such a constrained space. To say nothing of the fact that he has no food, nor any means to relieve himself. The tight space makes it impossible to do anything but stand in the dark.

It is a tomb.

Behind the locked door, I hear a strangled, choking sob.

We all know that Kommandant Dieter Kirch will not open the door for days at the very least. The last man who was punished in this way nearly died. When he emerged, he was pale and shaking, unable to do more than crawl out of the kommandant's office on all fours, begging for water.

Kommandant Kirch turns to me and Johann. "Dismissed," he says pleasantly.

11

FRITZI

Manacled, I wrestle crates into a crude pile in the cellar, fueled by my rage.

Verpiss dich, jäger.

I climb, dragging crates higher, stacking them as I go; only to climb back down for another, up again, stack it; down, another, up again—

Verpiss dich, jäger.

Sweat pours down my face. The manacles bite angry raw circles around each wrist.

I have never cursed someone so much, so repeatedly, in my *life*.

Verpiss dich, jäger.

My legs are liquid by the time I have a stack high enough to reach the opening in the ceiling.

I'm exhausted.

I'm hungry.

Every muscle aches.

But I climb, wobbling, sweat burning my eyes where it slips past the rim of my wool hat, and when I heave my body up out of the cellar, I shriek in victory.

If he thought he could manipulate me with that nonsense about trying to *save* people…

If he thought I would just buckle under my fatigue and grief…

He was *wrong*.

My lips curve into a smile, hair sticking to my face as I splay out flat on my back and collapse there, panting. The blistering cold of this room makes me shiver and shake, cooling the sweat on my skin, but my smile stays, my victory too sweet to let go of just yet.

I lie there for a moment, gasping, willing my heartbeat to slow. No matter what kind of lock the kapitän has on the door to this building, I'll break it, and—

My thoughts tumble to silence.

Lying here, staring up at the ceiling, I see a ladder out of the corner of my eye leading to another opening for the second floor. I see some kind of pump, likely connected to the aqueduct tunnels down below, but I see nothing giving off the soft light that filtered down into the cellar, that is even now setting this room with a soft gray glow. It's coming from the second floor, not this one.

I bolt upright.

The wall in front of me is flat, unbroken by a window or door. And when I shove to my feet and turn in a complete circle, I see the same on the other three walls.

No windows.

No door.

I'd assumed the cellar was only one floor beneath the first level, and that I would be able to escape onto the street from here. But the jäger put me somewhere deeper in this house.

My jaw grinds so tight that pain shoots across my scalp.

Damn him. *Damn that man.*

But at least this level has a ladder, thank the Three.

I trudge over to it and scramble up.

Ah, finally—a single window big enough to maybe be a door, shuttered, but with a gap running along the base, the source of the light that still pulls me with embarrassing drive.

Outside, that light says. *Freedom.*

I stumble across the room, not even bothering to stop and study my surroundings *Get out, Fritzi. Get out.*

I grab the door's handle and pull.

It rattles but doesn't budge.

Fury starts to fester in the base of my gut. I anchor my feet on the floor, wrap all my fingers around the handle, and *yank*, hard, with all my weight.

Nothing.

I scream and throw my shoulder into the door, but it remains as unmoved as the kapitän had been at my feeble blows. I hear rattling again, the telltale shaking of irons—he's locked the door from the outside.

What kind of torture house is this?

A scream rips out of me again, and I batter the door with everything I have left in me, every last scrap of strength, every dying flicker of hope that I could escape this fate, that I could save myself, save Liesel, and salvage even one small piece of goodness from the wreckage of this horror.

You cannot pull yourself out of this alone, says the voice.

NO, I force myself to respond. I can't leave it unanswered, can't give it space to grow. *No, no, no.*

I spin my back to the door and sink to the floor, every muscle deflating, one by one. I'm too spent even to cry—this game of anguish to hope and back again has tapped the last vestiges of my strength so expertly that as I sit here, on the floor of this inescapable house, I think only, *I should sleep.*

Why even sleep? The kapitän will return, and who knows what will happen then? My brain still cannot piece together any semblance of reason from his words—he means to *save* the hexenjägers' prisoners? I'm delirious. I have to be. I'm giving in to insanity to keep myself from truly realizing the dire consequences of my actions, as if I deserve any kind of softening, any kind of reprieve.

I sniff and scrub my nose with the back of my hand, the manacle clanking against my chin.

Do I just accept it, then? Wait here for him to return and give myself over to whatever fate he's chosen for me?

That question has one last surge of resilience rushing through me.

Absolutely *not.*

A *hexenjäger* does not decide my fate.

If I will go out by his hand, at whatever grueling torment he devises, then I will go out fighting until my last moments.

Like Mama.

I rock forward, hands to my chest, trying to shove the shards of my heart back together.

Yes. Like my mother. I will *fight.*

I push to my feet, surveying the contents of the room now, eyes blurry and half-lidded with exhaustion and sweat. This floor is one large room, same as the lower level, but cupboards line the wall to my right, and a little table with a single chair sits at the back. There's a cot in the far corner as well, looking mussed and recently used. Has the kapitän had other prisoners? The thought earns me a jarring shiver.

I head for the cupboards.

The first one has oddities, spoons, and bowls; the next is empty.

In the last one, I stare at the contents for a full breath, afraid if I blink, they'll vanish.

Food.

And not just rations, hard cheese and bread and a flask of beer; there are small vials of *herbs*. Cooking herbs, no doubt, but *herbs*, and I cry out with joy, snatching up the three little glass bottles before this hallucination vanishes.

But it doesn't. It's real. They're real. *Herbs*.

I uncork the three bottles and sniff each of them. Salt, cloves, bay leaves.

Two of these I can use. Two of these could save me.

My heart starts to beat hard. Not with horror or fear.

With hope.

Again.

How many times can one soul be yanked out of hope and back again before it breaks?

One more time, I think. *Always one more time.*

I grab the knob of hard cheese and bite off a huge chunk, eyes rolling back in my head at the aged salty tang—it honestly isn't even *good*, it's just *food*, but it's the best thing I've ever tasted. I grab the bread too—there's some mold on the corner, but the rest is fine—and I balance my haul as I hobble across to the table.

The rest of the room gives me one more treasure: a blanket from the bed. I should keep it to ward off the chill—it's freezing here too—but I'm manic now, driven by muscle memory, sheer will, and my slowly filling belly.

Between bites of bread and cheese and sips of hoppy beer, I first use the blanket as a makeshift broom. This is a hexenjäger's house, so cleansing the energy here is a laughable feat, but I start in the center of the room and sweep counterclockwise in ever-widening circles.

"*Holda, Abnoba, Perchta strong*," I repeat on each new circle, "*Goddesses cleanse from energy wrong.*"

Will this even work? I'm still connected to the Well. I haven't said the wild magic spell. It has to work—I'm following the rules, cleansing the space before I work. I wasn't able to prepare the herbs the proper way, and I don't have a ritual space or altar, but there's only so much I can do.

It has to be enough. The goddesses *have* to hear me; I'm following the guides they gave to witches.

I finish with the cleansing and rip off sections of the blanket to create little satchels. Into each go some of the cloves and bay leaves. The wood carved into two little spoons in the first cupboard is something I'd recognize it anywhere: aspen. The spoons snap easily, and I drop chunks into the satchels too. I only have enough to make four, but four protection satchels is far, far better than I had a moment ago.

I pop the last of the bread and cheese into my mouth and sit cross-legged on the floor, positioned so I can see both the shuttered window and the hatch that leads to the lower levels.

There, I whisper protection spells over the satchels, and I wait.

12

OTTO

I'm almost to the door when I hear the kommandant's voice calling for me. I pause, turning.

Inside me, panic boils like acid through my veins. *I am harboring a witch, a real one, and I am plotting to break your empire of fear*, I think. But nothing shows behind my eyes.

I hope.

"Otto, friend, walk with me," Kommandant Kirch says.

I want to rush down the stairs and take the aqueducts to the house where I've hidden Fritzi. She's no doubt confused and afraid. She deserves an explanation. And I deserve to know where she sent Hilde.

But it is not wise to go against any suggestion from the kommandant.

We head down to the ground floor of the Porta Nigra, a church used to praise Saint Simeon. It is empty now, save for some pilgrims and a priest praying. I can just hear the mutters of one of the pilgrims, begging God for blessings for his ill wife. I am glad that the hexenjägers share a building with a church; the pilgrims remind me that not all who claim to be Christian are evil.

We step out the front door onto the stone courtyard. The sun is high in the sky, but it casts neither warmth nor shadows.

This may be the ground floor of the Porta Nigra, but only because this is a repurposed ancient Roman building. With age, the city has sunk deeper and deeper into the ground. The courtyard can only be reached by a wide staircase that opens up before the street that leads to the main market.

Dieter moves around the building to face the river. It's quiet here, colder, more private even than inside his office, where Bertram no doubt beats upon the door of the closet, pleading to be released.

"Tell me about the witch," Dieter says, leaning against the wall and looking at the Moselle River. "The powerful one."

He doesn't know, I think, forcing myself to believe it. *He doesn't know Fritzi is safe in my hidden house; he doesn't know what I plan to do. He does* not.

"She is unlike any other we have arrested," I say truthfully. "She chanted—something—and smoke filled the cottage. My sister... disappeared."

Saying it out loud makes bile rise in my throat. Hilde is still missing. I have only the word of a witch that she's safe now, but—

"What did the witch chant?" Dieter presses. "Can you remember the words?"

"Er..." I frown, struggling to recall the moment. I was fully engaged in the duplicity of arresting Hilde, of appearing to the men to be the hero hexenjäger who would sacrifice his own family. I was so focused on what *I* said that I had not really taken note of what Fritzi had said. "A spell of some sort."

"Obviously," Dieter replies dryly.

I'm lost in thought, visualizing the moment. "She had herbs too," I add. "I could smell herbs in the smoke. Rosemary perhaps?"

"Herbs?" Dieter straightens, turning to face me fully. "Herbs, you say?"

I nod. "Is that important?"

"There are different types of witches, Otto. Some speak to animals. Some see visions in fires. Some use herbs to cast spells."

"Huh."

Dieter watches me closely. Fritzi—she means something to him.

"The other men have filled me in on descriptions of this witch," Dieter adds, rattling off an approximate height and weight for Fritzi, as well as her hair and eye color. It's mostly accurate, but also generic. "Can you tell me anything else about the girl?"

I pause. Silence and guilt go hand in hand. Before I can speak, though, Dieter adds, "A name, even? The men say that you spoke to the witch privately."

Her name is Fritzi, I think.

I snort. "I spoke only to try to get the hexe to tell me the location of my half sister, so that I could find and arrest her too," I say. "My threats fell on deaf ears. That witch had more spirit than any woman should, and no respect at all."

For just a moment—a flash, barely there and gone again—Dieter seems to...*smile*. I narrow my eyes, and he, seeing my expression, quickly schools his face into a blank mask.

"The solstice burning shall be in two days," Dieter says. "It will be a good purge. We have over a hundred." He casts his pale, eerie eyes at me. "You shall have the honor, I think. To light the first flames."

I duck my head, mutter my thanks.

"It has not escaped my attention that this honor has been denied you," Dieter continues, turning his gaze to the sky. "I watched your training. You are an excellent fighter, a position that led you to patrolling the diocese more often than working directly in the city, and your literacy and intelligence have, of course, aided the archbishop's decrees behind a desk."

"I serve in any way God desires," I say. I had not been aware that Dieter had watched me so closely. Has he realized that my patrols are always fruitless? Has he noticed the misfiled paperwork, the delays that have led to escapes? I had thought myself clever, my tracks covered, but...

"Your lineage aided your aspirations, but it is...wrong, don't you think, that you not feel the heat of God's love through a burning pyre?"

"It would be an honor," I manage to say without choking on the words. "A hundred witches to burn at once."

"And you with the torch in your hand." He looks at me with lips curved up, but that is no smile. "The bigger the fire, the more souls saved. One hundred." He says the number as if it is something to relish, something to *enjoy.*

I do not think about that number.

Instead, I focus on the other one.

Two days for me to realign my entire plan, for me to save them all.

And, hopefully, disrupting the largest burning of witches that Trier has yet seen will be enough to rattle the rest of the citizens, for them to throw off the shackles of fear and say, as one, *no more.*

That is what I hope for. I do not deceive myself, though. I may not be able to spark the revolution I desire. I may not be able to save all hundred.

A hundred and one, I remind myself—one hundred falsely accused witches and one real one.

"Yes, it will be a good day," Dieter says, noting the smile toying on my lips. Schiesse. I had not meant to show any emotion. "Better, of course, if we can add that other witch to the flames. I have sent more men out. There are places she could hide in this city. But not for long."

My stomach churns. "Perhaps she's left the city?" I suggest.

Dieter barks in humorless laughter. "No," he says in full confidence. "She has not left Trier."

How does he know?

While Dieter stares placidly at the river, panic surges through me. Black dots dance in my eyes. I'm so *close* to making my move, but if I fail now, more than a hundred lives hang in the balance.

Including my own.

I wait for Dieter to go back into the Porta Nigra before I leave, walking down the stairs toward the street slowly.

I take careful, measured steps. My back is straight. Even now, I may be watched. I cannot tip my hand. I cannot. Even if my heart thunders in my ears, I walk away from the hexenjäger base as if I bear neither sin nor worry.

I carry two maps in my head. One is of the aqueducts beneath me. The other is here, the real city of Trier, the paths that once started as organized Roman grids and have slowly evolved into chaos, with little alleys connecting one side street to another, wooden planks on roofs linking one building to another, hidden doors providing passage from one home to another.

That's the difference between a village and a city. In a village, all the people are connected—my mother knew every single person who gathered around her pyre to watch her burn. She helped midwife some of the women's babies; she sold beer to every family. But in a city, the people aren't connected.

The buildings are.

I head from the Porta Nigra roughly south, toward the Hauptmarkt. There's a noticeable shift in my reception as I near the market. Close to the church, men call out greetings, some salute me or bow before the black cloak. But it doesn't take long for me to see a child skid to a stop and race off down an alleyway to avoid crossing my path. A woman crosses herself and mutters a prayer of protection when my cloak swishes past her door. An old man pretends to cough, but I see the smirk when his spittle hits my shoulder.

Not everyone loves hexenjägers.

And that gives me hope.

The main market of Trier sells a little bit of everything from sunup to sundown, but currently, with Advent already begun, it's a Christkindlmarkt. While the staples are still available, every open space is now crammed with stalls selling something seasonal. Warm spices fill the air, scents flickering like candlelight. There are more people in the city now than there were a month ago; fall is a busy time for harvests, but there's little to do in winter other than make a day's journey into the city and imbibe in too many sweets and too much beer.

This, too, was part of the plan. I have spent the past few years finding small ways to undermine the hexenjägers, saving individuals, but it was never enough. This was to be the coup de grâce that would light a spark for a revolution instead of a pyre.

The prisoners in the basilica were to escape through the tunnels, the aqueducts providing the perfect route. Hilde was going to instruct the prisoners on the paths I'd been secretly teaching her in our private correspondence, telling them the best ways to disappear and splitting the groups up so that a handful went down one path, another cluster went a different way, and so on.

We were going to work *with* chaos, using the confusion of the breakout to mask the way groups of prisoners split up in different directions. I had carefully selected the routes, ensuring the aqueduct passages provided an outlet into abandoned homes or empty buildings. I had already stockpiled old clothing for disguises—from there, the plan was for the prisoners to disperse into the Christkindlmarkt, disappearing into the crowds as one more shopper, one more worshiper, one more random villager out for the day.

I'd factored in everything but Fritzi.

"Beer?" a pretty girl with braids says. She carries a yoke with buckets across her shoulder, a ladle in her hand. Her eyes drop to my cloak, the enameled brooch marking me as a hexenjäger. Her voice trembles when she adds, "Just one pfennig to wet your lips and warm your gut." I glance down at the beer open in her bucket, and she dips the ladle into the liquid, holding the frothy brew out to me. Her hand trembles. "You can have it for free, jäger."

I shake my head, and she shrugs, turning to offer the brew to another man, one who pays a penny to drink from the communal ladle. I ignore them, striding through the market, shoving past the men drunk on beer and the children drunk on honey. I whip my black cloak off, shoving it under my arm and hiding the brooch that marks me as a hexenjäger. I turn away from the main crowd, down a shrouded street blocked off with a plastered-brick stone archway. There's no sign affixed atop the archway, but everyone in Trier knows—this is the Judengasse.

The Jewish Quarters in Trier were originally robust and vibrant. The Jews lived close together, not by law, but because their temple was nearby. Eventually, the Judengasse became an eruv, allowing activities in that area that would otherwise be forbidden on the Sabbath.

But with every plague, every drought, every flood, the Jews were blamed, over and over again. They were banned more than once, exiled from the city if not the entire diocese. Perhaps banishment years ago was safer than if they had stayed. Perhaps I only tell myself that to assuage the guilt of my people against theirs.

There are many abandoned areas inside the city walls. But none more empty than the Judengasse.

I learned long ago, however, that there is rarely a truly empty place. Orphans—there are quite a few these days—and the homeless scavenge scraps and live in the shells of homes. While many buildings were seized and sold for profit—I mean, of course, for the benefit of the Church—the archbishop turns a blind eye here, preferring to pretend the entire Judengasse does not exist rather than deal with the starving homeless lurking in its shadows.

A pebble bounces off my shoulder.

I turn and see a pair of wide eyes looking at me from the doorway of a house with broken glass windows. I reach into my pocket, pulling out a coin and tossing it to the little girl waiting for me. She snatches it from the air and disappears. Little Mia keeps both my secrets and my pennies ever since I first saved her and her brother.

Turning my back to her doorway, I look up at the building across the street from her.

Several house forts dot the city of Trier. They're old—not as old as the Roman buildings, but older than the city wall, and several centuries have passed since they were first built with the wealth of Crusaders and the jewels of Jerusalem.

This one—the only one in the Judengasse—is a bit worse for wear. The white plaster facade is cracked; the colorful arches over the windows have faded and chipped away. But I don't care about appearances.

What makes a house fort special is the fact it has no way in.

At least not on the ground level.

There is no door, no window, no access point within reach at all. Inconvenient, yes—the only way into the building, by its own design, is by a ladder to the second-floor front door. But it served its purpose at the time. If Trier were under attack, the inhabitants merely had to lift the ladder, and no one could come inside and pillage the wealth behind the walls.

Now, though, this abandoned building serves as a natural defense for me alone. No one bothers trying to scramble up the decrepit crates I carefully piled under the door, and even if they did, they'd have a hard time getting inside without me knowing, thanks to a few strategically rotten boards and a shaky foundation. Plus the shutters over the only door are bolted with a heavy iron padlock.

I have an apartment in the city, near the Porta Nigra. It is filled with the signs of wealth I've accumulated being a hexenjäger, the paraphernalia I cannot sell off to fund my rebellion.

I hate it.

I spend most nights here.

It feels safer, somehow, knowing that the only way inside this building is through a second-story door or by the cramped, unlit aqueduct that opens in the basement.

My apartment is for Kapitän Otto Ernst, second-in-command of the hexenjäger units of Trier.

But this building is for me.

Knowing that only little Mia and her brother can see me on this shadowed, abandoned street, I hop atop the first crate, scrambling for a foothold, scaling part of the wall. A bit of plaster breaks off, skittering down. The sound is lost in the overpowering noise from the nearby market, but I cannot help but wonder if the witch inside has heard me approaching.

I left her in the cellar—there's a chance she's still down there. I *had* to rush, and she was safe there, at least. But somehow, I think she's found a way through the house. I glance up—my padlock is still in place.

She's got to be mad, though. Furious. I left her cold, alone, scared, and—*schiesse*. I didn't have time to take off her manacles. Those heavy iron bands on her wrist must be chafing and hurting her.

For a moment, I imagine Fritzi, eyes on fire, with a skillet raised to brain me the moment I step through the door.

I freeze, one hand on the ledge of the door, one wiping over my traitorous mouth.

What in the hell am I thinking, smiling at the thought of that uncouth witch plotting my murder? But her rage is so... It's like a storm at night, full of lightning, beautiful in its fury.

No. *No*. Where did *that* thought come from?

I shake my head and heave my body up to the door, fitting the key in the lock, listening for the witch and whatever trap she surely has laid for me.

13

FRITZI

At first, my exhausted, fear-strained mind attributes the creaks outside to the noises of this old building. It's shifting in the wind, groaning with age—

But the creaks turn to thuds. The unmistakable noises of a body climbing closer.

Then the rattling of the iron lock being lifted, a key fitted, twisted.

Alertness jolts through me, a flame flashing in the dark, and I launch to my feet, my four satchels gripped in both hands.

I cross the room to stand next to the door, my body flush against the wall.

The moment he opens that door, he'll get a face full of protection spells, which should stun him enough that I can shove him aside, leap out, and run like hell.

My heart slows as the lock clicks.

I sip in a breath, muscles coiled, pulse thudding in my clenched jaw. The manacles clink against themselves as I readjust my grip on the bundles, and I go rigid, willing them to silence. The air around me smells of earthy bay leaves and rich cloves, such familiar scents that every blink tells me I'll wake up in my own bed, in my own cottage, and all of this will have been a horrific dream.

The door opens.

I watch his arm push it inward, but he pauses. Letting his eyes adjust to the darkness; outside, it's afternoon, but in here, there are no other light sources, nothing to break the shadows.

Which works in my favor.

I flatten my body to the wall by the door, satchels held to my chest.

The kapitän eases forward. He hooks one leg inside, then the other, and the moment he's standing fully next to me, all of time seems to stop.

His gaze is on the bulk of the room. Searching for me. His face turns, turns, in another breath, he'll see me—

I move.

One protection satchel flies, striking him directly in the chest, and the air explodes with a powder of wood and herbs and magic.

Is the cloud bigger than it should be?

Does it...*spark* a little, like a fire, like more magic than I should be capable of?

I don't think about it. I can't. This is my one chance, and I *will* take it.

I heave my body into his, knocking him off-balance, and I spin, not hesitating as I hurl myself out the window. The clear, empty space opens for me—

But then—

Then—

There's nothing there. *Nothing.*

But my body rebounds off that nothingness as though I tossed myself onto a wall, and I bounce back into the room, the breath knocked out of me.

The kapitän is still coughing behind me, still distracted by my spell, so I leap again—

And bounce right back into the house.

What—

What did he do?

I whirl on him and launch another protection satchel. He dodges it, teetering left so it vanishes down the lower level shaft.

"What spell did you cast on this place?" I shriek at him. "Are you—are you a *witch*?"

He's not, though; I would have sensed it. I would have *felt* it, the magic humming in his blood.

The kapitän lurches for me, but I hold up one of my last two satchels, and he stops, arms out, a fine dusting of spell powder graying his hair and skin.

"Of course not," he says, voice gravelly. He coughs again. "There's no spell. It's a house fort."

"A house—*no*, I can't *leave*!" I point at the door. "You put a barrier so I can't—"

The blank look on his face stops me.

There's no magic in him. He didn't cast anything, but there is magic around that opening.

So *someone* cast a spell.

I feel the weight of the protection satchel in my hand. A satchel I'd intended to use to stop only *him* from harming me.

My eyes go to the opening. It's a two-story drop; I likely would've broken at least an arm.

Was it my protection spell that kept me from jumping out of this building?

It shouldn't have been that powerful, that uncontrolled. The spell I cast was against *attackers*, not against all bodily harm.

My mind heaves.

I remember the spell I cast on the kapitän's sister. Hilde.

How she was just...gone.

Did she run away? Or did my spell actually *send* her away? Somewhere safe, somewhere the hexenjägers *couldn't* reach her.

Unease crawls up my spine. Something isn't right. With my magic. With me, maybe.

I didn't give in, though. This isn't wild magic. It *isn't*.

The kapitän twists toward me, but I'm not quick enough. He knocks the satchel out of my upraised hand, and when I spin to smash the other one into his face, he ducks, grabs my wrist, and flips me around so my back plants against his firm chest. The last satchel falls from my hand, and he kicks it down into the lower level.

"I'm not going to hurt you." His growl vibrates down my spine.

"You can't with the spell I cast," I say, breathless, "but that doesn't stop *me* from hurting *you*."

I slam my heel down on the top of his foot. He wavers, and I shove out of his arms, but where can I go? Back down to the inescapable cellar? Maybe if I climb purposefully out the window, my spell will let me pass—

The kapitän tackles me to the floor.

Panic sends cold sweat across my skin as I drop, the breath huffing out of me, but through it, I can feel my heart hammering on the wood, the floorboards indenting into my stomach, and the weight of the kapitän on my back, the full hard breadth of his body against mine—it's too much, too *real*, too far past the point of no return.

I can't help it—I scream.

The kapitän lifts up off of me, just a breath of space, and it makes me realize he *didn't* land his full weight on me. I'm struck again by how huge he is compared to me, how immovable, and how fragile I am at his mercy.

My scream pitches, catching in my throat, tripping on my own hesitation—if he *is* so much stronger than me, why hasn't he hurt me yet?

"Schiesse," he hisses, mostly to himself, and he moves only to press my arms over my head. I scream again and writhe, trying to buck him off, *something*, fight *back*—

He reaches up to my wrists.

And unlocks my manacles.

"*I'm not going to hurt you*," he says again, punctuating each word.

He moves away from me, taking the manacles with him.

I scramble off the floor, putting my back to the corner, breath hoarse in my lungs. My wrists burn at the freedom, the cold air hitting the raw skin like knives.

He's standing between me and the door, which he leaves open, maybe realizing how dark it is in here, how abyss-like. But even the pale glow of the clouded sun outside does little to shed light on us, casting him in oblong gray shadows.

"Prove it," I snap. "Let me go."

"I can't do that."

I laugh. It's cold and brittle.

"I can't do that," he repeats with force, "because every hexenjäger in the city is looking for you. And I need you to tell me—*exactly*—where you sent my sister. Also"—he pauses, and I see his tongue run across his lips, a self-deprecating look of exhaustion that ages him in the low light— "I need your help."

I go slack against the wall. "What could you possibly need with a *witch*?"

He frowns at me. "I told you. I'm going to save everyone."

What he said to me in the cellar. That wasn't a hallucination?

None of that was.

This hexenjäger...

...wants to set all the prisoners *free.*

I don't move. Not to fight back. Not to run. Not to protest.

The kapitän takes that as tentative agreement, and he reaches into a bag at his waist, pulls out a lantern.

When he lights it, his hand goes to the door. My whole body stiffens as he closes it, too aware of how alone we are, of how no one still knows that this hexenjäger has me.

My fear isn't as potent, though, giving way to acidic confusion.

And that confusion surges up even more when the kapitän motions to the table at the back of the room, that one chair.

"Sit, please?" he asks. "I have a lot to tell you, and little time in which to do it."

14

OTTO

I want to glare at the witch—but I do understand her confusion and rage. I wipe a hand over my face, schooling my emotions.

"I can't tell you where your sister is." Fritzi speaks before I can press that question further. There's a manic gleam in her eye, and I think she's not telling me everything, but I can wait. If I answer her questions, she'll answer mine.

I hope.

I take a deep breath. "The first thing you should know is that you ruined *years* of plans to stop the hexenjägers."

Okay. From her flashing eyes and the snarl blossoming over her lips, I could have perhaps stated that better.

Her eyes rake over my body. I've taken off my hexenjäger robes, but I may as well still be wearing them for all the hate she directs at me. Before she can say anything, though, I tell her about my sister and our plan to take down the hexenjägers from within.

I watch her closely, seeing the shift from distrust to doubt to tentative acceptance. She's wary—which means she's smart—but I think she believes me. I hope she does.

When I finally finish, there's nothing but silence and darkness between us. I wait for her to say something.

"How many?" she asks finally.

My brow furrows. "How many?" I repeat.

"How many innocents died as you went along with this charade?" she asks, her voice rising. "How many people were burned alive while you waited to make your move?"

"Too many," I whisper.

It was an imperfect plan, but… "We tried other plans first, some to limited success, some that failed," I say, the only excuse I have. "We…we *tried*. It was just the two of us, separated and young and inexperienced, but it wasn't enough."

Fritzi remains still and motionless. She has learned the same lesson I have, it seems—silence begs its own form of confession.

"I had first thought that I could dismantle the hexenjägers from within." I meet her accusing gaze head-on. "It's tough to break through the indoctrination. Not just of the hexenjägers. Of the people, too, who learn that it's simpler to obey, to look away. They don't start with murder."

"They ease you into it," she says bitterly. "So why didn't you succumb?" She waves her hand at my confused look. "To the *indoctrination.*"

"My father," I say.

"He taught you to reject cults and see through lies?" Her voice rings with mocking.

"No," I say. "He taught me the consequences of succumbing to them."

She casts me a doubtful look, but I explain my stepmother's fate to her.

"Aren't you the little paradox?" she muses.

I can see why she says that, but she never knew my stepmother. When

Father wasn't around, she'd tell Hilde and me that religion is half politics anyway—which prince you serve determines how you pray. And the Holy Roman Emperor himself doesn't seem to pray to anyone but whatever lover he currently has. True faith, she said, was personal. Not political.

But that's the problem, I suppose. Because if you serve a prince that's Protestant, and he's killed by one that's Catholic, suddenly you're slaughtered for treason and damned for heresy, all in one fell swoop. And the Pope's in Italy and the Emperor's in Bohemia, and there's no one to stop anyone else from raising a stake one way or another.

My stepmother didn't really care about any religion. My father turned his into a weapon.

"So...you just wear a black cloak and crucifix as a disguise, huh?" Fritzi asks.

I pause. I feel her trust in me is fragile at best, and one wrong word will have her going for my throat. But I also feel like she deserves the truth.

"I believe in God," I tell her. "I am Christian. But I reject the Church."

Her lips snarl in disgust, and I see her whole body tense.

"There is a difference," I say quietly, "between someone who holds a personal belief and someone willing to kill anyone who doesn't share that belief."

It's not enough to convince her. I can tell that immediately. Her hands are curling into fists, her eyes darting back to the door, even if she knows she cannot throw herself at it bodily. To her, I suppose, the God I pray to and the one the archbishop murders in the name of are the same god. Maybe they are. I don't know. I only know that when I pray, I do not pray for death.

I pray for forgiveness.

And I know that I am not alone. It is that knowledge, that faith—not just in God, but in the good Christians who do not wish to paint the city streets red with blood. The people who look at my cloak in disgust, the ones who dare to spit on me... They are my only source of hope.

Fritzi's eyes are big and round as they watch me. She's still wary, still unsure.

Still untrusting.

It would not help, I know, to point out that not every person who bends their knee in prayer agrees with the archbishop and his reign of terror. I don't even bring that up.

Fritzi is a woman who doesn't need words and promises. She needs truth and action.

I meet her eyes, and I do not flinch away. "I have shown you from the start that my actions are my own, and they're not violent. And now I am asking for your help."

She cocks her head but doesn't answer.

"Can you bring me back my sister?" I ask, my voice cracking. Hilde would know what to do. She always did.

Fritzi's eyes shift away from mine. "I cast a spell of protection on her," she says. "I was trying to save her. That was all it should have done—just kept her *safe*." She pauses, face falling. "I can't undo it."

"Can't or won't?"

She bites her lip. "Can't as long as bringing her back would put her in harm's way."

That twists my stomach. Being beside *me* puts *her* in danger, a danger that's so dire a magical force keeps Hilde away from me. A few days ago, I would not have believed this possible. But I saw the way Fritzi leapt out the window and magic pulled her back in. I *saw* magic protect her.

"But then where is she?" My voice rises in my desperation. It kills me that Fritzi flinches in fear, but I can't help it.

She throws her hands up. "She's safe; I swear!" But the worry in her eyes belies that statement. I have to take it on faith then. If she will trust me, I will have to trust her. And pray that Hilde is safe.

"Is the kommandant back in Trier?" Fritzi's voice is so soft that I almost miss the question.

"Yes."

I watch her body closely. I have seen her shake with rage before, but never fear. Until now.

"Did he bring back a witch? One like me?" She meets my eyes, emotion warring in the pale blue depths of hers. "Younger than me, but with magic? My cousin." Her voice breaks. "Liesel. Does he have her? If you can free her and bring her to me, she can help us find your sister..."

Her voice trails off when she registers my sorrowful face. I know of no prisoners Kommandant Kirch brought back from Birresborn. At least, none were registered in the records. To my knowledge, Kirch and the troops returned with nothing more than the stench of smoke clinging to their cloaks.

"Can't you do something to find your cousin?" I ask. "And my sister?"

"I'm a green witch," Fritzi says, as if it were obvious. "I use herbs for spells that offer protection, strength, and things of that nature. My cousin is an augur—she can read the future in flames, or ask questions of the fire, and it obeys her. Not every witch is the same. We have different affinities."

This makes me freeze, but I don't think Fritzi notices the way my blood runs cold. Her words echo what Dieter told me this morning, outside the Porta Nigra. *He knows*, I think. *About real witches, their powers.*

"Kommandant Kirch did not tell me he had another real witch," I say.

Fritzi's jaw sets. "He *does*," she snarls fiercely.

"Then you have an incentive to free the prisoners. Will you help me?"

She narrows her eyes. "What do I need to do?"

I don't believe she'll like the plan Hilde and I came up with, so I say first, "What can your magic do to help? If I can get you into the basilica where the prisoners are kept, can you do...something? To free them?"

She snorts in bitter laughter. "I told you, magic can't just do anything. It depends on the witch's affinity. A little rosemary isn't going to be enough."

I shake my head, still confused. When Fritzi sent Hilde...elsewhere, it *seemed* enormously powerful. And just now, with the protection spell she cast on herself, that was clearly strong. Why can't she just save the others?

"Think of magic like a well," she continues, sighing at me. "Each witch can use their affinity to tap into the Well, and pull up a draft of magic. Protecting one or two people is like pulling up a bucket. Magicking out a hundred people from a well-guarded prison would be..."

"Like pumping it dry?" I guess.

She nods. "Sort of. Things that take a lot of power put strain on the Well. There are people who protect the source of magic, who ensure that doesn't happen. I would simply be unable to pull from the Well if it was something that big."

I frown at her, trying to understand her analogy. "Perhaps, if these keepers of the Well understood that we were trying to save innocents' lives..." My voice drifts off as she shakes her head. "Do you *have* to get your magical power from the Well? Is there some other source...?"

"No," she says, her eyes flash with rage. "No, we are not touching that sort of magic."

Interesting. She did not say it was impossible. Merely forbidden.

I don't press her on that—not yet, anyway. Instead, I pivot. "You *can* save one person, though, as evidenced by Hilde. Do you know other witches? If we have enough, perhaps you could all work together. My escape route and your combined powers..."

There's a different look on her face now. Not fury—sorrow. Her eyes slide away from mine, but she cannot hide the grief painted within them.

"Birresborn," I say. I'd guessed this before, when she mentioned the kommandant, but I'm certain of it now.

Her head whips up.

"You were a witch in Birresborn. Where Kommandant Kirch took an entire unit to root out a coven."

She nods slowly, once, a quick bob of her head.

Everyone in the village had been murdered. Almost everyone.

Liesel—Fritzi's cousin. That's how she knew she was a prisoner.

"Dieter took Liesel," Fritzi says. "I *know* he took her alive."

Two girls—all that remains of a whole village. My heart mourns for her grief. But then my mind locks on what she actually said.

She called Kommandant Kirch by his given name, Dieter. She spoke of him as if she knew him.

I open my mouth to question her, but I bite my tongue. Now is not the time to raise her ire, and besides, it could simply be a matter of her overhearing his name in the chaos.

"If we can't use magic," I say, "we'll have to use my original plan."

"Well, what is it?" she asks when I pause.

"You're not going to like it," I say.

Fritzi rolls her hand for me to continue.

"Okay." I take a deep breath. "Step one, I arrest you."

"No!"

"I told you that you wouldn't like it."

"Absolutely not."

"I need to get you into the prison, next to the prisoners, so you can teach them the escape routes."

"There has to be another way!"

I stare her down as she glares at me.

I see the moment when something breaks behind her eyes.

There *is* no other way.

"I can teach you the paths in the aqueducts." I draw my finger in the dust on the floor, tracing the outlines I have memorized. "There's a door that leads directly to the aqueducts from the basilica, and, once inside the tunnels, there are paths that split up and branch off. I teach you; you teach them."

"They can't stay in the tunnels forever," Fritzi says. "They'll be found."

"Each route ends at a safe house with supplies and disguises. From there, the market—"

"—it'll be crowded—"

"—then from there, out the city walls—"

"—and to safety." Fritzi blinks at me. "How are you going to get them out of the cage and to the aqueduct?"

"Gunpowder and a hypocaust," I say.

"Gunpowder, I get," Fritzi says. "What the hell is a hypocaust?"

"A heating system under the floor," I say. "When the ancient Romans built the basilica, they built a heating system using hollowed-out spaces under the floor to keep the building warm." I'm actually really proud of this—it took a lot of research to formulate this plan, and I've had no one but Hilde to appreciate my efforts. Fritzi raises her eyebrow, so I sketch the basilica's floor plan in the dust.

"See?" I say, drawing arrows, "This is where the cage is. The floor is made of brick, but *underneath* the floor are pillars. I'm going to blow up this part," I say, drawing a squiggly line, "which will open up one section of the flooring. You simply have to tell the prisoners to be on *this* side of the cage. Then the floor will give way, they drop down, and the hypocaust is linked directly to the aqueduct."

She frowns at my rough sketch.

"You thought of everything, didn't you?" She says the words flatly.

"I tried."

Her jaw tenses. "You really do need someone on the inside."

"I cannot warn the prisoners myself, much less teach them the routes."

She looks up at me, and I see the fierce determination in her eyes. "When?" she asks.

"The burning is in two days."

She swallows. "So you'll drag me to prison tomorrow."

"If you can memorize the routes tonight."

She nods tightly. "That'll give me one day to communicate to all one hundred prisoners."

My heart thuds. It's too risky; I can't ask this of her—

"Yes," Fritzi says. "I'll do it. I know Liesel's been imprisoned—she'll help too. We can work together."

She's just agreed to my plan, and both she and her cousin have actual magic that could aid it. But still, my gut twists with bile as I think about how this means I'm going to have to drag Fritzi into the prison and lock her behind an iron cage myself.

When I first pulled Fritzi through the tunnels, I had only thought of saving her to use her in this plan of mine. But now that the time has come... I am reluctant to let her leave my safety again. It's a ridiculous thought; I cannot very well leave her in the house fort for all time, and she's likely safer in the prison than out of it, with the way the kommandant has the men searching for her.

The thought makes my fists bunch. I will do this to save the innocents. But if anyone hurts her, they will pay.

15

FRITZI

I cross my arms. "This goes both ways, though. If I'm going to help you, you have to help me too."

He doesn't respond, doesn't seem to have heard me—his eyes have dropped low. I think at first he's staring a bit *too* intently at my breasts, but his face hardens, and I realize his gaze is fixed on my wrist where it's crossed over my chest.

I look at the angry red welts bleeding across the back of my hand.

I yank my arms down.

"You're injured," he says.

"Tends to happen when witches are around hexenjägers."

He's standing over me, the lantern flickering on the table beside me, and its unsteady light pulses the emotions on his face.

Regret.

Fury.

Pain.

I have no time for his self-flagellation—the Three damn these Catholics, really. "I'll need supplies to—"

"Sit."

"I—excuse me?"

"*Sit*," he repeats and brushes past me, back to the bag he took off during our conversation. He rummages in it for a beat before he turns with a jar and a knot of bandages.

I can't stop the surprise that flashes across my face. "I don't need your pity. I'm fine."

It's a lie—my wrists burn terribly—but I'll be damned if I accept that kind of help from him. I need to get Liesel and get out of Trier, not waste time tending to wounds *he* inflicted.

He crosses the room. I'm still standing when he stops in front of me.

His brows raise, and he eyes the chair against the back of my legs, the implied command heavy in his gaze.

My chest tugs, defiance sharp and biting. But he still says nothing, just stares at me in a long, weighted silence, and I know, in the clenched set of his jaw and the steadiness in his eyes, that he won't break.

I thought I knew stubborn.

I thought I was stubborn.

This man makes it a religion.

I suck my teeth and drop back on the chair. When I reach for the jar and bandages, he bats my hand away and lowers to one knee.

My heart heaves against my ribs.

"I'm not tied up," I tell him, hating the waver in my voice. "I can bandage my own wounds, thank you very much."

That earns what must pass for a sardonic look. "I don't doubt that you are very skilled at taking care of yourself."

Is that an insult? It feels like an insult, but I let him take my wrist.

His fingers are...gentle.

So gentle that it renders me immobile, and every argument I'd planned drains out of my mind.

How can someone so large touch me like I'm an eggshell? This doesn't feel like his natural state, *tenderness*, but he deftly rolls up my sleeve and gets to work smearing balm on my skin.

He stays quiet. He seems comfortable in silence, but I decidedly am *not*, and I shift on the chair, hating this closeness more each passing second, the way his dark eyes droop with sorrow when he finishes one wrist only to see wounds just as bad on the second.

There are flecks of green in his brown eyes. He has half his jaw-length dark hair pulled back, showing the way the tops of his rigid cheekbones redden slightly, and I realize I'm staring at him, and he knows it.

Schiesse, stop.

Focus on something else. Literally *anything else.*

I sniff the air—mint. Lavender. A few other herbs in that salve he's using.

I smile. "We'll make a witch out of you yet, jäger."

He flashes those eyes up to me. "The healing balm?" he guesses, tipping the jar.

I nod.

"Then every hexenjäger is a witch, for we all carry this in our supplies."

"Which is one of the many holes in your theology."

"It isn't *my* theology, need I remind you."

"No, merely formed from the tenets of your religion, jäger."

The kapitän sighs and finishes tying the last bandage to my wrist. "Otto."

I pull my arms in, surveying his work, but I stiffen. "What?"

"My name. It's Otto. Otto Ernst."

"I know your name." It cracks out of me like a whip.

He blinks.

There's another of his pauses. But if he seeks to make me use his name, that's one battle he will *not* win.

He seems to realize that, and he pushes to his feet. His shoulders tense—I hadn't even realized they'd been relaxed.

"If you're to take my sister's place in the jail," he starts—is his voice rough? I upset him. Good. "We need to start getting you to memorize the aqueduct layout—"

"Of course." I stand and smooth my skirt. "We can go over that later tonight."

He frowns at me. "And until then?"

"I need supplies. I'll make potions before I go into the jail. If I'm going to be a prisoner again, I will *not* be defenseless."

"You won't be undefended. You'll have me."

He says it so simply, like he's already guaranteed my safety.

I give him a look. "Reassuring. But *undefended* and *defenseless* aren't the same thing. I'll need more than a few healing spells for the prisoners who are too ill to move; and I'm not going into that prison without enough spells to protect not just myself, but the other prisoners, should your ironclad escape plan go awry."

His plan *is* fairly ironclad, actually, but I say it with sarcasm anyway.

His lips twitch. "I thought you said we wouldn't use your magic?"

"No—I said we wouldn't use the type of magic you were asking about. But the potions I'll make are perfectly acceptable to ask of the Well. I need to make them all tonight, though. I can't exactly whip out a cauldron, pointy hat, and broom in the middle of a hexenjäger cell, now can I?"

His frown deepens. "You—you really need those things?"

"No." I roll my eyes. "I just wanted to see if *you* thought I'd really need those things. Schiesse, jäger, what do you know about real witches?"

"Not enough," he offers. His eyes go furrowed and considering. "I don't understand your powers, but if I did—perhaps we could find a better potion or spell for the situation. Can you explain it to me?"

My brows vault up. "You want me to explain potion making to you."

"Yes."

"My entire life's work. In one evening?"

His cheeks go a little red. The sight is more charming than it should be.

"Ah." He clears his throat. "Then what about—are there any particularly powerful potions? One that we could focus on that would make the largest impact? Something that would make us both more powerful?"

I stare at him for a long moment.

He has no idea what powers he's asking to meddle with. Potions and spells aren't things that can be toyed with in a panic, frantically pieced together without forethought and planning.

And even if he is trying to undo the horrors the hexenjägers have wrought, I can't forgive him entirely for what he represents, and I want to remind him of what *I* am, too, of the fact that he should be a little afraid of me.

"Oh, yes, jäger," I say, sickly sweet. "There is one such potion. If we had time to brew it, that is—it uses a simple beer base, common enough. At the end of the brewing, you add a few more harmless herbs—but you also add belladonna and henbane, and then I'd speak the spell to complete it as it all bubbles and boils. You know what those ingredients are, don't you, jäger? Even non-witches know poisons that drive the takers mad before killing them."

The kapitän's interest turns to hesitation. "The resulting potion is a poison, then?"

"Not if I do it correctly. My spell would turn it into what's known as a bonding potion. It would allow someone like you to connect with a witch."

Mentioning the bonding potion is a jab in my throat. A seizure of muscle. I fight down any flinch at memory, any whiff of thought, and focus only on terrorizing this jäger.

He blinks. "It would give me some of your powers?"

I nod. "I would act like a vessel, funneling my power into you. But if it goes poorly, it could sever my connection to the Well entirely. Or so I've heard. No one I know has ever used such a potion. Who would risk it? Besides." I give a demonic smile. "It would first require *you* drinking the potion under your own will, trusting that I brewed it correctly. The risk is not only on my end with the magic—it is first on *you*, that the magic transformed the poison into potion at all."

The kapitän's narrow confusion goes to a slow building awareness that grows as I step closer to him. He can tell I'm playing a game, even if he might not yet see the reason, but to his credit, he doesn't back down. His gaze holds on mine.

"Now tell me, jäger," I whisper. "Do you trust me enough that you would take a potion like that? Do you trust that I wouldn't try to kill you? It only works if you take it willingly. Could you?"

His jaw works. I watch that tension flutter down his neck as he swallows.

"Would you even let me take it," he pushes back, the same whisper, what with how close I've let us stand, "knowing it would possibly link you to me?"

I smile. It bursts across my face so quickly that it surprises him, and he flinches, recovers, only to give a cautious, questioning grin in return.

"Then we're at an impasse, it would seem," I say. "Even if we had time to make this potion, which we don't, neither of us would see it worth the risk. So maybe you should stop asking questions about things we also don't have time to teach you, and just let me do what I do best? You have your escape plan. Let me have my potions."

With a disgruntled sigh, the kapitän bats his hand in surrender. "So what ingredients *do* you need? Give me a list."

"Ha! No. You think I'd trust you to be able to pick out the *good* myrrh from the bad? I doubt you could even tell the difference between nettle and nutmeg."

His lips twitch again. "I know what nutmeg is."

I step around him, aiming for the door, and I pat his shoulder as I go. "I don't doubt that you are very skilled at identifying nutmeg." My grin is feral. "But I'm going to the market."

He seems to trip on my touch, or maybe my joke—either way, there's a full beat before he flips a glare at me. "You are *not* going to the market. I told you, the city is flooded with hexenjägers looking for you. The kommandant himself wants you. If you get caught before we prepare, then a hundred people will *die*."

As though he needs to remind me.

I have a chance to save people from the fate of my coven, so of course I'll take it, and I have a chance to save Liesel too.

But he says it as if he's reminding *himself*, as if he never gets a chance to say his truths out loud, and now that he's told me everything, he can't help but to say it again, and again, speaking the forbidden words into the air.

I can't even fathom the weight he's carried all these years. The people he's watched die, the lies he's had to tell, the walls he's built around himself—

But he aided death too. He's part of the dark wave that has choked this country and destroyed my people, and even if he's tried not to be directly complicit, he's still *guilty*.

Isn't he? What if his words are true—what if he has, from the very beginning, worked against the murderers?

I turn away from him. I can't look into his eyes with these thoughts banging around my head.

"Well," I start, clear my throat, and stand up straighter. "If I don't get supplies, I can't guarantee the safety of all those prisoners, and I'm not going in that prison without my own guarantee."

"Fine." His agreement comes gruff. "But I'm coming with you."

"Fine," I relent. "I need you to pay, anyway. Unless you're all right with me using my wits and wiles to obtain what I need."

One corner of his mouth lifts. Is that a smile? The Three save me.

"No need to steal," he says. "I'll pay."

I turn for the door, but his fingers on my shoulder stop me cold. It's not just that he's grabbing the bruise his elbow left there yesterday; it's that his touch shocks through me, gentle now, such a stark contrast that my body can't decide what to do with it.

"At least—can you conjure some sort of disguise?" His voice is thin.

I stare at him for a full breath.

He really has no fear of my magic. Our whole conversation about his plans and his truths, he hadn't once flinched at any mention of magic, and he doesn't now. He speaks of it as any other skill or tool.

I fight a smile. "That's not how magic works. Besides, I don't have any herbs here—I used what few you did have." I press my finger to his shirt and swipe up a bit of the powder still coated on him.

His chest is just as firm as when he'd held me against him in the aqueducts.

He sighs and crosses the room. From under the cot, he pulls out a box I'd missed, a small trunk—from it, he draws out a thick cloak. "Wear this, then."

It's brown, not the black of his hexenjäger robes, but my body goes stiff. It's *his*, and something about dressing in his clothes sends a shiver through me.

It isn't a bad shiver.

Which is why I jerk back from him. "No."

"It has a hood." He nods at my head. "They're looking for a witch with yellow hair."

"I have a hat," I say. I pull it off—the Three, it's absolutely *wrecked* with grime now—and flip my head upside down to twist my matted, equally filthy hair up inside the hat. What I wouldn't give for a bath.

The desire squeezes the breath from me, and when I straighten, I'm winded, shaken.

A bath.

Helping Mama fill our tub, laughing over some stupid joke.

Her fingers pulling the tangles out of my hair. Her voice, airy and light, singing—

I straighten my own cloak, holding it tighter to my chest, and stare at the closed shutters, hoping the hexenjäger doesn't see the tears in my eyes.

If he does, he says nothing. Once he's dressed in his own sort of disguise—that simple brown cloak, the hood pulled low over his face—he turns to the door.

"What if your magic doesn't let you out?" he asks, and I can hear the hope in his voice—that I might have to stay here while he goes to the market alone.

"Then I'll rip your house down to its foundation," I spit, and I shove past him.

The magic does let me climb out, thank the Three, when I go slowly and don't try to hurl myself into untold danger. The kapitän points out the safe footholds—a few boards and crates are broken—and I wait on the street as he locks the door and climbs down behind me. It gives me a moment to get my bearings—not that I'd know *where* in Trier I am—and I turn in a slow circle, surveying the neighborhood.

It's abandoned.

Mostly.

The buildings are all quiet and dilapidated, held together by old boards or tattered sheets. There's a...*feeling* that I can't quite place, like this neighborhood is cloaked in some sort of protection spell.

Only it isn't a spell at all. It's grief, I realize with a jolt. This street, these buildings—whatever happened here left a stain of sadness in every stone and plank.

It knocks on the grief in my own heart. Like calling to like.

Aunt Catrin would have been able to communicate with whatever spirits are here. Birresborn felt like this before I left—like the dead were pressing up against the veil between our worlds, unable to move on just yet.

The kapitän starts walking, and I follow. "What happened here?"

He glances down at me. "It's the Judengasse."

The realization punches me in the gut. It's been decades since that edict. I'd forgotten, and my body washes with disgust—at myself for forgetting, and the hexenjäger for being so cavalier about it. A whole people were *forced out of this city*.

The Church leaves a trail of displaced souls in its wake.

"I don't understand how anyone can believe in your church," I whisper. "The corruption is so obvious, it's blinding."

The kapitän cringes. "Normalcy has a way of breeding acceptance—when darkness is all people know, they forget to ask for the light."

"This isn't seductive darkness though. How can people—"

"Seductive darkness?"

His question makes my words snap off. I hadn't meant to say that. Not...like that.

I swallow, eyeing him, gauging how much he might press for clarification. "Your church speaks of the lure of the Devil. There is no *lure* in this kind of evil." I wave at the Judengasse. "I can't imagine seeing this kind of treatment and *choosing* to step into a church."

His jaw flexes. "This is the Church's doing, as you said," he whispers, "not my God's. And people recognize that. I have to believe so, anyway."

I shiver, folding my arms tight. The rage that wells up when he speaks of his faith is equal parts disgusting and...familiar.

I remember someone who had unwavering faith in the Three.

Someone who believed our magic had no end.

Someone they disappointed.

"You can't separate your god from the evils committed in his name." It comes out harsher than I intended. It's this *place*. This neighborhood. The evil that lingers from the cruelty of the atrocities that happened here.

There are faces peeking out of some of these windows. People hiding in these abandoned structures. People driven to desperation by the hexenjägers.

Two faces in a house just behind us are easiest to see. The rest duck down quickly when I look at them, but these two stay. Staring. Watching.

They're children. Maybe seven, eight years old. I can see the dirt smudged on their faces even from here.

Fury rages up my throat, making me liable to scream at the hexenjäger, lay this blame on him, force him to see what's happening in his own city.

But I think he already does.

And I don't know what to do with that.

"I know."

I glance up at the kapitän. He's looking where I was, at the window with the two faces; he nods at them, smiles softly, and when his eyes drop to mine, my lips part.

"I know much of what has happened has been in His name," he says. "Faith is...complicated."

"The right thing isn't."

"I know that too. Which is why we're going to save the innocents."

"And then what?" The question knocks into my stomach. *And then what*?

After I get Liesel. After I get us out of this city. I take her, and we run to the Black Forest—*and then what*?

The threat is still here. Kommandant Kirch is still *here*. And I'm just going to hide away while he grows in power? What else can I *do*?

Stop him.

The voice is relentless now, and steady.

Stop him.

This neighborhood aches with that same goal. Everyone who had been here—every person killed or forced to live in exile for decades, centuries even—I can feel all of their desolate souls thrumming at the thought of the lead hexenjäger being brought to justice. Even if they weren't persecuted by hexenjägers themselves, the evil is the same.

Stop him.

How? How can I stop him? Mama stayed in Birresborn far longer than we should have as she tried to figure out some way to reach him, too, some way to convince him to give up this crusade. But if there is no way to stop him—what do I do?

I'm hit with a sudden image, the memory of Mama tied to her stake.

Instead, though, I see the kommandant, bound in irons, burning alive.

"We don't kill," comes Mama's reprimand from my memory, the lessons all elders taught us. *"Witches never kill. It feeds wild magic—and we do not* touch *wild magic, Friederike!"*

I brace, waiting for the voice to slither in, to push me over into temptation with wanting to see Kommandant Kirch dead.

But nothing comes.

Nothing but my own aching need, buried deep under my grief, and that is somehow worse, that the voice doesn't even *need* to tempt me. The will is already there.

I wince, black spots across my vision, the street spiraling, shaking—

"Fritzi?" Fingers grab my upper arm. "Fritzi!"

I lurch forward and slam into the kapitän's hard chest. He catches me, anchoring me as I gasp, shaking, sweat beading down my spine.

"I'm just—" I look up at him.

He's holding me on the street.

His face is close, so close, pupils blown wide with earnest concern—schiesse, how is a hexenjäger kapitän so *earnest*?—with a tuft of his dark hair breaking free to swing across his forehead, the edge of his cloak's hood dipping back, just slightly.

I sigh, for a moment letting him take my weight.

For a moment, just resting.

I waver again, eyes snapping shut.

"I'm just tired." I push away from him.

I've been alone since Birresborn, that's all.

I'm scared and grieving and *alone*, and he's the first semi-friendly face I've seen since my world fell apart.

That's *all*.

"Come on, then," he says, and his voice is so *kind*, I hate him. "Let's get to the market. Oh, schiesse—you have to be starving!"

I slit my eyes open. "Not terribly. I may have eaten your rations."

He smiles. Full. Broad. It does something to my stomach.

"Good," is all he says.

I don't just hate him.

I hate myself too.

16

OTTO

It's not a far walk from the house fort to the market, but I keep an eye on the girl beside me, making sure she's both protected from sight and isn't going to pass out from hunger. Besides, I'm hungry too.

I steer Fritzi around the Christkindlmarkt. I know exactly where I want to take her—and soon enough, her nose tips up at smoke that smells of pine cones.

"Hallo," I call to Hans, the man bent over the fire. Glowing edges of burning pine cones blaze inside a ring of stones, creating an outdoor firepit right on the cobblestones of the Hauptmarkt square.

Hans nods toward me without lifting his head. He turns a trio of wurst on a stick, sniffing the air as the fat sizzles.

"Two, please," I tell him, and Hans nods. Fritzi watches, her brow furrowed in curiosity. "With brötchen," I add, and Hans pats the ground at his side, finding a pile of bread rolls on a wooden platter beside him. He takes one, then turns his spit toward the bread, stuffing the sausage at the end of his stick into it. It looks ridiculous—a fat, round roll wrapped around a long and skinny sausage, bits of ash and black char speckling the meat.

I take mine; then I nudge Fritzi to take hers from Hans, who holds his hand up, head still bent. As soon as she plucks it from his fingers, Hans turns his hand around, palm up. I press two coins into his hand and don't step away until he feels it with his fingers and nods, slipping the money into a pouch.

"Danke," I say as we turn. Hans nods again, adding a new wurst to his spit.

We walk a little into the heart of the market, where it's crowded. I eat quickly, the meat still hot.

"He's blind, isn't he?" Fritzi asks, looking over her shoulder.

"Among other ailments, yes," I say. Hans took up selling in the market a year ago, after his daughter—the only person who cared whether he lived or died—was burned as a witch. Her accuser was a man angry that she'd spurned his advances. He claimed on oath, in front of the archbishop, with his hand on the Bible, that she had cast a love spell on him to make him lust for her. He swore that Hans had lost his sight as a result of his daughter's deals with the devil.

I think about that a lot. The way he swore before God something that was clearly a lie. The way he used a father's misfortune and ill-health to condemn a daughter. The way it meant nothing to him. Nothing to the archbishop, either, who heard the truth from Hans. Hans pleaded for his daughter's life, but he'd had no gold to back his testimony.

Fritzi takes a bite of the sausage and moans in delight. "I've never had a wurst like this before."

"Hans is from Coburg," I say by way of explanation. His method of cooking the wurst over a fire of pine cones, though, is catching on, the smoke adding a special flavor to the meat.

"Coburg?" Fritzi raises her eyebrows at me—Coburg is to the east, one of the cities where Martin Luther led the Protestant Reformation. Heretic to the Catholics, leader to the Protestants, his mark forever changed the principalities of the east. Coburg was the city where Luther translated the Bible from Latin into German, allowing any man—at least any man who could read—to have access to the Lord's Word.

To the archbishop of Trier, such free access to God is a treachery. But then again, if every literate person could see the context behind the passages of scripture he weaponizes, perhaps the blade of vitriolic words he sharpens in the fires of the accused would dull.

Last year, the archbishop sent me to Mehring with a mission to root out and destroy the source of rising Protestant sympathies along the border. I found the priest who was converting the formerly faithful, but rather than murder him, I spoke to him. My hopes that here, perhaps, was a church more open than the archbishop's reign of terror were squashed. The Bible may be free to be read, but already people within the Protestant religions are seeking to limit interpretations different from their own. The same old prejudices are rising up against the Jews, against women, against the other.

I may believe in God, but no church has earned my faith.

I look up from my dark thoughts to see Fritzi drinking a long pull of beer from a ladle. The girl with the bucket turns to me. "She said you would pay." The girl's flirting smile is far different from the smile of the other girl who offered me a drink earlier, the one who trembled when she saw my badge.

I pass the girl a coin. Fritzi takes another long draught of the spicy beer, and I hand over another pfennig.

"Come on," I tell Fritzi before she can guzzle a third draw.

"That's good beer!" she calls to the girl, who giggles at her.

"It's hardly good beer," I mutter when the girl can't hear. Fritzi cocks an eyebrow at me. "My sister brews good beer."

"Seasoned with *nutmeg*, I presume?" She gives me a little jab in my ribs.

"Yes," I say, unable to keep the grumpiness from my voice. "Cooked in the copper cauldron our mother passed down to her."

Fritzi eyes me but doesn't comment. However, at the thought of Hilde, my thoughts turn dark again. "We need to find—" I start, but already Fritzi is gone, slipping from my grasp and perusing a stall of glass baubles. The rickety wooden table doesn't seem sound enough to bear such delicate wares.

"I didn't think you'd be the type to like trinkets," I say.

Fritzi shoots me an affronted look. "I like pretty things."

So do I, I think immediately, and praise Christ Almighty the words didn't slip past my lips by accident.

"This one," Fritzi says, pointing to a bit of glass swirled with blue flecks, strung up like a necklace on a leather thong. "When I was a little girl, one of my cousins broke an old blue bottle, and I cried and cried because it had been so pretty. My mama put a piece in a dish with some sand and water and told me that if I sloshed it around enough, it would become a jewel. I know it was glass, but..." She eyes me. "It was magical."

I can't help but grin at her secret play on words, and I can imagine little Fritzi smoothing the sharp edges of the glass until it became a bead. "I went to Venice when I was younger. My father was on a pilgrimage to Rome, and we made the extra journey. I saw the glassblowers."

Fritzi's eyes light up as I describe the way a glassblower stood in front of a blazing furnace, turning a long tube, then pinching the red-hot molten glass with metal shears. "And, just like that, he'd made a horse."

"A horse?" Fritzi's eyes are wide, charmed by my story.

"I studied in Venice," the man behind the table says, drawing our attention. "A *Venetian* bauble for your girl?" He jostles the table, and the glass tinkles.

I bow my head in mock respect. Any glassblower claiming Venetian skills would certainly merit a high price, but I can tell he thinks he can capture me in a sale to impress Fritzi. He probably thinks I was boasting when I mentioned the pilgrimage, but the Italian I speak is real. "Sai come fare il culo di un cavallo?"

"Ah," the man says, eyes going wide. "Of course, sir, I, er. I met the man you speak of." It's obvious he has no idea what I said, even to Fritzi, whose laughter rings clearer than the glass on the table. "Oh, buy me some pretty Venetian glass, Liebste," she says in an exaggerated flirtation. I know she's mocking me by calling me "sweetheart," but the man behind the table doesn't. He grins sheepishly at me, still hoping for a sale.

"We have other things to purchase today, *darling.*"

Her face immediately falls, and she walks away. I shoot the man at the table a glance, and he smirks. "I may not know Italian, but at least I know how to talk to women."

I race through the crowd to catch Fritzi. She shakes my hand away when I grab her elbow. "I *know*, all right," she says. "I didn't really want you to spend money on something frivolous. I know there are more important things to buy right now."

I would have dumped all my coins on the table to make you smile, I think. She has had nothing but grief ever since she burst into my life, and for one brief moment, we swapped tales of joy and wonderment, and her smile was true. I'm asking her to risk her life for my plan, and that glass bauble is nothing compared to that.

"I wasn't chiding you," I tell her awkwardly.

She wraps her arms around her slender torso, not meeting my gaze. I feel as if our brief moment of camaraderie was as fragile as the glass, and I've already broken it.

We've somehow drifted behind a busy line of people waiting to buy Reibekuchen, the smell of frying potatoes weaving around us. Fritzi strides past them, but meets nothing but a dark wall on the edge of the market.

I'm careful not to corner her, but I wait until she meets my eyes before I say, "If things were different, I would have bought you a necklace."

She snorts and rolls her eyes. I can already see the sarcastic comeback forming on her lips, but I speak before she can: "You deserve a bit of magic."

That elicits the tiniest of smiles. "Come on," she says gruffly, shouldering past me and back into the crowded market. "I still need to get my ingredients."

I close my eyes and imagine a night of joy and merriment. I'd buy Fritzi a mug of glühwein. My mother used to say that beer was life, but hot spiced wine was the reason to live. We'd dance and drink and after...

But already, both the vision in my head and the girl in front of me are slipping away.

I shake myself and charge into the crowds after Fritzi. I lose sight of her a moment, but then I hear her shriek. I race forward, prepared to fight any hexenjäger who's identified her, but instead her scream turns to laughter, along with all the people nearby. A man towers above her, tottering on wooden stilts. He makes a show of falling, the stilts clattering over the cobblestones, but even as the growing crowd around him gasps and screams, he regains his balance, laughing as he holds out his hat for coins.

"Toss them all to me!" he says loudly. "For soon Peter shall take my spot in the market!" The crowd roars with laughter as the man dances his stilts over some cobblestones marked with paint—the place where the archbishop plans to install a grand fountain in honor of Saint Peter. Paid for, in part, with bribes from the rich who do not wish to be accused of witchcraft. A fiddler dances past us, bow gliding across waxed strings. "Kerzen!" a woman calls. Hand-dipped candles are draped by their connected wicks across her arm. "Kerzen for sale!" Nearby, a man stands over a cauldron bubbling with hot oil, dipping mushrooms into it. "Champignons," he calls in a French accent.

Fritzi starts toward that stall. "More food?" I ask.

She shakes her head, and something in the furtive movement makes my muscles tense. When she approaches the stall owner, she points to the mushrooms that are plucked and white in his basket, not yet fried in the oil. "Can I purchase three?" she asks.

The man scoops some fried mushrooms up.

"No," Fritzi says, shaking her head. "Three of the raw ones."

I step forward. "Nous voulons trois champignons frais," I say in French.

"Voulons?" the man asks.

I nod. "Ma femme est étrange," I say with a shrug.

The man looks at Fritzi and barks in laughter. She scowls—she's probably picked up at least a bit of what I said, but her expression changes as the man tosses her three fresh mushrooms. She slips them into the pouch at her skirt as I pay the man.

"'Your wife is strange?'" Fritzi whispers to me, so soft only I can hear. She snorts. "As if I would marry you."

So, the witch is more offended by being called my wife than by being labeled strange.

After several more stops, Fritzi tells me she needs only one more thing. She takes me to a building along the square. A painted sign declares it *Löwen-Apotheke*—the Lion's Apothecary.

"Don't talk," Fritzi says in a low whisper as she steps inside.

The building is brightly lit with both lamps and a fire in the hearth. A man looks up as we step inside, but Fritzi makes a show of looking away, seeking past him. To a woman—his wife, I think, or a sister.

Fritzi rushes to her. The apothecary scoffs, waving his hand in a dismissive way as he turns to a different customer.

"Have you any rue?" Fritzi asks the woman in a low voice. When the woman hesitates, Fritzi drops a hand to her belly. "Please," she says, her voice cracking over the word.

Grumbling, the woman steps behind the apothecary counter. She bends down, opening a small wooden box and shaking out a sprinkling of dried herbs into a piece of scrap cloth, which she wraps up.

"You didn't get that here," the woman says, passing the herb to Fritzi.

"Of course," she murmurs. Then she elbows me. Hard. I drop coins in the apothecary woman's hand, and Fritzi strides out of the building.

On our way back to the house fort, I question Fritzi's last purchase. "What was that?"

"Rue," she says. In a low voice, so no one else can hear, she adds, "It's generally banned—too close to witchcraft, ironically—but it's too useful to get rid of entirely."

"What's it for?"

"Menstruation cramps," Fritzi says matter-of-factly.

A flush creeps up my cheeks.

"Ironic, that," Fritzi goes on. "An herb that specifically helps only women, and it's associated with crime. If rue was an herb to make your"—her eyes rake over my body, lingering on my midsection—"*staff* stay firm," she says, smirking, "every apothecary would sell bushels of it on the corner." She shrugs. "But it's not. It's an herb for women, so it must be hidden and sold in secret. Especially here."

"Is…er…" I pause. "Is it an herb you need now?"

"Yes."

I feel my flush deepen as we leave the market and walk through the shadows toward the house fort.

Fritzi rolls her eyes. "For the *potion*. Just because it's helpful for cramps doesn't mean it's not also a useful ingredient in potion making."

"Oh."

She laughs at my unease, pushing against my shoulder. And while we just spent the evening gathering ingredients on the last night before I must arrest Fritzi and we risk everything, there's a lightness in the way she walks now.

Hope, I think.

She walks as if she has hope.

Hope that this plan will work. Hope that what I've done is not in vain.

Hope…and maybe something else.

17

FRITZI

I am humming spells I know by heart, their words tumbling from my lips, half song, half prayer. I am grinding herbs and packing them into little vials. I am covered in the smells of earth and life and magic. My belly is full, and though this house fort is still freezing, I'm protected from the worst of the chill.

For the first time in little less than a week, I am, if not happy, then content.

My mind shies away from any thoughts about *why* I am doing this, any ruminations over the coming day or memories of the past, and I lose myself in the repetition of these tasks, the familiarity so comforting that my chest stops aching.

The kapitän intersperses my work with explanations of the aqueducts. He draws a map on the floor and goes over the routes with me, over and over again, making me recite them back to him between potion spells.

Even just a few hours ago, I would have snapped at him and his insistence that I say it "again, just once more. And what if they go left instead of right? Which path? Again, Fritzi."

But now, I can't ignore the fear on his face. The tension in his shoulders, his hands. The way he points at his crude map and his finger shakes.

It's fear mixed with eagerness mixed with hope, powerful, dangerous hope, and any retort I might have given falls flat in my throat.

It still amazes me that a hexenjäger is capable of pure emotion this strong. It's…hypnotizing.

He really means to save everyone.

He really believes we won't be found out, caught, and executed; he really believes we can show the people of Trier that they don't have to live under the fear they've become all too used to.

I don't know if I'm capable of the conviction he has. Every inch of him is saturated in belief of some kind—faith or hope or certainty—and here I am, mixing potions, humming to keep my mind off of all my failures and betrayals and—

You aren't telling him everything, says the voice.

I channel my jolt of alarm into mixing another healing potion. *There's nothing to tell*, I cut back. *My past won't affect this.*

Won't it? You're a fool. Watch as you destroy his plan even further.

My jaw sets. *No. No, that won't happen—*

There is a way still to avoid any mistakes at all. There is a way to avoid having to tell him everything. You know it. It will be here, waiting for you, when you are finally ready to give in.

"Fritzi?"

I shiver, blinking through my fog.

The kapitän leans forward. He'd taken the chair while I spread my potion-making supplies around the floor, the diagram of the aqueducts sketched in dust between remnants of herbs and mushrooms.

After a pause, he stands. "It's getting late. We should sleep. We'll need rest just as much as any potion."

As if in response, I yawn, and there is my exhaustion, rearing high and strong. I'd been so distracted by getting to make potions again that I'd almost forgotten I haven't really slept in days.

"You'll take the bed," he says.

I'm too tired to protest. I've finished what I can make, and the potions are all now tucked in little vials that I'll carry in the leather pouches on my belt. I lay the bulging pocket on the table and stretch, my body aching at having spent the past few hours crouched over my work.

When I turn, I catch the kapitän's eyes on my waist.

He looks away, his hand snapping up to rub the back of his neck.

Silence holds. I know he was looking at me; he knows I caught him looking, and it wasn't even the first time. Yet I don't yell at him, don't draw a firm line.

Why?

I should.

But still, I say nothing, and I cross the room to descend the ladder to where he showed me a garderobe I can use to relieve myself. I clean as best I can with the fresh water pumped up from the aqueduct—it still isn't a full bath, but it's better than nothing—and by the time I come back up, the kapitän is seated on the floor in the corner opposite the cot, his hexenjäger robes strewn over him in lieu of the one blanket that I'd torn to make my protection satchels. The lantern next to him burns low.

Another cloak is already spread over the cot. The brown one he'd worn in the market.

I have my own cloak still, but I don't point that out.

"I'll wake us at dawn," he says, his eyes shut. "You can spend all day tomorrow teaching the routes to the prisoners and healing any who need it. Then, the day of the burning, you'll have a few hours before the Christkindlmarkt will be crowded enough to provide cover. The midmorning bells are when everyone will need to be in place for the explosion. And you—"

"Midmorning? I thought we were moving on the afternoon bells?"

The kapitän's eyes flare open, and he gives me a look of such panic that I immediately feel bad for teasing him.

I splay my hands. "Kidding! Midmorning bells, I know. I know the aqueduct paths for the prisoners to take and where Liesel and I will meet you at an offshoot tunnel afterward. I do. I promise."

He doesn't settle, his body wound and stiff, even under the cloak. "This isn't a joke, Fritzi."

I sit on the cot and bend to take off my boots, my hair hanging over my shoulder, some of it heavy with water from where I'd tried to wash the dirtiest curls without drenching my whole head and risking a chill. "I'm well aware," I grumble to the floor.

It was easy when I had my potions to distract me.

It was easy when we were in the Christkindlmarkt, and every turn brought a new, glittering distraction.

But here, now, in the silence of his house fort, knowing there will be nothing stretching between me and the rising sun of tomorrow...

I should have gotten ingredients to make a sleeping draught.

The cot creaks as I curl up on it, facing the room, my eyes level with his. I pull his brown cloak up to my chin, and that, along with my thick wool kirtle and the cloak I'm still wearing, almost offer warmth. It'll still be a verdammt cold night.

The cloak smells like the Christkindlmarkt—spices and frying oil and holly—but something else. A musk that I recognize as *him*, just him.

My stomach tightens, and I nestle in deeper.

He reaches to extinguish the lantern, but he's watching me still. The way he's been looking at me these past hours is heaped in such intensity that I wonder how he has the energy for it, a focused scrutiny like he can unlock all my secrets just by observing the way I tuck hair behind my ear, the way I pull my bottom lip between my teeth.

But now, his look breaks with a sigh. "I don't mean to be short-tempered. This is a delicate situation on its own, but without Hilde..." He rocks forward, his brow creasing. "I *need* you to meet me afterward. I need you to help me find her. I cannot—" His breath hitches. "I'm trusting you in that, Fritzi."

"You think I'll run off," I say.

His lips thin.

I roll onto my back, gaze on the ceiling, the long beams of wood turned to ebony shadows in the fading light.

My eyes flutter shut. "I promised to help you find your sister, and I will. Liesel will be able to find her. I know you have no reason to trust me, but we will meet you in the tunnels."

"It is a fair trade—you have no reason to trust me either."

The edges of my lips curl in a smile. "True. Still, I shouldn't have teased you. I don't take this lightly, I swear. My mother used to say my cheek would be the death of her."

Speaking of her is like swallowing a barb. Tears burn the backs of my eyes; my throat swells.

"There are certainly worse ways to die," he says, then inhales sharply. "I didn't mean—that came out wrong."

My body tenses, my eyelids pinching shut tighter, and I hold there, in silence, letting the quiet swallow his words, the memory they stoke.

I will not think about her body tied to the stake.

I will not think about how agonizing a death that was for her.

The light is still pulsing beyond my eyelids. The kapitän hasn't turned down the lantern yet.

"You need me to sing you a bedtime song?" I try to make it come out short, but it's just as brittle as everything in me suddenly feels.

A huff comes in response, followed by the light fading, until all is darkness, even when I open my eyes. I gasp in it, shocked by the depth of this black, though I shouldn't be—there are no windows in this part of the house fort, no slivers of moonlight pushing in—

"*How many stars are in the sky?*" the kapitän suddenly sings, a soft, pitchy croon.

My whole body goes tense, face contorting in an expression of amused horror that gets lost in the darkness. "What are you singing?"

"A lullaby." A beat. "Do you not know that one? I thought it was rather popular."

"I—I know it. But—"

"I assumed you asking me if I needed a bedtime song was a thinly veiled request for one. *How many stars are in the sky?*" he sings again.

I shove my hands over my mouth, but it does nothing to stifle my sudden fit of laughter. "What are you—"

"*How many*—don't make me sing the same verse again. You said you knew this one. It's a call and response."

"I am not singing with you, jäger."

"How are we to sleep?" he asks, voice hung with mock sincerity.

I flop onto my side, but I can't see him in the dark. "You're mad. Utterly."

I swear I can feel his grin in the darkness. And the sensation of him smiling in this space of sightlessness but being unable to see it is unbearably intimate, shaking down through my core in a relentless quiver.

With a defeated sigh, I give in. "*Count them all as we fly by.*"

"*How many clouds will come at dawn?*" he sings back immediately.

"*Count until we start to yawn.* All right, I am sufficiently tired, I think. Gute Nacht, you crazed man."

The kapitän chuckles. The low, deep rumble of his laughter palpitates the air, and I'm glad I ended this back and forth, because I'm not sure I can draw in enough breath to speak.

"Gute Nacht," he whispers in return.

My fingers bleed.

I tear at the dirt wall of the cellar, rocks and knobs of mud raining down in my attempt, but no matter how I climb, I never get to the opening just above, just out of reach.

"Mama!" I scream. *"Mama—"*

She appears there. In the square of light.

"Friederike," she says, and my heart swells to bursting at the love in her voice. I can barely see her face—the light behind her is too bright.

"Give me your hand!" I slip a little, sliding down the cellar wall, and when I look, I can't see the bottom, the floor long gone; maybe it was never there at all. "Help me! *Please,* Mama—"

"Help you?" She rocks back on her heels. "Why on earth would I help you? You let him in, Friederike. You did this."

A shadow rises behind her, growing, growing through the light until her outline blends and bleeds into the silhouette of a massive tree, gnarled branches reaching into the endless white light. Her shoulders protrude from the tree, her elbows and knees, but my eyes cannot focus on where she ends and the tree begins.

"What? No!" Another slip down. I cling to the wall, thrusting my weight against it, fingers aching and legs trembling at trying to keep myself on these crumbling footholds. "That's not what happened—*please*—"

"Oh, it's far too late, Fritzichen," says someone else.

I know that voice.

My body goes ice-cold, a thousand warring memories fighting to be felt.

I look up slowly, the stench of earth overpowering, mildew and decay and dying, breaking things.

And there, kneeling next to the tree, is Dieter.

Kommandant Kirch now.

Resplendent in his hexenjäger uniform.

Mama is gone. The tree remains, with Dieter over the hole, separate from it, seemingly unaware of it behind him.

"It's too late," Dieter says again. "You had your chance."

Come to me, Fritzi, says the voice. Only the branches of the tree shift, those ancient limbs flicking and twitching like in a wind, but I know, *I know*, the tree is speaking, the tree is the voice I have been pushing against for so, so long. *He lies. It is not too late. You can still stop him. Come to me. Say the spell.*

My body wracks with a sob, tears relentless, choking.

Dieter reaches down into the hole. My heart tangles with hope and fear, and before I can decide whether to trust him, he grabs my hands, wrenches me off the wall, and drops me into the darkness.

"Auf Wiedersehen, Fritzichen," he calls, and I scream as the nothingness swallows me—

But I'm not falling alone.

Next to me, the wind of the fall billowing her blond hair, is Liesel, little Liesel, her eyes gaunt and bloodshot, bruises on her cheekbones. Her thin fingers scramble to reach for my shoulders, clinging to me as we both fall into nothingness, down, down into darkness.

"He'll break through," Liesel gasps at me. "He'll break through the barrier with me. Get me out, Fritzi, *get me out*—"

"I'm trying!" I grab onto her, but the darkness of the cellar is thicker and thicker the farther we fall, and when I look up, the square of the opening is a pinprick, and I can barely make out the silhouette of Dieter there, motionless, staring down at my unraveling as the tree looms larger and larger behind him.

Come to me. Say the spell. Come to me.

"Liesel!" I grope for her in the dark. "Mama!"

"Fritzi!"

A different voice in the dark. The bony arms of my cousin are broader now, heavy and solid, and hands grab at my shoulders, pat my cheeks.

"Wake up—Fritzi, *wake up*!"

The dream releases me with a ripping surge, and I careen into the present, gasping the frigid air of the night-drenched house fort. The lantern is relit on the floor next to the cot, and its unsteady orange light shows me the kapitän sitting next to me, his hands on my shoulders, his pinched face flickering in and out of shadows.

"Fritzi?" He prods my name, the barest echo of care, and I come apart.

Sobs send me rocking forward, and I cling to him, my forehead pressed against his chest. He goes stiff for only a moment, then his arms fold around me, cradling me against the wide set of his chest.

I don't deserve it. I don't deserve his comfort, his help. I deserve to fall, I deserve the way Mama looked at me in my dream, like there was nothing left to save.

Schiesse, I sound like a Catholic. Self-deprecation and flagellation.

My sobs start to abate, but only because I'm shaking too hard. It's absolutely *frigid* in this house fort—every part of my body is numb with cold, and I'm almost grateful for that discomfort to yank me out of my sorrow.

"Did you even manage to fall asleep on the floor?" I ask, teeth chattering.

The kapitän shrugs. The motion drags the rough linen of his shirt against my cheek. "I've slept in worse places."

"Ever the soldier." I turn my face, press it to his chest, and breathe, willing my heart to slow, willing my limbs to stop shaking. Maybe it isn't just cold; maybe it's grief, too, my body unable to hold onto this pain anymore.

His hand starts to rub my back, building heat with his rough strokes. "You called out for her," he says, his voice low, careful. "Your mother."

Slowly, my shaking calms. Slowly, I go from needing his support and warmth to thinking only how good it feels to have someone here, holding me.

"Did you see your mother burn?" I ask against him.

His hand on my back stops. "Yes."

I don't want him to pull away. I don't want to be alone.

I twist my fingers into his sleeves, holding my forehead to his chest, keeping him here with me, however selfish. I don't have room for anything but self-preservation right now.

"How did you breathe again?" I choke out.

He adjusts his grip on me, tighter, and something in me releases, more tears slipping free.

The smell that was in the cloak is stronger now. The musk, a richness, deep and heady.

His chest rises, and I realize he's taking a fortifying breath, holding my body against himself as he fills his lungs and exhales just as gently.

"One breath at a time," he whispers. "Until you can trick yourself into thinking you've gone a few moments without thinking about her."

I give a brittle laugh. It isn't in the least funny, but I feel the deep rumble of his bitter laugh, too.

Is his hand in my hair, stroking it? What parts of me had calmed wind tense again, and he notices in the way he goes absolutely still.

"It's not yet dawn," he says, his words stunted. "We should steal a few more hours of sleep."

I hum my agreement. I don't want to sleep. I don't want time to pass at all.

In a few hours, I'll be a prisoner of the hexenjägers again. I'll save Liesel and countless others, but my mother will still be dead, and I'll still be buried under the crushing weight of all the things I've done wrong.

So when the kapitän stands, I tighten my grip on his sleeves and move my fingers to lock around his wrists. The tendons there strain against my fingers.

"Stay," I beg. "Please."

He holds, half on his feet, crouched over the cot. The look on his face is one of utter shock, and I can see the war that pulses in his eyes.

"You don't get under my skirts that easily, jäger," I say with a forced smirk. The tears on my face cut through any humor I might try. "It's just... cold. And I don't want—"

I shudder and press the back of my other hand to my lips.

The Three save me, how broken am I if I can so easily ask this *stranger* to keep my nightmares away?

But Otto sits again. "Of course," he says, a gruffness in his voice that he counters with a soft smile.

I lie back down before I can think better of this. Otto turns out the lantern, casting us into pitch blackness, and the narrow cot groans as he arranges his cloak over the both of us. He stretches out beside me, and I feel the puff of his breath—he's facing me where I'm curled toward him.

I asked him to stay, didn't I? So what more shame do I have left, really?

There's hardly any space between us, but I close it, nestling my head under his chin, draping my arm around his hips. Warmth floods me, and I think I moan—which wouldn't that just be *perfect*, after everything—but if I do, if Otto hears, he stays firm in his silence.

A beat passes, then his arm folds over me, pulling me to him, encasing me in that smell, musk and heat, the steady rush and lull of his breath funneling in and out.

I suddenly regret telling him that this was all I wanted, nothing more.

We need to sleep.

But I need to not think, to not feel, to just *not* in every way. I'm still in pieces from my nightmare, still driven to mania in the cold, and so my body starts shaking again, and Otto pulls me closer.

I arch into the motion, head rising, and in the darkness, I can feel his face level with mine now. Can taste the way his exhale re-forms the air, the spark and spice of his breath coming in a quaking gust that sizzles across my tongue. I can't tell exactly how far away he is from me, but I can feel the space, or lack of space.

I shift closer.

The darkness is consuming again. It is delirious and hypnotic and dangerous, spinning a web of perceived absence, a dreamlike void, as though nothing that happens here really exists.

So the way our lips suddenly rest against each other.

The way we both hold there, kissing but not, bodies entwined.

It is a figment.

It isn't real.

His head tips, mouth sliding against mine, rough edges and soft, pillowy bottom lip. I think I feel the flick of his tongue, for a second, the quickest, tentative prodding at my mouth.

Heat flames to life in my belly, soothing the tremors, launching out to the tips of my fingers and the arches of my feet. It's that heat that melts through the frozen part of my brain, the numbed echoes of me, and I yank down, curving into his chest, holding my head into the space between our bodies.

Oh, schiesse, what did I do?

What did *he* do?

My hand fists in the back of his shirt. I'd move away if there was room, if it wasn't still freezing. I should ask him to go back to the corner. I should tell him to leave.

"Get some sleep," I whisper into the hollow against his chest.

I can feel his heartbeat thundering. It matches the pulse I feel in my throat. Rapid, clawing thuds.

"You too," Otto whispers, and save me, it's hoarse, so hoarse I can hear the restrained thoughts whirling through his head too.

I tuck my chin to my chest and force myself to lie as still as possible.

18

OTTO

The morning comes too soon, but I have been awake for hours.

We were born to kill each other.

And yet she tucks her body close to mine.

I can feel her heart beating. Her soft breaths coming in little huffs. Her delicate eyelids closed in slumber, the long line of her bare white neck centimeters from my lips.

Heat flushes my body at the thought of how close we are.

How close we *were*. She pulled back last night, but a part of me—most of me—longs for her to look up at me now, to tip her lips to mine, to cross that bridge we did not cross in the dark.

I never wanted to wear the black cloak of the hexenjägers. I am no hunter. But dear God in Heaven, I think I shall be seeking the quiet peace I feel when she lies in my arms for the rest of my life.

She stirs, murmuring in that liminal space between sleep and awake, and I close my eyes, wishing for the sun to eat itself in fiery death and cast us in perpetual darkness rather than rise.

"Otto?" she asks softly. It's a tentative whisper, an uncertain question, an olive branch.

"It's not morning yet," I insist.

She lifts her hand, a stray sunbeam cutting across her wrist.

"It is," she says. And then she slips from the bed, leaving nothing but cold empty space behind her.

I sit up and stretch, hiding the smirk that wants to erupt from my lips when I see her eyes dart down to the place where the hem of my tunic lifts as I raise my arms over my head. It's nice to know she looks at me the same way I look at her. I catch her eyes, and furious crimson stains her cheeks. I can tell the exact moment she remembers last night, how close we were. I feel an echoing flush; how does it feel so awkward? We didn't *do* anything.

But we wanted...

But then she says, "I suppose today's as good as any to be arrested and thrown in prison, no?"

No. The word boils like acid inside me, but I swallow it down.

Automatically, she starts rattling off the paths she's memorized, the ones she'll be informing the prisoners of. "From the hypocaust, there are two directions. Half go left, half go right. The left split up at the second fork—one group left again, the other takes the middle path..." She continues on, rehashing the routes perfectly as she pulls out a heel of bread and a jar of preserves from the cabinet, dividing the food for the two of us to break fast together.

I chew as slowly as possible, but soon enough, it's time. I stand and drape the black cloak over my shoulders. The enameled badge glints in the early morning light as I open the shutters. I hear her stand up, adjust her clothing, gather her clinking glass vials.

When I turn around, we are no longer Fritzi and Otto.

We are witch and hunter.

And it is time.

"I'll go first," I tell her, one foot already past the frame, touching the crate that works as a ladder to the second floor. "Make sure no one can see you." She nods. We cannot give away the ruse so soon. It would be simpler, of course, to use the aqueducts. But I also don't want to draw too much attention to them, not now, not when we're so close to needing them.

It's early yet, and the streets are empty. Fritzi descends the crates with ease, hopping down lightly beside me.

"I'm sorry," I whisper to her as I pull the iron manacles out. Her skin isn't yet fully healed from the first time I shackled her, pink and raw from where the bandages I'd made had protected the new skin. She must have taken them off before descending. Silently, she holds her hands out to me, and I clamp the iron over her slender wrists.

The house fort is about half a kilometer to the basilica where the prisoners are held. I don't have to cut through the Hauptmarkt, but I do. I twitch my black hood over my face and walk a pace ahead of Fritzi, careful not to tug too hard against the chains holding her. Iron clinks behind me, drowning out her soft footsteps.

The market in the morning is far less cheerful. The Christkindlmarkt stalls are shuttered; the morning is for necessities. Cloth merchants dominate the area closest to me, the sellers using measuring sticks to cut out equal portions of wool. On the other side, the area where farmers sell produce after harvest, there are meager offerings—bundles of wood for home hearths; a few late vegetables like onions, cabbages, and parsnips; and a salt merchant hawking his wares. There are no cheerful songs, bright beers, merry dancing. Not in the morning. The morning is for work, even during advent.

Even for a hexenjäger.

Everyone who sees us averts their eyes, crossing themselves as we march resolutely past the ancient Roman cross in the center of the market square, then veer to the basilica-turned-prison. My black cloak makes me a shadow of death that all who see try to avoid.

Rebel, I think to myself. *See me, and rebel. See* her, *see what I'm doing, and for God's sake, rebel.*

No one does.

Not yet.

I walk quicker, careful to make sure Fritzi can match my pace as we make our way down the street. The buildings here are richer, with none but servants to witness us. As we approach the basilica, the street opens up to a courtyard paved with stones, filled with the sounds of the heavy boots of hexenjägers reporting for duty.

I take a deep breath. "Make way!" I bellow.

Black cloaks part before me. The hexenjägers peer curiously, snapping to attention when they see my resolute face.

I march up to the door near the curving asp of the basilica. A hexenjäger guard on duty salutes me, then moves to take Fritzi's manacles from me.

"I have the prisoner," I say, unwilling to relinquish her just yet. Then I cut the guard a second glance. "Bertram?"

It's not been long since I last saw Bertram, trapped in the tiny cell in Kommandant Kirch's office, but already the man has a haggard look about his face. He nods at me. "The kommandant shortened my punishment," he says. "Thank God. All are needed to help with the solstice burning."

"You had a spot of good luck, then," I say, but from the haunted look in Bertram's eyes, I'm not so sure of that.

"Unlike this witch, caught the day before the fires are to be lit." Bertram tries to peer past Fritzi's hood. His eyes widen. "It's *the* witch!"

"They're all witches, Bertram," I say. I don't want much attention. Especially as Kommandant Kirch took such an interest in Fritzi.

"But this is the one that got me punished," he snarls, his hand raised as if to strike her.

I move like lightning, shoving him back so he staggers against the brick wall. "*You* got yourself punished for being a fool," I growl. "What was it you claimed? A dozen demons on her side? And yet look." I sweep my arm toward her. "Just a woman."

So much more than just *anything.*

Fritzi smiles sweetly at Bertram, fluttering her eyelashes. I shoulder past him, dragging Fritzi closer to me. I hide the flinch on my face when I hear her stumble on the steps, her toe catching on a raised stone. I cannot help her. I cannot express any sympathy at all.

My hands curl into fists. My jaw clenches.

I have been suppressing my true thoughts for years now; why am I suddenly blinded by the need to protect this woman? I *prepared* for this—I cannot ruin it now, not when we are so close to such a major coup against the tyranny of the archbishop.

"You!" I snap my fingers at a different guard. "Let's get this witch in the prison. She can burn with the rest tomorrow."

He nods at me, moving over to the heavy padlock on the cage door. Meanwhile, I hold Fritzi to the side. Her eyes dart past the bars, looking for her younger cousin, the girl she was so certain had been taken by Kommandant Kirch personally.

"She's not here," Fritzi whispers so that none but I can hear. My heart sinks. If the little girl isn't here, where could she be?

"I'll find her," I swear, my voice low. But I have no idea how I'll do that.

"Bring the witch through!" a hexenjäger calls to me, motioning. Near the door, three people—a woman and two children—crouch in moldy hay. Hexenjägers point swords to push back the woman and the two little ones huddled to her side as if they were dire threats.

"On your knees, witch," I snarl, yanking Fritzi forward and kicking her down. She skids across the stone floor, tossing her hood back to glare at me. "Get in." I shove her shoulders, pushing her toward the door. It is a mockery, a final form of shame to make the accused crawl into the cage. Her skirts smear across a damp bundle of hay sticky with brownish-green refuse. Seconds after her ankles clear the door, the hexenjägers let it slam shut, trapping her inside.

She stands and rushes to the bars, gripping them, the metal clacking around the manacles on her wrist. "At least take these verdammt irons off," she demands.

I pull the key from my pocket and step forward.

"Careful, Kapitän," one of the hexenjägers warns me. I pause long enough to shoot him a withering glare. He bows his head respectfully, remembering my rank.

Fritzi holds her shackled hands to me, palms up. I fit the iron key into the lock. My fingers brush a newly opened, raw blister made by the rusty metal, and she winces, the barest hint of pain flashing across her face, and it's enough to make me want to rip this prison down brick by brick.

The iron manacles clatter to the ground. Fritzi steps back immediately, rubbing her wrists.

I bend down to pick them up and pull them through the bars toward me.

A shiny black boot stops beside my knee.

I feel the cold aura of fear settling across the basilica—not just from the prisoners, but from the guards as well. Fritzi turns her back, pulling her cloak up over her face, but I catch the sheer terror flashing in her eyes as she moves.

I stand slowly.

And meet the icy gaze of Kommandant Dieter Kirch.

"Good work, Kapitän Ernst," he tells me, but already his eyes are roving past my shoulder, through the bars, right to Fritzi.

She's trapped behind iron in the heart of the hexenjägers' prison. There is nowhere for her to run, no way for her to hide. I watch as her shoulders square, the realization of how trapped she is settling upon her. But no—this is something more. More than the natural fear of imprisonment. This is not a primal terror, but something deeper, something born of knowledge, of dark memories, of realized terror.

She's hiding from the man standing beside me. Only there's nowhere for her to hide.

She turns, lowering her hood, meeting Kommandant Kirch's eyes, her jaw tight.

When she speaks, her voice is quiet, but everyone can hear her words slice through the air toward him. "Hello, brother."

19

FRITZI

The warding spells that Mama kept around Birresborn started a few paces outside the village and lapped the town in a circle. She was famed among other covens for her warding abilities.

It was why we lasted so long, when other covens fell or ran to the Black Forest.

It was why we alone still stood so close to Trier.

I went with her every full moon and helped her reinforce them; I knew the wards as well as I knew her face.

So all I had to do was sneak out while she was asleep the morning of my eighteenth birthday.

Our small kitchen was still flour-dusted from her cooking frenzy—the finished schupfnudeln sat in a bowl under a towel, ready to be fried the next day; the Gaisburger Marsch was still simmering low over smoldering coals; there was even half a bottle of the sweet apfelwein left on the table, only because Mama forbade me from drinking all of it in one sitting.

I pulled a cloak around my shoulders, slipped past the table illuminated by the haze of almost dawn, and slinked outside.

The path to the warding wall led just down from our cottage. My heart twisted, anticipatory joy, anxiety, dread, everything all at once. This was a *good* thing, what I was doing. I was reuniting my mother and her son. It was just the sort of act Mama encouraged all in our coven to do. Good deeds fed the Well; bad deeds fed wild magic. So much goodness—healing a broken relationship, returning love lost—would make the Well overflow.

And maybe it was for myself a little too. To see my brother again.

I reached a small bundle of trees at the edge of the forest around Birresborn, and I jogged up to the tallest one. A mighty yew.

The moment I drew near, a shadow peeled off from a tree farther into the forest.

Dieter uncovered a lantern, casting yellow light onto his face, and grinned at me. It was a grin I couldn't help but return, as if this was just some dumb prank we were pulling on Mama like when we were younger.

He'd smiled at me like that when we'd snuck into Mama's room and read the book on wild magic. Mischief and fun and an air of *Trust me, Fritzichen—have I ever let you down before?*

Breathless, I fumbled for the potion to lower the warding spell. The way Mama cast it, no witch could pass unless they were a part of our coven.

Dieter hadn't been a part of our coven for five years.

My chest ached, being this close to him after so long without him and not even knowing *why*. All I knew was that a week before Dieter's eighteenth birthday, Mama and the elder witches had a meeting. Their shouts had carried through the whole village.

"He's a threat, Astrid! You are blinded by your maternal love when you

should be thinking like our leader. Perchta spoke to you. You must heed the Mother goddess."

The next day, Dieter was gone.

Mama said that the coven had voted to banish him and that was all I needed to know. I had sobbed for weeks. Did he even *know* he'd done something wrong—and could I do something similar without being aware of it?

When I'd confessed these fears, Mama had wrapped me in her arms and kissed my forehead. "No, mein Schatz. They will never take you from me. I promise."

That hadn't answered my question. Why had she allowed Dieter to be taken from her, but she'd fight for me?

The years passed, and our coven moved on—but I hadn't, and I knew Mama hadn't either. She ached for Dieter. She never spoke of him, but she grew solemn on his birthday or whenever we found one of his belongings. His affinity had been in healing, in the body, wounds, and blood—whenever someone fell injured or sick, Mama would take it upon herself to heal them now, as if trying to prove that we did not need my brother's gifts.

I missed him too. I'd been nearly thirteen when they'd cast him out—I'd idolized him, my fearless, quick-witted brother.

And after five years without him, just shy of my eighteenth birthday, I'd asked my little cousin, Liesel, to track him—her affinity in pyromancy let her find anything, anyone, by reading flames. She'd thought the whole thing great fun, this secret between us.

I got a message to him. He wrote back.

This meeting at dawn on my birthday was arranged. He'd said he was eager to come home and make things right with Mama. He'd said he missed me more than I could believe.

Surely enough time had passed that he had atoned for whatever had made the coven banish him. Any threat he once posed had long passed.

I shook the potion over the warding spell line as he smiled at me now. "Are you ready?"

"You have no idea," Dieter said with a wink.

The potion crackled and hissed as it poured through the air, disintegrating the invisible line Mama wove with her own hands. I felt the moment it snapped—a wash of electricity, like lightning striking nearby, and then—

Then—

What was that?

My shoulders tensed, brow furrowing, all the muscles in my body straining against an unspoken threat. Like there were eyes on me I couldn't see, instincts flaring in a wordless warning that something, *something*, was wrong.

"The ward should be down now," I said anyway, still smiling, but it was stiff. "Want to try?"

Dieter took a tentative step forward, then another. No great seizure of pain grabbed him, and after a moment of standing in the middle of the warding wall, he gave me a relieved smirk.

"Good job, Fritzichen."

I threw my arms around my brother.

He was so much taller than I remembered. More rugged, worn by his time away, and I wanted to ask him all about it, every moment he'd been gone. Where had he been? What was the world outside Birresborn like—I went with Mama occasionally to nearby towns for markets, but *beyond* that, far beyond—

Dieter hugged me back with one arm and spun us in a circle. A bag at his waist bumped against my thigh, and he set me down quickly, but not before I felt a shudder run through him, some errant twitch of repressed eagerness. He'd get like that sometimes when we were younger, so fixated on a goal that his whole body would shudder and shake with need.

"Fritzichen," he said, one hand on my arm, the other reaching into his bag. "You don't know how I've dreamt of this day."

I smiled. It felt forced, and I couldn't figure out why. "Me too—"

"No." His voice was a hard drop, his fingers spasming on my arm.

He held up what he'd drawn out of his bag: a bottle, typically used to store beer.

My frown was question enough. The wild excitement in his eyes didn't let any words form on my tongue.

"You have to drink this," he told me. He pressed the bottle to my chest.

I didn't take it. "What? Why? Dieter—"

"Fritzichen." Another hard snap, his tone bouncing from eager to unarguable in a heartbeat. "Together, we'll save the world. The voice has told you, hasn't it? It's what we're meant for."

My body went cold. A pond freezing slowly in mid-winter, the edges first, then the middle, all of it crystallizing one particle at a time.

"Sever from the Well. Take this bonding potion," he said, eyes glinting in his lantern's light. "Bond with me. Together, we'll be the most unstoppable force of wild magic the world has ever seen."

Too many things were rushing up on me. Too many realizations. His words, his mania, wild magic, the voice—all of it was coalescing, and I couldn't *breathe.*

That sensation of a threat, an unseen danger, grew and grew, my body shaking with building unease.

And I knew its source now.

It was in front of me.

"It's our destiny, Fritzichen, sweet Fritzichen." Dieter released my arm to tuck a curl behind my ear. "You and I. We'll join our magic and dismantle this whole corrupt system. We'll burn it all down."

The bottle sloshed where he pushed it against me again. Still, I didn't take it, my hands numb at my sides.

My focus caught on the forest behind him.

The trees were moving. Or, no—not the trees.

Soldiers.

Soldiers in the forest, marching toward us, toward Birresborn.

"Dieter." His name left my lips in a burst of air. "What is—what are you doing? Who did you bring?"

Dieter touched my cheek. "You have to start by severing from the Well. Say the spell. *On this day and from this hour,"* he started with a singsong lilt. *"I sever here the Well's one power—"*

The spell to sever the connection to the Origin Tree and its Well, to open a witch up to wild magic.

"You remember it, don't you, Fritzichen?" Dieter tipped his head. "Have you said it yet? No. Mama would've thrown you out too. Dear, perfect, obedient little sister. But it's time to not be so obedient anymore, yes? Time to be naughty now. Sever from the Well. Take the—"

"You broke your connection to the Well?" My mind was a chaos of realizations, and I fixated on this one. "Mama—she knew?"

Dieter breaking his connection to the Well had never been a possibility. It was such an unforgivable, irredeemable thing for a witch to do, dangerous and harrowing, and it would *destroy* him—he wouldn't have severed from the Well. He wouldn't have chosen wild magic.

That was why he was banished?

He wanted me to do it too. He wanted me to take a bonding potion he'd made—he'd brewed one? It was so dangerous to make, it could kill me and cut off his magic entirely if he'd made it wrong. He wasn't adept at potions. How could he trust it?

I couldn't trust it. Not from him. Not that look in his eyes, the desperate, hungry gleam of a man on the edge. He would connect with my magic and drain me dry.

It was absurd. No one made bonding potions anymore. It was too dangerous; all of this was too dangerous; it didn't make *sense*—

"No," I managed, throat like sand. "No, Dieter. What have you done?"

His face fell. Instantly. Fragile hope and manic need to a flat, dull fury.

"Oh, Fritzichen," he moaned. "Don't make me do it this way. You have to take the potion *willingly,* you see. It doesn't work if I force you. Make the better choice, sister."

"*No*—Dieter, I don't understand— "

He lunged to grab my arm again. I dove to the side, narrowly missing him, my pulse rocking through my veins as the soldiers drew closer. I could see their uniforms in the moonlight—they were hexenjägers.

Dieter wore their badge and uniform. I hadn't noticed, under his cloak—

He reached for me again, and I took off running back for Birresborn.

"There's no escape, Fritzichen!" he shouted after me. "You let me in! Together, you and I—this is our fate!"

Dieter stares at me, the bars between us, but oh, far more than that separates us now.

When he smiles, I have to fist my hands beneath my cloak, every bit of my focus on staying upright, on not collapsing in a mess of sobs and questions at his feet.

"Fritzichen," Dieter says, his voice airy with relief and excitement, all of it so pure that I can barely see him through his insanity. "I heard you were in the city, but I had feared you would do something rash. I did not believe you were capable of going quietly."

He doesn't let me respond.

Dieter snaps his head to look at Otto. I don't have the strength to move, even to follow his gaze, but I can feel Otto's eyes on me, the heat of his attention.

He will give us away if he keeps looking at me like that.

My thoughts are disconnected, a thing outside myself, as my brother makes a satisfied grunt.

"Good work, Kapitän," he says. "Where did you catch her?"

There is a pause. An almost indiscernible hitch in Otto's throat.

"In the slums, sir," he manages. A swallow, and he regains himself, his voice leveling—he really *is* skilled at deception, when he needs to be. "Just within the walls of the city."

"Trying to flee Trier, were you?" Dieter turns back to me, but my eyes have fallen to the floor.

The cobblestones are covered in molded hay and excrement, yet I see people huddling all across them, this space packed with convicted witches. Will we even be able to move enough away from the far spot on the floor to avoid the explosion?

Wouldn't *that* just be great: Otto and I do all of this, then inadvertently blow up these prisoners rather than save them. Myself included.

My head drops back, an exhausted, self-deprecating smile tugging across my face.

"What is humorous?" my brother asks, and there is the slightest twinge of annoyance in his voice.

How far has the corruption of wild magic taken him? Five years wallowing in it. Is there any part of who he really is left?

I will not speak to him. I have nothing to say. Nothing that wouldn't destroy me, and I cannot be destroyed, not now.

But—

Liesel.

She isn't here.

Do I dare show that desire? Do I let him see that he still has that piece to play against me?

My eyes find his lazily, and I can feel the tears gathering, all sensations dulled by how impossible this situation still is.

My brother killed our coven. He burned our mother.

Because of me.

Because I helped him.

Because I didn't know what he'd become.

"Where is she?" I whisper. "What have you done with Liesel?"

His face doesn't change, not really. But something in his eyes, an emptiness in the pale blue depths, makes my chest buck with renewed panic.

I'd become distracted with preparations for the prison escape. I'd smothered my fear for Liesel under action, blissful, ignorant action, but now, I see a hundred possibilities play across my brother's face.

He could have done anything to her.

He'd spent his years in Birresborn studying healing—how to reknit wounds, how to soothe aches. But he'd always been more interested in the *cause*, hadn't he? Asking Mama how much blood a person could lose before they died. Wondering which organs were necessary, which could be removed. Questions that had seemed a part of his studies at the time, but are now so horrifying my stomach fills with lead.

I know—*I know*—he has Liesel alive. And suddenly, that is the worst possible outcome for her.

Dieter steps back with a renewed grin, all teeth. I teeter after him, one hand going to my chest, trying to smash my heart back together, but I'm falling, falling—

"Well done," he says again. His cruel smile slides to Otto. "You have earned the honor coming to you tomorrow."

Honor? But I can't breathe, each gasp too short, my stomach cramping, lungs burning.

Otto bows his head to Dieter. He looks at me, and he risks both of our lives in the way he lets his eyes soften, pleading.

I feel the memory of his arms around me.

The rush and swirl of his inhale beneath my ear, a fortifying breath as he held me in the house fort.

I manage a choked breath. In, steady, out. Another.

"Your sister, sir?" Otto asks. When he looks back at Dieter, his face is hardened again.

My brother beams. "Indeed. Did you think yourself the only hexenjäger cursed with a traitorous family?" Dieter slaps a hand on Otto's shoulder in camaraderie, but I see Otto's lip curl, just a flash. "Your sister will similarly be brought to justice, Kapitän, once we find her. And have no fear—we *will* find her." Dieter glances at me, and I know those words were meant to spike fear into my heart. He knows Liesel's skills. "For now, we rejoice in our great diocese being soon purged of yet another witch."

"Praise God," Otto intones, but it's hollow.

"Praise God, indeed," Dieter says, and it sounds even more fake, a mockery, and I wonder how he has led them all to believe that he follows this doctrine, that he has given himself over to the Catholic god.

His eyes glitter with an evolved childhood mischief, one now fixed on madness and greed.

Dieter smiles at me one last time. I am stone.

"I will see you soon, Fritzichen," he coos. "We'll have a nice bonfire for you. And we'll see if you scream when I brand you—Mama didn't. But you know that, don't you?"

I do. Intimately.

Bile crawls up my throat, and I fight not to touch the spot between my breasts, where he branded her, where he'll brand *me*.

Except he won't. I'll escape long before he gets the chance to.

Dieter walks off, taking Otto's arm and pulling him along.

Terror floods my limbs, pins me even more immovably in place at the sight of my brother holding on to Otto. But he has been at Dieter's side for years. He knows how conniving my brother is, how deranged. I have to believe he's capable of outplaying him, and that this plan will work.

But Otto doesn't know that my brother is a witch. That Dieter draws his power from wild magic. That the head of the hexenjägers came from the very power that they root out and burn.

Because I didn't tell him. Because I did to him what Mama did to me, let him go into this with incomplete information.

What have I done?

A hand touches my elbow. "Fräulein?"

A shriveled old man stands next to me, a head shorter than me, his sagging skin speckled with age spots and pox scars. His mouth stretches in a prodding smile, showing gaps for missing teeth.

"Come," he says. "Sit. We will make room."

He bats his hand, but already people are adjusting, shifting to make a space for me on the soiled cobblestones like I'm some welcome guest at their home.

That breaks the tears down my cheeks. I dig the heel of one palm into my eye, fighting to remember the sensation of Otto holding me, showing me how to breathe.

Does he regret helping me now that he knows what information I kept from him? Does he hate me as much as I hate myself?

"Come now, Fräulein," the old man coaxes. "All is not grim. We are innocent, hm? Innocence shall prevail."

Will you let it prevail? the voice demands. *Or will you continue to ignore what I can do for you?*

Stop, I tell the voice. *Leave me alone.*

I have seen what giving in to wild magic has done to my brother.

Nothing, *nothing*, will make me follow his path.

Leave me alone, I say it again, only this time to the agony in my heart, the grief that ever seeks to make me collapse. *Leave me alone.*

I have work to do.

I force my eyes open, tears still wet on my cheeks. I may have failed Otto by not telling him all my secrets, but I will *not* fail these people, this one chance at stopping my brother's horror.

There are no hexenjägers outside the bars, all relegated to their stations around the basilica now that I've been locked safely away.

My eyes turn to the old man, blazing suddenly, and the concern on his face twitches into surprise.

"You're right," I tell him. "All is not grim. Not now that you have me."

20

OTTO

I do not have to ask where Dieter leads me; we're heading straight to the Porta Nigra. He walks without speaking, but it's as if he's having a conversation silently with himself. He smiles, tilting his face up, a chuckle in his throat before he pauses, counting the fingers of his right hand against his left palm. His head cocks, and he nods as if agreeing with something, then strides forward, setting such a quick pace that I must jog to keep up, my black cloak flapping behind me.

It would be odd if I had not seen him act this way many times before. Dieter Kirch is often focused in such a single-minded way that it is as if the entirety of the world around him evaporates. It's easy, I suppose, to walk through the city as if only your own thoughts matter when everyone else makes way, the crowds parting before him like the Red Sea.

He pauses at the steps leading up to the Porta Nigra, his pale blue eyes finally focusing on me. "You've earned it," he says, nodding again, clearly agreeing with himself. A decision has been made, and I have been found worthy.

"Thank you, kommandant." I don't ask what, exactly, it is I've earned—any questioning of Dieter could rescind whatever my prize may be.

The prize for capturing his sister, I think, bile rising in my throat as I ascend the steps a pace behind the kommandant. Everything I've learned in the short time I've known Fritzi has taught me her strength, her resilience, her *goodness*. How could Dieter Kirch have come from the same blood, the same home as Fritzi? I push the thoughts down. My father would ask the same of me—how could I be his when I believe and act the opposite of him?

The answer is simple.

We are not born into our nature; we choose it. And although the people and places around us may influence our lives, our decisions seal our fate.

Dieter holds the door for me as I step inside the Porta Nigra, at the ground floor church. The bells start tolling for Terce. A fair number of people stand inside as the priest prepares the liturgy, everyone pausing in their morning work for the psalms and prayers. Dieter and I move along the back of the church, skirting the narthex. No one glances up at us; it's common enough for hexenjägers to enter the church and make their way up the stairs to the offices above. But more than that, the people are focused on repentant prayer. Christ's mass at the end of the year may be about the celebration of his birth, but Advent is a time of contemplation, a remembrance of the end—not just of the end of the year, but the end of life, the end of all ages.

Advent is the dark before the light. And while Christmas is coming, Advent lasts four weeks. A month of solemnity before we can have a day of joy.

"Nunc, Sancte, nobis, Spiritus," the priest's voice intones as Dieter and I mount the steps in the south transept. I pause at the top as the hymn ends. Dieter strides ahead of me down the hall, but despite my years of practice, I need to work to school my features. My hands are shaking; my heart is racing. I can't give myself away, not to the kommandant, but…I don't know how long I can wear this mask. Not with her behind iron bars.

Not when all I want to do is murder Dieter for all the suffering he has caused the world in general and her specifically.

I bite my tongue until I taste blood, focusing on the pain. Downstairs, the priest switches from Latin to German.

"This is a time for peace," he says, a law we all know. By the decree of the Pope, no violence is allowed during this time of year. "And we must thank the archbishop for bringing us peace now, through the deaths of the evil witches plaguing our city."

There is a murmuring of thanks and agreement throughout the people in the nave. From my position at the top of the steps, looking down at the congregation, I stare hard at the faithful.

An old woman near the back, glaring defiantly at the priest, her lips pressed firmly shut. A young couple, turning away together. A man covered in grime and soot—he must have come into the church between jobs—his head down, his jaw set.

There is still hope for true peace. That gives me the strength to go on.

I let the door slam shut behind me as I step onto the second floor of the Porta Nigra, the private headquarters of the hexenjägers.

"Come," Kommandant Kirch orders me, annoyed at my lingering pause. Dieter leads me into his office, and I eye the little closet that Bertram had been locked up in. Bertram had said he was given a reprieve from his punishment, but I suspect it is less about Dieter forgiving him and more about the kommandant finding another prisoner to enclose in the tiny torture chamber. I wonder which jäger had the misfortune to find himself in such a fate.

Dieter sits easily at his desk, his long arms draped over the sides of the chair. "There is an irony, don't you think, in how you went to fetch your sister but brought me mine instead?"

I nod silently.

"I think you see that my sister is the more valuable witch to burn, though, no?" Dieter asks casually. His voice is conversational, as if we were discussing our evening meal options.

I am unsure of what to say. We had already acknowledged that Fritzi was a true witch, but that was before I knew she was Dieter's sister. Now if I lay such a claim upon her, it may seem as if I'm indicating there is something wrong in Dieter's family blood.

Her mother—his *mother—was also a witch*, I think. *It* is *in the blood. But not in him...?*

Is that why he hates witches so much, because the power should be his birthright, and he has no magic of his own? Such rage as his must be fueled by something, and envy is as much a reason as any.

"The men often compare you to your father," Dieter continues. He waves his hand, indicating that I should sit. "But I have noticed that you never do. You rarely mention him."

I perch on the edge of the seat, my nerves alert. "No," I concede.

"I don't remember my father. I barely recall Fritzi's. My mother raised us alone." Dieter picks up a knife and starts scraping the tip along the inside of his nails, cleaning them. His blue eyes flick up at me. "I killed her. My mother. I watched her burn. I did not step away even after the flames turned her skin black and her head bald. I watched every second of it."

My blood is ice water, but I do not move. Dieter's voice is so calm, so casual.

"The stench was—" He shudders, as if that was the worst of it, the smell. "But you know, it was fascinating too. You'd be amazed at how resilient the human body is. How long it can last."

"God made us in his image," I say hollowly.

"It eases my soul," Dieter continues, "knowing that you would be willing to do the same to your sister." The knife in his hand stills, the point still driving under his nail in a way that makes me wince. But his eyes turn to me, burning with intensity. "You would, wouldn't you?" he asks, now with a manic fury beneath his words, his voice rising. "You would watch Hilde Ernst burn. You would hear her screams and not flinch away. You would cut her, crisp, from the stake after, yes?"

A tiny bead of red blood seeps from under Dieter's nail from how hard he drives the point into his nailbed. "Yes," I whisper, watching the blood stain his cuticles red.

"I knew you were the man for the job!" he says buoyantly. He spins the knife around, driving the blade into his desk, piercing a parchment that bears the archbishop's seal. "You light the fires tomorrow morning, and then there's something else you may be able to help me with."

"Kommandant?" I ask.

Dieter stands and moves over to the tiny stone closet, unlocking it. He shoots me a shy smile, as if he's naughtily sharing a bit of stolen cake. With his boot, he kicks at the door, opening the closet and exposing the person trapped inside.

I go perfectly still. I cannot trust myself to show any reaction at all, so deep is my disgust.

The girl inside the stone chamber is small enough that she can sit on the floor, her knees drawn to her chin, but there are cuts and scrapes all along her pale skin to show how uncomfortable she is in such a cramped space. Her cheeks are hollow, her skin sallow—she has been denied both sunlight and food. She blinks as if pained, clearly trying to adjust her eyesight from the pitch black inside the stone closet. She holds her hands up over her face, and I see that she has clawed away her fingernails, red blood on each tip, in a futile attempt to fight against the immovable stone.

Dieter squats in front of the child, bouncing on his heels. He cups her cheek, and the girl snarls, trying to bite his hand, but he is too quick, chuckling at her.

"Is she to be burned tomorrow as well?" I ask hollowly.

At the sound of my voice, she turns her eyes to me. There is such fury in her look, such pure, unadulterated hatred. She is no more than ten years old, but I have no doubt she would kill me in an instant if she could.

"Liesel? Oh, no," Dieter says. "No, I have different plans for her."

I frown, wondering what power this little girl has. She must be able to do something Fritzi cannot do; why else has Dieter kept her here rather than burn her alongside Fritzi and the others?

Dieter doesn't notice my consternation. "Something else for Liesel, yes." He turns to me. "And you will help." There is a finality to that last sentence. His voice went from cheery to flat in the space of a breath, assuring me that I *will* help see his plans to fruition whether I want to or not. He barks in laughter, the sound so sudden that both I and the little girl jump. "Fire, for Liesel? Oh, no, no, no." He stares into her, his tone going vicious. "No fire for you, Liesel. No. Fire. For. You."

With that, he slams the door shut again. I hear a short scream from the girl, and I hope she wasn't injured further by the abrupt, unyielding door.

Dieter turns and meets my eyes, that eerie pale blue color piercing into me. My mind is in a panic. This is Liesel, Fritzi's cousin—another true witch, the one Fritzi hoped to save. And Dieter has her. But not with the other prisoners.

Even if my plan tomorrow works and Fritzi is able to free all the innocents from the basilica, Liesel will still be Dieter's prisoner, trapped in a stone chamber above a Catholic church in the heart of the hexenjäger headquarters. Unreachable. Doomed to a fate worse than the stake.

21

FRITZI

Murmurs ripple and sway around me as I crouch on the soiled cobblestones. Everyone is careful to only speak as loud as is necessary, eyes darting to the cell door in furtive glances that grow bolder and bolder.

They are reciting the routes they must take.

The groups I have divided them into.

I hear their whispers—

"The midmorning bells."

"We go left, left again, then right, up a ladder."

"In these clothes? We look like prisoners; we'll be spotted for sure."

"No, there will be supplies waiting; we'll be fine."

—and I sink further into myself, eyes on my lap, body utterly spent as the setting sun bursts orange haze through the one high barred window.

The bag of potions hanging from my belt has only three remaining vials now, two protection, one healing that I selfishly keep for Liesel. *When* I find her. I have distributed the rest, carefully calling them *healing tonics.* Or rather, Jochen, the old man who'd first spoken to me, distributed them—I am the kommandant's sister. They're willing to trust the whole Three-damned floor erupting underneath them at the behest of a rogue hexenjäger, but their eyes went round in terror at the idea that the kommandant's sister smuggled in things to help heal them. Until Jochen downed a vial and was able to stand up straight for the first time in months, he'd said.

More than one person is gravely wounded, sad excuses for bandages hanging around pus-thick cuts. Others cough into rags spotted with blood. One woman has a child whose face is gaunt and green, but she cradles him to her chest, the lot of them sipping gently on the few healing potions I'd managed. The prisoners think the potions are simple healing tonics.

All I can do is sit here now, mission fulfilled for today, playing over and over in my mind images of what Dieter is doing to my cousin.

He left when she was small, but even then, she'd been incredibly powerful. Mama and the other Elders had taken her under their charge early, teaching her advanced spells and preparing her for the great destiny that the Crone goddess Abnoba had planned for her, whatever it might have been.

I flinch.

Whatever it might *be*.

She was the one who helped me find Dieter in the first place.

Liesel had crouched over the low-burning embers in my cottage and held her hands closer to the heat than anyone else could bear, her brow furrowed in concentration, her little lips puckered tight.

"He's...close," she said with surprise. "In Trier. A big, dark building there. I see him...in an office? He's important."

"He's alive?" I gasped. Alive—and close enough for a letter to reach him in a few days. I could address it to him and send it just to Trier, and hope that, if he truly was important enough, it'd find its way to him.

Liesel nodded. Then she winced and yanked her arms back and stared at her hands in a darker sort of surprise, confusion and caution as she rubbed her thumb over her palm.

"Something's wrong, Fritzi," she whispered. "With him, maybe. I don't know."

"It's all right—we'll help him now, whatever it is." I gathered her into my arms and kissed the top of her head. "Thank you, cousin."

She wriggled. "Stop—Mama just braided my hair! You'll mess it—"

"Danke, danke!" I gripped her tighter and planted kisses all over her cheeks. "Kindchen, schnucki—"

"Stop! Friederike!" She went limp enough to slip through my grasp and rolled away across the floor. "The Three, you're the worst. We're not children anymore."

"Oh, yes. You're ten years old and a full maiden now, hm?"

She patted her hair, checking that it was still in place. "Of course."

"So you wouldn't have any interest in, say, sneaking into the stash of sweets my mother just brought back for my birthday?"

Liesel paused, hands on her braids, lips in a flat line.

"Well," she said. "Maidens like sweets, too."

What does Dieter want with her?

Is there something he wants her to find? Something to do with wild magic, maybe—or other covens? Wild magic needs evil to feed on. Does he not get enough from the hexenjägers?

What more could Liesel do for him?

She'll fight him. She'll fight him with every ounce of strength she has, fire at her command and in her soul, and my stomach heaves, because Dieter *will* break her. There was nothing in his eyes, no sanity or love or empathy.

He'll break her.

And he'll enjoy doing it.

I do my best to curl up as small as possible on the damp floor, using my arm as a pillow and wholly ignoring the stench of whatever is streaked on the stones. My eyes close, my breathing evens, but I won't sleep.

All these people will escape tomorrow; Otto will make sure of it. I know I promised to help him find Hilde, but I am not leaving this city without my cousin.

You will die, the voice says. *Both of you. Without me.*

I pinch my eyes shut tighter.

And hum to myself

That lullaby. The one Otto sang to me.

How many stars are in the sky?

Count them all as we fly by...

Morning comes, a dull gray sky that threatens snow, a heavier chill in the air as the cage of condemned begins to stir. Coughing and shivering wrack bodies with equal measure, and I can't tell if the trembling is from the frigid temperature or nerves. Either way, I am up well before the midmorning bells, my body rigid as I stand in place.

Jochen has taken position next to me, though I know his legs must ache to stand so long. He gives me a reassuring nod.

Too early, some people begin to shuffle toward the far wall, away from the coming explosion.

"Don't draw attention," I hiss.

Jochen repeats the command, and it catches; a few people peel back, treading uneasily over the doomed portion of the floor.

Three hexenjägers stride past the cell door.

Two more. Checking on us silently, then away.

Half a dozen come. These ones jeer and kick the bars. "You scum ready to meet your fate today? God Himself smiles on this purge of evil!"

The prisoners nearest the door flinch, but they don't respond. If the hexenjägers notice that their silence comes from an intense focus, they don't show it; they continue out, their laughter echoing over the stone walls.

My heart aches, cold and weighted in my chest, each thump a second passing, and I have nothing to do but count the time.

It should be almost sunrise, the first bells of the day. Almost—

The churches throughout Trier seem to take a collective breath, and then a cacophony of chiming and gonging rings across the city: the sunrise bells.

They won't ring again until midmorning.

I count the spaces after, minute by minute, swaying back and forth on numb feet.

22

OTTO

The night before the purging, I do not bother attempting to sleep. I am deeply aware that Fritzi is sleeping on a dank and soiled prison floor. That her cousin is trapped in the claustrophobically small stone cell without even a moonbeam of light or the chance to stretch out or relieve herself. That my sister is somewhere else, unreachable, perhaps scared and alone.

Instead, I spend the night in my office, working. I know that, come the morrow, I will end the day no longer a hexenjäger. I will either be successful and leave the city, or I will be dead, killed by the men who I pretended to be comrades with. And so, I use all the time I have left to leave my final gift to the witch hunters—absolute chaos in all the records. It would be simple to burn it all, but instead, I stay awake, painstakingly altering every map in the network of couriers I helped to build, ensuring the reliable and quick paths are no longer marked. I change the records of payments so that the archbishop and executioner's money handlers will misdirect funds, doing all I can to pilfer away their fortunes and aid the poorest in the process. I write notes to the hexenjäger patrols and outpost guards scattered among the towns, commanding them to go on fool's errands, and I send the missives out before dawn.

There is, even now, a limit to what I can do. But I do all I can think of while I can. I burn every bridge and cross every line I did not dare to before, when I could not risk being caught and ruining what little chance I had to make a difference. And in between every pen stroke, I go over the plan in my head again and again.

When the bells ring for Prime, the first hour of daylight, I light a candle to better keep track of time. It would not do to work through my own heist. Timing everything will be key—I must not leave too early, when Kommandant Kirch may notice my absence, but I can also not let too much time pass before I go to the tunnels with my flint and steel to light the fuse to the gunpowder.

My work takes on a frenetic pace, but when the candle gutters hours later, I know.

It's time.

I open my door and am surprised to see that there is no one about. Some hexenjägers are working to build the pyres, of course, and some are guarding the prisoners, but I suspect most are at the cathedral, basking in the archbishop's presence as he lavishes them with praise and favors. I have only attended one such morning blessing; that much self-gratification and supplication sickened me. But at least it seems that most of the hexenjägers chose to go to the cathedral early; let them stay until Sext, let them believe they have until the sun is at its zenith before they must fetch their prisoners. The more men at the cathedral, the fewer guarding the prison at the basilica.

It will make escaping all the more easy.

I start to make my way to the stairs, but I pause. I glance across the hall at the kommandant's office, firmly closed.

What if...?

What if I simply walked into Kommandant Kirch's office and freed Fritzi's cousin, Liesel? I stare at the wooden door. I'm alone now. No one would suspect me of such a crime. I could take her, go immediately to the tunnels, and then light the explosion and free the prisoners. The kommandant would not notice his special prisoner was gone until it was far too late. All night long there had been the occasional patrols in the hall, the sounds of others talking outside my door, but now—I'm alone. No witnesses.

Without allowing myself to second-guess the thought, I cross the corridor, my hand on the iron ring to pull open the door. But before I can grip it, the door swings open.

I leap back, and Dieter shares my startled, shocked expression. "Ernst?" he says, closing the door behind him and stepping over to me. "What were you doing at my door?"

"I smelled smoke," I lie. There is no quiver in my voice, somehow. "I thought you had left a candle burning, that maybe it tipped over..."

"All is well," Dieter says pleasantly, as if he does not have a child trapped in the torture chamber behind him. Then his face falls, and he leans closer to me, his thumb rubbing the sensitive skin under my eye. His touch is a gentle caress. "You have stayed up all night long," he says. "There are shadows under your eyes. And you have not joined the other men at the cathedral to celebrate our greatest purge yet."

"There is much to be done," I say. My words are a strangled whisper.

"And little time to do it in," Dieter says, agreeing. "But you have earned this honor, Kapitän, and I will see that you relish it."

He doesn't give me a chance to refuse; he just walks toward the steps, expecting me to follow. *Shit*. I glance back at his door once—*Wait for me,* I think, even though I know Liesel cannot hear my thoughts, cannot know my silent vow to return to her. I traipse after the kommandant, counting the minutes in my head. I seriously consider just shoving Dieter down the iron stairs, but his absence would cause an immediate investigation. It would ruin the plan.

Tempting, though.

A priest prays at the altar in the church built below the hexenjäger headquarters. He stands when he hears our boots on the steps. Dieter motions him over.

"A blessing, father, please," Dieter says, bowing his head. I emulate him as the priest intones a personal blessing under God, praising our holy work and making the sign of the cross over Dieter's body.

The priest shifts to me, repeating the blessing. As he makes the sign of the cross over me, I look up.

I meet his eyes.

My jaw sets, and although I do not speak, I cannot keep the revulsion from my face.

God has no part of the hexenjägers' plans this man blesses.

The priest's voice trembles under my intense glare. Out of the corner of my eye, I see Dieter turn to me, and I quickly duck my head, forcing my face into a mask of benign acceptance.

"God be with you," the priest says in German, not Latin.

If He is with me, He is against you, I think.

"And now to business," the kommandant says. He turns to the door that leads outside the church, expecting me to keep pace. I do, even though all I want is to flee to the tunnels. Dieter pauses before he opens the door. "Is there anything you want to tell me before we proceed?" Dieter asks me in a soft voice.

His strange, pale eyes watch me carefully, colder even than this December morning. Panic ignites in my belly—has he discovered my plan? Does he want me to beg for forgiveness?

"*You* are lighting the fires of the biggest purge in Trier's history," Dieter prompts me.

"Thank you?"

A smile cuts through his shadowed face. "You're welcome," he says, clearly satisfied by my gratitude for such a treat. He swings open the door, motioning for me to follow him outside.

While Trier has had many pyres, I have never seen the streets lined with so many stakes. They start here, at the Porta Nigra, going down the street named for Saint Simeon before skirting the market and curving toward the archbishop's cathedral. One hundred poles set into the center of the street, hay and fodder for each fire piled up below.

"It's clever, don't you think?" Dieter says. Before I can ask him what he means, he says, "You won't have to light every single fire, you see." He points to the way the dry straw links one pyre to the next, a sort of domino effect of flame. When I light one, the fire will spread to the next and the next and, as long as there's no wind or a damp spot in the line, it will eventually light it all.

"Imagine the last person," I cannot help but say. Whoever is tied to the last stake will hear the screams of the others the longest, will see the clouds of black smoke, smell the burning flesh, all the while awaiting their inevitable fate.

"Oh, yes," Dieter says eagerly. "That's going to be Fritzi."

I dig my nails into my hand, focusing on the pain, keeping the rest of my body still, my face blank.

Dieter points to the distance. "The fires will start at the cathedral, of course."

The archbishop gets a front row seat to the reign of terror he commands.

"And then will end here." Dieter smiles fondly at the stake just at the bottom of the steps of the Porta Nigra, as if he can see Fritzi already tied to it. "Now to the cathedral. I know you've had a long night, friend, but I'm sure the archbishop would like to see you prior to the day's duties."

A different sort of panic twists inside me at those words. I spent too long in my office, intending to go straight to the tunnels. Dieter's idle talk and the priest's worthless blessing have eaten up precious moments when I could have been heading toward Fritzi. And if Dieter drags me to the cathedral…

"Kommandant, I am sorry, but first, I must speak to the priest."

Dieter shifts, and I can see the doubt painting across his features.

"I must go back inside," I say earnestly. I even open the door again, and the priest looks up at me from his prayers, curious that we've lingered. "I need to confess. It is too great an honor to light the fires with any sin upon my soul."

"Kapitän Ernst," Dieter says flatly, "do you not think the archbishop can hear your confession just as well?"

Shit.

I stare at him blankly, unable to come up with a lie quick enough to get me out of this.

And then Dieter shrugs. "Do as you will," he says as if he doesn't care. "Just be at the cathedral at least an hour before."

"I will," I lie.

And he walks away. I turn and reenter the church.

"You seek a confession, my son?" the priest asks.

"No," I say without looking at him.

I head straight to the stairs, descending down and down into the depths of the water system below the streets. I'm running before the first turn in the tunnel. I'm not even halfway to the basilica when the midmorning bells start tolling, the sound a cacophony that reaches even below ground. I race through water, splashing and cursing, but I know—

I'm not going to make it in time.

23

FRITZI

I grab Jochen's arm.

He tenses beneath my fingers as the screaming of a hundred midmorning bells overlaps across the city, yanking the murmurs in this prison to utter silence. All of us are away from the left edge of the cell; it is obvious that we are grouped together, and we are one mass, one breath held, one cluster of equal parts dread and hope.

The bells cease.

Silence hangs dense and choking, and I lick my dry lips.

The floor is still intact.

No. My chest buckles. No, no—Dieter caught on to our plan. He has Otto, he has Otto the same place he has Liesel, and he'll destroy them both—

"Calm," Jochen whispers to me. "Calm, Fräulein—"

I am shaking where I hold him, shaking because eyes are turning to me now in growing distrust. This woman came into their cell, the sister of the kommandant, and she lied, didn't she? She led everyone to believe in salvation, but there will be no salvation, no escape.

A few of their accusation-heated gazes pin on me in funnels of violence. These people have nothing to lose now, and I gave them false hope.

How many minutes have passed since the bells stopped? Five? Ten?

Footsteps bound up the hall along with gruff laughing, a barked command.

"Begin manacling them," a jäger out of sight orders. He's coming closer; they all are, keys rattling to unlock our cell. "It's time to get these—"

The floor blasts upward with a shuddering, percussive explosion.

Screams tear through the crowd, and where we were pressed together already, bodies shove closer, scrambling for cover as rocks and pebbles and debris erupt in a clouded spray.

My ears ring, eyes blurred with soot and the air clouded with dust, but I shove into the crowd without hesitation.

"*GO!*" I bellow, voice tearing with my own fear, and bodies are frantic to obey.

The crowd heaves, and I vaguely see shapes writhing over newly displaced stones, angling for the hole in the floor leading down into thick, inky darkness.

I turn to Jochen, dust coating his skin in a fine film. He leans on me, and the two of us begin climbing over the hazards and rubble, some of it shifting threateningly beneath our weight.

Outside the cell and the prison, voices shout. I could take one of the protection potions and throw my body as a barricade between these people and the coming jägers, and hope that magic is still as unpredictably potent as it was in Otto's house fort and when I protected his sister. But nothing I do could help as much as the fog of chalky dust that blankets the room; the jägers can't see the hole in the floor, the prisoners pouring out to safety. They don't know exactly what is happening, merely that something exploded.

We climb down, desperation making us unsteady. I feel a sharp rock cut into my shin, but I push on, holding tight to Jochen as we leave the cold swell of the ruined prison chamber and plummet into the aqueduct's shadows.

Water splashes in all directions beneath the patter of running steps, but otherwise, it is silent, fear wrapping everyone in a blanket of focus. No one cries, no one screams, just the rush of panting breaths.

"Leave," I tell Jochen, wiping dust off my face, the taste of it bitter on my lips. "Leave—I have to go elsewhere."

"Danke, Fräulein Hexe," he says, and before my body can even feel the shock of his words—he knew? He knows what I am, what I *really* am—he's gone, the slush and stumble of his hobbled gait taking him off down the tunnel.

People still clamber down the rubble, and now I can hear hexenjägers shouting above.

"Stop! *Halt!* Hexen escaping—"

I shiver, arms around myself, and duck to the side, out of the way of the remaining prisoners.

Otto was due to light the fuse on the explosion, then run. He should be at our meeting place now; the routes he had me memorize took everyone out of the city, but the intersection where we're to find each other is the only route that goes *toward* the Porta Nigra. A risk, but there's no way we'd find each other in the chaos of dozens of people rushing through tunnels.

What will he say when I tell him that I'm not leaving?

I promised to help him find his sister. But no one could find her better than Liesel; he'll have to understand that.

He still doesn't know what Dieter really is, does he? the voice whispers.

I shake my head, too disoriented in the blackness, my ears still ringing, my chest permanently tight with worry. Not now. Just get to Otto. If he won't stay to help, I'll find Liesel on my own.

I spin in the dark, feel for a wall, and hold there. I'm facing…east? I think? It's all disorienting down here. But the Porta Nigra route should lie ahead, then two lefts, a right, another left—

I take a step forward.

Turn! the voice shouts. *Turn around, Fritzi!*

I stop, cold.

It's never…*yelled* before. And it sounded panicked? Afraid?

Numb, I turn. I turn because I am sleepless and sick with worry and being told what to do, where to go, with even this modicum of authority has my body moving of its own accord.

My fingers scramble for the pocket in the slit through my skirt, and I yank out a protection potion. Wild magic *will not* get me—I down the potion, the earthy, metallic taste a small comfort in the darkness. What will a feeble protection spell do against *wild magic*, though?

I wait for it to laugh at me. For it to wax on about how I can't hope to fight it.

But it's silent now, which is even more unnerving. Did the protection potion cast it away?

I take another step, heart hammering, lungs burning, all sight deadened but sound coming in muffled bursts so I'm not even sure this is the right way, or if back was better; why am I following the voice, why am I *listening* to it *still*—

I reach a turn. If this is the correct way, then I need to go left.

I walk. Each step I take draws me farther from the sloshing of feet in water, the shouting of hexenjägers. Are they in the tunnels yet?

I start running. In the dark. Hands out in front of me. All of my faith in the protection spell coursing through my veins.

Instinct seizes me, and I come up short, palms going flat on a wall.

Turn.

I run; my body stops moments before another wall. On I go, wholly given over to my basest of abilities, sightless and senseless and driven by manic terror—

When I stop this time, it's different. A pause only.

Ahead of me, an arm's length away, I hear a rush of breath that I recognize. A quick, shuddering exhale in the lightless nothingness.

Then, "Fritzi?"

I dive forward.

My arms lock around his neck, and Otto makes a startled cry that pings off the stones.

"Verdammt, Fritzi! I wasn't sure if it was you!"

"Sorry, sorry—"

"Warn me before you tackle me *in the dark*, schiesse."

"Next time, I'll be sure to."

"Good, I—next time?"

I drop my face into the curve of his neck, my racing heart thundering to stillness against the wall of muscle that is his chest. In the vast, sweeping place of senselessness that these tunnels create, I'm consumed by the smell of him, the feel of him, a quick respite.

I realize then that I hadn't thought I'd see him again. And I'd been terrified by that idea.

Which is just *maddeningly* annoying.

I don't release him, but I smack his arm. "You were *late*. *'The midmorning bells, Fritzi,'*" I badly mimic his voice. "*'Remember, the midmorning bells—we move on which bells? The midmorning—'*"

He curses again, but he tightens his hold on me, lifting me off the floor. "I know, I know. I'm sorry—I was held up." He pauses, and I feel the hitch in his chest, a quick gulp of breath. Held up by what? "You're all right, though? Everyone escaped?"

"Yes, they're all on their way out. The explosion worked perfectly." It rocks through me, again, how well planned this breakout was, how brilliantly Otto brought all this together.

He saved the lives of a hundred people in the span of five minutes.

"And you're all right?" he repeats, giving me a gentle squeeze.

I go rigid. When he feels the change, his grip intensifies, and a part of me melts entirely.

Eyes shutting, I keep my face pressed to his neck. "I can't leave without Liesel."

"I know." His hand splays flat on my lower back, his thumb moving so slightly against the wool of my cloak that I could be imagining it. "I know where she is."

That makes me draw back. I can't see his face, but I can feel the feather of his exhale from his parted lips, the warmth emanating off his skin.

"You saw her? Where? Is she alive?"

"She's alive. I—"

"Where? Where does he have her?" I wiggle against him, trying to get out of his arms, but he doesn't relent, and I give him an exasperated look he can't see. "I have to get her. I don't expect you to help—"

"*Fritzi*," he says in that tone like iron, the one that demands obedience so instinctively that I do stop struggling against him, only to roll my eyes at myself and flush in the dark. "Do you really think I'd save a hundred people only to leave a child behind?"

"I lied to you. About who Dieter is." *What he is.*

Otto finally sets me on the tunnel floor, but his hands move to my hips, and his fingers curl into me, binding me in front of him. The imposing force of his presence, even in the dark, coupled with the tugging command in his tone has me grappling for purchase with a handful of his tunic, trying desperately to pull myself together.

"I'll hear the full story after we save your cousin," he says. "But right now, we need to *move*. She's in the kommandant's office in the Porta Nigra. The headquarters were already fairly empty this morning; the explosion should draw all jägers to the basilica. We have a window now, and we have to use it."

I don't know why I'm challenging him about helping me. I just want another moment in the dark, another second to pause.

But Liesel doesn't have another moment, another second.

I feel through the vials in my pouch to find the one I need and press it into his palm. "For protection," I say. "If you're willing."

He doesn't hesitate. I hear it uncork. A beat later, he presses the empty vial back into my hand.

Maybe the Three are watching over me still. If they brought him to me.

Heart in my throat, I twist so I'm holding his hand. "Take me to her."

24

OTTO

Her fingers are laced through mine, her palm warm, her grip strong. We splash through the tunnels, the water icy cold, the darkness overwhelming, but all I can think about is how her hand is in mine.

The trust in me her touch implies.

We start to see more light slowly, as the main passage into the Porta Nigra comes into focus. Waterlogged, we pound up the iron staircase, speed more important than silence.

They'll all be gone by now, I tell myself. The explosion had to have been heard by the entire city. Everyone would have rushed there.

As Fritzi and I wind round and round the spiral stairs, going straight up from the tunnels to the floor for the headquarters, I repeat that mantra: *They'll all be gone by now.*

But I'm wrong.

I push through the door at the top of the stairs and am met not with silence and shadows, but a man, sword already drawn. "*Schiesse!*" The curse bursts out of me, pure verbal shock.

The man in front of me adjusts his grip on his weapon. Bertram. His lips snarl. "Everyone else went to the basilica," he says. "I heard you stayed behind. For *confession.* And I've been thinking about the way the hexe escaped in the tunnel. I did *not* imagine how she was ripped from my grip. It was you."

"Don't make me fight you, Bertram," I say, still standing in the doorway, one hand on the iron ring. I feel Fritzi behind me, trying to push ahead, but if she has any spells, I don't want to waste them on this excuse for a man. There are other foes for her to fight.

Bertram is mine.

He looks past my shoulder, and his eyes go wide when he recognizes Fritzi. "I knew you were shit, Ernst, but this miststück is what you gave up your holy quest for? Her? She's not worth hell, Kapitän."

"That's where you're wrong." My muscles tense. I know without a doubt that this will not end without blood. Not now.

But Fritzi is behind me, and after hearing Bertram's insults, she wants to attack. And while it would be pleasing to see Bertram crushed under her power, I need to focus on him while she keeps watch for anyone else.

"Here's the thing," I say, as much for Fritzi's benefit as Bertram's. "I know you. And I know there's only one reason why you're here alone."

Behind me, Fritzi stills. Now that she knows there's only one man—one whose weaknesses I've dealt with before—she can strategize safely. I shift my leg, my boot touching her foot, nudging. She understands the subtle movement, and she goes down a few steps, giving me room.

"Who says I'm alone?" Bertram snaps.

I make an exaggerated show of looking down the empty corridor. I could be wrong, of course. The doors are all closed. But, as I said, I know him. "You want to bring the kommandant my head yourself. You are not the type to share glory."

Bertram snorts, but there's pride in the sound. He thinks he's already won.

"I have a sword," he says, turning his wrist so the blade gleams in the morning light streaming through the windows.

"And I have the strength of a dozen demons, don't you remember?"

With a growl of frustration, Bertram lunges at me, but his blade glances off nothing, as if there were an invisible shield between us. *Fritzi's protection potion,* I think. I leap back, boots thudding loudly on the iron steps, and pull the door shut. I can hear both Bertram's curse as well as the sound of his sword striking the heavy wooden door. Before he can recover, I push the door open, slamming into his body and knocking him off-balance. Stunned, Bertram staggers back, but he's lost neither his footing nor his weapon.

I flick my wrists, calling forth the blades hidden in my cuffs.

I may not be a true hexenjäger, but I dressed for the part.

"Daggers? Against a sword?" Bertram mocks, steadying his stance and relaxing his shoulders. The fool thinks I intend to cross blades.

But I don't hesitate.

I throw a dagger straight into his neck.

Blood bubbles up his throat, over his open mouth, staining his teeth red. He drops his sword, his hands going to the wound. Even as he pulls the dagger out, his fingers tremble, droplets of red trickling between his knuckles as a spray of blood pulses, falling short of reaching me. He has only the strength to hold the weapon weakly in his hands before it clatters to the floor, and he falls to his knees. His back sinks against the wall as his limp hands open, palms up on either side, as if he were a supplicant in prayer. His head falls forward, hiding the wound, but nothing can hide the blood.

I turn to Fritzi, who's on the steps, waiting for me. "It's safe," I say.

She mounts the last steps and enters the corridor, gasping when she sees the body, the blood.

"That was so...quick," she mutters, shaken.

"Never hesitate," I say. "The first part of our combat training." I remembered the lesson, even if Bertram had not.

Still, before I step away, I say a prayer. Not for my soul, but his.

I motion for Fritzi to follow me, and I ignore the way one of my boots sticks against the stone corridor, leaving behind a bloody print.

When I reach the kommandant's office, I kick the door in.

"Where is she?" Fritzi asks, eyes darting around the room.

I cross the chamber in two strides. For once, I am glad I know Dieter well enough to know where he stores the key. I grab it and unlock the tiny closet, straining my body weight against the stone door. Fritzi chokes out a sob when she realizes what my movement means—that her beloved cousin is inside.

The door scrapes open, stone grinding on stone, and the limp body of the child falls onto the floor.

"Liesel!" Fritzi cries, dropping to her knees.

"She's not dead," I say immediately, noting the flicker of the girl's eyelids now that she's been exposed to light again.

Fritzi brushes her cousin's dirty hair from her face, her touch as gentle as a mother's. "Liesel," she whispers, her voice soft.

The girl blinks several times, as if slowly coming out of a trance. Her eyes settle first on Fritzi, and her entire body sags in relief. Then her gaze shifts to me.

She screams, eyes wide in horror, the sound cracking and choking in her throat. She has screamed so often within the stone chamber that her voice is barely audible now, but her horror at seeing me is just as real.

"Shh, shh," Fritzi says, her own voice tight with emotion. "He's not one of them, he's on our side."

I rip my black hexenjäger cloak off and let it flutter to the floor; I would rather freeze in the winter cold than wear it a moment longer. Liesel's red-rimmed eyes are still a mixture of disgust and horror and fear, but she turns to press her face into her cousin's shoulder, clinging to her and hiding from me.

It does not matter what my subterfuge was used for; there is blood on my hands and fear in her heart, and I will never be more than a man in a hexenjäger cloak, even when I grind it under my heel.

25

FRITZI

Dieter kept her in a closet.

I glance back into it, the stench emanating from it sour and vile.

Liesel shivers against me.

She cannot create fire from nothing, but even so, she usually runs hot, and I would beg her to sleep at my cottage during the winter so the bed would be cozy—but she's *shivering* now, and that rocks me into biting clarity.

I scramble for the healing potion and nudge her away, doing a quick sweep of her body for wounds. A few scrapes, a few bruises, but nothing severe—and no brand. Would it even burn her, who controls fire?

Still, I encourage her to drink the healing potion, and she gulps it down and clamps her arms back around me.

He imprisoned her. In a closet worse than a cage. In darkness and foulness and fear.

I hold Liesel to me as I stand, fury draping in a red veil over me.

Stop him, says the voice. *This is his office. You have to stop him.*

Liesel clings to me like she used to when she was small, arms around my neck, legs knotted around my hips. Her weight makes me stumble, but I survey the room, eyes snapping from the desk, to the shelves, to—

"Fritzi," Otto says, low at first, then again. "*Fritzi.* We don't have time."

"His office. His secrets are here. We could—"

"He doesn't store anything of importance here."

I whip a look at Otto and shift Liesel in my arms, wordlessly saying, *Oh, he doesn't?*

Otto holds up his hands. "Nothing he doesn't want anyone else to find. It's too public. We won't get anything else worthwhile here. Trust me—I've looked in the past."

My jaw clamps, lips stiff.

"I want to burn it," I whisper.

Liesel pushes back to look at me, and I recognize my own rage in her sunken, bloodshot eyes.

"Set me down," she tells me.

I comply.

Otto's brows pinch, his gaze flashing between us tentatively, as though he knows he should intervene, but holds himself in restraint.

Good.

Liesel takes a shaky step toward Dieter's desk. She fumbles in a top drawer and pulls out a tinderbox—she must have seen him use it. Did he taunt her with it? My stomach turns.

My cousin flicks the flint against the steel and cups her hand over it.

Her palm begins to turn red. Scalding, wavering heat palpitates the air over her skin, and a spark flares. She twists her hand to place it palm flat on the desk, and flames start to eat across the top, hungry, tearing fingers of orange and yellow.

"Let's go," says Liesel. She snuffs the flame and pockets the tinderbox. When she takes my hand, her palm is still warm.

The two of us are halfway to the door when Otto finally manages to speak. "How far will it spread?"

Liesel blinks up at him. Then looks at me. "Who is he?"

"A…friend," I say dumbly. "A rogue hexenjäger."

"He doesn't want his precious church destroyed, hm?"

Behind us, the desk is a slowly building inferno, the chair catching now too. A few sparks drift off, snag on scrolls stacked on wall shelves; soon, the whole of the room will be engulfed in flames. Then the hall, fire spreading through the grout of the bricks and the wood in the ceiling. Then the floors beneath, the chapel and altar and pews, all of it burning, burning—

"I've laid traps of my own for them," Otto says. His tone is soft, talking reverently, and I know that's the only reason Liesel doesn't set her blaze on him. "I falsified records and made a mess of their organization. If you burn it all, they'll regroup far faster, out of spite."

Liesel sniffs. When she gives me a probing look, I shrug.

She snaps her fingers and all the flames go out. But her mark is left in Dieter's office, the lot of his things utterly ruined.

It isn't enough.

But Liesel sways, eyes fluttering in a dizzy rush, and when I support her again, Otto puts a hand on my arm.

"We won't make it ten yards if you have to carry her," he tells me, and then he crouches down to Liesel's level. "I know you don't trust me. But please, let me help you."

He holds out his arms to her.

Liesel stares at Otto for a long moment. "I can scorch you to your bones," she says placidly.

Otto swallows, the muscles in his throat working. "I believe you."

She nods and takes a step toward him. He lifts her, cradling her gently in his arms, and she wilts into him, her eyelids fluttering shut. It's a further mark of how exhausted she is, that she so easily manages to relax with him, and my heart fully knots in my throat.

"Back out through the tunnels," Otto says to me. "For as long as we can. If we have to cut up to the surface, we should still have chaos on our side, but it'll be easier if we get all the way to the river. I have a boat waiting."

I nod, nod again, throat too thick, the lingering stench of the smoke starting to sting my nose and lungs.

Every blink, I see Mama on her stake.

Birresborn.

Stop him, the voice pleads. *You can use me to find out more about what he's after. Use me! Stop him!*

The way the voice is speaking to me now...I don't even respond. Something in it has changed. It no longer feels evil; it feels human, desperate and weak, and I ball my hands into fists at my side with a shivering flinch.

I'm falling for it, aren't I? This is another step toward losing myself in wild magic: thinking that it *doesn't* sound evil, that it *isn't* trying to trick me.

Otto starts back into the hall. I trail him, watching Liesel's snarled blond hair bounce over his shoulder. Her eyes are closed, so she doesn't see Bertram's body still lying in the hall, but I do. I glare at his corpse as I step over it—

I have one leg on either side of his thighs when his head snaps up.

I shriek and flail back into the opposite wall. Otto wheels around, eyes going from my face to my focus, and when he does, he goes absolutely immobile. Liesel, in his arms, moans, but exhaustion has taken her utterly.

The lids peel back slowly over Bertram's eyes, his pupils spinning wildly until they fixate on me.

"Fritzichen," sings a voice that isn't his. His lips move in wet, bloody smacks, jaw clicking on each puppeteered motion. "Where are you going, meine Schwester? Are you stealing my toy, just like you used to? Naughty, naughty Fritzichen."

"Dieter," I gasp, hands splayed on the wall, fingers gripping the bricks like I'll find a weapon there. But I have nothing, I have *nothing*—no more potions, no more herbs, not even a knife.

You have me, the voice whispers. *Use me!*

"Go ahead and run," Dieter croons through Bertram. Blood leaks down his lips and out of the gaping hole in his neck in twin trickles. "Just like we used to play when we were children, do you remember? Run and hide, Fritzichen. I'll come find you. I'll find you and your hexenjäger whore." Bertram's head lolls to the side, rights itself, lolls again, fighting the slice in his neck incrementally until the corpse fixes a blank look up at Otto. "Tsk tsk, Kapitän—"

I slam the sole of my boot into Bertram's face.

A sickening crunch echoes down the hall as his nose caves in, coagulated blood squishing out along the wall. But it silences Dieter's ravings, and I push a fist into my stomach to fight the pulse of nausea at the smear of gore that now coats my boot.

Otto stares and stares at Bertram's defiled corpse.

I grab Otto's arm. "We have to go," I'm the one to say now. "We have to—"

"He used magic," Otto says, flat. His eyes slide to mine, wide still, and I see pieces connecting in him, holes filling. "The kommandant…I thought perhaps he had no power, and that was why he was so angry at witches, but…*he is* a witch. Like you."

"No," I counter immediately, and Otto flinches. "Not like me."

Disbelief flashes in his eyes, but it breaks, and he gives me a hard look. "We're going to have that talk as soon as possible, and you're going to tell me *exactly* what is going on."

"Yes," I agree, breathless. It's all I have to give him right now.

Otto starts to turn, but I hold fast to his arm.

"He *isn't* like me," I say again. Begging.

His face softens. "I know. I know, Fritzi."

Another too short moment, and then we take off down the hall. I trail him through the Porta Nigra, delving back into the deep, dark tunnels beneath Trier.

26

OTTO

This is the route I had planned to run with my sister. I have spent months walking all the tunnels to ensure there were safe passages for the escaped prisoners, but I walked this one the most.

I run along it now, carrying Liesel's limp body, with Fritzi splashing behind me. The only sound is our feet in the water, our panting breaths in the dark.

It helps, the movement. Standing still lets my mind work, and when my mind works, I see the gaping hole in Bertram's neck that I put there, I hear the sound of Dieter's voice coming from his broken lips, I feel the crunch of his dead face even though it was Fritzi's boot and not mine that smashed it in.

No. Movement helps. Focus on holding Liesel. On running.

On reaching the drainage gate.

We stop short in front of the hole burrowed into the bank of the river, where the cold water drains back into the Moselle. It's strange, the way the smooth carved stone the Romans built hundreds of years ago gives way to mud and packed earth, but it serves its purpose. I have to put Liesel down, and all three of us crawl the last few meters, with me in the front. Branches have been shoved in front of the hole, mostly to keep debris from clogging the drain, but I've tested them before, and they break with little effort.

I turn and help Liesel up, then pull Fritzi from the mud and water. The three of us are streaked with grime, ash and silt and sweat and blood, but I am grateful for it. The niceness of my clothing is disguised now, and although I no longer have a cloak for warmth, I also no longer look like a hexenjäger, save for my boots, far nicer than any peasant would have but a luxury I am unwilling to give up. I let my heels sink into the mud a little, hoping for the camouflage it can provide.

"This way," I say. The drainage tunnel put us north, outside the city wall, but not far enough away to avoid being spotted. I know the girls are tired, Liesel especially, but we have to get on the water as soon as possible.

The prisoners I helped set free will be able to disappear, either in abandoned buildings in the city or among friends and family in the country. Their accusers will hopefully be satisfied; the victims will fade from memory and make new lives for themselves. I hope.

But I have no illusions about what will happen to me, the traitor, or Fritzi and Liesel, true witches, if we are caught.

"Where are we going?" Fritzi asks as she follows me. "We don't even know where we need to go to find your sister, or...." Her words fade as the events of the day catch up to her.

"Right now, the only place we are going is as far away from here as possible," I tell her, the confidence in my voice spurring her to keep moving.

When I had planned the escape with Hilde, we had intended to take a boat from the Moselle to the Rhine River, then south to the city of

Straussberg, and restart our lives in France. We have a distant relation in that city by the border, and it seemed far enough away from Trier.

Now? I don't know where Hilde even is, but I do know where Dieter is, and that is where I don't want to be.

"The river is fastest," I say. "We have to get out of this diocese." I already weighed the options even before knowing fully what was at stake, and the plan doesn't change now. "If we go east, with the current carrying us, we can go faster than we could ride by horseback."

"Not that we have horses," Fritzi muttered.

"Dieter does," I remind her. She pales and nods grimly. "Once we get to Koblenz, we..." I take a deep breath. "We figure out where next to go." At least that city is larger, right on the Rhine, and we will be able to disappear among the crowds. And we'll be at the very edge of the archbishop's power. Deeper along the Rhine Valley, the Protestant princes rule. The politics of religion may work in our favor.

The boat I bought earlier is small, clinker-built, and with a pair of oars. I purchased it for far more than it was worth as the seller saw my desperation, but the size is to my benefit—I am able to pick it from the hiding place under some brush and half carry, half drag the thing to the water. Two satchels inside hold spare blankets and clothing, dried food and empty skins to fill with water if we have to leave the river. I keep all my money on me; enough gold, I hope, to see us through the journey.

Once the boat is on the river, Fritzi helps Liesel clamber in, then steps inside herself while I hold the bow.

"I can help," Fritzi says, picking up one of the oars.

I push the boat deeper into the river and then use my momentum to throw my leg over the side and get in. Dripping, muddy, and tired myself, I grab the oar from Fritzi's hand and use it like a pole, getting us out of the shallows. "No need to row," I tell her. "The current will do most of the work."

Still, I grab the other oar. She raises an eyebrow at me, but I ignore her, rowing us so we'll move faster than the current. My hope is that the hexenjägers searching for us are still in the city or the tunnels. Speed is the only thing that can save us now.

The river is always crowded—it's cheaper and faster to transport wine and hay and lumber by water. My little boat is typical of those used to ferry people across the river for less coin than the toll at the bridge; I look like a ferryman, hunched over the oars with two female passengers who keep their heads ducked, huddled under their cloaks for warmth.

I row until my shoulders ache, and then I row more. Liesel sleeps, her arms spread wide, and Fritzi pets her hair, murmuring to her.

There are shouts along the river—larger boats vying for better positions, good-natured calls among the men from one boat to another. Several of the boats have sails, but without wind, oars and poles are used more often.

Trier slips away.

I focus on the oars. The slap of wood on water. Splashing and creaking. I am a cog in a mill, cranking the boat forward, forward.

"It's midday." Fritzi's voice cuts across the cool air. I glance up, sweat stinging my eyes, and see that both girls are sitting, their eyes on me. Fritzi's brows are creased in the middle, concern etched on her face.

Midday. The time Dieter had intended to start the fires.

"You can stop for a second," Liesel says, as if my attempts to save her life have annoyed her.

I flex my fingers, realizing for the first time that they're numb.

"Where are we?" Liesel asks.

"We shouldn't stop until Zell or Cochem, if we can help it," I say. I try to force my fingers around the oar, but my shoulders scream in protest. I look up at Fritzi. "Do you have any potions for strength?" I ask. "Something to keep me rowing."

"No," she says in a small voice.

"Okay." I nod, thinking to myself. There are remarkably few boats here, away from the main city. "I can go ashore, find some herbs, just tell me which ones. You can make something that will help me row faster, yeah? I don't need to sleep."

"Yes, you do," Fritzi says. "And no, I will not make you such a potion."

"But—!"

"I don't care," Liesel says. "Let his heart explode from overwork."

"I care!" Fritzi snaps at her.

"You care about his heart?" Liesel says snidely.

A blush creeps up Fritzi's cheeks, but she turns to me with ferocious eyes. "We are too exhausted." She turns to the side of the river. The trees are thick. "If we pull the boat up, we can hide here and rest."

I don't like stopping. But if my body gives out, it leaves Fritzi and Liesel in a dangerous position.

"And we have a way to find a path," Fritzi adds. "We're running aimlessly. We need a direction."

That's what Liesel can provide for us. *If* she's not too exhausted to work her magic.

I find a place where a fallen tree grants easier access up the bank, and let the girls out before hauling the boat up onto the shore, dragging it between the trees until we're a safe enough distance from the river that I'm certain we won't be spotted.

Fritzi sweeps a flat area nestled among the trees with a fallen evergreen branch, and when she tells me to rest, I do, gladly. Liesel sits on the knot of a root, her hand playing with the flint and steel from the tinderbox, flicking a spark between her fingers.

I remember what Fritzi told me about her cousin and her affinity for fire. A type of augury, using flames. My gaze focuses on the little light dancing around her tiny knuckles. My thoughts go immediately to my sister. Can Liesel tell me where Hilde is? I bite the question away. The girl doesn't trust me, but more than that—she's a child who's just been abused for her power. I cannot press her now.

Just as I come to that thought, I notice that her eyes are on me, almost hidden by her hair. She darts her gaze away, but I caught a glimmer of the same pale blue in Fritzi's eyes. The little witch is as curious about me as I am about her.

I sit up, holding a small branch from the forest floor. With a flick of my wrist, my spring-loaded holster hidden by my shirtsleeve brings forth my dagger.

Last used to pierce Bertram's throat.

I push the thought away, even if the image is seared into my mind. Instead, I turn the piece of wood over in my hands. It's still pretty green, but my blade is sharp, and even if I'm tired, I've whittled enough in my day to make short work of it. In moments, I've carved a crude horse with evergreen needles for a tail. Fritzi bustles around the small camp, checking supplies, getting fresh water.

Out of the corner of my eye, I see Liesel's flicker of flame has died. She's watching me, but when I look up, she jerks her head away, staring into the forest.

I toss the little wooden horse at her, and she snatches it from the air.

I chuckle, and she scowls, dropping it as if I'd thrown her a dead mouse.

I lean back against the tree trunk and notice that Fritzi has stopped to watch our strange showdown with an unabashed smile on her face.

"It's not made of the finest Venetian glass," I mutter with a shrug.

Fritzi grins as she bends down and sets the wooden horse upright. "It's dear."

Fritzi sits down between us. When Liesel thinks my attention is on her cousin, she reaches out, grabs the little toy, and stuffs it into her skirt pocket. Fritzi and I both pretend not to notice.

For the first time, there's a light of joy in Fritzi's eyes.

But it quickly fades.

"We need to talk." Fritzi's voice is quiet, but it pulls both my and Liesel's attention directly to her.

"About your"—I can barely say it—"Brother."

Fritzi folds her hands in her lap and doesn't look away. "Yes," she says simply.

"Why did he want to kill you so much?" I ask, unable to wrap my head around such depravity. He kept Liesel alive, torturing her to force her to use her magic, but he was going to kill Fritzi. He didn't want to use her. Why?

Pain flickers behind Fritzi's eyes. "He believes that great acts of evil feed his power. My death would have made him stronger."

There's so much I want to ask: H—how does that work? Why is he so hungry for more power, especially as he'd kept it hidden for so long? But I look at Liesel, at the tears stinging her eyes, and I remember that this is their family member. That he would have killed Fritzi, and likely Liesel too, after he was done with her, despite their blood bonds.

Their fury is encased in sorrow.

"Rather than talk about your brother," I say, "let's talk about my sister."

"Is she a witch too?" Liesel asks innocently.

"No."

"Pity," Liesel says.

"I accidentally sent her...elsewhere," Fritzi says. She fills in her cousin quickly, giving her the rough details of the past days.

"A protection spell shouldn't have done that to someone," Liesel says.

"There's something wrong with my magic." Fritzi's voice drops. "It was stronger than it should have been with Otto's sister. It didn't act as I meant for it to in the house fort either."

"And your protection potion deflected Bertram's blade too," I add.

"It can't do that." Liesel pointedly speaks only to Fritzi, mostly ignoring me.

"But it did," Fritzi says. "Have you noticed that? Magic...stronger than it should be?"

Liesel cuts her eyes at me. She doesn't like speaking about magic in front of someone who still, even under the grime, looks like a hexenjäger. She pulls Fritzi's ear down, whispering something to her, and whatever she says makes Fritzi's grim face fill with sorrow and worry.

"Do you think you can do a little?" Fritzi asks her cousin.

Liesel nods tightly.

"Let's start nearby. There was someone I met in the prison. His name was Jochen."

Liesel mounds some dry, dead leaves in front of her. The tinderbox flashes; a spark ignites.

"He's out of the tunnels." Liesel mutters. "Jochen. Wearing a hood. There's chaos in the streets."

Perfect. That's exactly what I'd hoped for.

Liesel shakes her head. "It's hard to follow one person," she says. "There are riots." She looks up at Fritzi, her pupils incandescent. "The people are rebelling."

My whole body sags in relief.

"What about Otto's sister?" Fritzi asks. The wires around my heart ease a bit. I did not want to push the child, but I'm grateful Fritzi asked about Hilde on my behalf.

Liesel frowns.

"Please." The word is raw from my lips.

The little girl heaves a sigh, then turns back to the small fire. There's an intensity in her gaze—not on the flames, but *through* them. She sees something none of us can.

When Liesel speaks, her voice is different somehow, calmer but with more authority. "Hilde Ernst is in the Well."

27

FRITZI

Otto stares at Liesel, expecting more. But when she leans away from the fire at her feet definitively, he looks at me in question.

"The Well is a place?" Otto frowns in confusion. I'd told him about the Well, but in the abstract—not as a place where his sister could go.

But Hilde *can't* be there. I didn't send her there.

Did I?

The lapping of the river a few paces behind us is almost deafening as I stare at the side of my cousin's face in the afternoon sun.

"Liesel," I start, "what are you talking about?"

She whips a glare at Otto, misreading my hesitation. "You don't have to pretend, Fritzi. He's one of *them*, and *they* know everything about us now because of Dieter." She pauses, noticeably flinches. "Almost everything."

Otto frowns and shakes his head. "Where is my sister? Is she—"

Liesel leans forward, teeth baring, and I think I should intervene, but I'm at a loss, missing something in what she's saying, my body gone to ice and stone. "The Well. In the Black Forest. The place where all good witches draw their power. The place your *kommandant* is trying to destroy."

I grab Liesel's arm. "What are you talking about?"

She turns her fury on me. But somehow, it's still directed at Otto, and it's breaking my heart.

"That's why Dieter wanted me," she hisses. "He wanted me to divine a way for him to break through the barrier of the Well."

My shock is too potent. It warps into horror and back again, and my stomach burns with nausea.

Because the Well, the coven in the Black Forest, is protected with wards even more powerful than the ones Mama put around Birresborn. Wards meant to let good witches in and keep bad witches out.

Only unlike Birresborn, there is no stupid, naive witch waiting inside the Well to drop the wards for him. He'd need a different way in if he wanted to go.

That's what he wants? To access the Well?

Why?

My shocked horror clashes sharply with the ever-present wall of my grief. I choke on it, rocking toward Liesel; I catch Otto's sudden spike of awareness, the way he twitches as if to lean toward me, but I'm fixed wholly on my cousin, on memories surging and biting.

Liesel's bottom lip trembles, and she drops her gaze to the small fire. Her fingers curl over the crackling orange and gold flames. "He forced me to look for ways to break the Well's wards. And I—I almost did. I would've broken, Fritzi. But I pretended the fire only told me where it's located in the Forest, that Abnoba wouldn't explain how exactly the wards work or how he could break them. It was enough to make him stop." Her voice pinches, and tears drop down into the fire. "I just wanted to make him stop."

I pull Liesel against me, burying my face in her hair. She smells of cinder and burning, a baked-in heat that she carries always.

Has she realized that I'm to blame? Has she realized that she helped me bring Dieter to Birresborn?

And because I refused to take the bonding potion he brought. Because I didn't let him use my powers and bleed me dry.

He was forced to abduct Liesel, to get her to ask the flames for another way to complete his goal.

"Liesel," I whisper, swallowing against my closing throat. "I'm so sorry. I'm so sorry I let him get you. I'm sorry I led him to us." I hiccup, a gag warping my voice, and I pinch my eyes against a rush of tears. "I'm sorry for everything."

She wriggles against me and digs her fingers into my arm, squeezing hard. But she doesn't speak. It's too big, I know; it's all too *much*, this day, this week, this month.

In a flash, she shoves away from me and glares at Otto. "But *why* is his sister in the Well?"

Otto looks at me, the same question on his face. "The Well is in the Black Forest?" he clarifies.

My tears freeze on my cheeks. He glances at them, back up at me, and I see his hands flex where they have gone lax on his knees.

I press the heel of my palm to my forehead, and on a deep breath, I explain one of the greatest secrets of my people. How the goddesses blessed a coven of witches to protect the source of all our magic and hid it deep in the Black Forest. How witches have run there over the past years to escape the hexenjägers, but the journey is perilous, to cross so much of the Empire, but some have risked it, if only for the safety it offers.

And that had been my sole focus when I'd stumbled onto Hilde's cottage. Finding Liesel, getting us to the Well. To *safety*.

That was the spell I cast on Hilde.

Protection.

"You sent my sister to the Black Forest," Otto says when I've finished.

I can't look at him. My eyes are on the forest's undergrowth, the flame still burning at Liesel's feet, kept alive by her grip on the magic. It warms this small clearing, but I don't think I'd feel any cold even if there was no fire.

"And that's where Fritzi and I are going too," Liesel tells him, drawing her chin up defiantly. She looks at me. "That's where Abnoba says we'll be safe."

"Abnoba? You keep mentioning her," Otto questions.

I finally meet his eyes.

There's no blame waiting for me there. No accusation. Just concern, patience, and somehow, that's worse, that he's able to still see us as somehow on equal footing after everything I've done.

Numb, I shrug. "Abnoba, the Crone. One of our goddesses. The protector of the wilds and life. Perchta, the Mother, is the overseer of rules and traditions. Holda, the Maid, is the goddess of death and winter. Abnoba blessed Liesel—she's been watching over her all her life."

Otto's brows go up. Which part is surprising—that our goddesses speak to some of us? Or that we have more than one?

Liesel tugs on my sleeve. "Dieter can't get us in the Well. She told me to come there. Without me or a connection to the Well, he'll never figure out how to get past the wards. They were set up by the goddesses themselves."

"He *is* connected to magic," Otto presses. "We saw what he can do."

"I told you, he isn't like me," I say. "He's a witch, yes; but he severed his connection from the Well. The magic he uses instead is corrupting: wild magic. There is no one who oversees it, no one who controls it, so it allows him to do anything he wants. But to access it, he has to feed it evil acts."

Or bond with another wild magic witch, and use her like a tapped keg he can refill and drain, refill and drain.

I shiver, pushing away the image.

"Evil like burning people?" Otto guesses. "So your brother is still a powerful witch, but his magic comes from an uncontrolled source that he can only access by slaughter. And my sister is currently in a hidden sanctuary in the Black Forest controlled by goddess-blessed witches who protect your source of magic."

Liesel puckers her lips. "He's not as dumb as he seems."

"But even if we're safe in the Well," I say, "Dieter will still be out in the world, wreaking horrors on innocents. When we reach the Well, we have to hope they're able to help us stop him. Somehow. This is so much worse than him just being murderous." Dread shakes through me, that there even *is* something worse than the murder of innocents.

"His magic explains why he pushed for the mass burning." Otto rubs his wrist, works his way up his forearm, massaging the muscles stiff from rowing. "He was going to use all the deaths to charge him with enough magic to break that barrier, with Liesel's help."

"Magic has been wrong lately," I say. "Because he's attacking the Well's barrier. But," I twist to Liesel. "*Why* did Dieter want you to get him into the Well? What does he want with it?"

Liesel brushes her palms on her soiled skirts. "He kept saying he'll get more. That little tricks like my pyroaugury would be child's play *after*." She looks up at me, tears brimming her eyes, and my guilt turns into a beast of teeth and claws at how exhausted she is. We haven't rested, she's barely touched the rations I laid out for her, and here I am, forcing her to relive what he did to her.

But she sits up straighter, her gaze boring into my soul. "He's not just trying to break the wards that protect the Well. He's trying to *break the Well.* He has wild magic, but if he has access to *all* magic without needing to be connected to the Well..."

There will be no limits on what he can do, no requirements of sacrifice or evil acts or rules. He'll have all the magic in the world. He's already started trying to break the wards from here, but nothing of what he's done so far has brought them down or even really hurt them.

My chest goes cold, matching the frigid wind that drifts past us, fluffing the hair around Liesel's face. "The forest folk will be willing to help us, then, if they know that that is his intent," I say, barely feeling the words.

Liesel shrugs, her eyes fluttering in a slow, tired blink. "I tried to figure out what all he knows, but—"

"No—you've told us enough," I cut her off. "Rest now."

I help her lie down on a cloak I spread out, and I pull the edges around her, tucking her in as tightly as I can. The fire stays burning next to her, casting orange and gold against her face, and her eyes are shut almost instantly, lips parted in a small *O*. Her hand is clasped under her chin in a fist, and I see the edge of something sticking out of her fingers—pine needles. The little animal Otto had carved.

My chest twists, aching.

I remember when she was a babe, how she'd slept like this in my Aunt Catrin's arms. Holding a toy. Innocent, soft.

Tears sting my eyes again, and I sniff, hard, looking up into the wind to dry them.

"Our paths align, at least," Otto says softly. "We can make for the Black Forest. Using the rivers, we can reach the town of Baden-Baden. It borders the forest."

I hang silent for a long moment. Wondering what conversation we would have if our paths did *not* align, if his sister was elsewhere, but Liesel and I still needed to get to the Black Forest. To the Well that Dieter is trying to break into, to corrupt.

"I'm going to get more firewood," I say. It's a lie—Liesel's fire will burn now without added fuel. Otto doesn't know that.

I shove to my feet and push into the forest, trying not to move too frantically, but the moment I'm far enough away from the makeshift campsite, I run. I only get a few paces before I realize how utterly stupid that is; I need to stay close, should any jägers pop up, should Liesel awaken with nightmares and only Otto is there to comfort her. But I need—I need to be *away*, to run, to *move*, to—to—

I drop against a tree, and all the sobs I've fought down, all the grief that's been waiting patiently in my gut to destroy me, finally comes out.

Sobs rupture up my throat and shake through my limbs, and it's all I can do to keep my feet. My mind plays over and over the image of Aunt Catrin holding Liesel in her arms as a babe, that one innocent memory breaking me when nothing else has been able to. But it's gone now, Aunt Catrin, Liesel's innocence—it's all gone, *because of me*. Because of my brother. Because I was a fool, a love-blinded fool who thought Dieter had been banished for something simple and childish, not for *wild magic*, not for—

A twig cracks behind me.

I whirl, hands up, body immediately going alert.

But it's only Otto. Palms out flat toward me, eyes wide in apology.

"I didn't mean to startle you," he says.

I grunt frustration and scrub at the tears I know he saw. "You should've stayed with Liesel. I'll be back soon."

"After you gather firewood for the fire that hasn't needed fuel once."

My hands go stiff, rubbing at my cheeks, and that stiffness surges down my body.

Otto takes a step closer to me. I fold my arms, jaw set and eyes still hot.

"It wasn't your fault," he says.

I laugh. It's hollow. "You have no idea what is or isn't my fault."

"I know your brother. And I know his madness is nothing you can control."

"But it is." My voice croaks, drags against my tongue until I swear I can taste blood. "Because I let him in. I let down the wards that protected my coven. I let him into Birresborn. *Me*. I did that. I'm the reason—" I gag on a sob, and then I'm falling apart anew, sobs ripping me in half, half again. "I'm the reason they're *dead*. He killed them all. Because I let him in and refused him."

"Refused him?"

It all pours out. Words I can't stop now, they're free. "He came to Birresborn to get me. He wants me to bond with him. That potion I told you about. The one that can connect a witch to another person—two witches bonded, though? Two witches who use wild magic, bonded by that potion—he'd have all the power he needs. He'd use my body like an extra store of magic, and he's so powerful I'd be unable to stop him."

"But you have to take the bonding potion willingly."

"Yes."

"So there is no fear of that happening." He says it simply. Like that's the only thing that mattered, and it's taken care of, so we're fine.

I frown at him, head cocked. "Didn't you hear what I said? *I* let him into my home. *I* betrayed my coven. All of this happened because of *me*."

I expect Otto to leave. He knows now. He'll walk away.

"Did you know what he'd do?" he asks quietly. "Did you know what he wanted before he came?"

I swallow once, twice, trying to force my agony back down again, but it's awake now, and it's demanding I crumble.

Hands over my face, back against a tree, I manage to shake my head. "No. I thought—I thought he'd just come *home*. I missed him. I didn't know what he'd become. But I should have known. I should have *stopped it*—"

It takes me a full breath to realize Otto's holding me now.

I feel the warmth of his body. The rush and grind of his exhale. The solidness of those arms, wrapped around me, pressing me into him, and it makes my whole body jerk to a pause.

"It's not your fault, Fritzi," he tells me again, more certain now. "His actions are not on you. It is not your fault."

He just says that. Over and over. And I'm crying again, sobbing into the cave of his arms, letting him hold me in this frigid forest, on the run for our lives, as if we have time to indulge in my grief right now. But he strokes my hair and murmurs reassurances—*It's not your fault; your family would forgive you; you're safe now, Fritzi*—and I have to believe I'm dreaming.

When I find my breath, tears ebbing just enough, that's what I say. Or demand, my tone low and surprisingly angry. "How are you *real*?"

Otto stills, hand in my hair. I push back to look up at him, knowing I'm well beyond a mess now, but he smiles at me, a confused tilt.

"You're all contradictions," I say, hands fisted in his shirt. "You were, until recently, an *honorable* hexenjäger. And now you're a man who's comforting a woman he should be furious with, at the very least, if not disgusted by—"

He shakes his head, hands on my elbows. "Why on earth would I be furious or disgusted by you?"

"Because of what I've done! To my coven. To *you*. To your sister. All the trouble I've made for you—"

"And I've made no trouble for you? Arresting you. Throwing you into my house fort without explanation. Dragging you into my escape plan. Arresting you *again*."

"Only because I messed up your original plan to start!"

"By rightfully helping who you thought was an innocent woman being accosted by hexenjägers."

"Don't try to rationalize my sins."

Otto waves at his face. "*Catholic.*"

Unexpectedly, it yanks a laugh out of me. That laugh bubbles up more, until his smile breaks into a matching laugh, and we really must be dreaming, or at least exhausted beyond all reason to find even a small bit of joy in this forest.

He coaxes me back to the clearing with Liesel, still asleep next to her fire, and we sit in companionable silence while she sleeps and the flames crackle. My tears are dried on my face and neck, but I feel the stretch of my laughter too.

We won't be able to stay here for long. Just enough to take the edge off of Liesel's discomfort.

But for this moment, in the aftermath of my breakdown, I focus on the feel of that resonant laughter. Not on the hollowness of my grief coiling back up, going dormant, ever waiting, ever living.

Otto and I trade off rowing the next day, interspersing our stints with letting the current drift us on. My arms burn and sweat slicks my underclothes to my skin by the time the sun slips beyond the horizon, throwing the river into pitch blackness, all light from above choked by a heavy barrage of clouds.

I shift my feet on the floor of the boat, trying not to bump beside Liesel, who has settled into sleep again. It won't be as comfortable as sleeping on the shore, but how many nights can we afford to stop? We won't be able to go like this forever, but for now, we'll push, just a little.

I can make out enough in the dark to see that Otto immediately hands me the waterskin and a chunk of hard cheese. I take them, my arm feeling like it's gone to jelly, and it's all I can manage to shove the food into my mouth.

"I'll do the first watch," he whispers. "I'll wake you after a few hours."

"I don't think so. I'll go first."

"Fritzi."

"I don't trust you to actually wake me up when it's time to switch."

"I wouldn't—"

"I think you'll let me sleep as long as I like because of your stubborn male pride, and then you'll just suffer being sleepless tomorrow. So *I'll* take the first watch, and I'll wake *you* up when it's time."

There's a pause. Then a rumble of his frustrated sigh.

"Verdammt, Fritzi, could you just—" He stops, and he takes a long, settling breath. "Please don't fight me. Sleep first. I'll wake you up. I promise."

If we could see each other beyond shapes in the dark, we'd be glaring.

I sigh dramatically. "I'll let you win this one."

I swear I can hear his eyes roll. "Whatever gets you to sleep."

"Gute Nacht, jäger." He grins at my teasing tone. I hold the oars out to him to be tucked on his side of the boat, since Liesel has taken up mine. "Here."

He finds my arm in the dark, his rough fingers tightening around my elbow, and something twists deep beneath my belly button.

His touch relaxes. Works its way up to my hand, increment by increment. He clasps his fingers around mine, and I feel the heat of his exhale on my wrist.

Maid, Mother, and Crone, I'm just *handing him oars*; this is not in any way *exciting*—

And yet my core is twisted and tight and I can't *breathe.*

"Gute Nacht, hexe." There's a smile in his voice as he takes the oars from me.

Schiesse. This trip will kill me.

I settle into the boat as best I can, my stomach fluttering, curling into myself the same way Liesel still is, using my arm as a pillow and knees to my chest.

It's only thanks to being racked with exhaustion—and hopeful that I will be less distracted once I've actually slept—that I'm able to even entertain the idea of sleep. The moment my eyes close, the sway of the boat wraps around my mind, and I slip deep into darkness—down, down...

The forest around Birresborn is burning. Every tree, every leaf, every blade of grass. I spin, but I cannot think of how to stop it; what spell can I use? What can—

Me. Use me. Stop relying on these limitations.

The voice comes from behind me.

I will not turn around. I will *not.* Smoke thickens, delves into my lungs, and I cough, tears springing to my eyes.

"Do you hear the voice, too, Fritzichen? You do, don't you?"

In front of me, Dieter materializes out of the smoke.

Use me! the voice begs.

I'm trapped. Dieter, the voice; both terrify me to my soul; both leave me grasping for what to do as the forest continues to burn, burn, burn.

Dieter takes a step closer. "You think you escaped me? Go ahead and run, meine Schwester. I don't need to chase you. I know where you are going. I know what you will try to do. I know everything, because we're the same, don't you see? We're the same, and before the end, you'll beg for my help." He grins. "Or for my mercy. Either way, you will *beg.*"

My mouth opens, but I can't speak—the smoke is too thick, the air choked with ash and the stench of fire, and I'm vibrating with fear, the look in Dieter's eyes.

This is a dream. I know it is. *Wake up, wake up—*

I stumble, frantic, turn away from him, try to run—

But the voice. The voice that was behind me. It's the tree again, the tree I dreamed about days ago, branches stretching high into the sky. It alone doesn't burn, limbs bare in winter's fallowness, and it towers over me in such a shock of presence that I go to my knees. Is it the Origin Tree? Why is it speaking with the voice of wild magic?

He lies to you, the voice says. The branches pulse, quaking. *He lies. You are not the same.*

And you will save us all.

28

OTTO

Once we reach Koblenz, we turn south, going against the current, which takes considerably more effort than I would like. But the Rhine is even more crowded than the Moselle, which works to our advantage. We are one small boat among dozens of others, slipping through the shadows of the larger ships. No one bothers to question us. When we pay the tolls at towns to continue down the river, the Catholics assume we're Protestants, and the Protestants assume we're Catholics, and neither bothers to ask as soon as my gold is in their palm.

Some nights, I pull the boat out of the river, and we make a campsite under the trees, stretching our legs and walking while we have the luxury. When it snows, we flip the boat and use it as a roof to protect us, curling together for warmth. Even without a fire, Liesel's natural warmth is enough to keep us all comfortable. Liesel may have hated me for the black cloak I wore when she first saw me, but she's warmed up to my presence. She only threatens to murder me in my sleep a few times a night, a marked improvement in our relationship.

Castles speckle the cliffs that rise on either side of the river. Some are monstrously huge; others are tiny, each one owned by a prince or a noble clutching at land. Most of the castles are so close together that, were we to stand on the parapet of one, we could see the next. These men are made rich from the vineyards the Romans built and the tolls their soldiers collect along the river, and they use those funds to squabble amongst each other.

One night, we make camp near a sheer cliff made of pale rock, dividing up my stores. I'll need to replenish supplies soon, but even Liesel can see the way my shoulders are more relaxed than they've been since we started rowing.

"What are you so happy about?" she grumbles. We're down to the hardest strands of jerky, so inedible that we have to soften it with water from the river before our teeth can tear through the dried meat.

"See that castle?" I point to the nearest one. "It belongs to the Count of Katzenelnbogen."

Fritzi and Liesel glance at each other and shrug, not grasping my meaning.

"It's the Cat Castle," I say, using the more commonly known nickname. "Protestant sympathizers. The one we passed earlier, though, the little gray rock castle? That was the Mouse Castle." Silly names, but easy to remember at least. "The Mouse is allied with Trier. But the Cat is not."

"Oh," Fritzi breathes, gathering my meaning. "We're outside the archbishop's influence now."

"Every day we row from now on, all the way to the Black Forest, we're pulling farther and farther from his reach."

Liesel hums a little tune to herself, about the katze that catches the maus.

But Fritzi doesn't seem to share my relief. "Dieter's not Catholic or

Protestant, Otto," she reminds me. "He doesn't care about the principalities or the borders. You're thinking like a man, not a witch."

I scowl at the little campfire we'd dared to make to warm ourselves and our food. I had wanted to make them feel safer.

But nowhere is safe. Not with Dieter following us.

The farther south we go, the flatter the landscape becomes. Fog clings to the shore, weaving around the trees that are barren of leaves but still speckled with mistletoe, bright green balls clinging to the spidery branches. Towns give way to villages, small clusters of homes that puff smoke from their chimneys into the already gray sky. We go whole days seeing nothing but fog.

Although the land near the river is still fairly flat, we start to see mountains in the distance, the dark green of the forest. We passed Speyer, and then the river bent farther south. "That's probably France," I say, pointing to the right side of the river. "If we go much farther, we'll hit Switzerland."

Liesel and Fritzi exchange a glance. We all knew that the river couldn't take us directly to where we wanted to be, but the boat has been a safe haven, a liminal place where time and danger seemed to be behind us.

"Do we know where in the Black Forest to go?" I press, glancing at Liesel. The forest is huge and mountainous; I don't know of anyone who's trekked through all its depths, not even the Romans, who notoriously feared the dark shadows of the impenetrable trees.

Liesel looks down at her hands. "I think this is right," she says.

Which is the best answer any of us has. I dock the boat when the river bends, and we all get off. Fritzi reaches for one of the two satchels, but I grab it first, shouldering both. She glares at me, but when I give her a wink in return, a red stain creeps over her cheeks. I know exactly what I'm doing, and the fact that she has anything but disdain for a man like me… I'll do whatever I can to make her blush like that.

"What do we do with the boat?" Liesel asks.

"I wish we could sell it." There's no one around, though, and even if there were, selling it may draw too much attention to us. My coin purse is almost empty after so much time on the water. I wonder what day it is—surely not the new year yet? I heft the bags on my shoulder again; they're far lighter than before. "We need supplies."

"We'll come across a town before we reach the forest." Fritzi's voice is full of confidence, and Liesel accepts her words easily, but there's a flash of worry in her gaze. We may have to live off the land, a hard thing to do in a bitter winter.

Liesel trots ahead, but I grab Fritzi's hand, rubbing my thumb across her knuckles. "We will get more supplies," I tell her. *I will protect you both.* I cannot put the full meaning of what I want to say into words, but she seems to read the promise in my eyes. Her shoulders relax a little, and together, the three of us venture from the shore into the hills.

About an hour of walking brings us to a cottage, built along a branch. There's evidence that the land was once used as a mill, an old, broken wheel still partly in the water, but the building is falling to ruins.

"We're probably close to a town," I say. I'm about to suggest that we stop and shelter from the cold in the mill house, but as I think the thought, the door opens. It isn't abandoned after all.

"Aye!" an old woman calls, stepping out. "What are you doing here?"

I hold my hands up, palms open, to show that we mean no harm. "Just passing through."

Her eyes slide from me to Fritzi, then Liesel. Despite our ages, it's clear that she guesses that Fritzi and I are wed, and Liesel is our daughter.

Still, we are strangers, and the one prevailing rule of the land is to not trust someone you don't know. It doesn't matter that we are all German; we don't belong.

Liesel pushes her way in front of me. "Please, Oma," she says in a pathetically small voice. "I'm so hungry."

"Liesel!" Fritzi hisses. We're far enough away that the old woman can't hear her.

"What?" Liesel whispers back. "We *are* hungry. And I'm tired."

I can see the old woman's resolve melt under Liesel's pleading gaze. That child has more venom than an asp in her veins, but God gave her shining blond hair and big blue eyes and the perfect pout on her lip to make the Holy Roman Emperor himself give her a castle just for asking.

"Come in, come in," the old woman says, gesturing for us to enter her cottage. She has porridge bubbling in the cauldron over her hearth and bottles of beer set on the table—wares she likely intends to sell in a nearby town. She scoops out a bowl of thin porridge for Fritzi and Liesel, but waits until I press a coin in her hand before she gives one to me. Apparently my silver is enough for beer as well, and the old woman pushes a bottle at each of us. I give her another coin, and she wraps up some bread and cheese in a cloth for us to take with us, pushing more bottles of beer toward me. I stow the goods in my satchel, grateful for the weight.

The day's work is not done, and my heart aches at seeing the work surrounding her, mostly mending and spinning. She's taking in extra work from town, not sewing for her own family. If I had to guess, this is a widow who is trying to find the means to survive alone. She took a larger risk than most would by offering us food. I offer to bring the woman another load of wood from outside so that she doesn't have to venture into the cold and lug it in herself.

By the time I come back, the old woman is sitting at the table and chatting merrily with Liesel as Fritzi looks fondly on.

"Tell me a story," Liesel demands sweetly.

I meet Fritzi's eyes, shooting her a look that says, *We need to go.*

Fritzi gives me a helpless half-shrug. Who can deny Liesel anything?

"I saw a White Lady once," the old woman says, as if she had been waiting for Liesel to ask for just such a tale. "It was a summer day, and she had hair so long that it reached all the way into the river. When the sun shone brightest, it made her hair look like gold."

"Was she a nixie, Oma?" Liesel asks.

The old woman laughs, clearly pleased at the way Liesel calls her "grandmother." "A water sprite? No, no. Have you not heard the tale of a White Lady before?"

"She means Holda," Fritzi says gently.

"Holda?" the old lady scoffs. Her fingers slide over the rough wood of her table, idly drawing in the dust and grime. "You worship the old gods, then?"

Something flickers in Liesel's face, disappointment, I think. The legend of the White Ladies is a story known throughout the Holy Roman Empire, but from the way Fritzi spoke, I think perhaps the story is more than just a fairy tale. It has roots in magic and goddesses that Fritzi and Liesel know. What is a folktale to me is history to Fritzi and Liesel. How many legends have been told about spirits and miracles, all to have their root in some real event?

"We should go," I say loudly, bending down and picking up the satchels. Fritzi and Liesel stand immediately, but the old woman stays sitting, her finger still making an outline in some pattern on the table. "Thank you for the hospitality," I start, my hand on the door.

And then I pause.

The old woman watches us, but her finger glides over the rough table with purpose. Fritzi, Liesel, and I all stare at the word she etches through the grime, the letters visible:

FRITZICHEN.

"Oma," Liesel says in a tiny voice, "do you know how to read and write?"

The peasant woman laughs. "Of course not, child," she says, an easy smile on her face. But her finger traces over the letters, again and again. It's as if her hand is possessed, separate from the rest of her body. She's looking right at us, not at the letters, and she seems unaware of what she's doing.

Fritzi sucks in a gasp of horror when the woman's pale white skin snags on a rough spot in the wood. With an audible snap, the splinter breaks off in the woman's fingertip, blood smearing over the letters. Despite the obvious pain that such a rough splinter must cause, the old woman doesn't even flinch, her face showing nothing but a pleasant smile cutting through the wrinkles on her face.

"Please stop," Liesel says, barely audible.

"Stop what, child?" the old woman says.

A cold, empty feeling washes over me. Is *this* what Dieter wanted to do to Fritzi? Drain her of her magic, her *self*, and leave her as a shell, an empty doll he can command like an automaton?

Fury, white hot and searing, replaces the horror.

I will *never* let him do this to her. I will kill him not only for what he has already done, but for what he wanted—*wants*—to do. I will kill him, and if God takes issue with that sin, let him stay my hand directly, for nothing short of that would stop my blade.

"We should go," I repeat, trying to keep my voice calm for Liesel's sake. I feel for the door behind me, too disturbed to take my eyes off the woman. I get the door open, and Liesel tumbles outside into the cold. I take a step back, grabbing Fritzi's hand and squeezing hard. Fear radiates off her, and I pull her close, letting her hide her face in my shoulder as we stagger back outside. I keep my arm tight around her waist, supporting her and hoping that she can feel how I will do anything to protect her.

The old woman's eyes lock onto mine through the open door. And for just a moment, as Dieter's possession of her body lingers, they are pale, eerie, and soulless.

29

FRITZI

He's following us.

In all our stops along the river, I tried to scavenge what herbs I could; but winter bears down relentlessly, and I barely had enough for one protection potion that I used to ward our boat.

A lot of good it did.

As we trek through thin, sparse winter trees, I grab handfuls of mistletoe from low-hanging branches. I rush ahead and use the time until Liesel and Otto catch up to shift through the snow and dirt, but there is nothing, *nothing* this time of year. I always relied on my dried stores through winter and early spring, and I feel their luxury now, how very useless I am without proper supplies.

Still, I gather the mistletoe into my empty vials. It's mostly for luck rather than protection, but it will have to do, and I whisper spells over the makeshift potions as we walk. I slip a vial into each of our pockets, and I stick sprigs of mistletoe in Liesel's braids—I'd used icy river water to wash both of our hair as best I could yesterday, and she'd heated her hands to dry the chill. My blond curls bounce wildly beneath my nearly ruined wide-brimmed hat, but with clean braids and green bursts twisted across her head, Liesel looks festive, like any other innocent child prancing through a forest around Yule.

It won't be enough, though. Dieter will laugh at these attempts to block him. He'll possess the next person we come across—or maybe Otto? The Three help me. He *cannot*—my brother *will not* take him—how is he possessing people? Could he do such a thing to me? No. It has to be willpower, him affecting those who aren't suspecting invasion. We'll resist him. We have to—

I'm locked in worry, murmuring another spell over a bundle of mistletoe in my hand, when Otto touches my shoulder. "Fritzi. Look."

I whirl, on alert instantly—

Before us, just down a slight decline, is a town hugged by the Black Forest.

It's the largest we've seen since sailing through Koblenz, not quite as large as Trier, and far less orderly; the whole mess of streets and buildings tumbles out from the thick edge of the Forest's blanket, rippling across this clearing, no walls to hem it in. A few bridges arch over swamp-like offshoots of rivers, and though it's getting late and the setting sun should be chasing everyone inside, each bridge is alight with torches and good-natured cheers. From deep in the town, music plays, a few different overlapping songs fighting for dominance from a bonfire-drenched center square.

The light and levity combats the heavy density of the Forest beyond, both sensations pulling my attention equally: the vast darkness of the Black Forest, just there, finally, we've made it; and the buoyant joy of a town in celebration.

"Baden-Baden?" Liesel looks up at Otto.

He smiles at her. "Just in time for a party, it seems."

Liesel brightens. Her cheeks are rosier, not quite fuller, but not as gaunt.

I have seen the way Otto slips her some of his rations. I have seen the way he always looks at her upon waking, making sure she's here still and safe, before we trade watches.

And I have seen the way Liesel has the little animal he carved for her in her skirt's pocket, the way she checks on it every once in a while.

Liesel starts down the hill, humming one of the songs we can hear playing. "Fritzi! I know that one—*hm hmm hm, there are angels singing; hm hmm hm, the bells are ringing!*"

"How do you know a Christian carol?" I call after her.

"I know things!" she snaps back, but she's smiling, and she continues down the hill, singing to herself.

"Did you not have carols in Birresborn?" Otto asks as we follow her.

"Not your Christian ones. I have no idea where she learned it. Likely doing something she shouldn't have—"

"What carols do you have?"

Otto's question catches me, and I look up at him, the mistletoe still in my hands, the spell half finished.

"Oh." I shrug. "We sing to our goddesses too. Mostly to Holda."

"The Maiden, right?"

He remembered. I smile. "Yes. This is her time of year—winter and darkness."

"You sing carols about winter and darkness? That hardly seems festive."

"About the chance for rejuvenation Holda brings us. The rest, the moment to breathe before spring's growth."

Otto nods, his eyes lingering on my face. He's done that more and more, like he's soaking up the final remnants of my words, and usually I drop his gaze first. But now I stare back at him.

"What?" I prod.

He grins. "Nothing."

Effervescence bubbles in my chest. The Three save me, it's ripping me in two—that he and Liesel can act so…so…*safe*. They saw what happened in that cottage, not two hours ago. They know Dieter can still find us.

Yet Liesel is singing Christmas carols, and Otto is sniffing the air as we come up on the first buildings of Baden-Baden. "Ah, cinnamon!" he says.

Liesel stops. She angles her head up, sniffing, and her face brightens. "Come on!"

She grabs my hand and off we go, and I let her take me, Otto in tow, the mistletoe falling out of my fingers.

Baden-Baden's Christkindlmarkt is bursting. Booths hawk similar wares: warm spiced glühwein, crumbly springerle cookies in fanciful designs, a big vat of savory kartoffelsuppe. Everywhere are families buying treats and singing hymns. A man stands on a stage, telling a wintry tale with puppets on strings.

There are no hexenjägers. No town guards at all.

It's such a stark contrast to the Christkindlmarkt of Trier that I stand in awe a moment, enthralled by the happiness.

Otto catches a passing reveler, and after a quick word, he turns back to us with a smile. "It's Christmas Day. We nearly missed it."

"Then Yule has passed." Liesel's happiness dips. She's fighting memories too. She's fighting the same sorrow I am, and I squeeze her hand in both of mine.

We would have had these similar foods and smells in Birresborn, only for Yule, not Christmas. The bittersweetness cuts me in two, how each scent and sight reminds me of a home that doesn't exist anymore.

"It's too late to venture into the Forest today," I say. "We should find a place to make camp."

Otto surveys the town square, the flurry of movement in the Christkindlmarkt. "I don't have enough for a room at an inn, but—"

He points over the buildings, to a hill towering off to the left. The sun's final rays hit it, casting it in gold—and illuminate the castle ruins woven in with the trees on top. Half of the structure looks decimated by some sort of fire, gray bricks singed to black, even at this distance.

"There could be others camping there too," I say.

"But it would provide shelter from the wind. Here." Otto digs into his coin purse and pulls out the last of his money. "This will be our final chance to get supplies before the Forest. What do you need?"

I snatch a coin from him. "Watch Liesel, will you? I'm going to find herbs in this market if it kills me."

Liesel tugs Otto's sleeve until he bends down to her. She whispers something in his ear.

His brows lift. "Well, then we have to, don't we?"

Matching grins cut across their faces.

My eyes narrow. "What's that about?" But I'm fighting my own smile.

"Oh, nothing," Liesel sings. "Get your herbs. We'll meet you back here. Otto and I have important business to attend to."

She drags him off into the Christkindlmarkt. The parting glance he throws at me pins me to the cobblestones.

I will find protection herbs. Warding herbs. I'll tear this town apart if I have to.

Liesel refuses to show me what supplies she and Otto bought until we reach the castle ruins. After a quick scouting of the remaining rooms,

Otto declares us the only inhabitants, and Liesel settles on the floor of the main room we've claimed, one with the most intact walls and the least amount of lingering burnt smell.

I immediately start warding the space. I managed to find burdock root and dried angelica, as good as gold for my purposes, and I murmur the warding spell Mama taught me as I walk the perimeter of the room in widening spirals, sprinkling the herbs in my wake.

Liesel gathers a bundle of twigs and lights them. It's a small fire, but it's all we'll need with her; one flick of her wrists, and we can feel the little blaze's heat in every corner of this room, though the light is low enough that it won't give us away.

And in this feeble construction of safety, my cousin dumps out the bag she carried up from Baden-Baden.

"Krapfen!" She declares proudly as she pulls a sugar-dusted pastry out of the bag. "One for each of us!"

"And bread, jerky, cheese, beer—but the krapfen seemed essential," Otto adds. His eyes sparkle in the firelight when Liesel hands him one. She tears into hers, smearing white sugar across her cheeks and nose, and the whole area smells of sweetness and yeast and the bitter earthiness of my herbs.

I finish the ward and dust my hands on my skirt. As if my skirt is in any shape to *clean* something—it's still crusted with grime from crawling out of Trier's aqueducts. I'd be all too aware of that grime if not for the fact that we *all* look a mess, but my cousin is halfway through a pastry as big as her fist, and Otto is smiling at her in a soft way that absolutely upends any thoughts in my head.

I kneel down next to Liesel. She tries to hand me my pastry, but I shake my head. "This first." And I take out the vial of potion I'd made with the rest of the angelica, a quick mix with melted snow. I dab some on my finger and trace a protective sigil on her forehead, a line through an oval with a few branching limbs.

The glossy outline holds on her skin for long enough that I see the tree in my dream. The branches reaching, bending, swaying with the voice.

The voice hasn't spoken to me in days. Not to try to sway me with Dieter's magic. Not to torment me or help me.

I should be glad that it's silent. Why do I feel like something's changed, something else coming that I can't see?

"Now, finish eating," I start, "then we should all get as much sleep as we can."

Liesel pouts. "But it's Christmas."

"We don't celebrate Christmas."

"But I missed Yule because I was on a tiny boat on the run from my evil cousin."

Liesel deepens her pout, and I catch Otto's bemused smirk, which he tries to hide behind a sip of beer that we got from the old mill woman. He makes a face at the taste, and I stifle a laugh.

I roll my eyes at Liesel. "You're impossible," I say, and she brightens. "Maybe the jäger would like to see one of our Yule traditions?"

Otto looks up, lowering the beer bottle from his lips. "Yes," he says, eyes on mine.

"It's only appropriate to leave an offering tonight, anyway, since we'll be entering their domain tomorrow."

"An offering to the forest folk?" Otto asks.

"And the goddesses." I shrug, encompassing the whole of the pantheon. At home, it was a simple tradition with the offerings usually going to passing cats or swept up by parents after the children went to sleep. But here, will actual forest folk come to collect our offerings?

"In Birresborn," Liesel starts, "we each leave offerings that are important to us, so the forest folk and goddesses know it's meaningful." She holds the last bite of her krapfen in her palms and sighs loudly. "Like this."

I push the bite toward her and pick up my whole krapfen. "How about this one is from both of us? It reminds me of home. That's a worthy sacrifice, don't you think?"

Liesel eyes me, clearly seeing that I'm only trying to make sure she gets to eat her treat, but she grins. "If you insist."

We both look expectantly at Otto.

He takes another sip of the beer and winces again. His eyes drop to the bottle, and an idea occurs to him; he rummages through his pack and comes up with one of the newer bottles, the ones he and Liesel just bought in town.

"This will be my offering," he says. "Good beer. At least I hope it's good. The girl I bought it from reminded me a lot of Hilde. She said that she brewed it using her mother's recipe, and that's what Hilde did, too." He pauses, eyes searching mine. "Is that a good enough offering?"

I have to inhale twice, fighting to catch my breath. "It's perfect."

"Well, the forest folk will surely enjoy this more than the piss water we got from the mill woman."

Liesel giggles, and Otto looks at me apologetically, but she's heard and said far worse.

I take the bottle from him, and we traipse out onto a little courtyard, or what was once a courtyard, a small space dotted with fallen stones and snow, the whole of the Black Forest spread out beyond. The trees blend into the sky right now, one never-ending swath of darkness. We'd walked through forests to get here, but *this* Forest is a thing apart; the density and size of the trees is otherworldly, even in the growing black of night, the clear sky and waning moon. It emits a presence that can be felt viscerally, like eyes watching in the dark.

There is power here. Ancient power. It sends a shiver down my spine as Liesel points to a spot in the center of the stones. I swipe a mound of snow there to serve as a makeshift altar, but I have nothing to cleanse the space, no way to follow any of the proper methods Mama drilled into my heart and soul about presenting offerings. And I realize, the cold of the snow burning my fingers, just how often these past weeks I've failed to adhere to our traditions, our regimens, our rules. What will the goddesses think of me? I haven't severed from the Origin Tree and its Well, but I've bastardized so many of our practices out of necessity and survival. Do the Maid, Mother, and Crone see? Do they understand?

I place our offerings in the snow, and when I kneel next to them, Liesel follows first, then Otto, eyeing us for direction.

Liesel takes both his hand and mine and bows her head.

"Abnoba, Holda, Perchta, accept these offerings," she starts. Otto cuts a look at me over her head, the edges of his lips rising in a smile. "Folk of the forest—hey, be respectful! Close your eyes!"

Both Otto and I snap our eyes shut, and I bite my lips together. Liesel squeezes my hand.

"Folk of the forest," she continues. There's a pause; she's fighting a yawn. "Grant us safe passage into your domain tomorrow. Please. We really need your protection. And goddesses—watch over Mama. She's with you now. Let her know I'm okay."

My heart seizes.

Liesel pulses her grip on my fingers. "Do you want to say anything?"

It's all I can do to get my throat to hum a soft *no*.

If I think too long about how this offering is such a sad reenactment of what we would have done in Birresborn. If I linger on the stillness when the air should be full of singing and rejoicing and my mother's clear voice leading us in prayers. If I speak, I'll fall apart.

So I just squeeze her fingers back.

Liesel throws her arms around my neck, rocking me back where I'm kneeling. It breaks me as much as these memories do, and I hug her fiercely, absorbing the warmth of her little body, until she stifles another yawn.

"All right," I say. "To bed now."

She peels away. "*Fine*. Happy Yule, Fritzi." She takes a step back into the castle, pauses, and looks down at Otto. "Happy Yule, Otto. I hope this didn't make your god too angry."

Otto's lips purse, fighting a smile. "No, I don't think it did."

She trudges off, taking the flow of warmth back with her into the little room. I watch her shadow move against the small fire until she lies down within the warding circle, and it's only then that I breathe, daring to let myself feel, for this moment, safe.

I turn to see Otto watching me.

We're alone. For the first time since Trier, but there's a tension in the air now, and it feels like truly the *first* time, something wildly new and terrifyingly expansive.

I pull the angelica potion out of my pocket. "I need to ward you. If it won't make your god too angry."

He grins. Schiesse, he's smiling more and more, and each time it strikes me utterly dumb.

"You two have had a poor introduction to my God, I know; but I promise, He won't rage over things like this."

"No, he just sends floods to drown the world."

"Fair, but He said He wouldn't do that again." Otto pauses. "Well, He said He wouldn't send another flood. He could make it rain fire or something, I suppose."

"Liesel would like that."

Otto huffs a laugh and motions at his face. "Ward me, hexe."

I stand, and he follows me up, crossing around the offering to plant himself before me. When he bends his head down for me, I immediately regret asking to do this, *needing* to do this, putting myself so close to him after Liesel has left. She's been a buffer, keeping me in careful check of my internal chaos, and now that it's just me and him, the moonlight casting us in wintry silver, I can feel the edges of my control fraying.

He was distressingly attractive already, but after seeing him work to earn Liesel's trust, after everything he's done to keep us safe, it's impossible not to be captivated by this man.

I put a little of the angelica potion on my finger and touch his forehead. His breath catches, and I have to hold my own to focus on what I'm doing.

"Thank you," I tell him. To keep from thinking about how close we are.

"For what?"

My finger glides down, from the edge of Otto's hairline to the apex between his dark brows, and his eyelids flutter shut. He moans softly in his throat.

Schiesse.

"What?" he asks.

Oh, the Three save me, I said that out loud.

I swallow and gather more of the potion on my finger. "For...for everything you've done for us. I know you give Liesel your share of the food. I know you'd work yourself to near death to keep us safe—and that's why I fight you, and will keep fighting you, because I won't have that be your end. Dying for us. I'll keep you safe as much as you're keeping *us* safe, whether you like it or not."

His face breaks into a wide smile, eyes still closed. "I have the sudden image of how it'd be to face your brother again. Both of us yelling at the other to run so we can take the danger."

"And *you* would be the one to run, because he's my brother, and it's my responsibility."

"No. You would run. He's my kommandant. The responsibility is mine."

"He's a witch. You're not. You'd run, and I would face him."

"Fritzi—"

"Shush now. Hold still."

"I am."

"No, you're not. You keep"—Distracting me—"distracting me." Schiesse, I really meant to say something else.

Otto frowns, and it creases his forehead, his eyes slitting open to look at me. He doesn't say anything, though, just keeps his eyes on mine as I draw the oval, the branching limbs of the sigil.

"I was trying to give you a compliment though. To let you know I'm grateful for what you're doing for us." It comes out as a whisper. "You're... exceptional, Otto Ernst."

"Exceptional?" he asks, arching an eyebrow at me.

"Well, acceptable, at the very least."

I try to laugh it off, but his eyes stay on mine, and I fight with every remaining shred of my pride not to look into them; then he speaks, and his voice sounds hoarse, roughened with restraint.

"You make it easy."

I slip the remaining potion into the pocket on my belt and lean forward to blow the sigil dry, and something about his posture changes as my breath rolls across his skin. Something in his shoulders, maybe, the tension there. But I watch the sheen of the sigil fade into his forehead, and I hold over him, lips parted, lingering so close that I can smell the beer he drank, hoppy and light, can feel the shuddering pulse of his exhale on my collarbone.

All of my insides quake, great building tremors that will shatter me inside out, and I start to sway, only catching myself by grabbing his shoulder, which just pulls me closer to him.

My lips brush his forehead. The dried sigil.

I go impossibly still.

His hands clutch onto my hips, all my senses drawn to the intimacy in those points of contact—my lips on his forehead, his fingers gripping my skirt, my hand on his shoulder.

The pause stretches, widens until it's as vast and deep as the Forest, and I can't take it anymore.

I whimper into him, the past days pummeling me, all my building desperation to be right here, to have him beneath my lips like this.

His fingers on my hips turn bruising, and his arms shake with a barely capped effort. "Friederike," he rumbles into the disappearing air between us. "There are about a thousand things racing through my mind. You need to tell me what's in your head. Now."

That demanding tone.

That consuming presence.

That overwhelming wash of control that I've become enraptured by.

"I'm thinking," I start, moving my lips down the side of his head, to his temple, to his cheek, until our noses align, and his mouth is so close I can taste the spice on him, "that I want you to throw me against the wall of this castle and make me see that god of yours."

"Verdammt, Liebste, that *mouth* on you—"

And then he takes that mouth. *Devours* it, his lips as bruisingly brutal as his fingers, crashing into mine with such force that I rock backward, only saved from falling by his arm sweeping around and clasping me against him.

The building desire erupts through me in a wave of sensation, shooting out to the tips of my fingers, which wind in his hair, to the center of my core as his tongue delves in to curl with mine. The kiss is every argument we've had, fighting for the other to feel pleasure; he advances, I push back; feel this first, feel this most—

He takes my head and roughly tilts it to the side, exposing my neck to glide his mouth down in such expert work that I'm on the edge of falling apart just from this. My whimper liquifies into a moan, and I relent, going limp in his victory.

I let him win because I cannot fathom why he lets me touch him, much less that he *wants* to touch me. All I have upended in his life, all I have broken in my clumsy grief, and this man wraps me in his arms and presses his lips to my skin with the reverence of a liturgy, as if in this moment, he sees something holy in drawing a moan from my body.

I'm given over to the power of his size, helpless but to fall open for him now, ride the motion of his tongue on my skin. But I need to taste him again, I cannot get enough of that sweetness, and I grab his face and guide him back. This is my own sort of worship, too, driving against him, savoring the beat of blood in his neck, the way he stumbles when I suck his lip.

"Fritzi?" comes Liesel's voice from the castle.

I stop, gasping into him, hand clenching into a fist in his hair. My skin is too tight, sensation everywhere all at once. He holds, too, just as breathless, one hand on the back of my neck, the other tangled up against the ridges of my spine.

"Fritzi," Liesel calls again. "I don't want to sleep alone."

I clear my throat, knowing it will still sound gravelly. "I'm—I'm coming," I shout to her.

"Liebste," Otto whispers again and presses another kiss to my jaw. *Sweetheart.*

I am unworthy of him. But I am selfish. And he has carried the weight of his own grief every moment since we met, but he looks at me like the world has gone silent. If I can be that for him, bring an end to his internal war, then I will, I will, I—

"I'm not done with you," I tell him, so wholly unwound that when he lowers me to my feet, I have to use my grip on the hair at the back of his head to hold myself right.

"We will find time," he promises, and I nip his lip again, because I can, because this moment has unleashed a torrent and I am at its mercy as much as I'm at his.

I take one last breath against him, gathering myself, and then I push around him.

He grabs my wrist and yanks me back, cupping my face in his hand. In the moonlight, I see his eyes shift through mine, the initial crash of need ebbing in this brief respite, the way he glides his thumb across my cheekbone, cradles the shell of my ear.

I don't expect him to say anything. There is an understanding in this look between us, a weight on both of our souls—unworthiness, guilt, shame. But somehow, we are here, undeserving of each other though we may be; and when he kisses me again, it is soft, his rough lips now like satin as they coax another whimper from the depths of me.

My hand doesn't leave his as I pull him back into the castle, into the permeating warmth of this small haven we've carved out in our world of stalking danger and flames.

30

OTTO

When the girls are safely curled up on the floor, I take a long walk in the cold December night air just to get my mind thinking of…anything other than the feel of her in my arms, on my lips. My mind replays all we did, all I *want* to do, and I grab a fistful of snow off a broken castle wall and scrub my face in the cold, trying to shock the lust from my body.

No priest would ever take a vow of chastity if he tasted a kiss like hers first.

And I am no priest.

By the time I return to the room and carefully step over the warding spell Fritzi laid to protect us, snow evaporating from my cloak, I find that the fire burning inside me, ignited by her touch, has not cooled in the least. I wrap my cloak tightly around me and lie down about a meter away from Fritzi, trying to put some distance between us, but still close enough to the fire that I won't freeze. I need sleep. We both do. Tomorrow we'll venture into the Black Forest and find God knows what—although, hopefully, also my sister—and we need our strength and our wits about us.

I count to a hundred. A thousand.

And eventually, I sleep.

When I wake up, she's in my arms.

Despite being asleep on the dirty stones of an abandoned castle, my entire body is relaxed because she lies beside me. The *rightness* of it, of this woman in my arms as I awake—it leaves me breathless. Fritzi is curled up with her back against me, her hands tucked under her face, the length of her body pressed against mine. Her hair spills over my shoulder, and my left arm is under her waist, my right draped over her side.

The dawn outside is gray and cold. Fritzi is still asleep; from her gentle, huffing snores, I know Liesel is too. I stay perfectly still, unwilling to break this moment. Even asleep in the dead of night, we found our way into each other's arms. I close my eyes, wishing for this moment to last. I smell her skin, her hair, *her*.

With a soft sigh, Fritzi stirs. My arms tighten around her. Her body tenses in confusion then relaxes into acceptance. She wiggles around so that she can face me.

"Good morning," she whispers, nestling into my arms.

We are millimeters from each other, and while a day ago I would have denied myself this temptation, I have no desire to ever deny myself anything when it comes to her. I lift my arm, brushing aside her blond hair and exposing her neck. My fingers trail along her soft skin, and she shivers, a delicious sensation that electrifies my body.

I lean up just enough to lick the shell of her ear and whisper, "It will only be a good morning after I have had a good night with you."

She arches up, her arms snaking around my neck and pulling me against her. My mouth trails down her jaw, nibbling and kissing and *tasting*. She is a feast I will spend the rest of my life starving for.

Fritzi stiffens. "Liesel is waking up," she whispers.

"Bespell that child to sleep more," I groan.

Fritzi smacks me gently, but not before I see a gleam of contemplation in her eyes, as if she is really considering my suggestion.

"Is there any krapfen left?" Liesel asks without opening her eyes.

Fritzi bats my hands away when I try to keep my hold on her. Groaning, I roll away from her, trying to realign my mind with the tasks at hand rather than indulge my body in the fantasies it wants to make real.

"You ate it all," Fritzi says.

Liesel shoots up. "If there's any outside, I'm eating that."

"That's an offering for the forest folk!" Fritzi protests.

"Maybe they left some for me!"

Liesel darts outside, and Fritzi and I both follow. She skids to a stop in front of the little altar of snow they made last night.

The krapfen is gone. While it's possible an animal came and snatched the food, the bottle I left is gone as well.

In its place is a different bottle, made of rare bright blue glass, not pottery, and stoppered with a wax seal.

Both Liesel and Fritzi turn from the bottle to me, eyes wide.

"Is that...normal?" I ask.

Liesel shakes her head, blond braids snapping. "I always leave out an offering at Yule, and I never get anything back."

"No one does," Fritzi says. "We leave the gifts because it's tradition. But..."

But someone left a gift for us in return.

"I think it's for you," Fritzi adds, rubbing her finger over the vivid color.

"Why did they have to leave beer?" Liesel mutters. "They could have given us more pastries."

I step forward, my hands shaking as I reach for the bottle. It's cold from being stuck in the snow, but the insides are still liquid, dark brown.

"Should I…?" I ask.

"Drink it?" Fritzi says, although her tone is a little doubtful. "Maybe. Open it, for sure, but smell it first…?"

I peel away the wax and yank out the cork. There's a hiss and a pop, the sign of a fresh beer. I sniff the content—nutmeg.

It…can't be…

Without hesitation, I raise the bottle to my lips and sip. I pull it back, eyes wide in shock. "This isn't just any beer," I say. "This is my sister's beer!"

"Beer is beer," Liesel says.

I shake my head furiously and take another swig. There's no doubt about it. Hilde used her mother's recipe, and even if the regulations on beer stated not to add extra ingredients, Hilde always added nutmeg to the brewing process, just as my stepmother taught her.

"This is Hilde's," I say again, wonder in my voice.

Fritzi and Liesel start discussing what this could mean. But as I drain the bottle, relishing in the taste of home, my eyes drift over the trees. This castle is ruins now, but it had been built in a highly strategic part of the province, a hill that overlooked not just the Black Forest, but also the town of Baden-Baden below, and—

Something's wrong. The peaceful, snowy landscape is dotted by jet black, cloaks winding up the road.

"Fritzi," I say, and the tone of my voice makes the girls stop talking immediately.

I point over the side of the broken wall.

An entire regiment of hexenjägers march up the hill toward us. It's impossible for us to see all the way into the city of Baden-Baden from this angle, but no doubt there's chaos on the streets. Has he possessed someone else? Is he coaxing the guards of Baden-Baden to work with him by using some magical influence to bend their wills to his? It doesn't matter. What army of man could survive when facing a witch like Kommandant Dieter Kirch?

"We have to run," I say, barely able to process the shift from feeling safe to knowing we're not. "*Now!*"

31

FRITZI

This castle sits high on a gray granite outcropping that sticks out over the Black Forest. That is where my eyes go; not to the hexenjäger contingent approaching, but to the trees. I realize that this is my first time seeing them in daylight, and I would be shocked at the remnants of greenery still clinging to their branches if I had room to feel anything more than terror and drive. Impossibly green, densely dark trees ripple off into the distance, taller and taller until the horizon takes them, and I arch out over the wall of the courtyard to survey the drop. We'd break our necks trying to climb down into the Forest from here.

"We have to get down the road before they make it too far up," Otto guesses the same plan forming in my mind. "There are more of them; they'll move slower. We can—"

"Get to that first curve of the road," I finish. "It leveled off just outside the castle's old gate. It looked like it accessed the Forest last night, didn't it? It was so dark—"

Otto is racing into the main room to gather our rations, still spread out from last night's sad mimicry of a Yule celebration. I follow, dropping to my knees to frantically stuff our other belongings back into the sacks.

"Yes—I know where you're talking about. Make for that. And we'll run off the path as soon as we're able. They'll be hard pressed to chase us on horses through the trees."

"And then we—" I stop cold when I see Liesel, still standing out in the courtyard, arms around her chest, eyes on the distant road, the black cloaks that move in and out of view through the winter-bare trees.

"Liesel." My voice pinches. I'm failing terribly at restraining my fear, and I can feel it creeping up through me, rising and rising like water lapping at a crumbling shore.

Last night feels so very far away. Krapfen and Yule offerings and—and Otto, who meets my eyes where I kneel on the floor, and I can see the same tug of regret in him, that our joy was so brief.

It may have been brief, but we will get more. We will get more.

"We'll get to the Well," I tell him. "We're so close."

"Yes." Liesel rushes back in, hands in fists at her sides. She stops in the center of the room, her eyes downcast for one beat, before she scrubs her face and pins me with a look. "Stay close to me. *Both* of you—especially you, hexenjäger. They won't take kindly to you trying to get in on your own."

We'll get to the Well. We have to. We've come this far—surely the forest folk will sense at least Liesel, the one blessed by a goddess personally. Surely they'll reach out to protect her. Maybe even Otto too. Why else would they have left a beer for him? His sister is there, with them. She'll fight to help him.

Otto slings the bag with our rations over his back. He tries to take the bag I have, but I shove him off as I stand and loop it over my shoulders, relishing in his lightning fast look of *Oh, really?*

Liesel takes my hand. "Let's go."

There's a determined set to her eyes, wise beyond her years, that strikes me dumb, and so I can only nod and let her drag me out of the castle, Otto on our heels.

The morning's frost and ice mingle with the castle path's uneven stones, either side of the road shielded by high walls that protect against steep drops down the rocky cliffside. The three of us sprint with all our might to break free of the castle grounds, risking the slip and unsteadiness of the ice in favor of desperate motion, the air fogging with our gasping breaths.

We follow the curving path, the crumbling walls, until, finally, the road widens and flattens out. There's still a drop into the jagged rocks on one side, but the wall falls away on the left, showing a border of trees so thick I wonder how we'll push into them at all. It isn't just trunks and branches and errant frozen leaves—it's an aura that pulses from the Forest itself, a darkness hiding in between these silent watchers that at once beckons and warns against.

"Here," Otto calls and is the first to duck off the path, angling for the trees—

Up ahead, rounding the bend that leads toward us, comes a hexenjäger at a sharp gallop.

The three of us freeze, Otto at the edge of the road, Liesel and I in the center.

The rider reins in his mount about a dozen paces down the road, the speed making his horse nearly buck him off. But he rights himself, canters in a circle, and when he faces us again, I recognize him. Not my brother—one of the jägers that had been under Otto's command. The scared one, the young one—

"Johann," Otto breathes. He lifts one hand, the other on a knife I know he has tucked into his belt. I stay rigid with Liesel, who grabs onto my skirts and hides behind me, burying a whimper into my side.

Johann eyes us.

Looks over his shoulder, back down the road.

"He's right behind me," Johann says, giving Otto a severe look. "Get off the road. *Now.*"

"Johann—"

But he cuts off Otto. "They're rioting in Trier."

Our tension shifts from fear to wonder.

Johann gives a watery smile. "The people who escaped turned on the hexenjägers. You started something. And for the first time *ever*, that city feels like it has hope again."

My heart lurches, imagining the people we freed, their gaunt, terrified faces in that cell. Jochen, the old man. They're fighting back? They're doing what Otto hoped they would do.

Johann's horse dances in another circle, feeding the anxiety that palpitates off us, and he shakes his head. "But you need to go. I'll cover for you, but he knows you're here. *Go*, Kapitän!"

Otto gathers himself before I do. He bolts back toward us, hauls Liesel up in one arm, and cups my face. "Fritzi. Let's go. Let's go, come—"

Johann shoots off on his horse, galloping back the way he came.

We can hear the pounding of hooves now. The woods around us echo with the murderous clomping of dozens of horses pushed into gallops.

Otto and Liesel plummet into the tree line.

I follow.

We narrowly squirm around rough brown trunks and branches like black reaching fingers. The forest floor is thick with undergrowth, spotted barrenly with what snow managed to fight through the canopy, and the air is somehow even more frigid than it was on the road, each breath crystallizing across my tongue.

"The road's clear!" we hear Johann call to the hexenjägers. "No sign of them leaving this way."

There's a long pause. I run with everything I have, darting behind Otto with Liesel, going, going—

"*Fritzichen*!" the shout rings up the road, snakes through the trees. "You've played with my toy long enough. It's my turn now."

Ahead, Liesel sobs and clings to Otto, and I barely make out the things she cries, half whimpers, half pleas. "Don't let him get me—*not again*—"

"He won't," I promise her.

I don't have magic anymore, no protective spells, nothing, and I'm so tired of not having supplies that can help us, that can *do anything*—but *I* can do something. If I don't have magic to stop my brother, *I* can still stop him.

I dare to glance behind us. To gauge how far my brother has advanced.

We've only made it a few paces inside the Forest. Dieter is there now, on the road, his horse dancing as he surveys the edge. He must realize it's fruitless to lead horses through these trees; he leaps down, snapping at someone to toss him a pistol.

Then he charges straight into the Forest.

A handful of hexenjägers follows him, pistols out, one already aiming.

I start to turn, to scream warning at Otto, but the moment Dieter vaults into the trees, his body goes airborne. He hovers there, suspended at the edge, and the same thing happens to each of the jägers who follow; an invisible force grabs them, yanks them aloft.

And, as one, they are tossed back onto the road, collapsing in unceremonious heaps of yelps and curses.

I whirl back around and race harder, each step putting more space between my brother and me. But his voice carries, rises with fury, a terrifying break from his normal collected control:

"You cannot hide, Friederike! *They will not protect you!*"

Otto starts to look back at me.

"Keep going!" I scream. Panic is welling higher and higher.

Otto redoubles, and he and Liesel pull ahead, speeding over fallen logs, around a hulking, thick tree—

I curve after them, and for a moment, I lose them, a dark blur in a world of dim shadows and massive rising trees.

"Fritzi! Here—there's a river!"

Otto lumbers ahead, and Liesel peeks over his shoulder. I catch a stain of tears on her cheeks.

"The mist, Fritzi!" she calls to me. "Go into the mist!"

Otto looks at her in his arms. "What? What mist?"

But I see it. Can't he? The river he mentioned appears, a narrow, gurgling snake of a thing compared to the Rhine. Wherever it comes from must be warm; mist rises off it in billowing clouds.

The steam blooms more and more, filling the air like an early morning fog.

I shake my head, trying to dislodge the blurry effect.

"Wait—*Otto*—" I trip on a root, catch myself, but when I look up, I can't find them.

I stumble forward, the thickness of the mist growing, growing, whiteness seeping through the trees in billowing waves.

"Liesel! Otto!"

The mist rises. The trees vanish. All is white and fogged, smelling of rainwater and mildew and dampness.

"Fritzi!" Otto cries, muddled, distant.

"It's all right!" Liesel shouts. "It's all right, Fritzi!"

I'm coming, I try. I scream it, my fingers tearing at empty air, but the words are nothing, the same emptiness as the fog.

Movement at the edge of my vision makes me spin. I try to call for Otto, but any sound warbles into a stifled scream as a weathered face forms out of the mist and launches straight at me.

I dive, shoulder cracking into a tree, and the wail that bursts out of my lips gets swallowed in the permeating whiteness.

I will judge her, says the voice.

It's been days since I heard it. And though I know I shouldn't be glad for it, there's a part of me that sighs in relief, in having something familiar in this sudden onslaught of uncertainty.

But as I stumble forward another step, the mist congeals into another face. Twisted and grotesque, hollow sockets for its eyes, missing teeth and gnarled hair, it writhes out of the steam and swipes at me, and I duck again, cowering, only to hit the cold, frozen ground with a jarring thud.

I will judge her! the voice declares again, shouting through me.

I push up, scrambling back to my feet, body drenched in a cold sweat. Shivers wrack me, teeth chattering.

Otto—Liesel—

You've had your chance with her, sister, says someone new. A dry, airy voice that ripples with agelessness.

Another face swells in the mist. Another. Screaming, mutilated faces, terror and fury and hollowness, death in all its twisted agony—no matter where I turn, no matter where I look, faces come, heaving and swaying. I was breathless from running before, but now, I am gasping for air in tightening lungs, fear choking the life from me.

She is mine, says the voice, the one I know, the one tied to wild magic, and I sob, but that sob is silenced. I want to rail against it—I have not given in, I do *not* belong to wild magic, I'm still a good witch, a good witch—

Who are these other voices? What do they want?

No, a final voice says. And this one sounds like a thousand voices in one, ringing, ringing, ringing with lifetimes of sight and wisdom and pain. *I will test her worthiness.*

All of the faces surging through the mist pivot, as one, focusing on me, just on me. My throat cracks with another soundless scream, and as the faces converge, plummeting through the air toward me, terror has me clawing backward until I trip again, and fall.

But when I drop, I don't hit the ground.

I hit water, and in a great, arching splash, I plummet beneath the river's surface.

32

OTTO

I'm holding Liesel in my arms. I'm holding her, and I'm promising that she will not be taken, that Dieter cannot reach her, that I will protect her no matter what. I'm holding her and then—

I'm not.

I stare down at my empty arms. She was there, solid, her weight pulling against my body, and now...she's not.

Oh, God. I've already failed her. "Liesel!" I scream, spinning around.

There's no one.

"Fritzi!" I am not ashamed of the fear piercing through my shout; I am afraid.

"They're not coming," a voice says. I spin around again, and there, sitting on the rocky edge of the river, is a young maid. Her hair is tightly braided and hidden behind a kerchief, and her long tunic dress is cut in the older style, a span of green wool with laces up the sides, cinched at the waist with a leather belt.

Her eyes, the exact same emerald as her dress, watch me curiously.

"Where are they?" I ask, breathless, on edge. The young woman is beautiful, but I have long ago learned that monsters wear human faces.

"Oh, they're here," the maid says, smiling. "But safe. So, not here. But here."

The maid.

This is magic beyond any I have witnessed before. But still, I think I recognize it. The old woman at the mill had told Liesel of the White Maiden. Fritzi told me the goddesses she worships were called the Crone, the Mother, and...

The Maid.

Doubt wrinkles my brow. I grasp at my thoughts, trying to remember the name Fritzi had told me. Which one is which? Abnoba is the old one, the one linked to Liesel. And the Maid is...

"Holda?"

She smiles, ducking her head. "I have many names. That is one of them," she allows.

I blink several times, unsure of what to do. What to think.

Liesel had shouted about mist to Fritzi, but I hadn't seen any mist. I see it now—surrounding me, isolating me with this woman. I don't recall stepping into it, but pale white clouds form a barrier around us. My hand drifts to my waist, my sword. Her eyes follow the movement, and her smile grows cold. I think about making a run for the fog, but even as I think that, the pale white barrier seems to glint, as if there are knives hidden inside the mist. It creeps tighter around us.

"You cannot go," Holda says softly. "Not until I've tested your worthiness to pass through to the Well. Testing one such as you—hexenjäger kapitän—may take quite a while."

That's right—Fritzi told me there was a barrier. Dieter couldn't get in because the goddesses know he is a threat.

I require a trial.

"Will you take me to Fritzi?" I ask the goddess.

"No," she says simply.

"What have you done with her? With Liesel? I swore to protect them!"

"Ah," the woman says, leaning forward. "Protect. Is that what you do? You are a *protector*?" She looks faintly amused.

"I—yes—"

"Is that what you did with the others, for all those years? Protection?" The woman stands, her green dress trailing in the icy blue water without, I notice, getting wet. "Is that what you did for your stepmother? Did you protect her?"

Acid rises in my throat. "I was a child," I start to say, but Holda's bitter laugh cuts me off.

"A child? When is that no longer an excuse?"

"You weren't there!" I shout.

She arches an eyebrow. "Wasn't I?"

My blood runs cold.

"You gave me a sacrifice, Otto Ernst, just last night, and now you pretend not to know me?"

My eyes rake over the goddess. She looks like a simple maid, like any of a hundred different girls I have seen in my lifetime. Her smile doesn't reach her eyes. "You don't know me," she says, a statement, not a question. "What a fool you are, to offer a sacrifice without knowing to whom you sacrifice. Or," she adds, cocking her head, "without knowing exactly *what* you are sacrificing."

She flicks her hands, and although nothing seems to change, my body is perfectly still. I try to yank my arms out, kick my legs forward, but it's useless. I cannot move. I can barely breathe; it's as if iron bands encircle my body.

"In the old days, we demanded sacrifices greater than a bottle of beer." Her lips curl in disgust. My offering offended her, although I had meant it sincerely. "We demanded sacrifices of blood and flesh."

She steps forward, and I see for the first time a blade in her hand, made of shining brass, the edge gleaming and sharp. She does not hesitate as she presses the tip of her blade right at the outer corner of my right eye. The thin skin parts easily, and blood makes my eye burn, mingling with a tear as she traces the tip of the blade in a curling line down the side of my face. The blade is so sharp that I do not feel the cut, only the pain after as my hot blood steams in the cold air. I cannot move; I cannot scream, not even with the blade tracing the edge of my jaw, down over my neck. I swallow, the movement enough to make the knife edge cut deeper.

"Don't worry, Otto, I'm avoiding your arteries," she says pleasantly. She leans back, inspecting her handiwork. I cannot see myself, but I can feel the cut she traced from my eye down to my clavicle. She cut deep, enough to make my mouth go slack on one side, the skin too loose to hold any expression even if the pain would allow it. Blood pours from my face. I will be scarred forever, if I do not die of infection.

"Is it enough?" I barely manage the words, blood spraying from my lips as I try to speak.

"Enough?" she asks.

"Is my blood enough of a sacrifice," I say, carefully enunciating my words, "to protect Fritzi and Liesel from your knife?"

She smiles again, this time a little more sincere. "I never wanted your blood, Otto Ernst."

In a blink, the pain is gone. I stumble. She's released me from the invisible bonds. My hands go to my face—there is no cut, not even a scratch. I look at her hands. There is no knife.

"What do you want?" I ask. If not my blood, my pain, what?

"I want to know if you are truly a protector," she says. "That's what I am. I am the goddess of protection." As she says those last words—*goddess of protection*—for a moment, her green gown brightens to glimmering white.

Maybe this test is only for me. Fritzi and Liesel know this goddess; perhaps they are already safe.

And then I remember something else Fritzi told me, about how her spell on my sister had been one of protection. "Hilde," I say, my sister's name escaping my lips. "Did you protect Hilde?"

Holda smiles fondly. "I did." Her look turns ferocious. "Not for you, stupid boy. I found her worthy, and, despite her lack of magic, granted her entry to the Well. As a favor. To my champion."

She means Fritzi, I think. Fritzi called to her goddess for protection, and Holda answered—perhaps a bit more enthusiastically than Fritzi had intended, but...

"Can I see her?" I ask.

"I haven't decided yet," Holda answers.

"You require a sacrifice," I guess.

"I require only the knowledge that you are worthy." Holda paces in front of me, and it's then that I realize the barrier of mist around us has grown smaller. There's only room for her to pace a few steps before she must turn around and go the other direction. The mist is thicker, utterly opaque but still glimmering with the same sharp edges. My right eye twinges.

"You say you are a protector," Holda continues, "yet there were dozens, hundreds of innocent people you did not protect."

She means those burned in the witch trials. "I tried, I—"

My voice stops working. My mouth moves, but no sound comes out.

"I didn't say that you *could* not protect them," she snarls. "I said that you *did* not protect them."

The weight of my failures falls upon my shoulders. I stagger back, and I hit the white mist. Fire erupts along my skin, and although there are no flames, I feel my skin cracking, my flesh burning. The deaths I did not prevent. Screams filter through the sound of sizzling, and I recognize every voice of every victim I did not save.

I tried—I think again, but did I try *enough*? I used the excuse of working in the background, of seeding chaos and attempting to help without being detected, but was it enough? People still burned. I did not help enough to save them all. I could have done more, been more, worked more—I could have killed Dieter. I could have killed the archbishop. I could have burned Trier to the ground. I could have—

The burning sensation evaporates, but my sobs do not stop. I fall to my knees. I am not begging forgiveness; I do not deserve any. But my sins are too heavy for me to bear.

"Tell me why you started working as a hexenjäger," Holda says coldly.

"To try to help others—"

"*Do not lie, mortal.*"

I force my sobs to stop. I force myself to look at what I have done, and what I have not. "I became a hexenjäger to spit upon my father's grave," I say, my words strong because they are true. I hated my father. I hated what he had done. I wanted to become the exact opposite of him. I joined not to save others, but because I knew nothing would have enraged him more than to know I made a mockery of his beloved religion, that I spent my life undercutting the beliefs he had built his life erecting.

I look up into the goddess's eyes. Her expression is unreadable, but I suspect that she has found me lacking. "I became a hexenjäger for revenge against my father. I didn't care that he was dead; I hope his soul burns in hell, and that it's tormented by the knowledge of the man I have become. And I do not regret that action." I take a deep, shaking breath, the air rattling in my throat, reminding me of how easily the goddess had made me believe my neck was cut. "But I remained a hexenjäger because I wanted to help as many as I could. And I failed so many more than I saved. I know that. That is the sin I live with. I am not a protector."

"You're not," Holda says, repeating my words. "You are not a protector." She kneels down before me, so that we are eye to eye. "But fortunately for you, Fritzi does not need a protector. She needs a warrior."

33

FRITZI

"It's rude to keep a goddess waiting."

I heave in a breath, lungs screaming, and a spasm of coughing grabs me. It sends me hacking onto my side, in the cold, wet dirt, coughing up iron-tanged river water.

The coughing spell passes. I'm on my hands and knees, and I spit the last of the water from my mouth, my hair hanging in knotted wet tendrils around me. My hat is gone, my clothes and cloak soaked; in this weather, I'll freeze quickly.

I need to get up. I need to—

My whole body stiffens.

Who spoke to me?

My head lifts, increment by increment, until I blink at the space before me. The river next to me is completely silent, still, as if all the world stopped spinning except for me, crouched here.

Me and—a woman.

She sits on a tree stump, back rod-straight, a thick braid of tangled gray and brown hair hefted over one shoulder, stretching down to rest across her lap. Her gown swoops over her legs and across the forest floor, a gleaming, iridescent blue, and when I blink, it might be water, it might be snow.

Her head tips. Her bright eyes match her gown, her crooked nose and wrinkled face curling in my silence. "You seek entrance to the Well. All who come to us for aid must be tested for worthiness, to ensure our haven remains intact. What will I find when I test your worthiness, Friederike Kirch?"

I'm shaking now. The cold and the sight of her rattles me like a quake. The test. The test of our worthiness, which keeps Dieter out—

"Otto." I shove to my feet. "*Otto!*" I scream and turn, scanning the forest. Distantly, the mist encapsulates us, but it's far enough back that I can see trees. No wind blows, the trees eerily still, their branches arched defiantly against any movement. My eyes snag on those branches, impossibly high up, stretching and stretching into a white sort of nothingness that stabs my eyes, and I wince and shrink away.

"You call out for the hexenjäger, but not your cousin?" asks the goddess.

I don't look at her. My chin drops to my chest, eyes staying shut. "It's not her I'm worried about. She'll pass. She's probably already in the Well, isn't she?"

The goddess shifts. I hear her gown rustle. Is she standing?

I'm not looking at her, but out of fear, not defiance.

"You should be more concerned about your own fate. The goddesses do not often take these tests upon themselves personally—we allow our magic to determine worthiness. But you, Friederike, and Liesel, and even your jäger—you have caused quite a stir among my sisters and I. We want to see for ourselves if you are worthy of the trouble you have caused."

That, finally, makes me look at her.

She is standing now. Her gown ripples around her, the long bell sleeves gathered around her wrists where she holds her hands to her stomach.

There's a look of proud disdain on her face when my eyes meet hers.

I'm looking at one of my goddesses.

And all I can feel is terror.

Did she hear the wild magic talking to me before I fell into this test? Does she know the voice has been talking to me all this time?

A detail surges past my worry, past my fear.

How did the wild magic talk to me after we'd passed into the Forest? Dieter had been kept out by the tree line—but even after I'd crossed the first boundary, wild magic was still able to speak to me. Shouldn't it have been kept out too?

The goddess sniffs. "Your jäger is being tested by Holda. She will likely let him through. She has long been the...softest of us."

Holda is testing Otto. The Maid.

Abnoba, the Crone, would have chosen Liesel. Abnoba has watched over her since birth.

"Perchta," I guess. The Mother.

The goddess smiles. It doesn't reach her eyes, blue iciness. "You do not grovel? You should."

She waves her hand and all the muscles in my body seize up, racked with tightness that surges a cry from my lips. She tugs, and I crash to my knees, a jarring thud clacking my teeth.

"You know who I am. The Mother. The goddess of upholding, of rightness, of *rules*." She steps around me, circling my frozen body, the wetness of the river seeping into my clothing, chilling me to the bone as I kneel there, utterly at her mercy. "I am the one who knows the true behaviors of all my children. I am the hand that rewards—and punishes. Now tell me truly, Friederike Kirch: Why have you resisted Holda?"

My brain fumbles over her question. I'm shaking and shivering, cold with terror, but when I look up into Perchta's face, her body backlit by the distant, blinding white light, all I have is confusion.

It shows on my face, and her lip curls.

"Do not pretend ignorance. Not with *me*. Need I drag the truth from you?" She lowers to my level and lifts a finger, twisting it in front of my face. The nail is sharpened to a point, curved like her nose, and in a flash, she slices it across my belly.

I cry out and grab for the wound, but there is nothing, no pain, even.

Perchta puts a tender hand on the back of my neck, and I go immobile again.

"Lie to me, and I will slit your stomach and stuff you full of straw," she tells me, voice like honey. "My sister has wasted far too much time on you and your brother. *Answer me*: Why do you resist being her champion? She has been talking to you for *years*. What more do you want than the favor of a goddess?"

Talking to me? Champion? My brother—

My eyes flit across the ground, searching for answers, pieces connecting, holes gaping like mouths.

She has been talking to you for years.

You and your brother.

"Do you hear the voice too, Fritzichen? You do, don't you?"

"Does wild magic...talk?" I ask.

"Talk? Heavens, child. It's a tool. A hammer or broom could sooner talk."

"No." I shake my head. No—it was wild magic. It was—it was tempting me to use wild magic, to sever from the Well, just like it tempted Dieter.

But all this time. The voice was *Holda*? The Maid.

Why would a *goddess* have asked both my brother and I to use wild magic?

"No?" Perchta's touch on my neck turns feral. She grabs a handful of my hair and wrenches my head back to glare down at me. "You refuse Holda's mantle? Very well. You are of no use to us—"

"No—no, wait!" I seize her wrist, clinging to her wrinkled, soft skin. "Please. Please—I didn't know it was her. I didn't know she wanted me to—" Should I tell Perchta that Holda has been asking me to sever from the Well? Dread numbs me, and I lick my lips. "To do what? What does Holda want me to do?"

Perchta studies me. I gasp in her grip, letting all my panic show, my confusion, my desperation.

"She hasn't told you?" Perchta rolls her eyes and releases me. "Too like her. She will be the end of us with her need to mask and ease."

I scramble back, rubbing my sore head, limbs still freezing, but the air has changed. It isn't the deadly chill of winter now—it's warmer, calmer. The air is scented with the faintest trickle of earthiness, like tilled dirt is all around us, though it's still just the river and rocks and muddy snow.

Perchta returns to her tree stump. She arranges her skirts around her legs, and I stay on the ground, cowering like I could sprint away at the first opportunity. But where would I go?

"Holda has been allowed to choose another champion because it is her mess that must be cleaned up," Perchta says. She winces, more in annoyance at herself for some slip. "Though Abnoba was also forced to seek a new champion—the threat of the hexenjägers whittled away previous chosen ones until all three of us had only your coven left to select from, to find someone worthy of standing against the tide of the hexenjägers."

My brows pinch. That's why all three of the goddesses' champions were from Birresborn. Because we were all that was left on the outside.

Perchta continues, "Holda first selected Dieter."

"She chose my brother to fight the hexenjägers?"

"The irony is not lost on us." Perchta flicks a nonexistent speck of grime off her spotless gown. "Her choice was ill-advised, to be sure. But we were running short on options. Abnoba had hers, and what a champion that girl will make! Holda swore she saw such promise in that boy with his healing affinity. And I had mine."

That sends me to my feet. I grip my arms around myself, shaking now for a new reason. "My mother. You chose them to fight for you?"

"Why else would one choose a champion?"

"We just thought it was being goddess-blessed!" I can't keep the shocked horror out of my tone. "We thought Liesel was blessed by Abnoba. We thought my mother was blessed by *you*. But not to *fight*, just to receive your favor!"

She bats her hand. "How very shortsighted of mortals. I would think that being *your mother's* patron would afford me more respect, but alas. You have forgotten many of her teachings in so short a time."

"I haven't forgotten. I—"

"Do not interrupt me, child. You want an explanation? Then be silent. You and your cousin are, as pitiful as you may be, our best chances of salvation—all because of what *you* allowed to happen to your coven and any remaining witches who could stand and fight. And, need I remind you, you got my champion *killed*."

I twitch back, eyes tearing as Perchta stares at me like she is a hunter and I am her prey.

"Oh, yes. We know all too well the truth behind Birresborn's fall," she says. "Our final coven in this part of the world. Our last chance at having champions out in the world who could fight against external threats. All of the other witches who managed to escape to the Well, who made it through the barrier, are broken and wounded and unfit to stand in a fight, let alone be our champions. Birresborn was our last hope in every way, and in one act of shortsighted loyalty, you destroyed our final chance to preserve our way of life."

Tears trickle down my cheeks. How was this goddess my mother's patron? But I know—she is the embodiment of all Mama's worst chastisements of me, lessons and scoldings and harsh, barking orders. And she's right. About everything. I've barely functioned under the oppressive weight of what I let happen to Birresborn, and hearing her say exactly what has weakened me all this time yanks a pitiful sob from my lips.

I wrap my hands over my mouth, trying to stifle it down, trying to cap it *again*. But it's coming and coming now, sadness and agony, and I fall to my knees again, sobbing at the Mother's feet, and I am a child utterly.

Blubbering, I cave forward. "Why didn't you help us?" I sob, hapless and broken. "Why didn't you *stop it*?"

I don't realize until I ask it how poignant the questions are.

Why was the fate of Birresborn entirely on *me*?

Why, if the goddesses knew we were the last coven, did they not step in and help?

Why didn't my mother tell me that Dieter had fallen to wild magic, that he was as dangerous as he became, that he'd been banished not for some familial disagreement, but because he was a *threat*?

When I look up at Perchta, the tears in my eyes blur the sight of her, that shifting blue gown, her pearlescent eyes.

Her lips purse, fury ripe and boiling. "Champions obey. They do not ask questions of the goddesses."

"What of the forest folk?" I sound so pathetic now, voice weak and wavering. "They can't be your champions?"

"They are the protectors of the Origin Tree and magic itself. They are not our tools in the mortal world. As Holda's champion, you will present yourself at the Well, and you will obey what the forest folk need of you to enact the will of myself and my sisters."

I hold, waiting, hoping she'll answer more, hoping she'll give me something that settles the roiling storm of confusion and doubt that she's unleashed inside of me.

The goddesses knew we suffered, and they didn't act to stop the hexenjägers until we were the only coven left—and even then, they chose one champion who is a *child*.

My mother knew Dieter was dangerous. Yet she hid the truth of what he was from me.

And Holda. Holda talked to me for *years*, and never told me who she truly was. She let me believe she was wild magic. Why?

Why?

Perchta rolls her eyes. "Dieter marches on the Well. We have not the time to hash out all your shortcomings. You are lucky, child; were it up to me, you would be cast out, severed from us, and banished like your brother."

"Even though you see what that turned him into?"

Perchta's nostrils flare. "Do you agree to be Holda's champion?"

"Will I be able to talk to her?" I scrub the back of my hand across my nose, regaining myself, finding strength I didn't know I'd possess here, scraped of everything. "Like this?"

Again, Perchta rolls her eyes. It's so like my mother's annoyance with me that the ghost of a smile lights on my lips. But there is no love hidden in her annoyance. Control only.

"Don't you already speak to her? Or she at least speaks to you. Simply *respond* now, and yes, you will be able to speak to her. If"—and here Perchta leans forward, pinning me with those sky blue eyes—"you agree to be hers."

I shrug. "Yes. I agree."

I don't know what it will mean, how it will change things. I will still fight my brother. I will still stop the hexenjägers.

But what about wild magic? Does accepting this accept wild magic too?

I need to talk to Holda. I need to hear from her what all this means, why she has been masquerading as wild magic in my mind.

Perchta leans back, hands folding over her bent knee. "Fine. But know, Friederike Kirch, that the moment you fail my sister, I will be the first to utterly eviscerate you. I have watched you, and I have seen how you toy with our rules and traditions. Do not step out of line."

I'm hit by the sudden memory of the weeks after Dieter was banished from Birresborn. How Mama cried and cried, and I did too.

She banished him because of Perchta's prodding. Because the Mother goddess had chosen my mother, and so she obeyed in all things.

So much remains uncertain, but I refuse to interact anymore with this goddess.

Perchta lifts her hand and snaps her fingers.

The moment she does, I'm thrown backward, tripping and stumbling to my feet. The force of her presence shoves me harder than I can manage, and I go flailing toward the river, back into the iciness, consumed by the flutter of prismatic light from her gown, from her eyes, from the threat buried deep in her watchful glare.

34

OTTO

"Fritzi needs a warrior?" I ask. But before I can even say the last word, the mist rushes at me, coming in from all sides. I flinch, remembering the way it felt like knives, like fire, but then—

It's gone. And so is the goddess.

"Otto!" Fritzi screams my name and rushes toward me.

"I told you he was fine," Liesel mutters.

Fritzi throws herself at me, and I catch her, rubbing my hands over her arms—her hair and clothes are damp. "Why are you wet?"

"Fell in the river." She buries her face into my neck, and for a moment, I feel the way Holda cut open my throat, cheerily telling me she had avoided my arteries, the warmth of blood—my blood—flowing down my body—

"Was it terrible?" Fritzi asks, pulling back and eyeing me.

"Just a normal chat with a goddess," I say. "She kept trying to cut me open or set me on fire. Did you meet one?"

"Mine was big on emotional torture," Fritzi said, shuddering. I hold her tightly, my jaw working. Holda had called me a warrior, but if those damn goddesses hurt Fritzi again, they'll see how much of a fighter I can be.

"It wasn't torture." Liesel rolls her eyes. "It was just a test. You both passed, by the way."

It's clear that all three of us have met with the goddesses. I suppose it's fitting; Fritzi had told me about "the Three" before, the Maid, Mother, and Crone. Three of them, three of us. But while Holda had seemed just fine causing me pain and while the goddess that tested Fritzi had clearly not been kind, Liesel seems oddly calm.

"I was tested by Perchta, the Mother," Fritzi tells me, guessing at my confusion. "Liesel was chosen by Abnoba long ago."

"We're friends," Liesel says.

Friends. With a terrifying goddess.

There is still an echo in my mind of what Holda told me—Fritzi needs a warrior. Of course I will defend her, and Liesel too, but...

From what?

I look around me for the first time since the mist closed over my body, one arm still protectively around Fritzi's waist.

We are no longer in the Black Forest. At least not anywhere near where we entered. The frost-rimmed river with snowcapped boulders outlining it is now a pleasantly warm bubbling brook with pale pink flowers floating on the surface. The ground is not craggy and treacherous; gently rolling hills covered in soft moss and meadow grass give way to trees three, four times larger than any I have seen before. The enormous trunks are smooth, as if the bark is made of silver, with long, low branches that swoop down, white blossoms amid the leaves and needles.

A warm breeze blows, and I throw back my cloak. It feels like late spring, not the dead of winter, with blossoms and the sweet smell of ripe fruit everywhere.

"Look." Fritzi's voice is an awed whisper as she points up.

Elegantly carved houses are nestled in the tree branches, grander than any palace. Bridges connect the trees, but they seem to have been grown, not carved—the long limbs extending out from one treeloft palace to another, branches twisting up to form covered walkways.

We head toward the village, but before we get very far, we hear chanting.

"What is that?" I ask.

Fritzi frowns, and she and Liesel exchange a look. "It's a spell," Fritzi says slowly, as if she's still muddling through it, uncertain of what the spell may mean.

"Smell that?" Liesel asks.

"Sage," Fritzi says immediately. "Rosemary. Protection herbs."

"We had to face a trio of goddesses just to get here," I say. "How does this land need further protection?"

Fritzi's jaw clenches. My heart sinks—not because the greatest threat to magic is Dieter Kirch, but because Dieter is Fritzi's brother, and the forest folk are reinforcing the protection to keep him out.

We round a hill, and we see a line of guards patrolling a well-worn path around the perimeter of the village. Other people hang in the distance, chanting and weaving their arms in some form of magic, but when they see us, they all freeze, turning to look at the invaders.

I keep one hand on Fritzi, unwilling to let her go after we were forcibly separated by the goddesses, but my other hand drops to my sword hilt.

"Otto, don't be an idiot," Liesel says flatly.

The armed guards step forward, while the magic-users retreat into the trees. The soldiers do not cower or hesitate. Men and women alike have long hair, most of them with elaborate braids, some glittering with shiny beads, some woven with greenery, some bound in strands of gold and silver.

Holda had told me that I would be Fritzi's warrior, but any of these soldiers would likely be a better candidate. I feel not only weak but childish in the face of such obvious power.

One of the warriors—she looks like a queen but carries the weapons of a soldier—peels off from the others. She has black tattoos in Celtic designs weaving over her bare arms, each line emphasizing her cut muscles. Rather than a crown, she wears a huge headpiece made of dripping moss and sticks, a chaotic nest that looks regal atop her braids.

She peers down at us, her lips parting slowly.

And then, from behind, comes a voice I know. A voice I love. "*Otto!*"

"Hilde?" My heart seizes, and I barely dare to hope.

A blur of mousy brown braids and red skirts hurtles toward me, and I'm nearly thrown off my feet as my sister launches at me. Fritzi chuckles, stepping aside so that I can wrap my arms around Hilde and twirl her around and around. She giggles, and for a moment, all is well. Sheer, perfect, calming relief floods my body. I knew Fritzi had sent Hilde to be protected, and I had long ago accepted that her magic was real and, by that same idea, Hilde truly was safe. But I hadn't really believed it until this moment, when she's here, laughing, exactly as I remembered her except, somehow, even happier. I clutch her to me, and a prayer of gratitude rises in my heart.

When I put Hilde down though, the soldiers watch imperiously.

"Oh, come *on*," Hilde says, glowering at the queenlike one. "Brigitta, it's my brother."

The leader—Brigitta, I presume—does not seem to care. But then her eyes glide to Fritzi and, finally, Liesel. "Champions," she says, bowing her head respectfully. Fritzi stands there awkwardly, unsure of how to react, but Liesel arches her head up, accepting the respect easily. That word clearly has some importance to everyone here but me, but it is a mantle I'm not sure Fritzi wants.

"The Three must have accepted your presence for you to accompany the chosen champions," Brigitta adds, turning to me. "Welcome."

Chosen champions? The way the woman says this twists inside me; there are things at play here that the goddess didn't bother to mention. To me, at least.

"My name is Otto," I say. And, because I feel the need to at least be worthy of being close to Fritzi, I add, "Holda chose me to be Fritzi's warrior."

That causes a ripple among the forest folk, and I'm not sure what I said that creates so much consternation.

"The council will wish to discuss this further," Brigitta says finally; then she turns her full attention to Fritzi and Liesel. "The champions are requested now."

"Requested?" Fritzi asks. "For what?"

"The Well needs your aid."

"Of course," Liesel says, striding forward. "That's why we came."

"It is?" Fritzi starts to protest, but Liesel tugs Fritzi behind her, and the guard close rank, escorting Fritzi and Liesel somewhere deeper into the trees.

Brigitta pauses, shooting Hilde a look. When I go to follow Fritzi, Hilde holds my arm. "We're to stay," she says.

"I'm not leaving them," I protest.

"This is one of those magic-witch-mysterious things," Hilde says. "But you can trust Brigitta."

I don't. But I do trust my sister, and I trust Liesel, who seemed sure that they should follow. From the crowd, Fritzi turns back to me, a question in her eyes. Her gaze slides from me to Hilde and back again, and I can see that while I was worried about her, she had concerns about leaving me behind. She gives me a little shrug as Liesel tugs her along, one I return, and she flashes me a smile.

Holda told me herself that Fritzi doesn't need protecting. Perhaps this will be the moment she will learn what battle I will need to aid her in fighting. Surely this centers on Dieter in some way; Fritzi's brother is a threat to all. But this also seems bigger...

Hilde beams at me, oblivious to my worried thoughts.

I pull her close. "You're well?"

She smiles at me brilliantly. "Better than well. I'm—I'm happy here, Otto. This is the most beautiful place I have ever been. It's *magic*!"

I laugh ruefully. "Who would have thought that witches were real all along?"

"What would the archbishop think?" Hilde says. She pauses, twisting her hands together, a nervous habit she's had since she was a toddler. "What of Trier? The forest folk were able to tell me some things, but they couldn't see past the walls of the city. Did our plan—" There is aching, desperate hope in her voice.

It wasn't just me who'd worked for years to find a way to disrupt the witch trials. Hilde had too. My sister was the one pushing me to do more, be more. Our secret routes and early warnings to targeted individuals had never been enough for her; it was Hilde who volunteered to be arrested, to work from the inside for a major, showy display of rebellion.

"Your plan was perfect," I say, watching as the fears melt away from her pinched eyes.

"Our plan," Hilde says.

"More than a hundred people were saved from the fires," I continue. "The prison is in ruins. And I heard—" I pause, catching the emotion in my voice. Johann had risked much to tell me of Trier, to try to deviate Dieter away from us when we ran into the Forest. "There are riots in Trier."

"Riots?" Hilde's eyes gleam. Riots mean that our protest was seen for what it was. The regular people are no longer willing to live in fear; they are fighting back against the archbishop's cruel trials. "Thank God."

God is another topic I want to speak to my sister about. Having seen real goddesses in a pagan religion I had thought was nothing more than myth, I have questions, if not doubt. But that is a topic for later.

Hilde leads me up toward the trees. She doesn't try to climb one of the ramps or rope ladders built along the trunks; instead, she shows me a small cottage under the shadows of the tree nearest the river. I recognize plants growing in the front garden, the little bowl of cream on the windowsill.

It looks like home.

"They told me some of what happened," Hilde says gently. "That the witch—Fritzi—asked for help from the goddess of protection, and Holda sent me here, the safest place in the entire world."

"And you have been safe?" I ask. "Truly?"

"Mm," Hilde says, smiling and opening the door of the cottage for me. "The forest folk are good, Otto."

Something about the way she says that makes me pause. I know my sister, even if we've been apart for the past several years. A blush creeps over her cheeks. Hilde has found not just safety and acceptance at the Well; she's found a sweetheart of her own.

I don't press the topic, but I do follow her inside. All the smells of home are here—the bubbling nutmeg-infused beer, the sprigs of rosemary, the scent of the soap my mother made, the recipe passed down to my sister.

For the first time in a long time, the fears that had wound inside my muscles loosen. I pull Hilde into another hug, feeling the warmth of her, the easy love that we share.

But through the window, I see more eyes watching us. Hilde may have been accepted by the forest folk, but I have not.

And I cannot help but wonder just what type of warrior the goddess needs me to be.

35

FRITZI

A few of the forest folk guide Liesel and me to a staircase that twists up a tree with a trunk wider than the cottage I shared with Mama. The bark glints and gleams in errant rays that break through the high, high canopy, other light sources flickering around us: elaborate silver lanterns hanging from elegant looping hooks, flashes of candlelight from within rooms nestled in the very trees themselves.

I crane my neck around, seeking through the branches, but I can't spot which one might be the Origin Tree. Surely it is deeper within, guarded fiercely, not holding buildings and homes.

The Well is a refuge. We were told stories of it from infancy, how we could come here for protection, kept safe among the witches chosen by the goddesses to protect our source of magic.

In the stories, I always imagined a village like Birresborn. A coven like mine. A tight community of witches depending on one another, scraping by.

But this is a city as sprawling as Trier, lifted into the treetops, and that gives it ancient importance.

The Well has been this society of resources and witches and power, abundance and wealth, while we were out in the world, clinging to whatever spell components and weapons we could scrounge up, fearing hexenjägers and prejudices.

How easily could the witches of the Well muster a force to not only resist the hexenjägers, but overpower them? This is no mere village. This is practically a kingdom.

Familiar anger rises up the back of my throat. The anger I felt talking with Perchta.

They've stayed here, in opulence and finery, while we've suffered.

Everywhere around me are witches rushing with baskets full of herbs, or arms full of protection totems, or hands lifted as they chant spells into the ether. Some of their arms, necks, and faces are splayed with a vast array of black tattoos in swirling symbols I recognize from my coven's books and scrolls. Sigils for protection, strength, endurance, foresight, and more—I've never seen a witch able to tattoo our symbols onto their skin before. The idea is too baffling—what if hexenjägers see? What if someone notes the symbology and cries witchcraft? But here, witches are free to show off every element of our practice in a way that hollows me to my core. I had not even known the full extent of the limitations I lived under, for survival.

Everyone we pass at least occasionally glances into the forest, past the edges of these trees set with buildings, their faces bent in such focus that I feel their urgency in my gut.

Dieter is weakening the barrier. I knew his effect was dangerous, with the way magic was bucking like an angry horse in the outside world; but to see the strain on the faces here—how far has my brother used wild magic to breach these walls? How many people has he killed to feed the evil that grows and grows in him like a disease?

Is it too late?

We climb, lifting up to a village that stuns me speechless.

It's built *into* the tree canopy.

Most of the buildings are carved into the trees that tower all around us, their branches curving to cradle structures and stairs like they were grown specifically to hold this village. The walls and windows match the trees in every way, from the sheen of gray to the twisting sway of the lines, so that everywhere is a forest caught in a gentle breeze, palpitating, dancing, a celebration of life.

Despite the fear and anger, I can't help but be mesmerized by this place.

"Is this whole area the Well?" I ask.

Brigitta looks down at me from a higher step. "Yes. In a way—we are tied to the Black Forest. In this world, but set apart."

That explains the massive size of these trees, the ethereal aura that permeates each glittering mote of dust we pass.

"Where is the Origin Tree?" My mouth is dry.

Brigitta looks off into the forest, toward the city-trees that race off farther than my eyes can see. "Deep within our borders. Well-guarded, don't worry—I've been a captain of the Grenzwache for five years, and I've only seen it from the barest of distances. Dieter won't get close enough to harm it."

Grenzwache. Border guard.

Brigitta gives a reassuring smile that does nothing to soothe my fear and carries on, leading us up, up, up, to a bridge that stretches to another tree. As I take a first step onto it, my eyes dip down.

I shriek and stumble back into the soldier behind me. I hadn't thought too strongly about the fact that we're being watched, hemmed in on all sides by what are clearly guards in leather armor dyed green and decorated with arching motifs of still more trees, because all of this is so overwhelming, so much a story come to life, that I'm half-delirious with the need to laugh. But the sheer *height* we're at up here, watching leaves drift lazily around us, down, down…

"It isn't possible," I whisper.

Liesel takes my hand. The way she grips it is insistent, and I manage to tear my petrified gaze from the bridge's railing to look at her. Her eyes are wide, a bead of sweat on her hairline. She's scared too.

I clutch her hand tighter. We're in this together. To the end.

"We wouldn't let you fall all the way," says the man behind us.

I look back. The guard has a brow slightly cocked, amusement playing in his eyes as he lets his words sink in. His copper hair hangs to his mid-back, pulled half atop his head with a woven leather braid that shows an insignia across his forehead: three moons. One waxing crescent, one full, and one waning crescent. A symbol of the goddesses.

"*All* the way?" I clarify.

He shrugs, arms behind his back. "It's only the last few seconds that would kill you, isn't it?"

It could come across as threatening, but that sparkle in his eyes intensifies, and he grins at Liesel.

He pulls one hand out from behind his back and holds something up for her to see:

A krapfen.

Liesel makes a startled gasp. "Where—where did you get that?"

Eyes flitting from her to me, he takes a huge bite. "Come on," he says through a mouthful of pastry and sugar. "The bridge is really quite sound."

He pushes around us and continues out onto it.

"We're nearly there," says Brigitta, who has realized we stopped. She looks back at us with the two other guards, the lot of them again not threatening. Just waiting.

Liesel tugs on my hand. "Fritzi. Your krapfen. He *ate* your *krapfen*. He got our offering!"

And while she sounds downright enchanted, and immediately darts out onto the bridge, I linger for a beat, watching the guard pop the rest of the krapfen into his mouth and give me a wink.

I manage a shaky breath.

Holda? I try. I've never reached out to the voice before. Never wanted to draw its focus. *We need to talk.*

I start across the bridge, doing my best to keep my eyes on Liesel's shoes in front of me, the way the wood of the bridge is half natural growth from thick oak branches, half boards nailed into it.

"Watch your step," the guard says, that tinge of amusement in his voice still, and this time, Brigitta swats his shoulder.

"Restrain yourself, Alois; she doesn't need your cheek."

"Oh, I beg to differ, Brigs."

"Don't—we're on *patrol*." She spins away with an eye roll. "*Pretend* you have decorum, the Three help me."

"She loves me," Alois whispers to Liesel, but his eyes flick to mine, too, and as Liesel giggles into her palm, I grip my jaw tight.

You can trust them, comes the voice.

I steady myself on the railing. It's different knowing who the voice is now. *What* it is.

My lungs shudder. *But do I trust you?*

Brigitta leads us to a massive chamber so high in the trees that the landing before the door takes us above the canopy. The wind here is warm springtime, winter held at bay by the magic of this place, but the height is what takes my breath away; we are at the top of the Forest, the top of the *world*. The blue of the sky is endless and infinite and makes me feel so startlingly small that I'm grateful for it. I am inconsequential beneath it. I am dismissible.

I manage a stuttering inhale before Brigitta opens one of two ornately carved doors, the pair of them making another triple moon symbol in polished birch.

"You will meet with our council," Brigitta says and ushers us inside. "They demanded to know the moment you arrived."

"Well, nice that they knew we were coming," I mumble, then hiss at myself. I can't let my nerves get the better of me. I can't make these people my enemy—at least until I decide what to do with all of...*this*.

Inside, the room is airy and light, the walls a soft lavender, with massive windows that show the top of the forest rippling out into the distance on all sides, green leaves stretching on into the swath of blue sky. The walls of the room are lined with shelves that hold books—*dozens* of books, actually, more than I've ever seen in one place—and scrolls, all manner of potion equipment, and magic relics of the sort we had in Birresborn: bones and twigs and satchels.

I'm so taken by the supplies here—more than my whole coven had at their fingertips, and the continued reminder of the Well's luxury leaves a tang of anger in my mouth—that I almost miss the flurry in the center of the room.

Three people are facing the door. They look up from where they had all been crouched over a table set with such an array of spell components that I can't guess what they're casting. Angelica and burdock root—warding? Two tall wax candles with a thread between them—severing? There's other things, but the eyes on me draw my focus.

Liesel and I stop just inside. I feel my travel-grime and river-dampness so heavily that my cheeks heat—these people are utterly spotless, their clothing so fine that I'd never hope to wear the like, their hair styled in either pin-straight sheets or done up in twisted knots with greenery set into the loops.

And here Liesel and I are, dirt-smeared and bloodied, hungry and thirsty and sore from sleeping on the ground.

Whatever flimsy upper hand I may have had shrivels and dies.

"Our champions," the center man says, his voice tight like he's fighting to stay cordial, to not recoil at our appearance. He rises from his bent position and claps his hands, hair so blond it's nearly white. "Abnoba has long prepared us for your arrival. Liesel—she is delighted by you."

"She talks to you too?" Liesel steps forward, a smile in her voice.

The man beams at her. It transforms his face, a fatherly aura in his kind eyes. "Not as much as she speaks with you, I imagine. Your bond with her far surpasses what even we can achieve. We are the priest and priestesses of the Well. I am Rochus. This is Philomena." He motions to the woman who stands straight and bows her head at us, her voluptuous curves hugged by a striking aqua gown that looks so like the one Perchta wore in my vision that I wonder if it's the same. "And Cornelia."

She looks around my age. With the same copper hair as Alois, she stays bent over the table, one finger tapping a rhythm on an unrolled scroll. I can't figure out the way she's looking at me, her eyes squinted, calculating.

"Dismiss your subordinates, Wächterin Brigitta," Rochus says, a noticeable dip in his voice as his formality breaks.

Brigitta's eyebrows lift. "I assumed we would remain and escort them to lodgings shortly. They have traveled far—"

"And will be put to use *now*, Wächterin. There will be time for resting afterward. Dismiss your subordinates. You may stay if you insist."

Brigitta looks at us, and her unease puts me even more on edge.

She nods at Alois and the other guards and ducks off to the side as they leave, and Rochus takes a step toward us, his arms spread.

"We are in dire need of your assistance," Rochus says, his smile tight. "You no doubt are well aware of the threat pressing at our borders. The goddesses have sent you to us at the proper time—"

"Because we are their champions?" I wave at myself, at Liesel, hoping he sees how absurd this is. Liesel is ten years old.

Her childhood has been cut short, and already Abnoba demands more of her.

Rochus sighs heavily. Behind him, Philomena has gone back to furiously grinding something in a mortar, her attention flitting from a scroll to us and back in simmering distaste.

"Her frustration is earned," says Cornelia. She puts a finger on one of the two unlit candles, follows the string between them with the lightest touch. "I think they're deserving of a full *explanation*, Rochus, before you jump right to using them."

Philomena glares at Cornelia. "You have felt Dieter's movements on us, and you wish to delay even more?"

Cornelia smiles icily. "Yes. I do. Because the goddesses chose them, didn't they? And so our champions are worthy of respect."

I don't like how they're talking about us. I don't like the way Philomena dumps more herbs into her mortar and grinds harder, her nostrils flaring at me like I'm the one who argued with her. Not that I wouldn't be arguing, if I knew what was going on.

"You want our help stopping Dieter," I say. "That's what we want, too."

"It is far more than stopping Dieter, I am afraid," Rochus says. "If he were to breach the Well and harm the Origin Tree, he could eradicate not just the magic witches draw from, but the very connection we have to the goddesses. And so"—he takes a breath—"for the protection of the Well, our goddesses, and magic's very future, you have come to help us."

"By running," Cornelia says. She waves at the table before her. "By taking the coward's way."

My eyes go to the magic supplies again. I spot other things this time—belladonna. Henbane.

A rock lands in my gut, a heavy weight of dread. A bonding potion?

There are other things they might use those herbs for than a bonding potion, though. I try to breathe.

Philomena shakes the pestle at Cornelia. "You would have us fight? We are not warriors!"

"We used to be." Cornelia's voice is low and controlled, a purr of fury, and I drop down one of the steps into the central seating area.

"Warriors," I echo. "They reacted to that word when"—I don't want to mention Otto, not yet—"when it was used, after we arrived."

"That was how we used to walk this world," Cornelia says, her fuming gaze still fixed on Philomena. "Warriors and champions on the outside of the barrier; priests on the inside. The old ways have been forgotten for too long."

"I knew this would turn into yet another fruitless argument with you!" Philomena cries. "Our decision has been made. Champions or no, we are not—"

"Warriors and witches," Cornelia snaps her gaze to mine. I go cold, frozen beneath the intensity in her eyes. "Pairs selected for their prowess, for their heart. Sometimes a mortal and a witch, sometimes two with magic in their blood. They took the bonding potion to connect their power, to share magic, but it was beyond that. Souls mingled. The apex of our powers."

My eyes go fully round. The rock of dread in my belly grows heavier. The ingredients on the table, this mention of the bonding potion—it can't be coincidence.

What do they want us to do?

"Creating bonding potions and performing the ritual used to be an honored calling for us," Cornelia says. She shoots a pointed, accusatory look at Philomena. "Bonded witches could save us more than any other plan. That combination of power could stand against Dieter."

"We agree," Philomena says, but it's biting. "A bonded witch pair will save us."

"Not as you intend," Cornelia snaps. "You would have us hide here, behind our barrier!"

"What do you want us to do?" My question yanks silence over the room.

"We're making the barrier around the Well impassable," Cornelia says. Her bluntness earns a hiss of warning from Philomena and Rochus both, but I'm staring at only her, fixated with horror as her words sink in. "We're blocking off the Well, the Origin Tree, all of it from the rest of the world. And the goddesses brought *you two* because one of us needs to be bonded with a champion to finalize a spell this large."

"What?" I rock forward. "What would that do to magic in this world?"

"The Well's magic will remain inside the barrier," Rochus says. "Wild magic will remain outside."

All the anger I'd been feeling drops alongside my dread, a toxic mix of fear and fury and concern and rage.

The Well and its witches have sat here, letting horrors unimagined pick us off in the real world, and now, when they have all these resources, when they could march out and *stop Dieter*, they would retreat even more. Permanently. As though we are not the same, as though we are not connected by the same magic, the same goddesses. As though this means *nothing*.

"Dieter would still have access to wild magic," I say. "The witch hunts will continue. And those accused now won't be witches at all—you'd leave innocents to suffer and die from prejudices started over us? You abandoned us already to die under the hexenjägers, so you're just lighting the remaining pyres yourselves!"

Philomena rolls her eyes. "I should have known Holda's champion would side with this prideful nonsense. Now is not the time to be haughty—it is the time to preserve what we have left. Your brother"—she cuts me a sharp, accusing look—"has managed to *weaken* our borders with wild magic. Our borders! If he is capable of that, what havoc will he wreak if he enters here?"

"Holda has been trying to get me to use wild magic," I say. No pretense. No softening.

A pause grabs the room.

"How *dare* you!" Philomena barks. "Accusing a *goddess* of trying to access that which is *corrupting*, which is *forbidden*! Do you even know what wild magic is, hm? It is the cast-off remnants created by performing evil deeds. And no goddess, not even one known to be unpredictable, would dare touch such a thing!"

But Cornelia looks back up at me. Her eyes narrow with intrigue. "She did?"

I nod.

"Wild magic is tempting," Rochus intercedes. "It disguises. It manipulates. It swayed your brother, after all."

"I'm starting to think it didn't." I glare at Rochus, who noticeably flinches. "I'm starting to think wild magic has nothing to do with good or evil. Why, if Dieter is weakening the barrier you keep around the Well's magic, has that made our magic in the outside world even *more* powerful? What is the barrier really keeping out—or in?"

Rochus's face goes white. Philomena blubbers behind him, a stain of red rising in her face.

"I think Holda chose my brother as her champion and tried to get him to use wild magic for whatever reason, just like she's done with me," I keep going, "only before she could realize what she'd done, he'd used what she showed him to hurt a lot of people. I'm starting to wonder if wild magic really is as evil as you say—or if my brother was just wicked from the start."

There. All the truths that have begun to sprout within me. All the horrors, all the fears. I rip them out of my soul and lay them at the feet of these strangers.

"I may be Holda's champion, but that doesn't mean I bow to you," I snap. "And that doesn't mean we'll blindly obey your misguided plan. *If* I ever did take a bonding potion"—the words ghost Dieter's face across my mind, his prideful smile, the way he'd extended the bonding potion to me and I'd known, deep in my soul, that he'd bleed me dry—"it certainly won't be with someone who is so eager to only *use me*."

"It's a bastardization of one of our greatest honors," Cornelia says, backing me up. "You have every right to refuse this misguided plan."

Philomena darkens, scowling at me, ignoring Cornelia. "We have the components for the barrier and bonding spells almost completed," she growls. "All we need is one of you to take the bonding potion. We did not bring you here to ask your permission, *champions*. We brought you here because you are necessary, and you *will* help us save our magic, or you will regret ever setting foot in our home."

36

OTTO

Hilde gives me a bottle of her best beer and sits down across from me. Although she has been here in the Black Forest since Fritzi first sent her, several weeks by now, she's worked to make the cottage hers. There are little hints of home all around—a quilt in the same pattern as the one our mother made, the furniture arranged the same way Hilde had it. But the cauldron over the fire is newer, not the same one Mother brewed her beer in. There are no scratches on the table from when Hilde cut the bread directly on the surface. There's no dent in the wall from when I played soldier with the fire poker as a mock sword when I was a child.

It's like home, but it's not.

Hilde smiles at me, guessing at my thoughts. "I couldn't go back."

"I should have," I say. "I should have found a way to preserve your belongings..." With Hilde arrested as a witch, her home was seized by the church. I had been so concerned about where my sister had disappeared to that I had not considered the consequences for the place she was born and had spent her entire life making her own.

Hilde shakes her head. "They were only things."

It breaks my heart, the way everyone has taken from Hilde but never given anything back. My father took her mother. My church took her home. I took her freedom—even if being arrested had been her idea.

"It's nice here," Hilde says. She leans forward. "They've told me I can stay, even if I have no magic of my own. I'm going to, Otto."

"You do realize I had to fight a literal goddess to get here, right?" I ask her. "This is going to make visiting you a bit…difficult."

Hilde shrugs. "Worth it, though."

"Obviously," I say dryly. "I mean, fighting a pantheon is part of an older brother's obligations, no?"

"I simply don't want you to get lazy." Hilde sniffs imperiously. "Honestly, traveling across the entire Empire and then having a fistfight with a god is the least you can do for me."

I throw a rag on the table at her, and she laughs, batting it away. I grin, but when she bends down to pick up the cloth, my smile dies. It hadn't been a fight as she imagined, and the ordeal against Holda still has me reeling. I cannot imagine going through that again, particularly since I suspect the goddesses may find new and different ways to torture me each time.

My cheerful mask is firmly back in place by the time she tosses the rag on the table. I nod to the window. "You have a visitor," I say.

Hilde goes to the door, swinging it open. "Are you here for gossip or beer?" she asks, her voice light.

"Why not both?" A boy with an impish smile strides into the room, long black hair streaming down his back. He's younger than Hilde, I think, but not by many years. Silver threads pierce the tops of his ears, dangling down. There are a few tattoos along his arms, highlighting stringy biceps, but he's not as decorated as the guards that took Fritzi and Liesel to the elder council.

"Meet Caden," Hilde tells me as the boy slings himself into one of the empty chairs at the table. "Brigitta's younger brother." She turns to him. "Where are the others?"

"Others?" I ask.

"Oh, there's always a gang of the young ones wandering around."

"We're not wandering!" Caden protests. "We're *patrolling.*" Hilde shoots him a bemused look, but Caden jerks his thumb at me. "They weren't sure about that one."

"Oh, yes, Otto is very intimidating." Hilde's sarcasm drips.

"Hey!" I say.

But Caden actually *does* look intimidated. He jumps at my voice, and I notice that he selected the chair closest to the door, furthest from me.

"He's a goddess-chosen *warrior*," Caden tells Hilde in a low voice.

"I'm also right here," I mutter. "Word travels fast."

"It does when it comes to warriors," Caden says, for the first time meeting my eyes. He reminds me of Johann and the other younger recruits in the hexenjäger units—desperate to prove his worth, to make something of his name. That sort of passion can drive a boy to become a man, but it can also drive a man to make the wrong choices, throw his loyalty behind the wrong group.

"What does it mean to you," I ask him, "that Holda called me a warrior? I met an entire cadre of warriors when I arrived."

"Brigitta and the others are *guards*, not warriors," Caden insists.

"A warrior is the stuff of legends," Hilde answers. "Goddess-chosen fighters that serve beside a witch. They have a 'destiny.'" She wiggles her fingers at the last word, part respect, part mockery.

"Hilde!" Caden says, eyes widening.

Hilde shoots him an impatient glare I know well. "If he's been chosen as a warrior, he deserves to know."

"He's not a witch."

"I'm also *still* right here," I say.

"I'm not a witch," Hilde argues, ignoring me.

"And my sister shouldn't have told you as much as she has!" Caden snaps.

A blush stains Hilde's cheeks, and she glances at me furtively. That's... unusual for her. "Your sister, Brigitta?" I ask Caden, my eyes on Hilde. Her flush deepens, and she looks away.

Caden nods, unconcerned and unaware that Hilde feels as if her connection with Brigitta is a secret. I stand and cross the room to get another beer as Caden says something to Hilde in a low voice. Little bunches of dried flowers hang in the window—roses, not herbs that would be used for cooking or brewing.

When I sit back down, Caden leans in his chair to look at me. "We haven't had a goddess-chosen warrior in...ages," he says. "But if Holda has picked him—"

"It's what she said," I interject.

"—then this could be the sign we've been looking for."

"Sign?" I ask.

Hilde takes over the explanation. "Some of the witches don't want to stay in the Well any longer."

I blink, confused. Where else would they go? This place is safe.

"We want to fight," Caden says, hammering his hand on the table. "We don't want to run and hide!"

Hilde shoots him a fond smile. It must be difficult for the boy, to have a sister so strong and respected in the guard, everything he wants to be.

"So, why do you stay?" I ask. "If you want to leave the Well, why not do so?" He couldn't just stroll around Trier bedecked as he is and speckled in pagan tattoos, but it wouldn't take much to hide those features. Villages such as the one Fritzi came from would certainly welcome him.

"The council values the Well more than *people*," Hilde answers for him. She emphasizes the last word, and I can tell from her sharp glance that she means non-magical people.

Caden looks down at his hands. "The Well was meant to be a safe place," he says in a low voice. "But it's become a prison."

I stare at him long enough for the look to become uncomfortable. My gaze slides to Hilde, and I know she understands.

Our home was supposed to be a safe place. But our father was a tyrant. We were children—where could we go? Who could help us? I approached the priest in our village church at Bernkastel once. I told him of my father's violence, and the priest merely nodded, praising my father for not sparing the rod against spoiled children. Hilde tried to reach out to a neighbor, but the woman, while sympathetic, told us of the horrors of being homeless, the hardships of a life without a husband and father to protect the family.

I can still remember what the woman had told us as she shooed us from her home: "Don't tell anyone else what you've told me," she said. "At least you have a roof over your head. At least you're safe."

Safe.

Caden is right.

Safety can be a prison.

"There are some among us," Caden says, meeting my eyes, "who hope that your arrival means we aren't going to stay besieged in the Black Forest any longer."

Fritzi and Liesel insisted that the Black Forest was where we needed to be—we have worked for so long, traveled for so far, just to end up in a place that may not be the haven we hoped for.

"There have been rumors..." Caden adds, shooting a significant glance at Hilde. "The council has been hinting that our protection spells aren't enough, not to keep out a witch who's turned against the Well."

Hilde frowns. "The council is too secretive."

"We don't know the full scope of their plans." Caden shrugs. "But if there's a goddess-named warrior here, maybe that will change things..."

He looks at me as if every hope he's ever held is pinned on my chest.

Warrior...

I have worn the label of "hunter" for the past several years. It was a mask to hide behind, but still a mask I wore well. I never truly considered wielding the sword once I left the hexenjägers. Not until a goddess called me a warrior.

Is that what Holda meant? That I would fight for Fritzi and the Well, and that if I fought well enough, there would be no need for a barrier?

Because as surely as it has kept Dieter out—at least for now—it has also kept Caden and the rest of the witches here trapped inside.

37

FRITZI

I gape at Philomena, her cheeks pinking in her righteousness.

Cornelia glares at Philomena too. "You cannot force them to participate," she whispers, aghast.

Rochus, though, is *livid*.

For the first time, his facade cracks, and he takes a surging step toward me. Liesel shrinks, and he notices her with a wince of regret, but the moment he looks up at me again, he's seething.

"You are ignorant of our ways," he says. "Of our customs. So you will be forgiven your outburst and your accusations. If you—"

"I didn't ask for your forgiveness," I cut him off. "I'm only ignorant because of *your* choices. You chose to abandon us. And you are currently choosing to abandon everyone else again. I will tell you right now—this *champion* will not be part of it."

Rochus draws back for a moment. "That is why the goddesses sent us not one witch to possibly take the bonding potion. But two."

Liesel looks up at Rochus. "I won't help you abandon everyone either."

"You are young, child," he tries. "You do not understand—"

He reaches for her. He will *touch* her, and I start to dive forward, but Liesel's lip curls, and all of the candles lit in this room flare brighter in a surge that makes Rochus jerk back.

"I do understand," she tells him in a tone like a void. "I understand more than you. Hiding up here. *Judging us*. I was locked in a closet. Did you see that? I was *tortured*. You had the power to intervene, and you *didn't*."

Rochus swallows, his throat working.

Philomena holds out her arms. "We saw, child. We saw, and we—"

"Abnoba is ashamed of you, I think," Liesel says. "She's ashamed. That's why she sent me and Fritzi. To stop you. We came here for help, to stop Dieter, and you're just hiding. You're not even trying. You're following your own rules so rigidly you've forgotten who those rules are even supposed to protect!"

"It is Abnoba's will that we make the barrier impassable," Rochus counters.

"She told you to do this?" Liesel's face breaks, a flash of agony.

The silence that follows is brief but weighted. Liesel's face is screwed up in concentration, and before I can interject, she shakes her head. "Abnoba is saying she let it be *your* decision. Not hers."

She takes my hand, her palm is scorching hot, the only other testament to her capped rage. It's offset by the way she trembles, the hollow exhaustion on her face, and my heart breaks.

"There are other ways to stop my brother," I tell the room. "*In the morning*. For now, my cousin and I have been traveling for a very long time. I think we could use some food. Maybe a bath. So far we haven't exactly been wowed by forest folk hospitality."

Cornelia steps around the chairs. "Of course. Follow me." She gives a withering look at Rochus and Philomena, and as she crosses to the door, Brigitta rejoins us and swings it open.

The four of us slip back outside, into the now blinding white light of the high, high sky, and as the door shuts behind us, I hear Rochus and Philomena hissing in low whispers at each other.

Something crashes to the floor, shatters.

Cornelia turns to me on the landing of the meeting room. Her eyes are all appraisal, but she bows her head solemnly. "I am sorry. You were ambushed. I told them it was wrong to rush you into it, but they feared exactly what happened—that you would reject their plan."

"And you reject it too."

Cornelia smiles. She motions at the flurry of activity below us, below the tree canopy. The forest folk poised everywhere, furiously working to strengthen the invisible barrier that Dieter has weakened.

"We've waited too long to act," she whispers. "And now, all we have remaining are drastic options that are just as harmful as the problem."

Liesel yawns so big that she staggers into me, barely covering her wide mouth with her hand.

Cornelia smiles down at her. "Come. You have done more than enough for today."

"Have we?" My stomach tugs. Dieter was on our heels in the Black Forest. If he's so close, and the barrier is so weak—

I spoke with confidence about giving us time to rest, but that was only in defense of Liesel; now, what options do we really have?

We came here expecting sanctuary, at the very least. But if all the forest folk have to offer is a cowardly retreat, then this will end just as I've begun to fear it will: with me facing my brother, alone. His terror is my burden to bear.

Otto won't let me do that though. He'll be there with me, his life at risk just the same.

My chest cramps, and I want to collapse right here, on the doorstep of this supposed haven, and sleep away the bad dreams.

Cornelia's smile softens. "Follow me."

Liesel stumbles a step forward, and Brigitta sweeps in, offering to lift her. Liesel agrees instantly, and I watch her eyelids droop shut the moment she's in Brigitta's arms.

We start back down through the trees, and as we near that bridge again, I eye Cornelia. There are about a thousand questions I want to ask.

But she looks at me, her copper hair even more fiery in the daylight, and there's a watery sheen over her pale eyes now.

"Thank you," she tells me. "I know it has not been the smoothest introduction to the reality of our world. I know you lost far too much to get here. But I am grateful for your presence."

"When I leave"—when, not if—"to face Dieter. To stop him. Will you come with me? Back out into the world?"

Part of me growls that it's too big a thing to ask.

But this society should bear some of this with me. That way I am not alone in bearing the blame for what happened to my coven.

So I ask it, and wait.

Cornelia hesitates. Her eyes drift around us, to the bridges and houses and tree-built structures. People move through them, going about their days. Some stop, stare, whisper to each other.

"Yes," she says, half to herself.

My shoulders stiffen. "...Yes?"

"It is what I have been pushing Rochus and Philomena to do. To leave here, to face this head-on. They have been terrified of the threats facing our kind for so long that we have been forbidden from leaving the Well, and that fear has clouded their judgment entirely. So, yes, *champion*," she says with a smile at me, "when you leave here to face your brother, I can tell you that there are plenty who would willingly join you against him. We have been held back too long, and I—" She sucks in a breath. Holds it. "I have allowed us to be held back."

A weight lifts from my chest. A weight and a sigh and a flutter of bottomless grief.

Honestly, the most uplifting part is seeing her take on some of the responsibility. So it isn't just me under this, me feeling the guilt.

"That would upset Rochus and Philomena," I guess.

Cornelia nods.

I swallow, eyeing the path we've taken, the way stretching back to that meeting room.

"Something has been building for a long, long while," Cornelia continues. "Even before my time as priestess. The goddesses have not said, maybe cannot say. But there is—"

"Cannot?"

"They are bound by the rules of their sisters and of the Well. There are limitations, even for goddesses, to keep magic pure."

Frustration itches my throat. "More and more it feels like purity is just a cover for control."

Cornelia's head twitches toward me. I glance up at her, expecting to see derision, scorn—

But she's smiling. "I think we'll get along just fine, Friederike Kirch."

"Fritzi. Please."

"Fritzi." Cornelia's grin pulses wider.

She sweeps her hand out and points to a series of houses built into a lower portion of the tree we're descending. Brigitta is walking toward one, and another woman is there already, wearing a maid's apron, her hair pulled up in a work kerchief. She takes Liesel from Brigitta, and the two quietly slip into a house.

"You can have these rooms to rest. We'll have food sent," Cornelia says. "That man you traveled with—he will stay with his sister?"

My mouth dips open. "I...suppose so." He'll want to spend time with Hilde. But the thought of not sleeping in the same place as him, of not being near him when every moment has been spent in his atmosphere for weeks, knocks hollowly in my chest.

Cornelia nods. "If you like, there is a section of bathing pools at the bottom of this—"

I squeal, startling Cornelia so she jumps and laughs.

"Just down the bottom of this tree," she explains. "Each one is secluded and has the supplies you'll need. I'll have new garments sent to you. And tomorrow morning—" She hesitates. "Tomorrow. I'll come fetch you myself. And we'll talk strategy for facing Dieter."

"Thank you." I clasp her arm. "Truly. Thank you."

Cornelia lays her hand over mine and squeezes my fingers. "No, Fritzi." There's a depth in her eyes that still speaks of things unsaid, decisions yet to be made. How we'll face my brother. How we'll stop him, and the hexenjägers, and fix the injustices weighing us down. But there is hope in her, too, and I dare to let myself believe in it, that maybe I've found an ally in all this uncertainty. "Thank you."

I make sure Liesel is settled—fast asleep in a cozy little bed piled high with quilts—and then I waste no time flying down the stairs to the bathing pools.

It isn't hard to find the area Cornelia mentioned. A narrow river meanders between the trees, with a series of offshoots blocked by thick oak dividers. A few have towels or robes tossed over them, presumably occupied; I walk until I find one that looks free.

It's so quiet here. Even with the hundreds of people I know are high above me in the tree houses, and those I can see peppered around, bespelling the barrier, silence reigns thick and relentless, that swollen quiet of a still glen or a spring morning. Is it part of the magic here?

It's peaceful. Deliriously so.

And that peace feels like a warning.

Dieter is just beyond this border, trying to figure out how to break his way in here to corrupt the Origin Tree with wild magic. Without me bonded to him, without Liesel to give him answers, he'll use more sacrifices to fuel his powers—but is that even right? What *is* wild magic, if it is connected to ours, if Holda wants me to use it?

What do you want? I ask Holda as I work my way to the bathing pool. The oak dividers are massive, folding one alongside another like a series of doors mended together, each pane etched with an image of a tree. *The* tree, I realize, the one from my dreams. The Origin Tree.

There is much I cannot tell you, Fritzi, Holda says. *You heard why.*

What Cornelia said, I guess. *You are kept from telling me by the rules you and your sisters exist by. So all this secrecy is because you're trying to tell me something, but you're prevented from saying it. You tried to get Dieter to figure it out too.*

Yes. No pretense. No delay.

And your sisters, I start, hesitation seizing me, *they disagree with whatever it is you want me to see. They don't want you to tell me. That's why this secret was bound in magic.*

Again, no delay. *Yes.*

I sigh, rubbing my forehead, feeling the dirt there. I can't deal with all of this right now, not now. After a bath, I'll find Otto and talk this through with him. Or just kiss him senseless, and—

I step around the last divider to see a small, dark pool fed by the river, surrounded by smooth stones large enough to lie on, the break in the trees letting sunlight pour in, warming the space.

Otto is in this pool.

Every thought in my brain fuzzes into echoing silence.

He's naked, waist-deep next to the largest river stone, bent forward. His face, hair, and neck are covered in some kind of lathered soap he works from a bar in one hand. A breath, and he plunges beneath the surface, then pops up again, the muscles down his torso and across his back flexing and shining in the water.

I make what has to be the most horrifically unflattering noise that has ever come out of my mouth. Something like a whimper, like a scream, like a strangled giggle.

He whips around, water spraying.

And sees me.

A blush starts in his cheekbones and flows down his neck, beneath the curled brown hair across the contours of his chest, his flexed arms, the smooth *V* that feeds down his hips and deep beneath the water.

I'm staring. And it's been silent between us for so long that Otto smiles slowly, wading a step closer. It raises him up, not quite *that* high, but the level of the water is lapping dangerously low now, and my internal thoughts are an incoherent jumble of panicked shrieking and desperate whines.

"You're all right?" he asks, dragging the soap through the water, leaving a trail of bubbles.

Always the first question. Making sure I'm fine.

The Three save me, he is not helping my chaos.

So I don't fight it.

After everything that's happened. Everything we've been through. We're *here*, safe for the time being, and I will take full advantage of this moment.

Because it might be our last.

Whatever tomorrow brings, it will drag us into stopping the hexenjägers and fighting my brother and his madness. Whether that involves all parts of the Well is yet to be seen. Tomorrow might even involve fighting Rochus and Philomena first.

The immensity of these possibilities and the weight of their outcomes has all of my insides cramping tight, seizing up the way Perchta grabbed ahold of my muscles.

My eyes fall from Otto's, severity descending over me in a wave of startling clarity, and I let my cloak drop to the forest floor behind me.

I kick off my boots, peel off my stockings.

Otto watches me, his eyes getting progressively wider.

"I met with the presumed priest and priestesses of the Well," I tell him matter-of-factly. My fingers shake a little as I undo the laces on my kirtle, and I lift it up, peel it off, leaving only my shift. It's stained up the hem and has been absolutely beaten with use, so I know the material is thin now, nearly translucent, some of it still wet from my earlier falls into the river. "They wanted Liesel and me to help them make the Well's barrier impassable. So Dieter would be given free rein to wreak horrors unchecked with wild magic in the world."

Otto staggers, the water rippling around him. "You—you refused them, I take it?"

"Of course." I drop the kirtle to the ground on a bed of moss by the river stones, and I can see the way Otto's breathing increases. The muscles along his abs clench tighter, and I track a bead of water that drips from his hair down his skin.

"How did they respond?" he asks, his eyes going black as he fights to stay focused on the conversation.

I pause for a moment, toying with the thin material against my stomach, a too-raw sensation from Otto's eyes on me, demanding I feel this, feel him.

"I don't want to talk about them now," I manage, voice quiet.

"What do you want to—"

I pull my shift up, off, and let it fall, standing naked on the bank of the pool.

The blush that stains Otto's cheeks is the single sexiest thing I've ever seen.

His jaw clamps, bulging by his ears, and his grip on the bar of soap tightens so much, so suddenly that it shoots out of his hand and sinks into the water with a heavy *kerplunk*.

I laugh. The effervescence of the giggles takes me, and I cup my face, unable to stop it.

Otto grins, still blushing furiously, but there's intent in his eyes now, something awakened, something feral.

He reaches up for me. "Liebste. Get in this pool."

I plant a hand on my hip and fix him with my most defiant look. But my attention has whittled down to his eyes on my body. His focus here, and there, drifting lower.

"How does it usually go," I start, throat thickening, "when you try to tell me what to do, jäger? Besides, we need another bar of soap."

"I'll find it later, hexe," he growls. The tendons in his neck stretch, restraint fraying, and I'm all but floating with the contrasting needs to obey him and tease him more. "Get. In."

"Are you sure? I think I saw more soap back by the—"

He surges to the edge of the pool, plants one hand on the bank's smooth stones, and heaves himself up to grab for me. My giggles sharpen into a squeal as his powerful grip wraps around my forearm, and he hauls me bodily into the dark silken water of the pool.

38

OTTO

From the moment she let her shift fall to the ground, I have heard nothing but the thundering of my own heartbeat in my ears, a driving pulse of *need* that pounds through my entire body. And now that she is in my arms, her lips upon mine, I am in the eye of the storm. The entire universe is a blur around me, but she—she is the center of my focus, the calm peace at the core, the perfect pinpoint of light my entire body is drawn to.

My hands, slick with water from the pool, draw up her bare back, fingers gliding along her spine, and she arches into me, and that alone nearly has me undone. I let out a shuddering breath.

"Nervous, jäger?" Fritzi asks, and there's an undercurrent of emotion in her voice that I recognize.

"I am certain of what I want," I say. "I want you."

"And I want you." Her words are a whisper, a promise.

"I need you to know, this is not some illicit tryst I ask of you," I say, searching her eyes. "When I say I want you, I mean all of you, for all of time. I do not want your body alone, Friederike; I want *you*, and I give myself to you, all of me that you desire."

Her eyes light up. "There is quite a bit I desire."

My grip at her back tightens, drawing her closer, in a way I know makes her feel what I too desire. Her head tilts up, and I claim her mouth in a deep kiss. The warm water lapping at our waists beckons us deeper. I pull us both back into the darker water as I worship at the altar of her lips.

At its deepest, the water comes just to the top of Fritzi's chest. I turn us, ripples flowing around our bodies, and pin her against the smooth rock wall. Under the water, my fingers tense on her hips, and she leans back, spine curving over the supple edge of the pool.

"Please," she whimpers.

I have spent too long hiding under false personae, checking my emotions, schooling my face. I know that when she gazes up at me now, she sees the full extent of my soul bared before her, the longing desire I cannot—*will not*—hide.

I will never hide who I am from her.

I let one hand drift out of the water, diamond droplets falling over her body. I trace her skin with my touch, finger lightly caressing her pale neck, down, between her breasts, lower, back under the water, lower.

I have wanted this—*her*—for too long not to savor every moment, every taste. I bend over her body, my tongue tracing the shell of her ear. I relish the way she writhes at my touch, the pleading moans that I pull from her pink lips. It is torture for me to resist, to wait, to draw this out, but it's the sweetest torture I have ever known.

"Otto," Fritzi groans, and I hear the command in her voice, the impatience as she bucks against my hand, her body demanding more from me. I cannot bite back the chuckle rising in my throat. A part of me loves the way she wants me as much as I want her. The much larger part of me is just as insatiably starving.

I float back in the water, just a little. She tries to hold me closer with her legs, but I let the water work for me, disentangling myself and letting her body float before me.

A feast I intend to savor.

Her hips lift from the water as I draw her core to my tongue, warm and sweet. The water rocks with the movement we create, gentle waves lapping up and darkening her hair. She sinks down, her shoulders kissing the surface of the pool as she lets herself fully unwind under the ministrations of my lips.

My hands slick over her wet body, floating along her curves, pressing against the muscles that tighten as she begs for more, more.

And more is exactly what I intend to give her.

I surge forward in the water, framing her body with my hands as I claim her mouth, my kiss probing. She meets me stroke for stroke, her arms gliding around my neck so that she can pull her body up through the water, tight against mine. Fritzi dips her head down, licking my jaw, nibbling my skin, and now I'm the one groaning, begging for more.

"You want more, jäger?" she whispers. "Then take it."

Under the water, my hands clench around her waist, my body finding hers, driving home. The coil of desire that wraps around us both tightens, tightens, and I can say only her name, over and over, a prayer I will never stop reciting.

After, we find big, fluffy blankets, folded up and warm by the entrance to the bathing pool, as well as clothing—a serviceable but basic tunic for me, and a new shift with a green split-hem gown for Fritzi, trimmed in gold embroidery. We make a little nest along the smooth, shaded stones on the far end of the pool, steam wafting over the warm waters.

"At least now you have something interesting to talk about in your next confession," Fritzi murmurs, giggling.

"Confession is for sins," I say, winding my fingers through her wet hair.

"That felt pretty sinful to me," Fritzi says in a teasing voice.

"No," I say firmly. "Love is *never* a sin."

Fritzi leans on her elbows, looking up at me. "You really believe that," she says wonderingly.

"Of course."

"But—"

"No buts. No corollaries or exceptions. Love is not a sin. It never has been, and it never will be. Anyone who tries to twist that simple truth is the one who sins."

She settles back down, tucking her head into my chest, idly running her fingers over the hem of my tunic in a way that makes me contemplate just how many more alleged sins I'd like to follow through with tonight.

"The thing I keep thinking about—" she starts, her voice slow, musing.

"Is the way we should take off these clothes and have another bath together?"

She bats at me playfully, but when she looks up at me, I see true concern in her eyes. I regret the way I tried to distract her. "What is it?" I ask.

"There's something here that's not right. In the Well, I mean, with the forest folk." Her voice drops, as if she's afraid we'll be overheard. "They said that witches were once bonded. Not just that they worked together, but that they were united."

I run my fingers through her hair, tucking a stray lock behind her ear.

I remember then the way she spoke of such a magical bonding potion when we were still unsure of each other, a lifetime ago. It was a powerful potion, one that would act as a channel between the witch and the person bonded to her.

"When you say, 'Bonded,'" I start.

"Using the potion I told you about," Fritzi says, answering my question before I can finish it. "They want either Liesel or me to bond with one of them, and then use our powers combined to sever the Well's magic from this world."

She had mentioned that before, although not the method. A protectiveness dangerously close to possessiveness surges inside me at the thought of Fritzi bonding with anyone else, but I push it away. One of the first things she told me about that potion was that it had to be taken willingly or it would not work, and I will never step in front of any choice Fritzi wants to make about her body or her power.

But I can tell she does not choose such a path.

"There seem to be some here who would rather fight than flee," I say. "Who want to see magic regulated but not eviscerated from the world beyond the barrier."

Hope flashes in Fritzi's eyes. "The world has sacrificed enough because of Dieter. Magic isn't the corrupting force. It's just the tool, one that can be used in different ways..."

I try to smooth the lines between Fritzi's brows, pinched together in worry, but there's no use. I don't fully understand magic the way she does, and I do not know the right questions to ask to help her find the answers she seeks. So I hold her, and I hope that will be enough.

After several long minutes, she relaxes into my body. Her breathing evens, and I almost think she's fallen asleep when suddenly she shoots up with a startled cry.

"Fritzi?" I ask.

Her eyes unfocus, looking at something in the distance, something I cannot see even when I crane my head around. Her face drains of color, her mouth going slack in horror as she stands.

"Fritzi?" I ask again, reaching for her.

"Dieter," she gasps, the word a strangled whisper of true terror.

I leap up, my hand going to my waist—useless; I'm not wearing my sword. I spin around, searching the shadows, but I don't see whatever she does. Fritzi walks forward, as if entranced, her hands extended, reaching for something I cannot see—

"Fritzi!" I yell, but it's as if she cannot hear me.

39

FRITZI

"Fritzichen!"

Dieter's voice rings through my skull, but it's...younger. It's the Dieter from my memories, from my childhood, and as I waver to my feet, I blink, and the pool glade vanishes and is replaced with a different forest—

I'd know the trees around Birresborn anywhere.

Strong oaks and thin birches, their steady trunks cutting gray columns of shade against the burning sun.

My head rings with the wrongness of this place. I shouldn't be here. I was—I was somewhere else. *With* someone else. I'm not—

It's summer.

It's summer, and I'm hiding by a fallen log, hands smashed to my mouth to stifle my giggles. Every quiver of my tiny body trudges up the scent of the forest floor beneath me—musty crushed mushrooms, earthy moss, damp dirt.

"Fritzichen!" my brother calls again.

He'll never find me here. He always overlooks this rotting log. He'll never—

A noise pierces the air. Like a scream, quick and jarring and high-pitched.

"Fritz—*Fritzi!* Come quickly!"

I'm on my feet in an instant, my airy, summer-light kirtle swaying around me, smeared with dirt stains, pockets stuffed with fragrant mint leaves from a plant I'd found a few paces away.

I spin in a circle, eyes stealing through the trees, the columns of shade and light, shade and light.

"Fritzi! Hurry!"

My body takes off like a shot, yanked toward him, *I'm coming, Dieter, I'm—*

I skid down the side of a hill, round a thick oak, and see my brother kneeling on the ground next to—to something.

My brain doesn't see it at first. It's a mound of dirt, bits of fuzzy mold.

Only that isn't mold.

It's fur.

It's a cat. One of Mama's cats. Something jagged has torn right down the side of her body, spilling dark blood across her orange fur.

I drop to my knees across from Dieter. "Oh, no. Oh *no*. It's Kleines Mädchen! Mama will be so sad!"

The tiny cat's stomach quakes still, lungs greedily dragging at a few last breaths. Her front paws twitch in futile kicks at the air.

"She's alive!" I start to stand. "Mama can save her—"

Dieter grabs my wrist.

I'm grounded in this moment. In staring into my brother's eyes.

Nothing else exists.

Just him. Those swirling, vicious blue pools that seize every spark of fire in my body and hold me captive as Mama's newest kitten lets out a mournful howl between us.

"It's too late for Kleines Mädchen, Fritzi," Dieter tells me. And he grins.

"No, it's not! Mama can—"

Dieter raises his other hand. He's holding a knife.

Why does he have that? What's he going to do?

I pull against his grip. "Dieter! Let me *go*! I have to tell Mama!"

"Mama, Mama," Dieter singsongs. "Mama! Hm. I don't think she can hear us."

He lifts the knife over the kitten's head.

And brings it down in a single, powerful swoop.

The blade crunches into the cat's skull, bone popping, the dirt beneath sucking the knife in with a wet plop. But the noise that comes out of the kitten's mouth, a warbling squawk—it palpitates in my ears, echoes on every heartbeat.

I scream. Dieter's grip on me clamps tighter, his knuckles vividly white, the veins in his neck bulging.

He cuts his empty eyes up to me, grinning.

"I needed to lure you out, didn't I, Fritzichen?" he says, teeth as white as his knuckles. "That's all I needed to do. Lure you out. And now I've won our game."

The Birresborn forest wavers, trembling at the edges of my vision, a vision quickly blurred by tears. I blink, blink, trying to clear my sight, but the fog of everything coalesces around me, and when I manage to see again, Dieter and I are standing.

Reality crashes through me, and I feel every bit of terror that the memory had repressed—it wasn't real, just a memory; but it *had* been real, and we're back in the pool glade in the Well now, I'm *safe* now—

Only Dieter isn't here. He's a dream still, a figment of memory.

He has to be.

My lungs ache from breathing so fast, that tight pinch in the back of my throat like I've been sobbing.

How did I forget that memory? But I feel it, deep in my mind, extracted from where I'd buried it under fear that hardened into scar tissue. Survival, denial, because he was my brother, he was my brother, and I loved him.

Dieter is in front of me now, somehow, holding his hand out to me. Beckoning. An apparition and a dream and—he isn't real, this isn't *real*—

The barrier is thinning. How many people has he killed to beat it back since we parted ways?

Does he even really need to do that to harness wild magic?

Does he realize how much we've all been lied to?

Distantly, I hear Otto shouting for me. I feel his hands on my arms, prying at me, but I'm staring at my brother, part of my brain still mired in memory and dreams.

Dieter beams, that smile I used to think was all confidence. Now, I see the holes in his facade, the madness he hides behind a veil of certainty.

"I will stop you," I tell him, pushing the words against the sourness of my shaking disgust and horror. "I don't want to save you. Not after everything you've done."

His smile widens. He's all teeth and twistedness, all horror and poise.

"You can't be here," I say, my voice rising. His silence is unnerving. "You can't get past the Well's barrier. Can you? Not entirely."

I don't know how to get out of this spell he's pulled me into. I'm frozen there watching him, this echo of him, that cruel smile, those callous eyes.

Dieter's smile bends, showing some of that cruelty unrestrained.

"Oh, Fritzichen. You misunderstand. I don't need to get in yet—I just need to get you *out*."

My fear starts to crack, panic slithering up through me, and I try to buck backward, to Otto. I strain, pulling, but this spell has me, whatever he's done. I stepped into it somehow, a snare, a rope tightening around my body and shackling me to him.

"Just like Kleines Mädchen," he coos. "I only need to lure you to me."

He snaps his hand shut.

I hear the crunch of the skull. The whimper of the cat.

I hear Otto screaming for me, frantic, one final claw of his fingers on my arm.

And then the whole world shatters into darkness.

40

OTTO

One minute, I'm holding her.

The next, she's gone.

I stare down at my hands, now empty, my mind stuttering over the concept of how a person can simply disappear.

"Fritzi," I whisper, my entire being bereft at the loss of her. I look up, the pool now eerily quiet and empty.

"*Help!*" I scream, panic raising my voice to a fever pitch. "*Help!*"

The bath was private, but in moments, guards come rushing in, led by Brigitta. They have weapons already in hand—some with blades, some with vials of potions or spells weaving through their fingers. Brigitta stops short when she sees me alone.

"Fritzi was here," I say urgently.

A look of confusion flashes across the guard's face.

"Fritzi was *here*," I repeat, "and then she *disappeared*."

Gasps filter through the crowd of guards, but Brigitta holds her hand up, demanding silence. "What do you mean?"

"She said Dieter's name, as if she saw him, but there was no one else around. And then she stood up, and I reached for her, and..." My hands open and close in the empty air. "She was *gone.*"

"Breach!" one of the guards shouts. I hear footsteps on the wooden walkway beyond the door, more yelling. "The wall has been breached!"

Brigitta turns to a man with copper hair who stands at attention beside her. "Summon the council," she orders. She sends more guards elsewhere, to check the perimeter, to inspect the trees, but that is useless.

Dieter hadn't been *here*. He had taken Fritzi by some foul magic.

"Come with me," Brigitta says, motioning for me to follow her. My heartbeat thunders in my ears, numbing my other senses, forcing me to replay the image of Fritzi fading from my grasp over and over in my mind.

As we walk higher into the trees, I pause, shaking my head. "Where are you taking me?"

"The council needs to be informed of this," Brigitta says.

I shake my head more forcefully. "*Liesel* needs to be informed."

"The council are the highest officials in the Well."

"And Liesel is not only a powerful witch with a direct connection to a goddess, she's also Fritzi's cousin." *And Dieter's cousin*, I think but don't say. "I need to go to her. First."

Brigitta hesitates.

"We don't have time for this," I say in a low voice.

She nods tightly and leads me in a different direction, but then grabs one of her guards and orders him to bring the council to the champion's room. Good. From the way Fritzi spoke of them, it will do this council well to be reminded that while they serve the gods, they are not themselves gods.

In moments, Brigitta knocks at a door. When Liesel doesn't answer, I push past Brigitta and open the door. "Liesel," I call.

It's a mark of how tired she is that she doesn't immediately get up.

The room can only be described as cozy, with fresh flowers spilling out of every jar and window, filling the room with a sweet, warm scent. Flickering candles burn low, and dozens of colored glass balls in various sizes hang from the ceiling. At a word from Brigitta, the glass balls light up, filling the room with a magical glow.

"What's going on?" Liesel asks sleepily from the bed.

I drop to my knees in front of her. "Dieter has Fritzi."

The girl's instantly awake, shooting up in the bed. She swings her legs over the side and rushes to the closest table, wrapping her hand around the candle flame as if it were merely a flower to pluck from a garden. She turns her palm over, the flame burning in her open hand, and stares deeply into the fire.

Behind me, I hear the arrival of more people—judging from the gold embroidery and haughty expressions, these must be the priest and priestesses Fritzi spoke of. They draw up short, watching Liesel perform her magic, but one of them—the youngest, a woman—pushes the others inside and closes the door so that we're alone.

"She's in Baden-Baden," Liesel says with authority. "But there's a... cloud around her. My powers are blocked." She grips her hand into a fist, and through the smoke rising between her fingers, she meets my eyes. "It's Dieter."

The priest behind me sucks in a breath. "He should not have been able to breach the protection barriers around the Well."

"I'm not sure he did," I say. "I didn't see him—only Fritzi did. I don't think he was actually here; I think he just found a way to pull Fritzi out."

"Still," the priest says. "It's a bad sign. His magic, at least, crossed the barriers."

He continues talking, and the priestesses chime in, conferring with each other about what this means for the Well. But my eyes have not left Liesel. I see the fear blooming inside her, the paralyzing, horrifying terror.

"We will get her back," I vow to her.

"I don't think she understood before," Liesel says, her voice a whisper, only for me. "Dieter is my cousin and her brother, but...there's something wrong with him. It's not the wild magic. I think he's just...wrong." Her eyes blur with tears. "He's going to hurt her," she tells me, carefully enunciating each word, as if trying to make me realize the depths of his depravity.

"I won't let him," I say, my voice cracking. This is the second time someone I love has been whisked away before my eyes, but I didn't understand fully what magic was when Hilde went away, and by the time I did comprehend, I knew Fritzi well enough to trust Hilde was safe. Now, though?

Now I *know* Fritzi is *not* safe.

I know that Dieter will not kill her outright. I know he will torture her. I am not there to protect her. I am not there to save her. What use is a goddess calling me a warrior if I cannot even fight? My breath comes out in a shuddering release, and for a second, I let the fears spooling inside me tighten around my mind, and I can hear nothing but Fritzi screaming, feel nothing but the hollow knowledge of my own uselessness.

And then I look at Liesel. I see her swallow down her fear, her tears. "What do we do next?"

Liesel meant the question for just me, but the others hear it. "Liesel, it's up to you now," the priest says.

"Rochus!" the youngest priestess says, abashed.

Rochus ignores her. He takes a step closer to Liesel, his hands out, but the girl shrinks into me, and I wrap my arms around her, glaring up at him. The priest squats down, eye level with her, ignoring me.

"Liesel, you need to bond with me. Champion and warrior, as the goddesses designed our people to work together."

"And together, we will go to Baden-Baden and save Fritzi?" Liesel asks.

He hesitates.

He *hesitates*, and I know at that moment he intends to leave Fritzi to her brother's devices. To leave her to die.

My arms tighten around Liesel, but that child has seen the way adults lie and manipulate, and she knows what Rochus means.

"You still want to run," she says coldly.

"We have to—" Rochus starts.

"What kind of warrior could you possibly be?" I snarl, and for the first time, the man looks directly at me. "Neither my god nor yours would choose a coward as a warrior."

"I'm not a coward for trying to protect my people! For trying to protect *magic!*"

A million curses rise to my mind, but before I can say a single one, Liesel speaks, her voice soft but certain. "You are," she says, and Rochus reels back as if he'd been punched.

"Well, I'm not." The youngest priestess speaks loudly, drawing attention to her. "Cornelia," she says by way of introduction, nodding at me. "I don't need my goddesses to tell me the right thing to do. Brigitta, summon every guard willing to become a *true* warrior. We do not patrol tonight. We go to war."

"The council does not approve of this action!" the other priestess snarls, blocking the door as Brigitta moves toward it.

"If the goddesses don't want us to fulfill our destinies," Cornelia growls, "then they should not have given us a destiny in the first place."

"Do you intend to fight the very gods you serve?" Rochus asks, eyes wide.

"Yes," Cornelia says emphatically.

"Me too," Liesel says, her voice still calm. "And if you don't get out of the way, Philomena, I'll just set this entire place on fire."

Sputtering, the priestess finally moves aside. She and Rochus storm out, Brigitta rushing past them, a horn to her lips, sounding an alarm.

Alone now, Cornelia turns to us. "I can reasonably count on fifty, maybe a hundred to join us tonight," she says.

"I don't think that will be enough," Liesel says.

I didn't get a full glimpse of the number of hexenjäger troops Dieter brought with him from Trier, but he has enough to turn this into a bloody battle. Even alone, however, Dieter is more powerful than I can comprehend.

"We need something that can take him down," I mutter.

Neither of the others heard me. Cornelia is focused entirely on Liesel, speaking directly to her. "The bonding potion is the most effective way to sever the Well from this world, but there are other ways. Messier ways. I don't trust Rochus not to try them if the battle fails."

"He would rather break the Well than let Dieter have it," Liesel says.

"Perhaps."

"That bonding potion you keep talking about," I say, loud enough to make the others listen. "That's what we need."

Cornelia looks confused.

"The goddess Holda called me a warrior, and not just any warrior, but *Fritzi's* warrior. I take the potion with her, and together we take down Dieter." I know this is the way it has to be. I cannot let Fritzi be in a position to kill her own brother; that would break her. But if I have some of her power, I can do it.

Cornelia, however, is shaking her head slowly. "You don't understand the danger of this potion."

"Fritzi warned me about it."

"It's a highly complicated spell. It's meant to bond, yes, but if it fails, a witch would lose all connection to magic entirely. One or both of you could die."

"Liesel can—" I start, but she interrupts me.

"I don't know that spell."

"But you do," I say, turning to Cornelia. "Fritzi told me you were making the potion already."

"Yes, but it's not complete. And I cannot get it now. Rochus and Philomena will stop us."

I squeeze my eyes shut, concentrating on everything that Fritzi had told me about the bonding potion. "A beer base," I say. "My sister can give us that."

"I could bring the last ingredients needed," Cornelia says doubtfully. "But this plan seems unwise. I am not a potion-maker; Philomena is, but she would never aid us."

"A last resort," I promise her, a new idea forming in my mind. "But when it comes to Dieter, we need every weapon we can get. If all else fails..."

Reluctantly, Cornelia nods. If this potion fails, it may kill me or kill Fritzi's magic, but everyone in the room knows there are worse things than death when it comes to Dieter.

Every second counts. Liesel and I rush from her room down to the forest floor, and I lead her to Hilde's cottage. Cornelia heads in a different direction to ensure the troops are ready and to procure the needed ingredients.

"That was a long bath," Hilde says, swinging open the door. "I heard the horns—what's going on?"

Liesel and I charge inside. "I need your beer," I say.

"Yes, let's get drunk when the alarms are sounding," Hilde says, staring at me flatly.

"It's for a potion," Liesel says. Hilde visibly melts in front of Liesel; the girl looks angelic, even when awoken from sleep in the middle of an emergency.

"What do you need?" Hilde asks.

I go over to her fireplace, looking at the murky liquid bubbling in the cauldron over the low heat.

Another knock on the door. Hilde opens it, and Cornelia steps inside. "Priestess!" Hilde says, shocked.

"I've brought the rest." Cornelia holds out a small basket, and Hilde looks inside.

"This is poison!" she gasps.

I take the basket from Cornelia and start adding in herbs, among them belladonna and henbane.

"Otto, what is this? No one can drink this now!"

Cornelia touches Hilde's elbow. "It will not be poison when it's finished." A dark look crosses her face. "Although I confess to not fully understanding your intent with this, Otto."

The door opens a third time, and Hilde whirls around. "What now?"

"Just me." Brigitta steps inside. Her eyes linger on Hilde, but she quickly turns to the priestess. "We're ready."

"The potion is not," Cornelia says. "This must be done with care." She casts a dubious look at the cauldron, and I can tell she's on the brink of telling me not to even bother trying this.

Damn it all. Every second counts, and while this potion may be key...

Brigitta moves closer to Hilde, quickly explaining the situation.

"This is too rushed," Cornelia adds, doubt lingering in her voice. "It's too dangerous. We need to go—*now*—and—"

"Liesel, help me bottle this," I say.

Liesel reaches for the ladle as Hilde hands me an empty bottle.

"Otto, a potion is not merely a mixture of ingredients. The spell must be spoken, and—" Cornelia starts.

I ignore the rest of her protests as I pour the brew through a funnel into Hilde's bottle. The hot liquid burns my hands, but I stow it in a pouch Hilde offers.

I tie the bag securely closed and glance up and see Liesel watching me. I have come to know the girl as well as I know my sister, and I recognize the look in her eyes, the slow nod of approval.

I straighten and look at Cornelia, who is still protesting this plan. "Fritzi knows the spell," I say. "I spoke to her about it before, in Trier. I *know* she knows the spell. All you have to do is get me to her, and she can complete the potion. We will be bonded, and together, we will have enough power to kill Dieter."

The bag weighs heavily on my shoulder, but I do not flinch as I meet Cornelia's eyes. Liesel steps a little closer to me, slipping her hand into mine.

"Potions do *not* work like that," Cornelia says in a low voice, but there is doubt.

"Magic isn't working the way it should," I remind her, pointing to Hilde, who was spirited away here in an explosion of power that belied Fritzi's intent. "It's worth it to try."

"We have to go," Brigitta says. She moves closer to Cornelia. "Let him have hope, even if it is false." Her voice is a low whisper; she did not intend for me to hear, so I pretend that I didn't.

I don't know why I don't tell them what my real plan is. I just keep thinking of the way Fritzi was furious at the council, the way her expectations for the haven of the Well, the safety of the goddesses, were belied.

Magic is not always the only answer, even if none of these witches can see it.

Hilde whips her head around to me, concern flashing on her face. I give her a silent look. In a house like our father's, we both learned to communicate without words. She frowns but accepts the way I shake my head, telling her: *Don't worry. I know what I'm doing.*

Cornelia sighs, defeated, then turns and leaves Hilde's cottage with a swish of her robes.

"Be safe," Hilde tells me, wrapping me in a hug made awkward by the way Liesel refuses to relinquish my hand. My sister turns to Brigitta. "And you too. Be safe." She stands on her tiptoes to give her a kiss. As they break apart, my sister shoots me a questioning look, and I grin back at her, thrilled to see her so in love.

I crouch in front of Liesel. "You stay with my sister. You can trust her. I will bring Fritzi back to you."

Liesel nods. I know she wants to come with us, but she is still a child. And I cannot live with the idea of allowing her to fight.

"And you bring Otto back to me," Hilde murmurs to Brigitta. The other woman chuckles, her lips on Hilde's neck, but Hilde pulls back, stands on her tiptoes, and whispers urgently into her lover's ear. Brigitta's eyes snap to me, so I have little doubt my sister was speaking about me.

As soon as Brigitta and I exit the cottage, I turn to her. "How are we going to get from here back to Baden-Baden in time?" I ask, a new worry twisting inside me.

"Do not fear," Brigitta says, her lips carving into a smile. "Transportation is the least of our worries."

41

FRITZI

Darkness shatters like I broke the surface of a lake. I gasp, chest screaming and arms aching, eyes flaring open in a wild panic.

"Shh, Fritzichen. Shh. You've been out for quite a while."

A hand pats my cheek. My sight is blurry, and I will it to clear, wild terror making every rational thought scatter. I am instinct only—I need to see. I need to see where I am.

My eyes focus.

Dieter is in front of me, reaching above us. I realize, then, that my hands are overhead too.

An iron lock clicks, and he steps back to survey his work. My wrists are in manacles fixed to chains that hang from the thick wooden beam of the ceiling, dangling me in the air.

Barbed terror burrows into my chest, and I throw my eyes around the room, desperate to focus, to *breathe.*

A bedroom stretches around us, something opulent and ornate. A wide canopied bed towers in front of me, a roaring fireplace to my left, with a table to my right holding a steaming porcelain cup of tea and a tray of delicate springerle cookies by a window that shows buildings, houses, things I think I recognize—

He has not taken you far, says Holda. *Fritzi, I'm so sorry. They're coming to help you. I promise, they're coming.*

My head throbs, and I dip my chin to my chest, arms stretching painfully over me, the tips of my toes barely brushing the floor enough for me to keep weight off my wrists. I'm barefoot. Barefoot because I'd just been in the bathing pool with Otto.

A tear leaks down my cheek, and my eyes snap shut.

How long until they get here? I ask Holda.

She doesn't respond.

"Tut-tut now, meine Schwester; no more sleeping." Dieter pats my cheek again, harder. "We have things to do before tonight."

I try to question him. To speak, in any way.

But I feel something in my mouth. Metallic, hard, like a bit on a horse's bridle.

I prod it with my tongue only to feel that it encases my tongue, pulling it out grotesquely so I can't speak, can only moan in a panicked rush as my gaze flies to my brother.

"I have to give credit where it is due—humans are ingenious when it comes to developing ways to stretch the body to its limits." Dieter tugs on a bar that runs along my jaw, and I feel how the whole thing loops around my head, yanking my tongue out. "They developed this to keep a witch's tongue from wagging during interrogations. Which seems pointless, doesn't it? How can you confess your sins to their most holy of men if you are as good as muzzled? But it isn't about confessing, we both know. All they want from witches is silence."

He uses his finger hooked through the bar to lean in closer, tugging my face to his, the heat of his breath scorching and vile. "But with this, you won't be able to cast any spells, will you? Go ahead and try. Mumble for your goddess."

I do try. It comes out garbled, a desperate, choppy churn of noise.

Dieter beams and releases me, my body rocking in the air. He turns, grabs something from a chair by the table, and faces me again, holding it up triumphantly.

The bottle he'd brought to Birresborn. The bonding potion he'd wanted me to take, to connect my magic with his.

"This is your last chance," he tells me sweetly. "If you agree to take this bonding potion, all this stops. Your mouth open like that, all *distended*—you can drink this potion easily. That's all you need do, sister. Nod—will you take it?"

He waits. He has to. The magic will not work unless I take the potion willingly. It's part of the spell—one person brews the potion, the other drinks it, and only then, with that level of trust, will the bonding spell work.

But if I become bonded to Dieter, he will drain magic from me, use me until I am nothing left but a shell of a person, refilling my body with power like his own personal store of magic.

Panic dizzies me so powerfully that I feel myself on the edge of passing out again, blurred vision palpitating, clouds of fog encroaching—

Friederike! Holda shouts, her voice ripping through my head. *Please—I know I have misled you. But please, you have to sever from the Well. Accept wild magic. Now, please—save yourself!*

How? I whimper. *How? I can't speak. I can't do anything.*

Tears burn my cheeks. I fight through them, fight for a squirming shred of strength, and glare at Dieter.

I shake my head.

His deranged hope falls. Crashes off his face in a tight glare. "Friederike. I do not think you understand what is at stake."

I hold my glare on his eyes. Maybe it's for the best that I can't speak; at least this way, I can feign resolve.

Inside, I'm falling apart.

Dieter's lips purse.

In a flash, he hurls the bonding potion into the fire. The bottle shatters, flames eating up the potion in a sudden gust of heat and intensity, and I flinch helplessly, manacles clanking.

Dieter straightens his tunic, smooths his blond hair back. "You chose this path, Fritzichen. Remember that. We did not have to do things this way. *You chose this.*" Then he grins.

He grins, and it pierces my stomach with cold.

"I have other ways of getting your magic," he tells me. "The bonding potion was merely the least...messy. But." He lunges toward me, hand clamping to my jaw, holding me close as he exhales down into my face. "We are fated, you and I. Did the voice not tell you? It told me. The great vision for us. You and I, champion and warrior, warrior and champion, bound together to change the world."

I go slack. *Holda? Is he—*

I'm so sorry, Fritzi. I told him many things before I realized the lengths he would go to. This—this is not what I intended. I had dreams of the greatness the two of you could *achieve, but he is—*

You didn't tell me. I'd be sobbing if I could. As it is, I choke down cries, tears dripping over Dieter's fingers on my jaw, and I slam my eyes shut. *You didn't warn me!*

There is silence. Heavy with guilt. *I am so sorry, Fritzi—*

"Oh, no, no, no, Fritzi! I told you—stay awake." Dieter turns away, toward the fireplace. "We have things to do. More now that you have chosen the harder path. Don't make me regret keeping you all to myself."

He crouches by the fireplace, his back to me, and I use this moment to look up at the manacles. They're locked tight, my hands white with strain, and I'm not hanging close enough to anything to try to kick at a weapon or break free.

Sweat beads along my skin, trickles down my spine, cold and hot all at once.

"My hexenjägers know it was you and the kapitän who made fools of them," Dieter says casually. He twists something in the fireplace and sparks rear up. "They'd love nothing more than to exact revenge on you, my pretty sister. Oh, how they cheered when I told them you'd been captured!" He laughs, something high and grating. "They do not realize the twenty Baden-Baden citizens I had them burn are the reason you were *captured*, but then again, they have not realized the truth in any of this."

He burned twenty people to get to me.

Betrayal gnaws in my gut, but I can't wallow in it now. I have to act. I have so little on my side; I can't afford to alienate Holda.

He didn't need to burn anyone, I say to her. *Did he? Wild magic doesn't need sacrifices or evil to use it. That's what you wanted him to see, what you want me to see.*

One of the things, yes, she says. *Please, Fritzi. You still can say the spell. You're talking to me, aren't you? Please. I cannot help you more than this. With wild magic, you will not need to adhere to the rules of the Well. You can fight back.*

Metal clanks from the fireplace, and I go rigid, hating the weak whimper that slips out of my throat, the only noise I can make.

Dieter stands. "If I was at all certain that my men would not kill you in their drive for vengeance, you would be at their mercy right now.

Morale and all—humans are so much easier to manipulate when they are high on bloodlust! So remember that, meine Schwester." He turns that beaming grin at me over his shoulder. "Baden-Baden is positively *crawling* with hexenjägers. And this time, there are no aqueducts to sneak through, no honorable kapitäns to save you. I doubt very much you will be able to seduce any of my men now—I promised that they would get to hear you scream and shortly see you burn, and they are *manic* for it."

He faces me and lifts the object in his hands.

I thrash against the manacles, tears leaking down my face, pathetic garbled moans cracking from my throat.

I need to say the spell to sever myself from the Well. I need wild magic.

But my mind is blank with terror as he closes the space between us and cups my cheek around the horrific gag, shushing my sobs, all the while holding a long iron bar out to the side.

At the top of it, glowing orange from the heat, is a brand. One I've seen before, singed into the chests of witches.

He twists it, bending it through the air like it isn't scalding hot and dangerous, and I see the letter *D,* the size of his palm, the iron thick in artful curls.

D for *dämon*.

The letter that he branded Mama with.

He follows my gaze to it and back. "The bonding potion would have let me access your power far more easily—but, well, you did say *no.* But this! See, this is one of the things I'd hoped you'd come to realize. Sigils are not something *holy*, something the goddesses designed for us. We *give* them their power. Sigils can be anything, anything at all, that we *choose* to give power to. And this sigil? This one makes you mine."

His?

It rocks through me. How could I have been shortsighted, so quick to believe he'd do something for the church instead of himself?

Not *D* for *demon.*

For *Dieter.*

For *him.*

He's been swinging the brand the whole time. Swinging it, swinging it, each pass of the metal through the air making it flare from orange to red to yellow—

Without warning, he straightens the brand and shoves it against my stomach, straight over the thin bodice of my gown.

Pain is an explosion behind my eyelids, a brilliant, searing burst of lightning and ignition. The expanse of it is too inconceivable to be felt immediately, and it isn't until he rips the brand away, tearing singed flesh, that I scream.

That noise is garbled, mutilated by the tongue gag, a shrill, careening wail.

"Shush now, Fritzichen. Mama didn't cry when she got her mark."

I look down, the need to retch sending sour bile up my throat. And I see the mangled flesh, burnt and blackened, bits of it now orange and glowing on its own, and I gag, hard.

Dieter lays his hand over the wound. "Shh, shh," he coos, and a wave of magic pulses into me from his palm.

The pain vanishes. Immediately.

No balms or potions. Just my brother, muttering slightly under his breath.

He pulls his hand back, and my stomach is healed. My gown lies gaping and scorched, but the brand is gone.

The sheer might of wild magic stuns me, even here, even now. He healed such a wound *himself*. None of our laws used, none of our rules followed. Just *him*.

I gasp, tears streaming down my cheeks, and when my eyes find my brother's face, he's giddy.

"This didn't work on little Liesel," he says to my stomach. He strokes a finger down the healed flesh, and I shudder. "The brand, I mean. So resistant to fire, that one. But you and I will have some fun with this, won't we? Some scars don't ever heal. And these scars connect us, Fritzichen."

He shoves the brand against my stomach again.

My scream this time is a crooning shriek, and I flail on the chains, trying to get away, trying to escape him. The heat and the pressure of the iron and the *smell*; I thought I had known every facet of how burning could smell, but this is a phantom of its own, a snarl of laughter that grabs me by the throat and sneers, *You thought you knew suffering? This is where it is born.*

He removes the brand, lays his hand over the spot, heals it again.

He was meant to be our village's healer, he was meant to help us—

"I wanted you to listen to the voice too." Dieter rests the length of the brand on his shoulder and props his other arm on a nearby chair so he can bend closer to me, catching my gaze through surges of tears. "I wanted you to sever from the Well and give into wild magic like I did so you would know how deep the lies run. Wild magic is not something to be feared, and the Origin Tree's magic is not the most powerful. We have been lied to, forced to grab up scraps so we can stay in their control. Mama, the Elders, our coven, the Well—all of it is a festering hive of deception bent on keeping us in line, and I will break it open. Oh, don't cry! You get to help me still. What was it you said to me? *I don't want to save you, not after everything you've done?* Well, likewise, sweet Fritzi. I don't want to save you anymore. But you are still very, very useful."

He pitches the brand toward me, and I flinch and writhe.

Say the spell, Fritzi! Holda begs, and I beg myself too; I'm so deranged by pain and horror that all I can think is, *Say it, say it, say it*—but what are the words?

On this day, I start. That's right. *On this day*—

"You have to know, Fritzi." Dieter steps away to stick the brand into the fireplace. I think he's done—he has to be done—but he holds it in the flames, eyes drifting to the ceiling, his head shaking in exasperation. "This is all the fault of Mama and the Elders, and those forest folk you met. *They* are the ones who kept the secret of wild magic from us, knowing just how powerful we could be! *They* are the ones who forced rules upon us! All the things I do—*they* force it. If they had given us the true strength of the Well from the start, none of this would be necessary."

He turns back to me. The brand glows orange again.

"Just like this pain." He nods at the brand. "It isn't necessary. You chose this route. Because, no matter how powerful wild magic may be, it showed me that the only way I will be able to change our world is with your power enhancing mine. You're *special*, Fritzichen. And this is the sacrifice you must make for freedom."

I blubber and beg through the gag, but it's all muffled, all nonsense, my world a swimming, flickering sea of pain, and I am rendered inconsequential but to experience this.

Dieter holds. The brand dips to the side as his head does, surveying me, his brows sharpening.

"Oh, pretty sister, you're crying out for him, aren't you? That traitorous kapitän of mine." He clicks his tongue and shows me the brand. "But you see, you aren't his anymore. You aren't Mama's. You're *mine*. And when you burn tomorrow, these brands will make sure that every drop of the wild magic your death generates funnels straight into *me*. The barrier will fall"—he snaps his fingers—"just. Like. That."

He shoves the brand high against my collarbone.

I pass out. Darkness yanks me down, down, and I see Holda there, see her screaming for me, but her voice is soundless, soundless like I am, her tongue in a gag—

Past her, I see the Origin Tree.

I see forest folk gathered around it, defensive lines, hands raised outward to face an enemy I can't spot—they weave spells around the tree. Creating the barrier, the Well, this is the start of the Well—

A jolt of magic rushes through me, and I snap awake to Dieter pressing his hand against my chest, healing me again.

I shake my head; it's all I can do: shake it and whimper when he lifts the brand, twists it between us.

His eyes roll over the wicked iron *D* before dropping to my healed skin, the holes in my gown.

He places it back against my stomach. Holds it. Holds it through my writhing, my screaming.

I pass out again.

The forest folk are around the Origin Tree.

This is what I wanted you to know, Fritzi. Holda's voice is different here. Clearer, less restrained, and something in this liminal space of unconsciousness and pain must finally be breaking through her layers of magic-kept secrecy, where the other goddesses can't see what she's showing me.

The forest folk protect the Origin Tree, she says, *but it was not always the source of magic. Magic used to be all wild. It used to run and flow freely.*

She shows me the world, the wide world of witches casting spells and their warriors guarding them, and none of the spells they generate follow our rules.

But there has always been threats to our kind. The hexenjägers are the latest iteration. The ones before them, the Romans, all but wiped us out just the same. And so my sisters and I gathered as much wild magic as we could and trapped it in the Origin Tree.

I see the forest folk again, creating the barrier, guarding the tree.

We set up rules to access the Origin Tree's magic and created the tale that wild magic is corrupting. We bestowed the responsibility of enforcing those rules on priestesses and Elders. We thought, if we made accessing magic more controlled, and convinced witches and normal people alike that the only evil magic was wild, that it would make good witches less feared. Less of a target.

We were wrong.

Wild magic is still in the world, though less of it, with what we took to fill the Origin Tree. My sisters do not agree with what I know to be true—that capping our witches' powers was never the solution. Controlling magic was never going to be enough to convince the world not to fear us.

You must fight back now.

You must break your connection to the Well and open up to wild magic. It is the same power. It will not harm you.

I am so sorry, Fritzi.

Dieter rips me into consciousness again.

I come, gasping this time under both pain and realization.

Clarity is startling and vile and a relief.

There is too much she wants me to do. Too much beyond this moment, and my brain retracts to only *this moment*, because I am all body and flesh under my brother's insanity.

Dieter didn't get this far in Holda's crusade, or he wouldn't be doing—doing *this.* He doesn't need to do this to me. He doesn't need to do *any of this*—this brand may act as a focus for his intent, but he doesn't realize how limitless his own power really is.

I try to tell him. If only to get him to stop.

I remember Liesel saying that. *I just wanted to make him stop.*

He reheats the brand, moves it to the spot on my collarbone.

Adds a new one, on my thigh, singeing through my skirt.

The air hangs heavy with the stench of burning flesh. I am screaming at a pitch I have never heard before, twisting against the chains, my wrists chafing, my toes scrambling against the floorboards slick from my sweat and tears, and I cannot escape this, cannot *think*—

On this day and from this hour. I need to say those words. I need to think them. I need, I need, I am all need, need to stop this pain, to get *away*—

Otto, Otto, *help me*—

Sever from the Well. Wild magic is the same as the Well's power, all along. The goddesses thought they were keeping us safe. They lied. They lied, they lied—

Dieter steps back, his head cocked appraisingly.

"Beg me to heal you." He says it so calmly, so straightforward, that I anchor to his words for their cold oddness. "Beg me, and I will consider it."

I whine, throat bruised and blistered, sweat and tears drenching me, but when I look into his eyes, I glare at him, utter, rooted hatred.

Dieter shrugs. "I did try to be merciful, over and over. What will your kapitän whore think? You, all damaged like this."

He reaches up above me. A click, and the loop holding the manacles releases, plummeting my body to the floor.

The resonant impact of the fall holds me captive, and I lie there, pliant and defeated, sweat-slicked and in such pain as I have never felt. I squirm to find a position that doesn't hurt, but my arms twist in the manacles, concaving my chest over the two brands there, and my skirt pulls at the burn on my thigh, goring it deeper.

Dieter crosses to the door and uses the iron rod to beat on it. "She's ready."

The door opens. Two hexenjägers enter, already laughing; the moment they see me, their laughter hardens into something hungry.

"Chain her to the stake," Dieter tells them. He folds himself into a seat at the table and lifts his tea, his face bathed in the fading evening light. "Spread word to find your stations after—the burning starts soon, and I do expect we'll have some misguided attempts at rescue."

The jägers approach me.

I will myself to pull away. To fight back. My mind screams to act, but I am nothing, I am *pain*—

One grabs the chain between my hands. The other swoops under my legs. The agony of shifting, of being yanked around—darkness throbs, beckons—

"Oh, do be gentle with her," Dieter calls from the table. "She is, after all, my sister."

One of the jägers chuckles. They haul me from the room, and I can't even whimper anymore. I'm a shell, scraped raw, watching my brother in a perverted hypnosis as I'm carried out.

How are we expected to defeat someone like him? No magic is strong enough.

Fritzi, comes Holda's voice, choked with tears. She says nothing else. Just my name. Just that plea.

My eyes pinch shut, my body swaying in the hands of the jägers. The agony palpitating out of each brand lives inside of me, building on each inhale only to build again, never ending, like the Forest, like those trees, like, like...

I want to cry out for Otto. I want to scream for him. The wanting and the missing wells up in my throat, but I am gagged and bleeding and ruined. He's coming to save me, Holda said he is; but he's too late.

What will he do when he finds me like this?

He'll get himself killed. I can't let him fight Dieter, not when I'm in pieces.

Delirium is taking me—I'm not sure whether any of this is real, or if I'll wake back up in my room in Birresborn to Mama bent in work over the kitchen table.

"*On this day and from this hour*," she sings. There is flour in the air. The sweet smell of baking pastries.

I sing along with her.

I feel the vibrations of the words throb through my body, past the pain, past the fear.

Once, I would have done this to prove the Well wrong, in a way that is so similar to Dieter's intent. To stand up against the control they enact over us. To willingly, eagerly prove what Holda showed me, that we can access wild magic *without* needing the evil sacrifices they said we did. To show them that wild magic is more powerful.

But now, in this whittled moment, I do this to save the man I love, and Liesel, and all the witches and victims of the hexenjägers.

I do this to reclaim myself because I have been brutally unmade.

"I sever here the Well's one power.

Soul thus rendered, alone I wait,

Only I will now hold my fate."

42

OTTO

I grew up with tales of the Wild Hunt. The Hunt, my stepmother told me as she tucked Hilde and me into bed, presaged war and death. An army of ferocious beings would storm across the land, chasing dragons, and if you saw the Hunters, you may be driven mad, or you may be forced to join their war and destruction, or they may simply kill you for the fun of it. The horses they rode were large and demonic, with red eyes and hooves sharp as swords. Hilde hated the story and would beg our mother to tell her that it was all false, but every time, before my sister fell asleep, I'd click my tongue to sound like horse hooves to rile her up. Our mother always warned me that if I continued to be naughty, the Wild Hunt would come for me.

I never thought it was real.

Until now.

The horses that carry us are larger than any I've seen, but their eyes glow like amber, not devilish scarlet. Most of the guards are already mounted by the time Brigitta escorts me, Liesel, and Cornelia to where they wait. I see now why the Wild Hunt has the reputation of fear that it does. This is not even the full number of guardians the Well has to offer, but those gathered here are ferocious, dressed in full battle garb, leather straps holding plate armor, spears and swords gleaming.

Cornelia mounts a white stallion, heading to the front of the troops assembled. Brigitta brings me to a black horse with gold-painted hooves. Its long mane is plaited with glass beads that are somehow silent even when the mare shakes her head. Brigitta hangs back as I hold my hand out to the horse. She snuffs, the scent of clover filling the air, but then she bends her head low, letting me rub her nose.

I glance back at Brigitta, who visibly heaves a sigh of relief. "She'll let you ride her," Brigitta says, as if that had been in question. I start to ask her what her concern had been, but the woman strides closer to me. All around us, the other horses stomp, blowing puffs of breath into the chilled night air.

Brigitta moves behind me, her lips close to my ear, careful that only I hear her words. "This is Skokse," she says. "The fastest horse we have, and the smartest. Our people are going to be focused on the fight. You, Otto Ernst, are not our warrior. You're *hers*." Brigitta gives me a significant look as she steps back, and I understand exactly what she means—one man on a swift horse can get to Fritzi faster than an entire army, should the opportunity arise. Brigitta and Hilde are close; my sister must have told her of what she knew I would want to do.

I swing into Skokse's saddle, and I can feel the power of the horse under me, eager to ride. Brigitta mounts her own horse—a dapple gray wearing a red leather saddle. She raises her arm, and silence falls among the army assembled.

"Tonight we protect the Well by leaving the Well. We defend magic beyond our border. Tonight," she yells, her voice ringing out, "we ride!"

She looks directly at me, eyes boring into mine, as she throws her arm down. I grab Skokse's reins and dig my heels into her sides. All around me, fighters and horses charge toward the border of the Well. My senses are overwhelmed with it all—thundering hooves on all sides, the scent of petrichor and soft earth spraying up, the sharp snap in temperature from warm to frigid as we break into the Black Forest.

I am at once a part of something larger—this strange, wild hunt with nearly a hundred warriors and as many mighty steeds—and also utterly alone. I lean over Skokse's body, my arms clutching her withers more than the reins, trusting the horse as we charge forward. My eyes squint through the darkness and the wind, and it feels as if there is no one, nothing in the world but me and my horse and our purpose. Skokse does not merely gallop through the Black Forest; she *flies*. I keep my head low against her neck so that I don't run the risk of being knocked off by a branch, but the horse knows the Forest well. Skokse does not hesitate as she leaps over running water, weaves between trees, and crashes through the undergrowth.

When we burst through the edge of the forest, I recognize the road where we met Johann and Dieter. Skokse's hooves crunch through fresh snow. It takes only minutes to reach the path, go past the old, ruined castle and toward the edge of Baden-Baden. Although Skokse has pulled ahead, the others catch up with us here.

A battalion of hexenjägers stands stiffly along the road leading into the city. Baden-Baden is not large enough to merit a wall like Trier, but the soldiers make their own wall, spaced out at attention, black cloaks billowing, silver enameled badges glistening in the moonlight.

I pull on Skokse's reins, slowing the impatient beast as I eye the hexenjägers. All around me, the other soldiers do as well, approaching carefully, weapons drawn. The hexenjägers have no right to be here; we're well away from the diocese and the archbishop's influence. Besides,

Johann said Trier was in turmoil—why haven't they protested Dieter bringing them all out here to the southern edges of the Empire? My hand drops to my sword hilt, but I don't draw it yet.

Why aren't they moving?

Over the horses, I meet Brigitta's eyes. She was watching me, hoping, I think, that I could excuse this strange behavior. I kick Skokse forward, taking the lead, and Brigitta holds up an arm, keeping the others back as I approach alone.

The men standing before us are silent, their eyes hollow, their muscles oddly tense. As I draw closer, Skokse stamping with impatience, I can see the ropy tendons of the men's necks sticking out. I swallow, uncomfortable at the sight.

Nearest me, the one closest to the road, is Johann. I lean over Skokse without dismounting, trying to meet Johann's deadened gaze. The boy attempted to help us on the road; he was happy that Trier rioted against the archbishop's terror. But now his eyes are unfocused, and even though every muscle in his body is taut, there's an emptiness to him. A spider has found its way to his shoulder, and I watch as the creature crawls over Johann's face, eight legs pricking over his cheek, and the boy doesn't flinch. Bile rises in my throat as the spider crosses the bridge of Johann's nose, up to his left eye, a thin line of its black leg crossing the red veins streaking the white eyeball.

Johann doesn't blink.

But, I think, perhaps his eyes are focusing, even if they don't really move. He's not entirely hollow inside.

There is horror there, a raw screaming horror that cannot escape his mind.

"I have to save Fritzi," I whisper to the boy. "But I will come back for you."

I wheel Skokse around, racing back to the Wild Hunt. "I don't know why they're frozen," I tell her, "but this is Dieter's work. No human can be this still."

"Then it is a trap," Cornelia says, pulling her white stallion up beside us.

Brigitta nods solemnly.

"We have to get past them." I meet Brigitta's eyes. Dieter has put these eerie human-toy soldiers to stand in our way. They will attack at any moment, surely.

"You go first," Brigitta tells me. Cornelia starts to question her, but Brigitta shakes her head, arguing that speed is of the essence. Cornelia may be an elder and a priestess, but on the battlefield, it's Brigitta who is wisest. Cornelia bows her head, agreeing that I should go on ahead.

"The youngest one—there," I say, as I turn Skokse around, pointing to Johann. "If you can, save him."

Brigitta scowls but nods. At that, I touch my horse's side. Skokse responds immediately, a coiled spring waiting to launch, turning and breaking into a trot, wending around the stiff soldiers.

A few paces behind me, the forest folk follow. I'm about halfway past when a ripple goes throughout the crowd of hexenjägers.

"Attack!" one of them bellows, Jäger Kock, a friend, I recall, of Bertram's. "Kill them all!"

The hexenjägers burst into a flurry of action, oddly rapid, given the stiff way they held before. Skokse easily dodges blows, and I use the hilt of my sword to smash into the skull of one that draws close. I don't want to kill them, but I can't let them delay me.

Fortunately, the forest folk draw most of the attack, and the hexenjägers surge past me, swords drawn, charging at them. I urge Skokse forward faster, but not before I get a look at the eyes of my former compatriots.

They are all eerily empty and blue, not brown or hazel or green.

Each man now has Dieter Kirch's eyes. While they attack using the same skills that were drilled into us as youths in training, there's an odd nature to the fight. I see one jäger slashing in the air, fighting an invisible enemy. Two others bump into each other, bouncing off their shoulders without any awareness of having come so close to an ally. They fight as if enchanted, as if they see something in their strange blue eyes that none of the rest of us can see. Their blows come low, at the horses' knees rather than at their riders.

Dieter has possessed them, somehow, I think as I break through the last of the hexenjägers and pick up speed, galloping down the road toward Baden-Baden. *He expected opposition, but not monstrously huge horses.*

I wonder what the hexenjägers think they fight, what hallucination is infecting their minds.

With the battle on the road behind me, the small city of Baden-Baden spills out, blossoming into a myriad of smaller streets. I head straight to the town's center square.

It is *so* silent.

Skokse's hoofbeats are thunderous. My hands tighten on the reins, fear stabbing at my heart. It's late, but not *that* late. And while Advent was a time of fasting and sacrificing and quiet self-reflection, Christmas to the end of the year is a time for joy and celebration and raising candles to cut through the darkest time.

There is nothing now but silence.

As I draw closer to the center of town, I see a series of wooden stakes along the road.

I pause to count them. Twenty black stakes, kindling now nothing but ash and soot at the base. Each one leads deeper into town.

It is a horrid trail made of the remains of innocent people burned as witches.

And it leads me to one last stake, right in the center of the empty town.

Fritzi is tied to an enormous pole made of yew, its pale color a stark contrast to the blackened stakes along the road. Her chin rests on her chest, her unbound hair swinging over her face, gleaming gold. For a moment—for a horrid, pain-wretched eternity—I think she's already gone. But then she twitches, and even though she's bound, even though she's unconscious, the sob withers inside me. She's still alive.

Through the veil of her loose hair, I catch a glimpse of dark metal. My teeth clench at the sight of the iron muzzle forced over and into Fritzi's mouth, a painful violation of her body that works to silence her as well. A slight breeze blows through the square, and despite being nearly unconscious, Fritzi gargles a sound of pure pain. My eyes widen—the breeze was barely enough to disturb her gown, but—

Her clothing has scorch marks all over. The center of her dress is burned away, exposing Fritzi's pale belly marred with black and red burns, the welts so painfully sensitive that the barest kiss of wind makes her writhe. Blood speckles her once-beautiful gown, which now hangs in threads across her body.

My blood boils.

I will take pleasure in smashing each of Dieter's fingers under my boots for daring to touch her this way. I will relish in his screams as I rip the tongue from his foul mouth. And then I will take even greater pleasure in crushing his throat beneath my heel and watching the life leave his already soulless eyes.

"Oh, look!" A male voice calls out, mocking me. Skokse prances nervously, as if she also knows that Dieter is a more formidable foe than any she has ever faced before.

I dismount, looping my reins on the pommel of the saddle so they don't drag and catch. "Go to Brigitta," I tell the horse, somehow confident she can understand me. "Lead them here. Hurry."

As soon as I take a step closer to Fritzi and the stake, Skokse turns, neighing, hooves clattering over cobblestones so violently that sparks erupt. The horse is gone in seconds.

Send help, I pray, to my God, to the goddesses, to any power that will listen.

I draw my sword and strain my eyes to see into the shadows. I expect Dieter to face me. I expect one man to approach.

Instead, hundreds do.

Their footsteps make the ground rumble—they are in sync, perfectly moving as one. There are old men and women who stumble—they should have a cane or an arm to lean on, but don't. There are children, Liesel's age or so, their paces oddly elongated to match the tread of the others. There are adults. A huge man with biceps the size of a tree trunk, probably a blacksmith. A slender woman I think I recognize from the market when we first passed through Baden-Baden. Another dusted with flour, another wearing a butcher's apron. Hundreds and hundreds of people emerge from the alleyways, skulk down the streets, pour from the buildings, all walking in even steps, all wearing the same empty, blank expression, eyes drooping, mouths slack.

Dieter is a puppet master, using these people as his unwilling army.

Movement on the stake makes me whirl around, my attention on Fritzi. She stirs, barely conscious. "Fritzi!" I shout.

Every single person turns as one.

My heart seizes in terror at the abstractness of it all. And then the townspeople speak.

Each person says the same words, at the same time, with the same inflection. The sound of it is deafening, rattling my bones. And although every voice is unique—cracked and old, young and high, deep and weary—the words are Dieter's.

"Look at the insignificant traitor, come to fetch his witch," the hundred voices say as one.

"Let them go, Dieter!" I bellow.

"Kapitän, Kapitän." Even though it is a hundred voices that speak, they all, somehow, have a condescending inflection to them that is distinctly the kommandant's. "How did you sneak past my men? You always were the cleverest little witch killer." Another laugh, this one darker. "The cleverest little witch killer who never did kill a witch, did you?"

"You'll be my first!" I shout.

The giggles from a hundred different throats, high-pitched and manic, are worse than the sarcastic chuckles. I weave through the people, trying to draw closer to Fritzi. Every step I take is blocked by another townsperson. I'm unwilling to cut my way through the crowd of innocents, but Dieter knows that he's not only mocking me; he's delaying me from reaching Fritzi.

A barking laugh that rings in different pitches but drips with the same sardonic bitterness on every voice echoes throughout the square, deafening. "She is not yours, Ernst. She is mine. Didn't you see the way I branded her? It was a *D*, mein kapitän, not an *O*."

I grip my sword, praying to find Dieter among the crowd. My hand grips the hilt so hard that my fingers ache, but there is nowhere for me to expel the hateful rage boiling inside me.

On the stake, Fritzi moans.

She's not dead yet, I remind myself. I reach into the bag slung across my body, my fingers wrapping around the neck of the brew I made. *It's not too late.*

Behind me, I hear the rising thunder of the forest folk warriors who've come to save Fritzi, to protect magic. Hope surges inside me. For a moment, Dieter's hold on the crowd breaks, and their bodies all bend forward, drooping as if they are puppets with cut strings.

He did not expect me to have reinforcements.

He has laid out traps—the hexenjägers, these townspeople—but I do not think Dieter truly expected to be met with a strong force. The forest folk were a sanctuary, not an army, and I doubt Dieter thought anyone would get past his first layer of defense.

He didn't expect me to have friends.

Because he has none.

With a bone-jarring jerk, all the bodies of the townspeople simultaneously snap to attention again, each one raising fists or holding out tools as weapons.

The forest folk burst onto the square, having fought through the hexenjägers. Cornelia, astride a white stallion, is in the front.

"Don't hurt the people!" I shout, hoping my voice can be heard over the thunderous arrival of the others. "They are being controlled!"

Brigitta's beside Cornelia, and I see her eyes flash. She, at least, heard me, and she calls back a warning command to the others. Horses are pulled up short, hooves stamping on the cobblestone.

The priestess pulls out a length of bright red string, weaving it through her fingers. She raises the pattern to her eyes, scanning the crowd, then points.

"*There!*" she screams.

I do not hesitate. I charge forward, knocking aside the empty puppets of the townspeople. They fall as if they were dolls. Hidden deep in the crowd, I see an old person hunched over a cane, a brown cloak pulled over their head.

The person is eerily, emptily still, just like all the rest, but there is not a flicker of doubt in my mind as I raise my sword and smash it down.

At the very last second, the cloak swirls as the person dives in the opposite direction. Off-balance, I stumble as my sword strikes the cobblestones.

A hundred townsfolk laugh, the sound an echo of Dieter's, but too even, too measured. "Ha. Ha. Ha. Ha."

The brown cloak drops, and I catch a glimpse of pale blond hair.

The townsfolk move, their steps jerking like puppets, surrounding Dieter, separating him from me.

Cornelia looks through her strings again, and the army, now aware of what's happening, all track her movements. "There!" she cries.

A dozen soldiers lunge toward a street corner blocked by a dense cluster of people protecting Dieter with their bodies, and the warriors fight as gently as they can, pushing through the crowd. The puppets, though, do not care about injuring either the forest folk or themselves. Their movements are jerky, but their bodies swing out, arms flailing, legs kicking, heads thrashing.

It will delay the forest folk, prolong the battle.

I whirl around at the scent of smoke, acrid and sharp. I don't know if Dieter used magic or if he merely controlled the townspeople to do it for him, but the kindling piled under Fritzi's stake sparks in flame.

This fight is distraction enough that Dieter cannot focus on anything more than pulling the invisible strings that control the people. In the distance, I can hear boots stomping—he's called the hexenjägers to join the fight.

But through the chaos and the smoke, I see Fritzi.

Let the entire world war around me.

I will save her.

43

FRITZI

Sensations come to me in bursts.

Footsteps. Dozens of them, hundreds, maybe.

Horse hooves.

Shouting.

A voice, one I recognize, distantly, fuzzily, but it's enough to guide me forward, out of the darkness—

Pain ricochets through me, and I cry out, recoiling into that darkness, the sweetness of its relief.

Fritzi—you have to wake up. You have to wake up, now!

No, no, I can't—it *hurts*, I can't—

"Fritzi!"

That voice again. Otto.

I rear back, spine hitting something rounded, jagged. My wrists tug, the skin scrubbed raw, and I'm only vaguely aware of my arms behind me, chained around a pole.

Not a pole.

A stake.

My nose stings, and that is what drives me fully awake, the jarring shock of smoke billowing into my lungs, acidic and as rough as sand. I cough—that iron muzzle holds my mouth still, and the cough turns into a gag as smoke drives into my throat, coats my tongue in ash.

"Fritzi!" Otto's voice is closer, frantic. Weapons clash now, swords on swords, pistols firing—who is fighting? The hexenjägers, the forest folk?

My eyes peel open, but there is only smoke, great billowing sheets of it, so thick I briefly wonder if I'm already dead. There's *so much*—my eyes fall, and I see the pile of kindling beneath my bare feet, flames licking all around the edges, eating up the snow-damp wood and puffing screens of gray into the air.

I cough again, gag again, and yank against the manacles. My heart stutters, so used to panic now that I've gone numb, and I just pull again, pulling, desperate, frantic—

My whole body goes still.

I severed from the Well.

What does it mean? I ask Holda. *What can I do?*

Her response is swift. A gust of cool air, a surge of light from the orange-gold sunset sky.

Anything, Friederike. Anything.

The only pause I have is in knowing that once I do this, Dieter will realize he never needed sacrifices to gain his power. It was the only gruesome cap on his mania we had—in a way, I understand the limitations that the goddesses sought to impose.

When I face him, it will be all of him, unscrupulous, versus all of me, broken and terrified.

I focus on the manacles. Can I just will them to break?

A sharp cry pierces the air. A shout, a plea. Bodies shove, and through a break in the smoke, I see townspeople, *townspeople* fighting the forest folk, and my mind rattles with confusion.

Within them, shoving through the crowd, is Otto.

His gaze collides with mine.

I sob, relief so potent I can feel its warmth in the pit of my stomach

He barrels forward, but townsfolk swarm him, beating him back; he tries not to fight, but they swing axes at him, butcher knives, whatever weapons they could find. Blades cut through the air, aimed at his neck, his side—

Otto—I try to scream for him. It's muffled and warped, but my throat tears over it.

Something pulses out of me. Soft and cool and…and *green.*

From the cracks between the cobblestones, thin plants begin to sprout. They launch up, narrow green stalks with vibrant yellow flowers, all wrong for this season, for this temperature, for this *speed*, but they grow and grow, surrounding Otto in a ring that stretches up to his shoulders, growing, towering—

Rue. Rue like in the protection potion he took so long ago, in Trier; rue that we bought in the Christkindlmarkt.

Otto falls out of a defensive stance and flashes a look at me, questions ripe in his dark eyes.

The rue had been to protect him. To aid *him.*

But the townsfolk around him go stiff. Their weapons freeze in midair.

As one, they look down, at their hands, their feet, and then back up, and suddenly they are shaking, weeping, some falling to their knees.

The potency of the magic ripples out to them, and they are purged of Dieter's touch.

The wind shifts; smoke clogs the air, bursts embers at me, and I flinch away, losing sight of the townsfolk, of Otto.

I did that. Didn't I?

I freed them from the spell Dieter placed on them.

Yes, says Holda. *Yes, Fritzi.*

When I sob now, it is in desperate hope, despite the fire crawling ever closer, billowing on the wind. The only thing stopping it from raging unchecked is the dampness of the wood, but the smoke gathers on that, and every breath now is choked more and more. I will suffocate long before I burn.

Strength. I need strength.

I tried to will the manacles to snap on their own, but my affinity is, has always been plants. And with wild magic now, I am not limited by rules, but my talents still lie where they always have—if I want to escape, if I want to harness all the powers of wild magic to fight back, I need to play to my strengths.

Cedar. A tree that gives strength. I can grow one—if I can control it now, if I can *will* it to help me, its branches will be strong enough to snap these manacles.

I imagine the tree, its size, its shape, the smell, woodsy and wet in a forest, the size, imposing and massive and commanding.

Behind me, the ground trembles.

The kindling at my feet shifts, and I stumble over it, sticks rolling away, the stones groaning far below.

I throw a glance over my shoulder and see a tree sprouting up against the stake, its young limbs stretching for me, *reaching* for the manacles. I push more of myself into it, tears racing down my face as I watch it climb, driven by *me*, just me; all this time, we were capable of this? All this time—

The tree goes from a healthy auburn to a sickly muted gray.

The whole of it shrivels, a puff of decay launching off as it wilts and falls.

"Ah, Fritzichen. Whatever are you doing?"

I whirl around, but he's nowhere near me, not that I can see—all is smoke only, gray and darkening, and I cough, wheezing, breaths like knives stabbing me inside, the brands aching outside.

"Did you find a way to sever from the Well?" Dieter coos.

But there's a heaviness in his voice. A twist of something dark that his control is usually too riveted to show, and it washes over me, a frigid charge of terror.

"But how are you using magic?" he presses. "You fed it no evil acts. You did not pay the sacrifice of blood it demands. Oh, my pretty sister. My pretty, *clever* sister. What have you discovered?"

No, no—this was what I feared. That he would realize that all the sacrifices he made, all the burnings, weren't even needed. He could access the whole of wild magic from the start. On his own. All the people he's burned to fuel his magic—he only *thought* they bolstered his power because we were all told that that was the way.

We were lied to, misled, and he's seeing that now.

"Oh, Fritzichen!" he purrs. "You *are* useful, aren't you? How long have you known the extent of the Well's lies, hm? How long have you *kept* this from me?"

The brand on my stomach flares with pain. Something within it seizes, the twisted, ruined flesh, and I scream, that muffled wail that slivers cracks in my throat.

"Naughty, naughty Fritzichen," says Dieter's disembodied voice, and this time, there is nothing controlled about it. He's *livid*.

I yank on the manacles and eye the tree, but it is dead, and when I focus again, I'm too frantic, the magic slipping through my fingers, bucking—

"Fritzi!"

My head whips around.

And there is Otto. Bolting over the crackling kindling, elbow thrown over his mouth against the smoke. He climbs the wood, scrambling higher, boots singeing in the embers, the hem of his cloak catching, sparking. He rips it off and fights up, up, and then his hands are on my face, and he's *here*, he's *here*, and I come apart.

"Liebste, I'm here." He echoes the thoughts in my head, a promise, his words roughened by the smoke and that coil in his eye, rage barely capped. "What has he done to you? Liebste—"

He touches the gag on my mouth, runs his hands around it to the back. It clicks, then the metal gag falls away, and my jaw *screams* with being able to close again, every muscle in my mouth feeling bruised.

"Otto," I sob. "You can't—you'll burn—"

I cough, unable to get a full breath, and I see him fighting a cough, too, his eyes going bloodshot in the smoke.

"I'm not leaving you," he tells me, and he ducks around me to work at the manacles.

The fire edges closer, the smoke thickens.

"Oh, *no*," says Dieter. "She does not get to be *free*."

The smoke parts.

He's standing at the base of the pyre, unadulterated rage contorting his face.

"My dear sister lied to me, Kapitän," he says. "She knew more about this wild magic I harness—and she kept it to herself! While I tried to share with her what I had found. And not only that." He cocks his head. "How many innocents did you let me burn, Fritzichen? To keep this information to yourself. That all this time, the only source of magic I needed was me."

That makes him grin. His rage toward me breaks in an undeniable cackle of glee, triumph ripe and vile.

"All this time," he gasps, staring at his splayed fingers. "*All this time.* Killing people was pointless. Well—educational. But not *necessary*. Oh, the goddesses are even more demented than I thought. Look what they made me do! Do you see?" He glares into the sky. "Do you see what you let me do?"

Dieter lifts his hands into the air, closes his eyes in something like reverence, something like awe. He whispers, a spell I can't hear, words weaving as his fingers flex and strain, the muscles bulging in his neck. He's using it to focus now only, using the words as a conduit to draw on the power we could always tap into.

"Otto," I beg. "Otto—hurry—"

His fingers fumble behind me. He curses, slips on the wood, tugs on the irons. "It's not coming off. Verdammt—I can't break it! It's like something's jammed—"

"He bespelled it," I gasp. "He bespelled the manacles."

Dieter's eyes pop open.

And he *pulls*.

The street, already a cacophony of noise from the battle, echoes with a thunderous percussion, like an explosion, like a burst.

And I know.

Deep in my heart. In the pit of me. The part no longer connected to the Well, but forever a part of it, magic in my blood.

He's ripped open a gap in the Well's barrier.

A look of pure joy floods my brother's face. He is, in that moment, all giddy happiness in a way that is disgustingly innocent.

Then Dieter staggers as if hit by an invisible force. His eyes, fuming, whip around. "Oh-ho, the forest folk want to fight me now, do they?" He shoves his hands back out, redoubling his effort, his face purpling with strain. "That tree cannot keep you safe. Those goddesses cannot keep you safe. *I will break open your magic, and you will cower at my feet!*"

The forest folk are resisting his rip in the barrier—but only barely. Their charms and spells work to protect the Well, but Dieter has funneled so much straight to it that it is only a matter of time.

There is wild magic to draw on all around us, but the goddesses still capped most of it in the Origin Tree. And he will get in. He will widen what he has started.

Then he will march into the Well, to the Origin Tree, tap into the massive amount of goddess-blessed power there, and destroy us all.

"Otto," I gasp his name. "Otto, *leave*."

He shifts back around to stand in front of me, my manacles locked fast. I watch his eyes go to Dieter, watch him see the inner struggle my brother is engaged in, and when Otto turns to me, I don't try to hide the brittle, teary-eyed plea in my eyes. His whole face unravels, emotions rippling in quick succession: fury, disbelief, revulsion, *refusal.*

"You have to leave," I tell him, wishing my voice sounded stronger. "You have to live to stop him. He's breaking through the barrier; he knows he doesn't need me anymore. Please, just go."

Otto bends closer, grinding his forehead to mine. "No," he says with such force that I go silent. "No, verdammt, Friederike Kirch, *I'm not leaving you*."

He pulls something out of his bag. My gaze fixes on it, bleary, exhausted.

The smoke is so thick. So consuming.

My eyelids grow heavy, drooping—

"Fritzi!" Otto shakes me, his hand cupping my cheek. "I have the bonding potion. It's the *bonding* potion, Fritzi. Share your power with me, and we can defeat Dieter together!"

Is he shouting too loud? *Yelling*, almost, or maybe the fire is roaring, my heartbeat thudding in my ears.

I eye the bottle in his fingers. "The bonding potion?"

"Hilde and I made it," his voice lowers, and I manage a look at him, confusion ripe. "When I drink *your* potion," he says, shouting again, "you and I will be bonded and share power, right? Then we can defeat him! You drank from it already!"

Behind him, Dieter looks up, briefly pulled from his focus.

His eyes go to the potion in Otto's hand.

"No. Otto. *No*. I didn't—you can't talk about this!" I shake my head, frantic. *Don't give my brother any other ideas; don't remind him of things he could do*—he has access to enormous amounts of magic now, but he is unpracticed in harnessing everything without focus or spells. He could still increase his power even further through bonding potions. He could still drain me, build himself even stronger. "That doesn't—that won't work. That's not how potions work!"

I would have had to make it for Otto to be able to take it. As it is, it would strip me of all magic, it would *kill* him.

But he will die either way, standing here with me, burning.

Everyone I love has been taken from me like this. My coven. My mother.

I will not lose him too.

This fate is mine alone. This was meant to happen, wasn't it? Dieter should have burned me in Birresborn. But I was spared, spared though I didn't deserve it; and through it, I found Otto, this man who has transformed me in irreversible ways.

Otto lowers the brew to his side. "Fritzi—"

"I love you," I tell him. It rips from me as the smoke builds, strangles out the air; as the flames roar, encroaching on him, swelling the heat to scorching. "I love you."

I scream.

The cedar tree behind me floods with life. I give it everything I have, shoving it higher, taller, *full*—only I angle its branches to arch around me, aiming for Otto.

His eyes widen, briefly leaving my face to catch on the eruption of the tree, but then he gapes at me, horror washing him white.

"*No*—" The plea is cut off in a startled cry as a branch shoves him back, back, through the smoke, out of the fire.

His body crashes to the cobblestones far from the inferno, far from *me*.

Right next to Dieter.

Otto still has the potion in his hand. His fingers pop open, and the bottle rolls away, unbroken.

Rolls, rolls—

Until it comes to rest under my brother's foot.

44

OTTO

Dieter Kirch, kommandant of Trier's hexenjägers, responsible for prolonging the massacre of innocents under the guise of witch burnings, bends at the waist and picks up the bottle of potion that I brewed with my sister's help in a little cottage in the middle of the Black Forest. Beer and nightshade.

He peels back the wax stopper.

My body aches, my throat coarse from smoke, as I struggle to stand. Fritzi is still chained to the stake, kindling burning hotter as the flames catch and grow. Her body sags against the restraints, defeat and despair exhausting her.

Dieter plucks the cork from the bottle and tosses it on the flames. I look wildly around, begging someone to see, to help. There's a perimeter around the fire, an invisible wall. I happen to be inside it, with Dieter. But all around the edge, the forest folk fight hexenjägers with eyes still enchanted blue. Some townsfolk, relieved of their bewitchment, flee or cry or huddle against walls, disbelieving the battle unspooling in their center square. Fritzi hadn't been able to free all of them, though, only the ones that swarmed around me. The rest continue fighting. But no one comes close to the fire. No one even looks at it. At us.

Dieter has narrowed his magical focus to this point, to Fritzi's death, and he has somehow ensured no one can get through, erecting this enchanted barrier only because I got so close and she got so powerful. He wanted to showcase his cruelty even among an audience of puppets and enemies; the fact that he's hidden Fritzi's pyre indicates that he's unnerved.

My gaze flicks back to him. He sniffs the bottle, nostrils flaring. "I know this potion," he says, his voice low, warm. "Oh, sister!" He strides forward, utterly ignoring me. Dieter rushes right up the edge of the fire, so hot that he must feel the flames, but he ignores it, holding the bottle up toward Fritzi even as she starts to kick out, her skirts igniting. "Sister!" he shouts again, "My darling Fritzichen! Did you think—did you *really* think you would bond with anyone but me?"

It sickens me, his giddy, mocking delight. I know so little about magic and potions, but I know this is among the most sacred, most powerful. And he wants to use it to drain his sister of her magic. Her life.

Dieter whirls around to me and barks in laughter, the sound disbelieving. "Did *you* think you could fight me with a sip of this?"

"We *can* defeat you together," I snarl.

His eyes widen in fake surprise. "Oh, you actually believe that. Otto, friend. If you bonded with Fritzi, you wouldn't make her stronger. Your blood is so weak. You are a detriment to someone like her. You would do nothing but drag her down to your lowly level."

I flinch as if he struck me, the words the worst blow he's ever dealt me. Deep in my heart, I know he's right. Fritzi's power—the goodness of her—it's far above anything I can even hope to touch. She is the sun, and I am not even a moon worthy enough to reflect her light.

Dieter raises the potion to his lips, but doesn't drink yet. "The irony of this. I could not force her to drink the potion I made. But you just give me the potion she made." He chuckles. "She's mine all because you wanted her to be yours."

"You can't steal her magic," I growl.

"Quiet down, dog," Dieter says casually. He flicks his hand, and I feel my joints hardening, my muscles tightening. I strain against his pressure, but I can barely move.

He tips the bottle up to Fritzi's writhing body in a cruel salute. "Prost," he says. The flames around her freeze—he will delay her murder long enough to attempt to steal her power. The fire doesn't disappear, the heat still radiating from static sparks, but it no longer roars and spreads.

Dieter brings the potion to his lips. "Your magic will be mine, Fritzichen. You can break with the Well, but you'll never break this bond with me."

Dieter downs the potion, his throat bobbing as he gulps the liquid.

I strain my body, still struggling against the magic paralysis Dieter placed on me.

And then, with a stomach-churning lurch, I break free. I stagger up.

Dieter whirls around, the bottle still in his hand. "I said, *'Down, dog,'*" he growls, a cough choking his words. He swipes his hand at me—

Nothing happens.

Dieter's eyes widen. A rush of noise swooshes over us, and people spill across the invisible barrier that had kept them out. At the same time, the flames around the pyre swoop up, stronger than ever.

"Save Fritzi!" I hear Cornelia call. More forest folk run forward. Dieter curses, twisting his arm, his fingers bent grotesquely—

Nothing happens.

"What did you do?" Dieter screams at the fire, even as Fritzi throws her head back, trying and failing to escape the flames.

"What did *I* do, you mean," I growl.

His head whips around to me. His eyes are wild, his skin sallow. The bottle drops from his fingers, this time smashing on the cobblestones, the remains of the liquid spilling out. He buckles over in pain.

"Fritzi didn't make the potion," I say. "I did." And without Fritzi's spelling the liquid as it brewed, it was poison. It won't kill him—but it will kill his magic.

Which was, of course, my plan all along.

45

FRITZI

The space between Dieter and I deepens into a vacuum, an echoing tug of absence that I feel as strongly as his rip in the Well's barrier.

Something is...*gone*. Like a light flaring on to show that what was once monsters and lurking beasts is now just an empty room.

Otto severed my brother's connection to magic. *All* magic.

Dieter is realizing that now, too, and as forest folk pour toward him, he turns on Otto, still on the ground at his feet. The look on Dieter's face is the most chilling he's ever shown, violation and malice unrestrained, and seeing it aimed at Otto sculpts everything in me to the finest of points, the sharpest of intentions.

The cedar tree's branches twist for my manacles, now free of Dieter's enchantment, even as forest folk guards start scrambling up the flames, fighting to snuff them with waves of their hands and muttered spells. Brigitta is an arm's length from me, shouting, but I scream and double forward, and the cedar tree snaps the irons like they're nothing more than another piece of dry kindling.

My hands flare in front of me. I am action only. Instinct pure and stripped.

Vines creep out of the ground, shattering cobblestones, slithering across the town square from the Forest. They come and come at my command, and in a heartbeat, Dieter is knotted up in dozens of thick green snakelike vines that lock his arms to his chest and ensnare his legs and keep him *there*, immobile, helpless.

He writhes and turns that withering glare onto me. "*Friederike*!"

I feel Brigitta's fingers on my arm. I hear the snap and crunch of footsteps on the kindling, smothering the flames easily now that Dieter's magic isn't keeping them lit. I hear townspeople wailing in the falling down of his magic, and hexenjägers, too, their weapons clattering from their hands as they are released from my brother's sway.

The kindling shifts beneath my bare, scorched feet, and my body is still a chaos of pain, but all I see, truly, is my brother.

The vines tighten on him. *Tighten.*

His fury holds, but his face begins to go red, his lips sputtering, spittle dripping.

I could kill him. So easily. There is no fear in it now, is there? No need to worry about feeding wild magic with a cruel act, because wild magic is only as evil as the intent behind it.

And right now, I embrace that evil, if it means seeing the light go out of his eyes.

"Fritzi! Fritzi—look at me!"

Otto pulls at my face, trying to get me to look at him, but my hands are still outstretched, and Dieter's eyes are on mine, and if I don't kill him, if he doesn't *suffer*—

"You have him," Otto says. "He's done, Fritzi. Stop. You can stop now."

He's done, echoes Holda. *Look, Fritzi. Look at the hexenjägers.*

With effort, I peel my eyes away from my brother.

Around him, forming a haphazard half circle of shaking weapons pointed at Dieter, stand some of his jägers. Many can't seem to decide whether to gawk at the forest folk or at their kommandant, but the pulse deep in their eyes speaks to revelations unfolding, truth emerging, awe taking root.

Johann is first to step forward. He looks up at me, and I realize the sight I must make, bleeding and burnt and disheveled on a now smoldering pile of kindling, forest folk flanking me, broken manacles dangling from my wrists.

He nods at me, apology heavy in his eyes, and he faces Dieter.

"Kommandant Kirch," he says, pushing his voice loud. "You are under arrest." A pause. His throat works. "For the use of witchcraft."

Two other jägers step forward, one pulling out a pair of manacles, and Brigitta, next to me, makes a choked noise of objection.

"He is *our* prisoner," she starts, but I seize her arm.

With my other hand, I reach for Otto. The rush of this victory is quickly catching up with me, and I can feel my legs straining to hold me, the ache from my brands demanding to be the center of my focus. He immediately sweeps in, his arm going behind my back, his grip tight on my upper arm.

I meet my brother's eyes again. I let him see every bit of my pain, every piece of my fury, as my thoughts roll over themselves.

The forest folk would imprison him. Maybe, eventually, execute him.

But I *know* what will happen if the hexenjägers take him. I have seen firsthand the reception awaiting an accused witch in a Catholic church, no less one who possessed an entire brigade of jägers and hid his power from them for years.

They will strip him to nothing. And only then will they burn him.

"No," I say, to Brigitta, to the forest folk who are poised to sweep in to push away the jägers. "Let them have him. He deserves a taste of what he has done to us."

It's Cornelia's gaze I feel on me. She sits astride a massive white horse, and when I look at her, she nods, her brow pinched, understanding resonating.

"Rochus and Philomena will hate this," says Brigitta. But there's a gruesome smile in her voice. "All the more reason, then."

She cuts her head at the forest folk, and they step back, giving the hexenjägers room to approach Dieter.

I let the vines fall from around his body.

The jägers grab him, wrestling him into irons, and he spits and kicks. "*Worms!* You don't know what you are doing! You will regret siding against me, *you will regret—*"

They haul him off into their swelling crowd, a mass of black-cloaked jägers, all solemn, all shocked.

Otto helps me down from the kindling pile. As my toes touch the cool stones of the town square, Johann alone lingers, his face dirt-smeared, blood caked along his neck.

"Kapitän," he says to Otto and comes to attention. But something in him weakens, a tremble of fear. "We could use you back in Trier. I know the archbishop will dismiss any accusations Dieter made against you, and—"

"My place is here," Otto says immediately. He looks at the side of my face, back to Johann, to the forest folk spread around the milling jägers. "Besides, I think we will have a need for an intermediary, now that the world has seen who truly lives in the Black Forest."

Johann's face pales. That hesitation is reflected tenfold in the jägers behind him.

What has revealing the forest folk done to their already ripe fear of witches and magic? The reason that the goddesses created the Well at all was to help soothe the violent fear that normal people have toward us.

Whatever the repercussions. Whatever the prejudice.

We cannot keep hiding.

No, Holda agrees, and I hear the smile in her voice, teary. *Now, thanks to you, we will not.*

My chest bucks. *Thanks to me?*

You are my champion, she says. *I have long searched your world, hoping to find one worthy of the task I set forth. I thought that it could be your brother. But no, Friederike—it was always you.*

I can't get air into my lungs. Black spots spray across my vision, and I stagger, leaning into Otto, shutting my eyes for one moment, just one moment of *rest*.

I will shield your connection to wild magic from the Well, she continues, *that you may show witches across this world what strength they have been denied. You will show the forest folk and my sisters that the rules by which we abide are stifling and false. You will reawaken our magic, Friederike Kirch, and save us all.*

I only wanted to stop my brother. To get Liesel to safety. And now, to be with Otto—and I have those things.

But it isn't over.

Holda chose me as her champion.

And I accepted. I'm so tired. Tired from the weight of what is still to come, the fight I know awaits me back at the Well from Rochus and Philomena—tired from the shake in my hands and the ache in my core and the tug that bids me to look into the crowd, to spot my brother once more before he's gone.

I will never see him again.

But suddenly it feels as though I have not seen him in years, since he left Birresborn, since the version of him I loved faded more and more into a dream.

"We're done here," Otto tells Brigitta, Johann.

Gratitude is cooling and sweet. I keep my eyes shut as he lifts me, and my body goes limp in his arms. The bend of my stomach makes me whimper, that brand tugging, but I can heal it now, can't I? Summon a healing plant. Use wild magic.

My fingers lift, stretch feebly.

"Hey, don't move. Just rest. I have you, Fritzi," Otto says into my hair, his lips brushing my forehead. "Cornelia! Can you help with—"

My focus fades out. Drifts into tempting darkness, something warm and velvet and consuming, because Otto has me in his arms, and I am, in spite of everything that looms, safe.

Hazy blue light speckles against my eyelids. Pulses of rose red. Swaths of orange.

I shift, blinking slowly, and a window comes into focus, stained glass pieced together in geometric patterns that catch rays of sunlight and twist them into rainbow riots.

For a beat, I lie staring at the window, trying to orient myself.

This is the room Liesel was given in the Well. The bed beneath me is soft and warm, blankets piled over me, a heavy layer of quilts.

I brace, expecting a swarm of pain in my consciousness—

But none comes.

Slowly, so slowly, I push up onto my elbows.

Someone stirs next to me, and then Liesel's head pops up from within the blankets. "Fritzi!"

She starts to dive for me, thinks better of it, and sits back on her heels. "Move slowly—Cornelia had her best healers work on you, but you're still...hurt."

I look down, one hand coming up to rest on my collarbone, the spot where Dieter branded me highest.

The thin white shift I'm wearing rubs against a scar there, something knotted and wicked, but it doesn't hurt. Much. An ache lingers, deep inside me, and I feel the same on my stomach, on my thigh.

"They did their best," Liesel whispers. "Dieter...whatever he did. It was deep."

I twist to look at her. Her eyes are watery, bloodshot, but she's clean, and her cheeks are pink.

I open one arm to her.

She doesn't hesitate. Her little body crashes into mine, and we go back against the bedding, her tears wetting my shoulder, her chest trembling.

I want to reassure her that it's all right. That he's gone, far off back to Trier to be tried and executed for the same crimes he forced on us. I want to promise that he'll suffer for what he did, but as her weeping stills, I can barely speak around the lump in my throat.

"I'm so sorry, Liesel," is all I manage. "I'm so sorry. For our coven. For our home. For—"

"I'm sorry too."

I push her away to look into her eyes. "You have *nothing* to be sorry for."

Her lips pull into a soft smile. "Neither do you."

Silence falls between us. She truly means that?

Can I ever begin to believe it?

"Where is Otto?" I ask, voice rough.

Liesel grins. "Oh, *him*? Why would you want to see *him*?"

My lips flatten, barely suppressing a smile, and she rolls her eyes.

"He's *sort of* been worried about you. He comes here all the time. It's really annoying. I told him: this is where *girls* sleep."

"How long have I been out?"

"About three days."

Three—?

My breath catches.

But Liesel squeezes my hand and wriggles out of the bed. I start to follow her, pausing with each movement to readjust to the soreness in my body, but she gets me standing, and I balance on her shoulder, my thin shift fluttering to brush the tops of my feet.

There's a bandage wrapped around one ankle. A series of bruises shows when I look at my wrist, splayed purple and yellow petals like a wildflower, the final kiss of the manacles that hung me from the ceiling of Dieter's room and bound me to the stake.

I can't even begin to think about what the rest of me looks like. I'm on the verge of healing. I'm *alive*. I should be grateful.

But each motion prods at the remnants of the brands. Scars my brother left on my body. Will I be able to heal them completely with wild magic? How will I try here, in the Well, without drawing fury from Rochus and Philomena—or even Perchta and Abnoba? And what about the barrier Dieter ripped; what has it done to the Well's magic?

How will I be able to convince everyone here that the Well and the Origin Tree are not only unneeded, but that we should do away with all of our laws and ceremony and embrace wild magic?

How does Holda expect me to fix any of this?

My heart thunders, and I have to pause, hand to my forehead, breathing deep.

Don't think about that now. Don't focus on tomorrow.

There is only today. Liesel at my side. My body, healing, repairing.

And Otto, waiting for me.

Liesel hands me a finely woven shawl from a nearby chair, silken soft and brightest blue.

"The council has been in constant meetings," she tells me as we work our way to the door. "They shout. A *lot*. But from what anyone will tell me, it's good. They were mad that Cornelia took guards into Baden-Baden, but the people in the city have been rejoicing over them. There's a big festival they've been having, thanking the forest folk; they're *happy* to know that all this magic has been nearby this whole time. Otto said that once you're better, we can try to go down to see it. It's like a bedtime story, Fritzi."

I smile down at her. "It is, isn't it? Forest folk coming out to be among us."

Her nose scrunches up in excitement. "I'm going to turn all this into a story, actually. I've been working on it! Something we can tell around the fireplace. Do you want to hear it?"

My muscles go stiff. But her eyes are so full of joy that I nod. "I would love to."

We reach the door, and Liesel opens it. "Not right now, though. Now is for—*Otto*!"

I jump and scramble to grab the doorframe as her scream rips across the treetop village, the swooping bridges and sturdy branches lit by the canopy-muted afternoon light. Forest folk scattered all around flinch and gape at us; some bellow laughter; others curse and pick up whatever she made them drop.

I fall into giggles, and Liesel shrugs.

"He's never very far. He told me to let him know the moment you woke up."

"By screaming at the whole Well?"

She shrugs again. "I took what Brigitta calls *creative liberties*. Like in the story I'm making—I can change certain things! I can make it different because I want it to be different. It's my story."

My grin softens. I smooth a lock of hair behind her ear. "Yeah, Liesel. It is."

Footsteps pound somewhere over us, a thundering run. My eyes cut up, and I follow the path they take, down a staircase, across a bridge, wrapping around a tree trunk—

Otto sprints into sight, leaping the last few steps. His eyes lock onto mine, and he doesn't slow, but his face breaks in a wide grin, and he hurries for me, arms extending.

He's as clean and bright as Liesel, his hair half pulled back into a knot atop his head, a crisp brown tunic belted around his waist, black boots glinting in the light. There's a bandage peeking out of his sleeve at his wrist and a red cut on his temple, but otherwise, he's whole, here, *alive*.

I stumble forward, smiling so wide my face aches, and barely clear the doorway when he swoops in, his arms encasing me gently, testing my limits, my pain tolerance.

"Is this all right?" he asks. "Am I hurting you?"

I squirm against him. "If I'm not fully in your arms in the next two seconds, Otto Ernst—"

He relents, lifting me against him, and I hear the rumble of his chuckle resonate deep in his core. "Demanding, aren't we?" But there's palpable relief in his voice.

I let him take my weight, ignoring the sting of the brand on my stomach, the tug of pain from the one on my chest, and just revel in him. The feel of his solidness and the smell of his warmth and the way he rests his mouth on the seam of my shoulder, half kissing the spot, half inhaling me.

Back the way he came, Cornelia appears, flanked by Brigitta and Alois.

"Brigitta!" Liesel cries and races toward her. "I told Fritzi about my story—"

Her voice fades, but I stiffen, knowing why they've come. They'll want to fill me in on what has happened in the meetings, and I do want to know, but I want to pretend, just a little longer. That everything is truly over.

Otto feels my tension, and he tightens his hold on me. "Not yet. Things have waited three days—they can wait a little longer."

"A little longer? How much longer?" I cut a grin, clinging to the insinuation he might not have even intended.

His chuckle turns into the rumblings of a growl. "Liebste, if I thought your body could at all handle that right now, I would leap from this treehouse and plummet us straight into the bathing pools."

A thousand jokes are on the tip of my tongue. A hundred ways to torment him, tease him, dissolve into this banter.

But my eyes fix on Cornelia, talking with Liesel, and everything awaiting me rears up again.

He is the single fixed point. The anchor that has quickly become my lifeline.

All I have to give him in return are the raw parts of me.

I push my face to the side of Otto's head and hold there, a tremor shuddering through my limbs. "There is no healing that can be done to me," I start, a whisper hung with yearning, "that is more potent than your hands on my body."

He stumbles, one arm snapping out to steady himself on the wall of the cottage. His jaw bulges beneath my lips, pulse firing against my fingers on his neck, and he dips his mouth to my shoulder again, the bare skin where my shift pulls back.

"You need to rest," he tells me, tells himself. He doesn't sound entirely certain, and that dip in his tone funnels every raging thought in me, every twist of fear, into nothing but blissful desire and heat.

Until Cornelia closes the space between us.

I close my eyes.

Otto holds for a beat, waiting for my response, but when I don't keep pressing him, he sets me on the ground and puts his fingers beneath my chin.

"Fritzi."

I manage a breath. Steadying, resilient, with him here, with Liesel's happy giggles tinkering just beyond.

And when I open my eyes, I look up at him with all the strength I can find. "I'm ready to speak to the council."

I'm not. At all. What will I say? That Holda showed me she made a mistake? That the very positions of power the council has enjoyed are what is stifling our people? That wild magic is actually no different from our magic, except that it's *more* powerful—

Otto's brows bow inward. "Speak to the—what?"

Even Cornelia, who comes up alongside him, frowns at me. "You are in no shape to speak to the council, Friederike."

I squint at her. "Then why are you here? I'm Holda's champion. Don't you need me?"

"Yes, but you did not think I'd put you to work so soon?" Cornelia asks, a laugh of disbelief. "I'm here to see how you are."

"No business at all." Otto points a threatening finger at her. "No updates. Not until she's fully healed."

"Updates?" I'm still half against him, one of his arms draped around my hips, and I push into his body. "What updates?"

"No. *No.*" He turns that faint reprimand to me. "Not until you're better."

"I will positively lose my mind if you expect me to stay in this cottage without speaking to anyone for *days*."

He seems to realize the absurdity of what he's demanding, but he sighs, and all he says is, "If you're certain."

I touch his jaw, my thumb brushing across his full bottom lip. His presence goes from fortifying to infusing. It isn't merely that he's here—he's here *for me*, and he really does want to shield me from the fear that had built, the heaviness of these responsibilities.

An anchor. A protective wall. A soft place to fall.

This man has me utterly enraptured. How could I not be?

"Thank you for watching out for me," I tell him, and my words are buoyant with how I feel the weight lifting under his protection. "How did I come to deserve you?"

"Oh, watching out for you is quite literally his calling," says Cornelia with a grin.

I eye her. Otto flushes suddenly, pink spotting on his cheeks, and my gaze goes sly.

"What's going on?" I press.

Cornelia winks. "I'll let him explain. But I am glad to see you are up—take your time, champion. I do not want you back until you are healed."

I reach for her, lips parting.

I should tell her what Holda showed me. She deserves to know, so we can strategize together, share this responsibility again—

But Cornelia gives my arm a quick squeeze. "Later, champion."

And so I trust in that. *Later*. That we will have a *later*, that she will be waiting there to bear these burdens with me.

Cornelia heads back to the steps, where Liesel is talking animatedly with Brigitta and Alois.

I look back up at Otto. "What was she talking about?"

His hand moves against my spine, the ridges concaved to perfectly fit his fingers.

"The council has agreed to begin the bonding ceremonies again. Starting with us," he tells me, and his head slants down to me, breath bathing my face from his unspooling smile. "I'm your warrior, Friederike Kirch. If you will have me."

My breath hitches.

After everything, the idea of taking a bonding potion comes with an expected jerk of hesitation.

But it's immediately soothed by the way his eyes dip through mine, full of such openness, such eager, unabashed desire that I'm breathless in the storm of him. And even though others are nearby, the force of his presence once again consumes me, and all the world falls away so there is only *him*, only *me*, only the sudden, vital texture of his lips as I arch up to meet him.

"Yes," I whisper into him, getting dizzy on his taste. "Yes, I will have you." But I pause, draw back. "Do you know what that means, being linked to me? What you'll be pulled into—this struggle with forest folk and goddesses? This isn't your fight anymore."

Otto cradles the back of my head, an amused smile playing across his face before I can even begin to entertain that he has any doubts about this.

"Oh, Liebste, you realize this is all just a formality, right? I have been thoroughly bewitched by you from the moment I found out that you ate all the rations in my house fort."

I reel back.

"That—*that* was when you fell in love with me?"

He grins.

"Of all the things that happened between us," I stammer, "I cannot *believe* that *that* is the memory you chose... The Three save me, jäger."

"What?"

"There are so many better things you could have said!" But I'm echoing his grin, I can't help it, my body going to giddy bubbles in his arms. "Like when you held me after my nightmare?"

"Yes?"

"That was so much more romantic than *rations*."

"Well, when you say it like *that*—"

"Or in the Christkindlmarkt, or any of those times on the rowboat, or—"

He silences me with his mouth, half a kiss, half a wide smile.

"Take what I give you, hexe," he says, jerking my body closer. "And what I give you is all of me, bound forever to you. I am yours."

A kiss.

"I am yours."

Another, deeper, lingering.

"I am yours."

I relent to his ministrations. It is both taking and giving to let him have this victory, and I know I will one day have my own, and on that day, we will find out whose triumph is sweeter, who is best brought to their knees before the other.

But for now, I surrender to him.

It is a promise.

It is a beginning.

EPILOGUE

DIETER

I let them cart me into Trier.

They are so afraid of me, the cowards. As well they should be. I did not merely control their bodies; I occupied their minds. I whispered their sins back to them and watched gleefully as they cringed away from me, shame fueling their fear, just as it should.

It's snowing when they open the door of the wooden prison cart they escorted all the way from Baden-Baden to Trier. I blink in the light.

Ah, home.

We pass by the burned debris of the riots that followed my former kapitän's traitorous act. More guards are posted in the streets; windows are boarded up. Winter approaches, the snow quenching the fire of rebellion. This will all soon be forgotten. In other times, perhaps, such resistance would take hold.

But I'm back now.

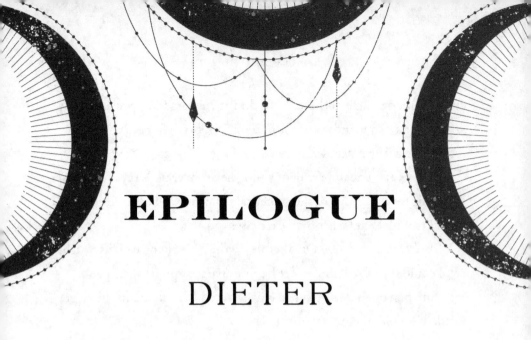

There is a pyre already built in front of the cathedral. Some of the city's residents have gathered. No doubt rumors have preceded my arrival—the kommandant of the hexenjägers, brought back to burn.

I smile at them beatifically.

"This way." The impertinent young hexenjäger pulls my chain, and I stumble forward, toward the cathedral's main door. That one, Johann, he was trouble. But he has his weaknesses too.

If only I had possessed Otto before. I would have known of his treachery. I could have used him before he tore apart my pretty little prison.

But then again, if Otto had not enacted his silly plans, he never would have found my pretty little sister.

A smile twists at the corner of my mouth, and I do not bother to hide it. I like the way it makes the hexenjägers "guarding" me cower.

"I must have caused quite a stir to be sent straight to the archbishop's office," I say as we step inside the cathedral. "How naughty I've been."

Jäger Kock, to my left, lets out a hiss of breath. I think he believed my skin would ignite the moment I touched foot on holy ground. I turn my head to look at him and slowly lick my lips, savoring the taste of his terror.

"Come *on*," Johann says, jerking my chains.

"I will kill you slowly," I tell him, my words light.

"Not before I watch you burn," the jäger mutters.

I chuckle, following along like a good little boy. I can do that, you see. I can be a good little boy, go to church, say my prayers, burn the witches. Such a *good* little boy.

Johann holds open the door to the archbishop's office, and I step inside, chains rattling. It is irksome, that metal rubbing my wrists. I hold my hands out to Johann. "Please, sir," I say sweetly.

Johann ignores me, and Jäger Kock follows inside, intending to be a guard to protect the archbishop from my foul evil. The two men block my vision of the archbishop temporarily. I hear the old man start to stand.

"This is..." he says in his cracked voice. Is that fear I hear? I bite back a giggle at the rhyming thought. *Fear I hear, fear I hear.*

"Dieter Kirch, witch." Johann spits the words out.

Tentatively, I feel for the magic. That potion—it broke me for a moment. I lost hold of my threads; they slipped through my fingers.

Just like my games with Fritzichen as children, those little links to magic are hiding in the dark, but I can still see them.

The jägers step aside.

I lift my head.

I meet the archbishop's eyes.

And I smile.

Got you.

The archbishop sits down placidly at his desk.

"You can go," he says to the jägers.

Johann's brow furrows. Thinking, thinking, that one! Did his training teach him nothing? Ha, the irony. I giggle to myself. What good training the others received, to learn how not to think.

"And take off his chains," the archbishop adds.

Johann's consternation grows, but I hold out my manacled wrists obediently. He fits the key into the lock, and the iron falls away.

Johann closes the door behind him.

The archbishop moves to sit behind his desk. I take the seat across from him.

"Well," the archbishop says.

"Well," I echo. Another laugh bubbles up. *Well*, like the Well of magic.

How strange that I once thought such magic as that was important. I thought I *needed* it. That damn goddess tricked me. Made me think wild magic wasn't as powerful. As *easy*.

The archbishop's watery eyes meet mine. "I think a burning is presumptuous," he says, hefting a sigh. "I'll dismantle the pyre. A quiet retirement would be best. People will forget. In the spring, as I continue the Lord's work..."

"The Lord's work?" I ask. "Sir, you've never done that a day in your life. You have *always* worked for *me.*"

The archbishop blinks several times.

I stand up and start pacing. I like being able to stretch my legs. It was harder to think, all cramped in that prisoner's box, but at least the men moved quickly, eager to be rid of me. "It's that damn tree I did not factor in," I tell him.

"The tree," he says blankly.

"Oh, I know what you're thinking—the tree that my little sister grew, that enabled her to break free of my bonds. Not that tree. That's not the tree I'm thinking of, you stupid man." I pause, take a breath. He cannot help that he is stupid. "No," I say, regulating my tone. "I mean the Origin Tree."

"The Origin Tree," he repeats.

"Yes, exactly." My pacing picks up a notch, step, step, step, turn, step, step, step, turn. "I had been so focused on the Well, but when I ripped the barrier, I saw much more than the forest folk ever wanted me to see. Something else Holda kept from me..." I sigh dramatically, even if the effect is lost on such a simple man. "Ah, well, I suppose I shall find out the truth about that tree soon enough."

"You shall find out," the archbishop says, nodding.

"That's the tree I meant," I tell him, leaning over his desk. In my excitement, spittle flies from my lips, but the archbishop is such a gentleman, not wiping it away, pretending it doesn't land on his face. "The Origin Tree. I thought, before, that wild magic was just an untapped source that must be fed evil, must be tempered in some way before it can be used." I giggle again. "How silly I was. Wild magic is wild, that's all. And so am I. We are made for each other, no?"

"No," the archbishop says, a flicker of something in his eye, something I do not like. No, no, no, no, *no,* you are not going to slip from me again, you are not going to hide from me. You are *mine.* I lunge across the desk, grab his arm, yank up those pretentious robes he wears.

There it is.

I trace my finger along the white lines of the scar on his arm. A decorative, curling letter *D.* Branding him had been difficult—getting close enough to do it half the battle—but the risk has paid itself off many times over. I can seep into any weak person's mind and control them like a puppet, but that requires concentration. At best, it is a temporary measure. The brand, however, is a magical sigil, one that allows me true possession of a human's body, of a witch's magic.

"You are mine," I whisper. *You are still mine.* There was just a little worry, before, when Fritzi nearly killed me, when she thought she broke my magic. But no. She did not. Not the way she thinks...

"I am yours," he whispers back.

And so too is Trier. The entire diocese. The entire Empire.

Mine.

Fritzi thinks this is over. Weak and wounded, she thinks I will die at the stake. I know what our dear Mama would have advised—that I should go into hiding.

A god does not die. A god does not hide.

Already, I can tell that my men's fear is spinning the legends of what happened to me into mythic proportions. Any of them—like that damned Johann—who would think to oppose me would *never* oppose the archbishop. And if they try?

I smile.

All will be well.

I pat the archbishop's arm and pull the robe back over the brand on his skin. "Now first," I say, "you're going to write a very clear decree that not only am I not a witch, but I remain the kommandant, your trusted ally in the face of evil witchcraft. Actually..." My grin is feral. "Let's go ahead and give me all the power of a prince. This diocese is a principality, no? It deserves a prince."

The archbishop picks up a quill and pulls over a sheet of vellum. The nib scratches on the surface, ink bleeding onto the page.

"Good," I say, looking over the desk at the praise the archbishop writes for me, the way he confirms that I did not bend to the temptations of the devil, but my weak hexenjägers did, led astray by evil. "What is it your Bible says? 'Sanctify them in the truth; your word is truth.'" For so many, all it takes is a word written for them to believe it.

The archbishop continues writing.

Taking him had granted me power, of a sort. It had allowed me access to the city, enabled me to become the leader of the hexenjägers. But that was never the type of power I needed.

I need power like my sister's. Magic. *Strong* magic.

Fritzi opened herself up to wild magic, and my brand opened her up to *me.* Will she feel it, I wonder, as I siphon off the power she taps into? Probably not. The wild magic is so much stronger than the Well's after all, and she won't notice as I divert a little back into me.

She is mine, I think, my mind stretching back, recalling the way her skin seared, her flesh burned, the smell ripe and delicious. My mouth waters at the thought.

She is mine, and so is her magic, and she doesn't even realize it.

"I told you, Fritzi," I murmur, "some scars don't ever heal."

"Some scars don't ever heal," the archbishop repeats hollowly as he lays down the quill.

I watch the ink dry, my smile spreading as I think of our mother's death, our mother who died without screaming. Pity, that. I had thought that the only way to take a witch's magic was to mark it as my own and then burn the body of the witch. With nowhere else to go, the magic came to me.

My sister showed me the foolishness of that. I do not need to kill for power.

I can do it simply for pleasure.

I frown, and the archbishop stills, like a rabbit under the shadow of a hawk.

That damn potion had been a surprise, enough to sever my original connection to magic, but not enough to break the ties that bind me to Fritzi and *her* magic. A clever trick, though, to use a potion like that. A trick I had not believed Ernst capable of manufacturing. I'll give him that. He played a good game.

But I play a better one.

Wild magic is a flood, one I drowned in. But I learned to swim. And even if they dammed the magic up and tried to take it away from me, a river stronger than the Rhine pours from my sister's brand, straight into me.

I flex my fingers, feeling the magic pooling inside me.

Oh, this is going to be *fun*.

HISTORICAL NOTE

This story is a blend of history and fantasy.

Trier remains a real city in Germany, home to the Porta Nigra, the cathedral, the basilica (known as the Aula Palatina), and surviving house forts—although we added a house fort in the Judengasse for Otto. The hypocaust under the basilica and the tunnels under the streets that Otto and Fritzi use to free the prisoners are also real, remnants of heating systems and aqueducts made by the Romans.

The Trier Witch Trials were also all too real. They began in 1581 and extended all the way to 1593, with an estimation of a thousand executions. One of the four largest witch trials in Germany and possibly the largest mass execution in Europe outside of war, the Trier Witch Trials were so impactful that news traveled throughout Europe, sparking a revival of witch trials as far as Copenhagen, Scotland, England, and eventually, the infamous Salem Trials in America.

While the hexenjägers, forest folk, and the Well are all fictitious creations, it is true that the Romans did not dare breach the Black Forest. The Forest was originally linked to the Celtic goddess Abnoba, and it marked a mysterious, dense border invaders didn't cross, perhaps simply due to the tough geography...but we're not ruling out a bit of magical protection.

ACKNOWLEDGMENTS

Night of the Witch came about thanks to the Overworked Moms Writer Club Slack group and those dark, uncertain months at the beginning of the COVID pandemic. Those two things, one a blessing, one a curse, paved the way for a conversation about the intersectionality of German medicinal women, brewers, and witches, and eventually, a book about a fierce witch and an honorable soldier.

We owe this book to that Slack group—thank you for bringing us together. But we do not owe this book to the COVID pandemic—we wrote this book in spite of it. Perseverance in the face of great sorrow, which we channeled into *Night of the Witch*.

Endless, heaping, gushing thanks is also owed to Sara's agent, Amy Stapp, who fought so passionately for this book. Without your stewardship, *Night of the Witch* would still be nothing more than a shared Google doc. We also want to thank Beth's agent, Merrilee Heifetz, for giving insightful notes and helping shape the story. And thank you to Taryn Fagerness, for being our overseas support and working so hard to bring this book to the world. Thank you, thank you, thank you.

Thank you, over and over for all eternity, to our editor, Annie Berger, for taking a chance on our witchy world. Beyond that, thank you for *getting* this book, for understanding it in a way that fostered our talent and confidence and joy. Working with you has been one of the great pleasures of our careers, and we are so infinitely lucky to have you on our team.

To Jenny Lopez—your enthusiasm will always make us smile! Thank you for being one of our support system pillars and for being such a rallying voice for this book.

To Madison Nankervis—thank you for your immediate and stunning championing of *Night of the Witch*. Knowing we have you backing us up means the world, and we cannot think of better hands for our book to be in.

To the additional members of the Sourcebooks team, who continue to render us awestruck with their support: Karen Masnica and Rebecca Atkinson for all things marketing and publicity; David Curtis, Liz Dresner, and Erin Fitzsimmons for providing us the beautiful cover art and design, gracing our story with an image both eerie and magical; and Thea Voutiritsas for shepherding the book through production.

To Trenton Bruce—thank you for tolerating Sara's many varied emails about German language nuances. You went above and beyond what is expected from any brother-in-law. (And let it be known that any errors in regard to the German used in this book are entirely our own.)

To our families, for giving us space to dream and create, and then bringing us back to things that really matter.

From Sara: To Beth, for giving me a light in the darkness of these past years with this book and your friendship. It still shocks me silly how well met my soul is with yours, and I am so honored to have gotten to write this book with you.

From Beth: Sara! Words cannot say how much of an impact you've had on my life! Thank you for reminding me of the beauty and power of words, and for taking a chance with me as we discovered this story. The book may be fiction, but the magic was real.

ABOUT THE AUTHORS

Sara Raasch has known she was destined for bookish things since the age of five, when her friends had a lemonade stand and she tagged along to sell her hand-drawn picture books too. Not much has changed since then. Her friends still cock concerned eyebrows when she attempts to draw things, and her enthusiasm for the written word still drives her to extreme measures. She is the *New York Times* bestselling author of the YA fantasy trilogy Snow Like Ashes, as well as four other books for teens (none feature her hand-drawn pictures). Her favorite German food is Pfeffernüsse—so many of her childhood memories are connected to the anise scent of those cookies that her grandmother used to bake.

Beth Revis is *the New York Times* and *USA Today* bestselling author of numerous science fiction and fantasy novels for teens and adults. Her debut, *Across the Universe*, has been translated into more than twenty languages, and her works have been honored by the Junior Library Guild, and received stars from *Kirkus*, *Publisher's Weekly*, *Booklist*, and more. Co-owner of Wordsmith Workshops, which aids aspiring novelists, Beth currently lives in North Carolina with her son, husband, and dog. Her favorite German food is spaetzle and lebkuchen, and in researching this novel, she was able to trace her own family roots to a village outside of Bernkastel.